THE SHADOWS

THE SHADOWS: Fire's Hope

ISBN-10: 1-7325704-0-X
ISBN-13: 978-1-7325704-0-5

Cover and interior by E. Kathryn
Edited by Tina Winograd

https://ekathrynsshadows.com

Exodus 3:7 And the Lord said: "I have surely seen the oppression of my people in Egypt and have heard their cry because of their taskmasters, for I know their sorrows."

To Jo, Mia, and Aurora for enduring endless emotional turmoil on my characters' behalf. You guys keep me going.

THE SHADOWS

Fire's Hope

E. KATHRYN

PROLOGUE

November 6, 2015

In the warm comfort of the night, sweat beaded on Hellen's body as the tension in her muscles faded. Her gaze lost on the furious pink infant with spindly limbs in her arms.

Tears finally dripped from the apples of her cheeks and a wave of relief washed over her as the droplets of water touched her daughter's contorted face. The child's lungs were powerful, and this fact assured Hellen her daughter was healthy and safe. She drew her closer, holding her tightly against her chest so the tiny girl's fingers curled around her collar bone.

Hellen sank back into the hospital bed, refusing to let her child leave her breast, even as the nurse urged her to rest. This labor had been long into the night, and the stale hospital room was now humid with the scent of blood and fluid.

It calmed her, and the sweet moisture in the air tickled her throat as she panted. Who knew where her boyfriend was? She didn't have a clue if he even knew their baby had arrived, or if he cared. He didn't matter now. All her cares rested upon her little girl's heartbeat as the infant helplessly relaxed into her mother's bosom.

"Miss Meyvise, we need to test her," the nurse urged at her side, reaching out to touch the pale-yellow blanket on the infant's back.

"No..." Hellen moaned, still caught up in the beauty of her daughter's face as she closed her eyes and fell asleep. "No, just let me have her, just give me a minute," she cried helplessly, overcome with love for the tiny creation she held.

"It's been an hour," the nurse whispered. "It will only take a moment." With elongated and ungloved fingers which were dry from excessive washing, the nurse pried the child from Hellen's grasp, and as gently as could be seen, the nurse carried the girl away from her mother. "What are you going to name her?" the nurse asked as she placed the baby within the curved bassinette.

Laying her head back against the pillow, Hellen heaved through the thick air. "Emilie..." she murmured, barely audible. Her eyes locked upon the nurse as the woman retrieved a small red film from a canister, similar to a litmus paper in purpose. Hidden from Hellen's view, she tested the child for a Shadow.

The woman waited for the reaction of the child's blood smeared on the paper. She didn't move for several long seconds, causing Hellen to worry.

The nurse turned, and Hellen could see over her shoulder the thin red film had turned black where the blood touched it. "No!" Hellen screamed, reeling up in bed, "No! Please no!" She couldn't get up. She couldn't rush to seize her child. She could only lay there alone in the hospital bed to scream. "No! I'm begging you, please don't take her away from me!"

Despite her heartbroken tears, the nurse's eyes darkened, and wordlessly, she wrapped up the baby girl and carried her away. Hellen's eyes lingered on the sight, scarring her more deeply than murder as she cried out, shrieking for them to let her hold Emilie a little longer.

1
SOME KIND OF MEANING

October 25, 2030

A red strand of hair fell between Mark's eyes as he sat hunched over a keyboard, his fingers flying across the keys, ignoring the pain in his back from the awkward position, adrenaline fueling every decision he made.

One by one, the party members came online, each name and icon appearing as new voices joined within his headset. With anticipation high, the dungeon opened, and after waiting a solid thirty minutes, the raid had begun.

Mashing the keys, Mark's simple character, decked to the teeth in armor, followed along the path closely behind his friend, who sat beside him at a separate laptop.

Gary sank back into the huge leather office seat in the basement of his home, far more relaxed than Mark, who was rearing to go as he charged into the dungeon. Without desire for the loot or the rewards, Mark was in it for the adrenaline surge he got from listening to the twenty other voices screaming over his headset as they got slaughtered.

His only consciousness pertaining to the real world was of his annoying bangs that kept falling into his face, especially the obnoxious red one which migrated from the sea of ebony to right between his eyes. It always fell, no matter how many times he pushed it away, and the red patch wasn't dyed either. Those strands of crimson hair that tumbled before his gaze were completely natural.

"Follow me to the left flank!" Mark fired into the microphone on his headset, getting more hyped as he led a stealthy trio around the army of ghouls, abandoning his party.

Gary stood among the trio, joining him in the enraged crusade up a path overlooking the largest opening out of the dungeon. Hundreds of monsters spawned, waiting right around the corner to smite the main party.

They hadn't been seen yet, and there was a thin path around the ancient cathedral, which was lined with chests of loot and gold, endless rewards for the one who got there first, but one could only be so stealthy with so many ghouls ten virtual feet beneath them.

"The bridge is out above the exit. Do you see that?" Gary pointed to a collapsed rope ladder. His nimbler archer inched closer to the ledge, crouching and casting a spell to hide himself.

Mark nodded to his friend, thinking over their next move. His brawny character could last far longer against the horde of ghouls than any archer, but a single arrow could equally stir up the beasts if Gary fired into them.

Gaming was all Mark thought about day and night, and with his best friend nearby who shared this passion, Mark's addiction flourished. This level of gaming wasn't exactly accepted within his own home. His mother thought he got a little too into it.

Gary addressed the third member of their trio, forming a plan and deciding it would be best to help the others deal with the ghouls in the first catacomb, then deal with this ambush later.

However, Mark tuned out. Gary saw it in Mark's dark brown eyes as he rationalized the situation, weighing his options, and jumping the gun. Greedily, Mark's character dashed forward, opening one of the chests along the path to snag some gold before flinging his character into the fray.

"Mark!" Gary shouted as the gray armored character disappeared into the sea of monsters. Digital blood flying, Gary slapped his face as Mark screamed, elated, quite effectively holding his own even though he was surrounded on all sides.

"You idiot!" Gary laughed, firing arrows into the beasts below. He took out as many as he could, but carelessness rapidly depleted his arrows, and he was forced to draw his sword and jump in.

"I got this!" Mark assured, starting to aggressively slam the keys harder to the extent he was becoming oblivious to how his *A* key was sticking. He was taking damage. His character veered left because his keyboard was breaking, and there was no way Gary could get to him in time to give him cover.

Utterly surrounded, Mark's heart raced, struggling to deflect oncoming blows and hold on to what little energy his character could regain.

The health gauge fell into the red. Gary threw his hands up and growled at the computer screen. "I died!" he spat. "This wouldn't have happened if you weren't so greedy. You had to go rile them up. Now there's nothing stopping them from annihilating the rest of—"

"Shut up!" Mark screeched so loud, he was sure Gary's parents would be slightly concerned about the noise. "Come on!" he yelled, mashing one key over and over. Nothing was working. Only a few more hits and he'd be gone.

The ghouls pushed him farther back to the passageway where the rest of the raiding party battled. "No!" Mark shrieked, and as the final blow struck him down, a party member charged in to be met immediately by the frenzied monsters. "No!" he screamed again, realizing he'd thoroughly ruined their chances of catching these beasts by surprise.

In horror, his dead character watched the rest of the party get slaughtered. Gary's character revived from the back, too far from the fighting to be able to do anything, and Mark stared at his own revival timer in fury. His fingers useless at the keys, his hands formed into fists, growing tighter and smoldering.

Shouting a curse, Mark slammed his fists on the keyboard harder than he thought he ever could in real life. The screen shut down abruptly, and Mark felt his heart and gut implode as his psyche grasped what he'd done.

Abandoning the game, Gary shrieked and burst up to his feet. "Whoa! Fire!" he cried out as Mark jumped away from the seat.

"No, no! Not my laptop!" he screamed, not sure what he was seeing because, indeed, his keyboard was on fire, destroying the computer entirely. Before he could think further, Gary threw a towel over the flaming laptop and Mark hurriedly patted it down with his hands to try to suffocate the flames. "Oh no, oh no! No!" He fretted, his voice finally coming down before the towel also caught on fire.

Smoke welled at the ceiling of the basement, and Gary coughed. However, Mark's only concern was for the expensive gaming computer he'd do anything to save. Losing his mind with worry, Mark ripped the towel off the computer, also knocking it to the floor, and he stamped the fire out of the towel. When he was sure the fire was out and the towel was ruined, he turned back to the fried computer in despair.

Kneeling, Mark froze, astonished. "I know I said the fan was acting up... but I didn't think it was this much!" Turning over the laptop, Mark observed the charred surface and sighed. "Maybe the hard drive isn't too damaged. I've got all my school on there and everything..."

"Mark, did you not just see that?" Gary screamed, standing back from Mark and staring, disturbed. Mark gazed at his friend, brows drawn. "Your hands..." Gary trembled. "Before you touched the towel—they were on fire!"

"What?" Mark gasped, not truly believing this, sure

Gary was exaggerating, but as he stared at his fingers, the smell of smoke rising. He clenched his hands into fists then rubbed them against his clothes, pushing down the fear of looking at his laptop. "Everything is ruined..." he murmured, drawing the laptop off the tile floor and picking up what shattered pieces had fallen away.

"That's what you're worried about?" Gary snapped, stumbling behind Mark and grabbing his backpack from a pile on the floor. Their basement hovel was the only place in the little house to set up the two clunky gaming laptops, and the spot near the window was the only area in the basement that got good Internet.

Mark's mind slipped away, lost in worry. It wasn't that he was at all materialistic, but his laptop had been expensive, and it meant a lot to him. It was one of the few things his father had given him that was genuine, a huge gesture, and a step forward.

Now the laptop was just another reminder that any kindness from his father was fleeting. Shoving what was left of his laptop into his backpack, he threw it onto his shoulder, wincing a bit as the school books inside hit him hard.

"What? Are you just gonna leave?" his friend said, ignoring the game he had stepped away from even though his character had gotten killed again.

Heaving a sigh, Mark hesitated, still staring into his palm, expecting the smoke to rise once more. Fear chewed at his heart. The sight of the red flames upon his laptop left him conflicted. He wasn't sure what he should be more scared about: his father's reaction to the destroyed laptop he'd only had since last Christmas, or the fact he might have caused the device to spontaneously combust. "You know the Addisons, right?" he murmured, sinking into his chair before the charred table.

Gary shrugged. "Name rings a bell."

"They're family friends. The girls babysit my sister a lot," Mark said, "and... they sometimes tell the story about their brother who would have been my age if they hadn't found out he was a Shadow."

"Shadows?" Gary lost all ability to be serious. "So, what are you? Some Shadow?"

Smirking, Mark adopted an air of sarcasm he got from his mother. "Oh yes, I must be some kind of Shadow creeping into your life to destroy everything you hold dear!" Hoisting his backpack up again, he grimaced at the weight of the dead laptop on his back.

"I'm not joking!" Gary hollered, grasping onto Mark's arm as he stormed toward the stairs. "Where you going, hothead? You don't have to listen to me, but if you're a Shadow, you better hide it! Most of the time Shadows are taken away at birth. Who knows what they might do if they find you."

Mark deadpanned, torn away from the stairs, "They?" he smirked. "You've been watching conspiracy videos again, haven't you?"

"Come on! You've seen the news, Shadows are freaking dangerous! None of them know how to control their powers, and on top of it, they've got access to another dimension where they can communicate telepathically!" Gary's enthusiasm worried Mark, his friend released his arm, but the intensity of his voice prevented him from budging from the bottom stair.

"Dude... you need to get off the dark side of the Internet!" he spat coldly, his feet stamping up the hollow wooden stairs as he turned his back.

"Says the guy who has to fight his sister for game controllers!" Gary called up, following him.

Mark waved at Gary's mom, saying nothing when she asked him why he was leaving so soon.

She called out to catch the boys. "If he's leaving, Gareth, you have dishes to do before dinner."

Gary protested Mark's every step, half-acknowledging his mom. Mark shook him off and at the door he forced a smile. "I guess we'll have to try that raid again someday... maybe when I can afford a new computer." He frowned.

"It's not like my dad will buy me another."

Gary shrugged it off. "There's always the console games you got. Maybe you can dig up your old games and we can brush up on some of the classics? If you can kick June off, that is."

"I'll get her off," Mark said, waving as he jumped down the two stairs from the porch and tripped through the grass to the sidewalk. Gary was a few houses down from Mark's home, and the brisk walk stung his face in the frigid October air.

In Mark's eyes, the only upside to autumn was his birthday, otherwise, he hated the cold that came with it. He walked as fast as he could, not quite running, but hurrying home to get out of the cold, gray weather.

When his house was in sight, he hurried a little faster toward the small, one-story home with a garage to the side of the front door, four small bedrooms, two bathrooms, and a window that didn't latch in June's room which was easy to sneak in and out of. This was only possible if Mark didn't wake June in the process of sneaking out.

"Mom, I'm home!" he called in a taut but quivering voice as he stepped through the door. He took off his coat as soon as he came in, savoring the warmth of home.

As he hung up his coat, he heard his mother, Marissa, in the kitchen. "You're back early," she said as Mark came into the kitchen and made his way to the refrigerator. "Stop! I'm making dinner!" With a grumble and a sigh, he closed the refrigerator begrudgingly.

"My computer... crashed," he lied, thinking over his words as he sat at the kitchen table. Restless, and a bit hungry, Mark rolled around his father's tea jars on the table. "How come Shadows are taken away at birth?" he asked, which caused his mother's shoulders to arch.

Glancing at him from the stove, she forced a smile. "Please tell me you and Gary didn't spend that whole two hours looking up conspiracy videos. You know your father hates them."

"I was just asking…" he grumbled, hating everything about how his father oversaw the family, when he even did that. "But… I did some research…" he admitted, then defended himself. "On my own. Did you know when Shadows turn invisible, they enter another world and all you can see of them is their shadow on the ground? That's where they got their name. They call the invisibility thing the Shadow Realm, and not a lot is known about it."

She moved from the stove to the freezer and get out frozen vegetables. "Actually, I did know that. Why the sudden interest? Something come up in your video game?"

Gulping a little, Mark shook his head. "Well… I was thinking, you know how you're always getting on me for being hotheaded?" He winced at the word.

Giving a small laugh, Marissa nodded. "All your life, but not as much as I fight to keep your head out of the clouds. It's impossible to make you focus on one thing."

Mark opened one of the jars of tea and smelled it. Reeling away, he never could understand why his mother kept it. She never drank it—only his father drank tea, and even then, it was a strong black tea he scoured international stores for. "Today… I think… well… I think I might be a Shadow… I…"

Setting down a pan for the vegetables, Marissa paused and stared hard at him for a long few seconds. "You know that's impossible. They tested you the day you were born." Turning her face away, her shoulders arched, fidgeting with bag the vegetables. She added, "It was negative. I promise you."

"It's not that," Mark replied a little too hastily. "It's just… I may have gotten a little too worked up during the raid… I kind of, set my laptop on fire."

Marissa didn't move, staring at him with her drawn eyebrows, then glancing at the lumpy backpack sloppily thrown onto his shoulders after ditching his coat. She studied his face, making him overthink his choice of words. Her all-knowing blue eyes scanned his soul, and a whirlwind of speculation turned in his stomach. "Listen, I don't want you getting too deep into this, your aunt was never the same after she gave birth to a Shadow. It changed her. Shadows, even young ones who can't control their abilities, are incredibly dangerous."

Suddenly, *Ode to Joy* started playing from his mom's pocket as her cell phone rang. He jumped at the sound.

She answered, and Mark let himself drift off again. He hadn't believed Gary, but to be honest, he wasn't sure. What if he could create fire?

Mark stared at his hands while his mother talked on the phone and was distracted in her cooking. The image of flickering tongues of crimson fire expanded in his mind as if he were dreaming. The warmth relaxed him, and he closed his eyes, letting darkness calm his racing thoughts.

The peripheral sound of his mother's footsteps kept him aware of her presence, but the darkness was broken by a very vivid white cloud of smoke in the shape of a woman. On the phone she paced, pushing around things on the stove which appeared like a box of contained smoke wavering about inside. Every physical object was made of intangible smoke, even the table before him. He could see no color or light but in the dark a vivid red orb, glowed within his heart.

His mother's ghostly form turned towards him and the burning phone fell to the floor. Blinking several times, Mark's gaze was flooded with light, but when his eyes adjusted, he saw his mother staring at him, horrified.

"What's wrong," Mark said now more scared than ever.

Marissa hastily bent down to gather up the phone, her hands shaking almost too hard to dial a number she knew by heart. She turned away, keeping her voice low to not worry him, but her hushed tones only worsened his fear.

"We'll be expecting you, thank you," she said as she hung up and then turned back to Mark. "You just, please… stay right here." Her request seemed frantic with anxiety though she hadn't explained anything to him.

Mark was completely unable to stay put for long,

wandering over to his younger sister, June, who sat on the floor in the living room playing. "Hey there, what are you doing?" he asked, kneeling with her.

"I *was* waiting for you to get home," June answered, giving an exasperated sigh which was comical for a six-year-old. "Can we play *CoursesGo* now?"

June preferred racing games over the violent strategy games Mark was addicted to, in fact, for her age, she was particularly obsessed with them and played as often as she could get her hands on a controller. However, she still required Mark's help setting up the system to play.

Mark groaned a bit. "I was going to get online with Gary..."

"Aww..." she whined, "but you'll be on for hours. Please, just one short game."

With her convincing argument, he mocked her previous sigh and did so. Setting up a race for the two of them, they started in third and fourth place out of twelve cars, and as he expected, June soon took the lead and was almost over-lapping him.

A loud, quick knock on the door made Mark jump and their mom hurried past them through the living room. As Mark whipped his head around, he wrecked his virtual car, losing to his sister.

They were here.

Setting down the oddly shaped controller, which June seemed to treasure like a doll, Mark stood. A short man leading the group of five entered the house and stared directly at him before acknowledging his mother.

The man stuck out his hand to his mother, shaking hers gently. "Thank you for calling us. Have you had any issues?"

Mark realized his mother was trembling even as she shook her head. "He only turned invisible, and he said he had set... his computer on fire."

The man's steady eyes accepted this, emotionless, professional, relaxed.

"My sister had a Shadow. Do you think it's possible it runs in the family?" Marissa fretted.

With an apathetic shake of the head, the man denied, "The Shadow is not hereditary." His entire posture made Mark nervous. Despite being rather short, the man was robust with thick arms and a militaristic demeanor. The man looked him over, assessing as much as he could before finally, he offered a false smile and a personable manner.

"It's good to meet you. Why don't we sit down and figure this out?" The man's offer was the fakest thing Mark had ever heard. This was a threat. Only silence was given to him as he complied, and the man signaled someone to rush to Mark's side with a small kit in hand.

"We're going to test you for a Shadow again," the man warned. "It's just a finger prick, you'll be fine."

Mark bit his lip as the kit opened. Inside was a stack of square cotton pads, a quarter-thick cylinder, and a thick pen. Before Mark could comprehend what each item was, the complete stranger took his hand, pressed the tip of the pen to his finger, and snapped a button on the side. A tiny lance shot into his finger, startling him, but the person didn't react, merely drawing out a small daub of blood and holding his hand steady. They retrieved a thin red film from the cylinder and placed it over the drop of blood, collecting it onto the paper.

Setting the film into the kit, the man squeezed Mark's finger tighter, then pressed a cotton pad onto it. He took the prompt to hold it there himself and wait for the bleeding to stop. By then the short man picked up the film and held it to the light. They waited, every second paralyzing Mark.

"Negative," the man said finally.

Mark breathed a sigh of relief simultaneously with his mother.

Personally, the short man took a seat beside Mark, placing the film back into the kit as his assistant cleaned up. "Tell me, what did it feel like when you turned invisible, do you think you could remember?" he asked.

Trying to make sense of it all, Mark's fingernails dug into his knees. "I don't know, warm, and alone in the darkness. Is that what the Shadow Realm feels like?" He pinched the cotton between his thumb and his pants.

Anxiety spinning in his gut, he reflected on the feeling he had drowned himself in, rage and adrenaline fueling his heart and it happened again. He vanished. It was getting easier now. He stared at those around him, knowing they still knew he was there, but all he could focus on was the expression on his mother's face.

Finding it now slightly easier to control, he released the feeling and returned to visibility. A little triumphant, he relaxed. Having even the smallest control felt good, but his mother stood with her hands over her mouth, horrified.

"How odd," the man hummed, very surprised. "Has he shown any signs like this before?"

Marissa nervously shook her head and in a low voice, as if she didn't want Mark to hear, she spoke to the man, "Not really," she whispered, and Mark's eyes widened, "but last February—he doesn't remember it well—we found him on the floor with massive tachycardia. I thought I saw him turning invisible, but I couldn't tell for sure..."

The man sighed. "As much as keeping his powers hidden was unsafe, waiting to confirm was wise..." he said, but Mark's confusion only soared higher. Powers? Tachycardia? What?

The man sat next to him in a friendly manner then strictly looked him in the eyes. "Mark, listen to me." Mark gulped. "From what you have displayed to us..." He noted the two men moving closer to him as the shorter man spoke. "You have proven that you are, in fact, a Shadow, and you will be coming with us."

"What!" Mark burst out, scarcely finding his voice. Many thoughts spiraled in his head, too many questions to be answered. But he wasn't given a chance to ask, and another strange feeling came to him.

At first, he thought it was like the feeling he had just

experienced when he turned invisible, only this one almost hurt. In a second, Mark realized what it was, his eyes widened in fear. One of the two men with the short man had revealed a small syringe and without warning injected the light blue serum into his shoulder.

In all his fear and confusion, he found a new sensation: he couldn't move, couldn't see, couldn't speak, and couldn't even force his own breathing. There was only blackness. His entire consciousness faded as he felt the second man taking hold of him securely but gently as he collapsed from where he sat on the edge of the couch.

11
ASH AND FIRE

October 26, 2030

The first semblance of consciousness returned as doors closed around him. Standing by himself, Mark stared at the cold metal, a space only six-feet by four-feet. He felt drugged and dazed but was regaining control over his senses. He became acutely aware he was in a holding cell.

The room rattled and shook like an earthquake, and Mark stumbled, clinging to the corner, and sinking to the floor. He was wrong. He was in an elevator.

A thousand fears took root in his mind with no idea where he was and nothing to him but the clothes on his back. They weren't even his clothes. He looked over his attire to find he had been dressed in lightweight clothes, just warm enough for October. Dark slacks, a plain white T-shirt, and a black jacket accented with red. It was neither warm nor comfortable, and Mark felt the material was eerily like a uniform.

Shuddering on the floor, Mark stared into his hands. Pushing down fear as his heart raced, his body prepared itself for anything, and adrenaline coursed through his veins.

Scared out of his wits, Mark's hands started to smolder and smoke, and in the tiny room, he feared he'd suffocate as the smell of smell filled his lungs. The fire followed, blisteringly hot and overpowering, but it didn't shock him. He stared at the steel door, feeling the elevator jarring as it rattled in whatever direction it traveled.

His hands trembled, and the fire wavered, absorbing the heat, and burning his skin. The fire didn't scare him. He didn't care if he was burned. The elevator reeled to a halt and Mark curled up tighter against the floor covering his head with his arms even though the flames tangled with his hair and the fire spread.

The two thick elevator doors opened and Mark froze, fixated on the sight as the warmth from his flames traveled out ahead of him.

Fifteen young teenagers clamored together, some bickering and entertaining themselves, others lounging on beds, which lined the far side of the room. A young boy fell to the floor with a yelp and Mark's attention locked on the sight. Tendrils of light scattered out as the boy's hands impacted the white floor. Like a solar flare, bright bands of light dissipated, and the boy hoisted himself to his knees, panting.

A girl stood over him, laughing uncontrollably. "You're not a sun, Kip. Flight is just not in your blood."

The boy jerked up, his hands consumed in light brighter than the sun. "Yeah, but fusion is!" he shouted, then slipped and fell again. Wild strawberry-red curls fell over his eyes, and Mark knew what Kip was. A Shadow.

Kip glared up at the girl, bright coals in his eyes as water flowed clearly from the girl's hands. This water extinguished the light he had created, and he sat in the puddle, now soaked.

Scanning the others in the room, Mark got lost in how each of the fifteen teenagers possessed their own unique ability, each with a strange countenance, some appearing inhuman, and others seeming completely normal. Kip was a bit smaller than the rest, and though he seemed incredibly powerful, he looked like he got picked on a lot.

Suddenly, Kip tensed and fought to get away from the water beneath him. Slick white frost raced under his feet, growing and spreading to fuse Kip's shoes to the floor.

Another girl near the argument gasped and whirled about at the culprit, "Silverstonarellena, let it off!" she shouted. She appeared like she could be the oldest in the room by the way her shoulders were a little broader than the rest, and her chest expanded with a bossy roar. Furious, she stormed over to one of the beds by the wall and glared down at a boy with white hair.

Mark saw the hair first, still going unnoticed as he stared from the elevator. Wild and silvery, it had numerous tangles and braids that made the boy's long hair look like a sharpened crown. His golden eyes spoke worlds of fear as he leered forward into the girl's soul. He shot a nasty glance past her at Kip and twirled a braid around his finger. "Just what can you do about it?" he threatened.

"Come on, Sil! What did Kip do to deserve that?" the girl snapped.

Sil brushed the strand back into the fray as he stood up gracefully. He retracted the ice from Kip's form by only looking at what he had created. His movements were slow but deliberate, bearing a heap of animosity over Kip.

He traveled past Kip ethereally, with a dirty look in his sharp eyes, but the boy dolefully endured it. Staring down at the dissipating puddle, Kip wiped the dripping droplets off his face, disguising his tears, then got up to scurry away.

Sil, however, took three long strides into the expanse of the room, closer to Mark. Glaring at the girls, Sil followed them with his gaze, only briefly taunting before gazing toward the only exit from their room.

Mark's face drained of blood the instant Sil spotted him, kneeling in the corner of the landing room, petrified.

Sil didn't move, assessing Mark like a predator. The stubborn fire on his hands rose. Sil's golden eyes flared brightly, shaking Mark to his core. Scrambling back, he pressed himself to the far wall of the elevator, panicking as

Sil took one step forward.

"What do we have here?" Sil whispered over him, his voice scarcely resonating as he took another step closer, then another, and with each step, Mark's heart raced faster, causing the fire to burn hotter.

Crying out, Mark's hands crumpled in pain as his skin cooked. "Get me out of here!" he shrieked at the ceiling, certain no one could hear him, no one would listen, and there was no way to make the doors of this elevator close.

In an instant, the fifteen teenagers drew near, curious of the new voice, but the crowd did nothing to lower Mark's panicked heart rate. With his hands before him, the fire raged even more, attaching itself to his clothes.

Sil's cold gaze locked onto the flames growing higher around Mark, and as the others rushed past him, he smirked. "Fantastic! As if one Shadow of fire wasn't enough!" Whirling about, he glared at Kip, who rushed from the back to see what everyone was looking at.

Kip hesitated long and hard before passing Sil, his hands forming into fists before he, like everyone else, crowded the elevator. Mark only saw this silent exchange before a third girl got into his face, getting far closer than anyone else in spite of the flames overtaking his form. "Are you all right?" she asked, forcing Mark to look into her Irish, emerald eyes.

The light in her eyes blocked out everything for a second, but Mark still shuddered, staring blankly at the girl's pale skin and thin red hair. All their eyes were unnatural, attempting to draw him in, and for a second, Mark was able to make out thirty inhuman eyes all staring at him. "G-get away!"

Thrusting his hands out, he tried to push them, but seeing the fire he clasped his hands against his chest, struggling to contain the flames and not hurt them. "You're Shadows?" he breathed, unable to summon his voice. Shadows were horrifying monsters, creatures with endless powers they could never control. These were kids his age.

Suddenly, in a flash of green mist, a Shadow appeared

next to the green-eyed girl with another ginger who could have been her sister. "A human?" she wondered aloud with a foreign accent in her voice. "What's he doing here, Elise?"

"No, not human," Elise said, then gestured at him. "See his eyes?"

He briefly looked up, but cowered when he saw them all staring, trying to catch a glance at his eyes. What was wrong with his eyes?

He couldn't face them. Drawing his knees closer to his chest and trying to convince himself he wasn't surrounded by Shadows.

One of the girls neared him, pushing past the others with a gentle fluid motion. Her thick brunette hair flowed in waves around her face, her oceanic-blue eyes mesmerizing Mark for they were far less inhuman other than the fact they seemed huge.

He sank into those eyes like deep water, oblivious to her smile and her kind gestures as she murmured, "What's your name?" A sweet touch spread cool water over his hands, the orbs of water enveloped the fire, enclosing it before putting it out.

He still shuddered as he struggled to take his gaze from hers. His mouth dry, he found he was able to speak only in a hoarse breath. "Mark Halo…but I'm not sure anymore." He attempted to wipe away a few tears, but they kept coming and he lost interest in trying to stop them.

She placed a tender hand on his shoulder, asking, "Why aren't you sure?"

Mark stared down at his reddened hands, observing what he thought would be severe burns, but instead, it felt as if he had dipped his hands into ice-cold water for an hour. He was not truly injured, but he was shaken up, for sure.

"Where am I?" His voice cracked. Placing a hand on the floor, Mark tried to stand, but feeling dizzy, he fell back. Just as quickly, the two ginger girls comforted him, unafraid of his flames despite how Mark hesitated to contact their hands for fear the fire would resurface. He felt like he had a fever.

"Fire?" Kip drew closer, wide-eyed and pushing his unruly curls out of his face.

With unnecessary help, they hoisted Mark to his feet and guided him out of the elevator and into the room. Not sure if he should feel nervous or accepted to this strange group of Shadows, Mark lost focus, feeling dizzy still, until Kip took his gaze once more, pulling him close. "I'm Kipling. My Shadow is plasma. We call it Shot, and you?"

Just a first name? Mark puzzled. But the following mention of a Shadow name confused him even more. It occurred to him everyone around him had a different power. He had only scratched the surface of knowing what these kids were capable of. The worst part was the return question. He didn't even know how to answer. "Shadow?"

Kip drew his brows together. "You don't even know what a Shadow is?" he puzzled, as if it was ridiculous that he didn't know.

Mark's brows knitted in sheer confusion before he frowned, reverting to sarcasm. "Of course, I know what a Shadow is!" he snapped. Letting loose his hotheaded, spitfire nature was the only way he could make himself feel comfortable.

The girl who created water laughed heartily. "We are all Shadows," she said. Finally, the others crowded around Mark, rolled their eyes, and turned away. As if they had heard it too many times to count and didn't want to hear it again, but Mark remained eager, yet mystified by her phrase. She seemed good-intentioned, and her four simple words intrigued him.

III
INDUCTION

Everything he knew was about to change.

"You've been a Shadow since you were born. You were always one of us, but it's possible your Shadow is different than ours and it cannot be detected by that strange test." The girl explained with an unbreakable smile, smoothing back her long brunette hair in an unerring grace. Mark took in her big oceanic-blue eyes. "Each Shadow has two abilities—"

"—I can..." Mark broke in, summoning some courage, "...turn invisible, and..." He stopped himself, again, hesitating to confirm what he thought. Clutching his fist, he felt the flames swelling and it hurt as it burned at his skin and clothing.

"We all can," she said sweetly, "but it's not simply turning invisible; it is entering into the Realm only we Shadows can see." Mark's heart lifted as he heard this, something about the Realm drew him in. "We each have our own unique ability, a deep understanding to the world, and also these."

The girl turned her cheek to him, pulling aside her long hair to uncover her right ear and display that it curved to a soft point. Mark's eyes dashed about the room at each of the Shadows around him, skittishly making out their pointed ears and ethereal faces. Hastily, he reached up, gracing his fingertips along the edge of his own ear. It was subtle, but it was unmistakable when compared to the Shadows around him.

How had he never noticed this? If it was such a telling sign of being a Shadow, why was it not more pronounced? And why had no one else in his life noticed until now, his mother, his father, or his friends?

He wanted to ask. He wanted to shriek out in protest. But he didn't speak fast enough. The girl lit up, giving a warm smile to everyone. "I don't mean to break this off, but I just don't want to be rude to the others, and you don't even know my name."

Mark studied her as she jumped to offer him a hand. "Oceana the Shadow Marine. You can call me Ocie."

One of the ginger girls pushed away from the group of Shadows, crowding him—a motherly, kind girl with sapphire eyes and ever-present spunk. "Give him some space! My name's Elise, Shadow Elastica, nice to meet you!" Her words flew together in one breath.

The four Shadows closest to him all seemed motherly, hovering closely as if he were a newborn child. Mark flustered to keep track. *Ocie's the brown haired one. Elise is bossy, and Kip...*

Mark glared at the smaller boy. He was a little too close for comfort, and Kip had an unusually high-pitched voice for a guy.

That left the other red-haired girl, the one with emerald eyes. "And what's your name?" Mark forced, gesturing to her.

She cackled with a chortling laugh. "Rita," she stated. Opposed to Kip, she had a quite deep voice and some kind of accent. "I'm Shadow Teleport." A green mist puffed around her form as she vanished from one side of Mark and appeared on the other. "I teleported over from Scotland a couple years ago, and they caught me pretty fast."

Mark found Ocie's eyes and gathered a bit of reassurance from them. However, while his eyes were distracted, Kip touched his shoulder, and his back straightened. Cautious, his hands clenched to quell the flames. Swallowing hard, he shuffled away from Kip's hand.

"What is this place?"

Elise gave him a smile and a chance to take in the room. Every inch of the walls, ceilings, and floors shimmered in white marble, and except for a pair of skylights in the roof, the stone was more or less unbroken. The L-shape of the room created two sections, a common area where they stood now, and a bedroom stuffed with a cluster of various beds against the walls.

It was a bland and seemingly empty space, but the bed area was crammed with tiny bookcases and eclectic belongings tossed among the blankets. "This is the ASH," Elise said. "Have you ever heard of this place?"

Pressing his lips together, Mark cringed on the edge of tears, his nose stung as he nodded. He bit his lip feeling the crackle of fire between his fingers snapping at his skin like a lit match. It stung, and he felt powerless to take his hands away from the flame. No amount of jumping or reeling back would allow him to get away.

Mark contained himself as they walked to the middle of the room, allowing the Shadows to surround him. Despite Elise telling them to give him space, they got closer, and his flames grew hotter.

"Just…" Mark hesitated, considering sticking his hands in his pockets but thinking better of it. "How many Shadows are there?" he asked with a stray glance at the crowded beds.

Elise shrugged, not an ounce of worry in her demeanor. "Fifteen of us in here, and I don't know… two hundred in the rest of the ASH."

"Two hundred!" Mark gaped. His cheeks burned with heat that felt like it was emanating from his eyes.

Ocie chuckled, an elegant hand curling near her mouth. "And so many more in the rest of the world. Haven't you heard anything about Shadows?" she asked.

"Plenty," Mark replied, his eyes glancing over each of the Shadows around him, "but they're supposed to be dangerous and out of control. You guys can't all be..."

Mark shivered, falling quiet and trembling. Suddenly cold, he reached to draw his jacket. The nervous feeling still lodged in his stomach, Mark paled coming face-to-face with the white-haired figure, Silverstonarellena, glaring down at him. He looked powerful and calculating, and Mark's horror, Sil's eyes flared in hatred, as he handed something to Mark.

Letting out a shriek, Mark looked at what Sil had shoved into his hand. Within his palm was a large snowflake with sharp spikes on every edge. Sil had done his best to jab it into his skin. Chucking it away hastily, Mark stifled a cry and gaped at the blood on his hand.

Elise hurried to help, but his gaze shot to hers, burning with crimson. "Don't touch me!" Terror in his body as he stood fully and did everything in his power to get as far from the Shadows as possible. But the white marble room enclosed him. There was no escape.

"I got it." Kip assured with a look to Elise, darting towards Mark. "Look, your fire can't hurt me. I can make fire too," Kip said, a glow in his eyes as he held out his palm to show off a small, yet intensely bright star within his hand. "Can you let me help?" Kip's eyes were gentle, but similar in color to Sil's, only much brighter and warmer.

A golden ray of light cast from within Kip's eyes reassured Mark, and the fire quelled gradually. Mark visualized himself pushing away Kip, but he did not. Even though he told himself over and over to do it, he didn't move at all.

Giving up, Mark shrank to the floor, losing his senses, and dragging himself to the wall where he let his fear consume him. He was surrounded by real Shadows, boys and girls who he had been taught were dangerous, but these kids were just people. He felt lost.

Kip gently placed a hand on Mark's shoulder, drawing him up and silently helping him as he took Mark out of the main room into a closed bathroom.

He felt dazed as Kip led him to the sink and forced Mark's hand under running lukewarm water. The shallow wounds stung as soon as the water touched them, but the coolness quickly soothed the pain

"Calm down, okay. I'm not going to hurt you or anything." He smiled, and Mark silently stared into the mirror.

His eyes sparked when he saw his reflection, a dim glow when he realized they were a deep ruby-like crimson. He tensed, and they flared brighter. Leaning closer to the mirror, he gazed at them long and hard. "My eyes changed color," he gasped.

Kip let out a gentle laugh as Mark awed at their new crimson color. "What color were they before?"

"Brown," Mark breathed. The intensity of his eyes paralyzed him. He wasn't sure if he was truly scared of them, but he couldn't stop staring.

"That's normal." Kip shrugged. "They'll get even brighter when you use your Shadow."

This did startle Mark. Unused to being a Shadow at all, it hadn't dawned on him that the fire was something he could *use*.

Kip leaned on the counter. "So how old are you?"

Mark shuddered to see his own eyes flash before he stammered, "A-almost fifteen." He let out a troubled breath as a sharp sting raced across his palm.

Suddenly overjoyed, Kip almost jumped from his place while nearly singing the words, "I'm fourteen too!"

Mark pressed his lips together. They might have been the same age, but they couldn't have been more different. Kip was a Shadow, and Mark... he didn't know what he was.

Shadows had powers they couldn't control; they were

dangerous. Shadows were... complete monsters. These were kids, people, his age. It made no sense.

Taking his hand out from under the water, Mark used his left hand, which hadn't been hurt, to brush his hair out of his face.

Kip brightened, his shining yellow eyes flashing as he noticed something. "You've got red strands in your hair too!" he said. The excitement in his voice confused Mark.

A pair of bright red clusters of hair situated in the middle of his hair line fell directly between Mark's eyes. A hand still scratching his head, he spotted another one had appeared, hidden within the obsidian ocean.

"Oh... I've always had that," he mumbled.

Kip's face lit up excitedly, and Mark grumbled. The strange discoloration made sense now.

He brushed the red strikes out of his face and over his head, but they stubbornly fell back into place. At the same time, Kip brushed several of his curly red locks behind his pointed ear.

Mark leaned against the counter with him, distressed. "So, will you tell me?" Mark asked, somewhat irritated.

Kip drew his brows together, "Tell you what?"

Almost smugly, Mark smiled, eyeing the boy with the crimson glow in his eyes. "I saw that look. You're comparing yourself to me. Tell me, how do you find us similar?"

Sighing, Kip looked down at the floor. "I can't say," he whispered.

Frustrated, Mark pushed himself off the wall. "Why not?" He raised his voice enough to startle Kip. An anger he'd never felt took control and combined with his fear and need for answers. New to feeling the flames forming in his hands and burning in his fingers and eyes, he tried to stop himself.

Kip kept silent as if contemplating. "I'm sorry," he whispered finally. "We're just told not to come to any conclusions before your Shadow name is decided."

"Why?" Mark demanded.

Kip's eyes drifted across the tile. "Your Shadow name is who you are. I just don't want to give you the wrong impression." Awkwardly, he brushed his hair behind his ear again. "I promise. I'll tell you as soon as Keller decides."

Mark fell pale and drew back. Who was he? Questions spiraled about in his mind, and fear overcame his senses. Why did he have to be here? Why couldn't he just stay home? It wasn't like he was a bad person, or he was even capable of hurting someone. Why did the world have to be afraid of him? He wasn't like these Shadows, not by any stretch of the imagination.

"Come on," Kip offered, gently nudging Mark's shoulder, "let's try again. We're not all that scary. I promise." Meekly, Kip didn't portray a lot of confidence, but Mark accepted enough to follow Kip out.

Standing in the doorway, all the Shadows stared at him again, waiting for him, curious about him, but unmoving. He couldn't look them in their eyes but let his gaze wander toward the skylight and the warm sunshine beaming inside.

A gentle laugh echoed from above, sweet and mischievous, but uncomfortably close to him. He wanted to contain himself, but he whirled about, nearly screaming as the figure of a girl sprung over his head and clung to the wall directly behind him as if gravity had no effect on her.

She pounced on him like a spider and grasped ahold of his shoulders firmly. In a handstand on top of him she balanced gracefully as if she were hanging there by her ankle.

From where she was, suspended aloft, she smiled widely, gravityless and upside down. "Ah," she practically sang, then glancing at the others, she grinned like she had vampire teeth or something. "This one's scared!"

Looking into his face, the girl's eyes were lightning green, and she laughed as Mark let out a cry in fear. Placing a feminine hand on his cheek from her inverted position above him, she whispered in his ear, "Don't be afraid..."

Mark's eyes widened by the lies in her tone. "You are in the Shadow of the wing!"

As soon as she finished, she pounced off him and vanished in midair. Mark stumbled to the floor. "Who was that?" he said under his breath.

Ocie knelt next to Mark, grimacing. "Emilie Meyvise," she hissed with a sour tone.

Just as suddenly as Emilie had struck, Mark's eyes widened as he repeated, "Emilie Meyvise?" A worse fear overcame him.

More than arriving in a strange place, more than being immediately resented, more than being surrounded by strange powers, more than being unfamiliar with everything going on, his fear this time was familiar.

"I know that name," he whispered with his eyes pinned open. "I know that name," he repeated. Emilie's eyes and her expression as she spoke to him, it all whirled inside him. "And I know that face."

The name shot through him like a bullet and the words "Hellen Meyvise," escaped his mouth. Standing too quickly and somehow knowing Emilie was still close by, he shouted, "Hey! Are you related to Hellen Meyvise?"

Appearing only inches from his face, Emilie grinned evilly. "As a matter of fact," she affirmed as she twirled in the air, her dark brown hair in a wave about her as if it were underwater.

Piecing things together, Mark brushed the red strike out of his face again. "My aunt's name is Hellen Meyvise..."

Emilie smiled and placed her feet on the floor from floating effortlessly. Suddenly, she let out a brisk laugh, and threw her hair over her shoulder quite theatrically. "Are you saying we are related?" she asked with a broad, wild smile on her face. Gulping, Mark nodded, adopting a pensive expression to try to seem surer. Emilie moved closer to him airlessly, threatening, before raising an arm.

Mark flinched, but his eyes went wide as he felt the arm, he expected to strike at him gently wrapped around his shoulder in what seemed to be an embrace. Bringing her lips close to his ear, Emilie whispered, "Whether we are cousins or not, you may call me Feather." Leaning away from him with a much kinder smile now, Emilie gleamed toothily, again vanished in a wild spiral.

As soon as she was gone, Mark spotted something that made the blood drain from his face. The elevator doorway, from which he had appeared, was opening again and the figure inside promptly declared in a raised voice, "Mark Halo."

Ocie placed a hand on Mark's shoulder and gestured him to go forward. To Mark's best assumption, if Ocie suggested it, it was a good idea. However, realizing he had only known her for a few minutes, it confused him to see his feet driving him forward. Then it occurred that since this had been the way he came in, this would also be the way he got out. It was over now. The nightmare was ending.

After stepping in, the elevator door lurched closed behind him. His eyes grew tender, and he relaxed, his whole-body loosening. However, as he looked out at the Shadows through the closing doors, he noticed their confidence as well as the mixture of unease. He could hear the mutters.

"He'll be back."

Mark felt the fear vanishing. He kept an empty expression on his face, and he felt comfortable knowing the man who stood next to him was completely normal unlike the freaky Shadows inside that room.

Recognizing this was the second time he had felt it, the fear of the elevator rippled through him. His heartbeat rose with the flames in his hands as the whole box shuddered. The floor was cold, and though the lights were firm, it seemed completely dark and overcoming.

"You go by Mark, correct?" the man standing next to him confirmed as soon as the door opened before them. Mark somehow nodded, and the man smiled as Mark noted how short he was. Letting out a distressed breath, Mark realized this guy had been the same man at his home.

Coming out of the elevator, the two of them stepped into an endless hallway. Turning to meet Mark's crimson eyes and not showing the least bit of fear, the man finally extended a thick burly hand to shake. "My name's Ian Keller. I'm sure they've already mentioned me down there, once or twice." Keller raised a brow as if to inquire, and Mark tensed, forcing a mostly nonexistent nod. "Now…" he breathed, his voice sounding almost excited, "show me what you can do."

Maybe Mark was wrong. Maybe this wasn't how he was getting out. Maybe this was his initiation. Maybe this moment would determine if he was staying. Maybe it all depended on how he used his power before Keller that decided when he was going to leave. With too many options available, Mark's eyes once again flared to the bright crimson against his will.

Frantically, he referred to the feeling that caused him to vanish, and once he did, a feeling of relief came over him, comforted and held by the Realm.

It was becoming easier to handle and control with practice. Hesitantly, he flickered back into visibility like a flame. He met eyes with Keller, trying to express that he had done all he could do. Keller raised an eyebrow, a little disappointed. "You do know all Shadows can do that, right?"

Mark's face burned with a mixture of embarrassment and ignorance before he murmured, having been told this by the Shadows, "Yes, sir." Like a bullet, a thought shot through him, and he used the adrenaline he assumed had caused all this to summon flames in his left hand. They burned harshly on his skin. He couldn't take the heat for long and he shakily let it off, unable to hold it any longer.

"Fire…" Keller whispered gently, then placed a hand over Mark's. "When you create it, you're sustaining it so securely that it will burn anything, even you. From now on when you create it, keep it in your mind that you don't want to burn yourself." Listening intently, Mark felt as if Keller's instructions were critique-like and meant to help him become better at controlling it.

Keller eyed him keenly. "Would you like to know where you are?" he asked.

Mark nodded.

Keller smiled a bit smugly. "You're in Culpeper, Virginia, where the Library of Congress used to be. Do you know where I'm talking about?"

This time, he shook his head.

Keller invited him to walk down the hallway with him. "The facility is known as the ASH on the inside while on the outside it is the Library. The goal of this facility is to bring the Shadows together, to forward their powers, and prevent them from misusing their powers in the public," he explained. "I and a few others started this facility twenty years ago. The entire building is surrounded by a machine I designed called the ASI which makes all Shadow activity invisible from the outside, like the Realm. And it keeps all the Shadows inside until the time is right and they know how to use their powers properly."

He felt calm speaking to Keller, and his words nearly passed over him meaninglessly. He also felt that while this normal person was touching him, his flames held back as if they didn't want to burn the man. It was like gratitude was forming inside him as Keller took something out of his pocket.

He folded Mark's fingers over the object almost in the same way Sil had shoved the ice ball into his hand, but far more gently. "Lunch is at noon, dinner is at six, from one to four you'll be free to go outside with the others, and the ASOs will be there if you ever need anything or lose something beyond the barrier. You'll make a fine part of the ASH, Mark."

Like a wooden beam had been sent through his torso, Mark felt as if he couldn't breathe. "Wait!" he spat like a nasty taste hit his tongue. Keller turned back to him as Mark stood like an awkward broomstick scared upright. "What did I do wrong? Why do I have to stay?"

Keller frowned. "Because you are a Shadow, and nothing more," he stated flatly then gestured Mark into the elevator. Mark stumbled back, the soles of his feet feeling weak. Every step was like falling over marbles. So, when he slammed into the far wall, it was as if he had been thrown in violently.

As the doors closed, Mark leaned against the wall, ignoring the startling shake of the elevator as it moved either up or down, the direction of which he was unsure. Hours before, he had awoken and was dressed in these clothes by people he didn't know and thrown into this room. Now, here he was again, lost in despair as he felt so utterly helpless against the Shadows consuming him.

Fighting the tears forming in his crimson eyes, Mark sank to the floor as he had the first time. *They're going to eat me alive in here.* There was so much fear in his mind, he could barely move. His thoughts flashed with the many faces of the Shadows in that room, Sil's especially. If he didn't figure out how things worked, that guy was going to kill him.

I can't be afraid, he thought, *there can't be any more fear.* The elevator jerked a bit as it came to a stop. Glancing down at the object Keller had placed into his hand, a thin sheet of metal reading:

MARK HALO #016
Room 13-15
Shadow Fire

"No more fear," Mark whispered as the door opened.

IV
A SAFE HAVEN

The elevator door opened, displaying the room of Shadows, no difference at all, they were even still standing about in the same places, though more cryptically. Mark stood wearily of his own accord and stepped into the room before anyone came to him. Upon exiting, the elevator door closed automatically, and he stared forward at the Shadows, hugging his arm.

Emilie appeared before him abruptly, upside down and in the air, but far less unexpected. Nothing could faze Mark. He felt numb. Emilie encroached on him, drawing uncomfortably close to his face whilst reaching to touch his hand.

Without speaking, she took the sheet of metal and read it silently. "Shadow Fire," she whispered breathily. Elation filled her voice, and with a wide grin she turned to the other Shadows to declare, "He is the Shadow Fire."

Kip smiled at the words as Emilie slipped the chained metal pendent around his neck. The younger boy placed his hand on Mark's shoulder. "Our powers are the same. That's what I couldn't say before." As he spoke, Kip's eyes flared.

Mark tensed. Staring at the floor, he held himself up, and despite his resolve, he was still insecure. "This is insane."

Kip half-shrugged. "I'll try to help you get used to it."

Ocie stepped between them. "Are you ready, Mark?" she asked, also placing a hand on Mark's shoulder, opposite Kip.

Looking up curiously, Mark fretted. "Ready for what?" Their hands on him made him feel restrained, surrounded, and easily manipulated. He dug his heels into the floor, desperate to hold his ground and achieve some kind of confidence.

Ocie looked toward the skylight. *Into the Realm of the Shadows,* her voice resonated in his mind. His knees trembled, and his heart raced. He was hardly aware of what the Realm truly was, other than a dark world he entered when he turned invisible.

His eyes blank, mindlessly gazing at the white walls, Mark couldn't focus on the Shadows coming closer. Then simultaneously, they vanished from sight. But when Mark paid attention, he could see dark shadows scattered across the floor where they stood.

His head whipped back to Ocie. She had vanished too and the same with Kip, but their hands were still on his shoulders. Ethereal and heavy, Mark felt as if he were being touched by spirits, and he shuddered until Emilie appeared again. With a cryptic voice, she whispered, "Come with me."

Mark stared at her ghostly hand. His own arm was made of lead, impossible to raise, but with incredible effort, he lifted his arm, then hesitated, drawing back. His heart clenched, every nervous thought turning a pit in his stomach.

With his eyes closed, his fingertips made contact with her soft palm. Instantly and with brute strength, she grabbed his wrist and yanked him headlong into the Realm.

Mark wobbled, his balance wavering as he no longer felt his feet on the ground and gravity's control on his body vanished. A rush of black flooded all around him like a dark ocean wave had submerged him in the Shadow Realm.

Shocked, Mark spun around, turning weightlessly and looking down, his feet floated above miles and lightyears of nothingness. He flailed, but he couldn't stumble, and it was impossible for him to fall.

Nothing about the muscles in his body, or his determination, held any power here. The only semblance of control he could feel in this dark world came from a pulsating, glowing, fiery red orb beset upon his chest.

His eyes dashed about the sight of his own form in the Realm, and all he saw was a glowing body of fire. He was completely engulfed in a burning deep red conflagration.

Getting a feel for it, Mark focused on the fifteen Shadows around him and how, instantly, he could feel everything about them. Each was identified by a glowing orb on their hearts, burning through a shell of vaguely human incorporeal beings.

Nothing separated him from them. As if he had known them all their lives, he could feel the essence of their hearts and every thought which traveled through their minds. They were all alit with their Shadows glowing brightly like stars in this endless night, the light to this wavering dark world.

One of the Shadows came near him, and all he could make out was a woman made of water. As if unrestricted by the gravity-free vacuum of deep space, the water wavered and bounced about in droplets which clung to one another on contact.

It took effort to perceptively feel out to her and acknowledge her presence was Ocie. Her hair trailed around her as heavenly blue waters, calm and crystal clear except for a light at her heart and her eyes. She was stronger than he was, far more powerful, and honed in her Shadow.

What do you think? Her voice came to him sweetly, fluid and moving like the water. *This is the Shadow Realm,* Ocie said with a kinder love and deepness in spirit than any human relationship. Mark didn't hear her voice; he felt it, moving all around him, in and through him, more personally and intimately than a love song.

He was completely unable to grasp that other people, beings of such incredible power, knew and could feel into, enter in, and move through, that secret place he had hidden himself in when he quieted his soul.

In his heart, he had always known about this place. He had seen it when he slept and closed his eyes. This was the place he saw when he lost himself in video games, the empowered state he could feel when he focused his mind. This was the place he only imagined, his safe place, his hovel, and it comforted him to know he was not alone.

Mark realized the Shadows around him could feel him and know his heart as he could feel theirs. They sensed his anxiety and reached out to him. The Shadows knew how precious this secret place was to him.

Above him stretched a million miles of black and empty space, and beneath glittered thousands of colorful stars. Like an endless field of jewels, each shined with different intensities and called out to him with their own voices.

However, on all sides of him, forward and behind, on this level place, he was surrounded by wavering, unstable white pillars forming the walls of the ASH, the beds across the room and every bookshelf. He could even see the elevator, a cold, closed door, and above it, the hallway where he and Keller had been.

He could vaguely make out the outline of the huge building, but more so, he felt the presence of a tree, an unremarkable thing, but it was the fact that he knew it was there that amazed him. Invisible to his human eyes, he could feel its physical structure.

There were three planes of existence in this Realm, the endless, blackness of space above, the physical muted form of the real world, and the star field far below. *This is incredible,* he thought, gasping in awe, but unable to feel any real breath escaping his lungs. The Shadows' glow brightened, and he tensed, recognizing they could hear his thoughts.

Looking at them, but unable to focus on a single entity, Mark leaned closer, weightless but able to control his location and see intangible objects to avoid them. *Where is this? Outer space?*

A voice chuckled uncomfortably close to him, and just by looking at her visage, a dull golden glow and a rush of summer air, he knew it was Emilie. *Of course not. This place connects all of us to each other, mentally, and on a more... psychological level.* A wavering body of water, closed in on his fiery form, nearing enough he could feel stray droplets of water evaporating in his flames.

Mark realized it was Ocie.

The purpose of this place is to bring unity among the Shadows, to create a like-mindedness that protects us and keeps our hearts pure.

So, we can't hurt each other? Mark wondered, enthralled.

Ocie shook her head, tendrils of water-like hair swirled about her.

Mark sulked, a little grief entering his psyche now that he could feel the Shadows near him. They invaded the quiet secrecy of the place he used to see in his dreams. Mark feared he could never feel alone again. He liked the solitude, and he wasn't sure how he felt about others in here with him.

From within his fiery form, Mark looked around. Feeling dizzy with no clear direction in this world, he grimaced, sinking lower in the airless void like falling to the floor. *I... I want to be alone...* he whispered to them through his mind, unused to sharing his mind's secret voice to speak to another person. They complied. Elise nodded and shooed out the others before leaving as well.

As soon as he felt he was completely alone, Mark looked around him, turning in circles. All to be seen for miles was the endless night and vast welcome lonesomeness of the Shadow Realm.

Closing his bright eyes, Mark breathed a sigh of complete release. Seeing the Realm for real for the first time, not feeling like he was crazy, Mark accepted this and let it into himself. This world was a sweet salvation, and despite how it felt—a little invaded upon—Mark let himself sink deeper.

The dark fumes of physical objects that could not take form embraced him, and he traveled through them until he came upon the colorful stars and gazed into them. No human could ever look down on the stars like this, not even through water.

And in that instant, he realized they were Shadows. He could feel them. Their presence was strong, pervading the whole area, and Mark didn't feel alone. He felt held and gently lifted. They whispered to him, Shadows speaking from far beyond him, *it's not time for you to come to us.*

V
SILVERSTONARELLENA'S HATRED

The Realm wasn't just a daydream, it was a real place, and he wasn't the only one there.

Mark stretched out, feeling stiff but surprised to feel cool sheets beneath him and the dim light of day touching his face. A smile washed over him. He refused to open his eyes for a long time, but when he did, he was still in the ASH.

Frowning bitterly, Mark was greeted by Kip who must've sensed the moment he left the Realm. Groaning, Mark looked around at the others, not seeing anyone near him but Kip. On the bed where he sat, he counted the three walls and six beds where the boys slept and noted the room divider was all that separated the girls from the boys. "What happened?" Mark's voice came breathlessly.

Kip chuckled, playful and childish. "When you came out of the Realm, you were asleep," he mused which made Mark very uncomfortable, "right there on the floor, so we moved you to a bed, and you slept for, like, two hours," he explained, checking the time with a bleary gaze up at the skylight.

His eyes narrowing, Mark eyed him skeptically. "Wait... how did you do that?"

Kip laughed again. He had a high voice and a somewhat

girly laugh, but Mark figured no one had ever told him otherwise. "I can tell time based on the position of the sun really accurately. My eyes also change color based on the time of day. I sort of have a connection to the sun," he admitted sheepishly.

At this point, Mark kept his mouth shut even though what Kip said sounded ridiculous. "Hold on!" Kip said suddenly, scampering to his bed to fetch a box from under the flimsy metal frame. He rushed it to his new friend and presented it. However, like an idiot, Mark stared at it confused. No way was this incredibly sheltered kid he'd just met offering him a gift.

Kip glanced nervously from Mark to the box. "This is for you," he insisted. Kip stared at him as if he thought Mark had never been given a gift before.

Mark smirked. Kip was incredibly sheltered. Hastily, Kip ripped off the top and made Mark look inside at the pair of black and red rollerblades.

"What for?" Mark asked, eyeing the skates as Kip urged him to put them on.

Kip only smiled wider. "So you can skate with me, of course!" he beamed, placing the skates in Mark's lap.

Mark hesitated, dumbstruck at the sight of the pair of inline skates, but as he looked closer at the boots, his eyes flared a little brighter with the fierce red he couldn't dampen. The black and red looked cool, and they appeared brand new. Years ago, Mark had gotten really into roller hockey, but his interest faded with the introduction of video games into his life. Mark realized he'd gotten so addicted to gaming, he'd forgotten how good real adrenaline felt, and maybe if he'd learn how to use that adrenaline outside of yelling at a computer screen, he wouldn't have found out he was a Shadow in the first place.

Kip was already wearing a similar pair, which were worn and well loved. "All right," he said finally, offering a smile which made Kip leap with joy and skid on the hard floor.

Mark knelt to tighten the roller blades securely, nervous from previous experience that loose skates meant twisted ankles. He might have been only slightly enthusiastic about joining Kip in something *fun*, but his curiosity compelled him to move.

It was easy to balance on roller blades, and even easier to get moving. Again, Mark studied Kip. He seemed childish but intelligent, eager and possibly carefree, powerful but innocent. It was a beautiful combination.

Mark trailed Kip, and other boys followed suit into the center of the common room where Mark had first arrived, and they skated in a circle, forming a rink by only their unity. The Shadows made their twists and turns around the room, some finding the coordination to go backwards. Their rhythm was perfect, and only varied around turns. Every motion streamlined and uniform.

Gliding forward, unstable, Mark skated on a small rink arranged by the Shadows within the room. *Innocent,* it was all Mark could think to himself as he mimicked the Shadows' rhythm. Kip rushed forward to playfully skate next to Mark. "Hey, you're getting it. Have you skated before?" he asked, slightly throwing Mark off balance.

Being unused to the skates, Mark flared his crimson eyes at Kip before responding, "I haven't skated in years."

Kip nodded, gracing along as if the eight wheels were a part of him.

Emilie whizzed past them suddenly, barely touching the ground as she flew around the wide circle. The tip of his front wheel collided with Emilie's skate ever so slightly and his balance flew to the wind.

He stumbled, fighting impossibly hard to stay at Kip's side. He couldn't focus enough on where he was falling to look forward. He swerved, sending him headlong into Silverstonarellena's path. Sil was traveling the same direction as Emilie, and Mark slammed into him at full speed, knocking both to the ground.

"That—" Sil got up before Mark even determined which

direction was down. "—is... it! If you're going to be stuck here with the rest of us, you need to get a hold of your Shadow before you kill someone!" Ice formed over Sil, covering his face with fractals, and stiffening his long white hair, even his golden eyes turned pale as ice.

"I didn't even do anything. Emilie just—" Mark said, wobbling, giving all he had to not slip.

"Emilie knows how to skate. You're the one who lost your balance." Sil twisted Mark's reaction. "Like Shadows, you need to know how to skate before you can ever skate around others. You're a hazard!"

"Sil's right." Emilie slid to a halt after reversing direction and taking sides as if it had been her plot from the beginning. "A Shadow shows control and strength; that is what a Shadow *is*. The only reason you would run into him is if you were attacking him... unless you're as big of an idiot as you seem." Engineered perhaps, she had designed it so Sil would have a reason to fight Mark.

"Are you kidding!" Mark burst, seeing through what Emilie was trying to do. "You tripped me!" He certainly didn't want to start a fight, but Emilie was making it unavoidable.

The other Shadows cleared the common area of the room as if it caused less damage to let any fight with Sil or Emilie happen. Elise stepped back from Sil's growing hostility and headed to the wall. She pulled a switch and Mark awed as the bedrooms were sealed off with a bright, glowing reddish-bronze shield.

"Sil, don't be ridiculous. Mark just got here, and Emilie, don't antagonize him!" Elise insisted with panic in her voice, though she tried to hide it in a leader-like tone.

Sil raised his hands bearing long sharp threads of ice, ten towering, glittering tendrils growing from his fingertips. "You ever wondered about the whole reincarnation crap Keller's tried to teach us? Our Shadows will always come back, different form, different body. It's been like that for generations!"

Sil swung his hand out, slinging thin, sharp needles at Mark. It was beyond Mark how he managed to summon the agility to dodge it on his skates, diving to the floor.

"Yes, but *he* won't. Quit screwing around. Haven't you lost enough!" Ocie cut in. Mark stiffened, Sil's words freaking him out. *Reincarnation?* Looking between Ocie and Sil, he realized Sil did this all the time. He picked fights. He antagonized everyone.

"It's been too long since we've had a good fight." Emilie flew over to Mark, crossing her arms with a sadistic grin. "Let's see what you've got, Shadow Fire!" With a simple touch, Mark began to float, but only with Emilie's touch could he remain in the air. Emilie took him higher and higher. At the skylight, she turned him around.

"What are you doing?" Mark panicked, flailing his arms and legs but unable to gain any control over his surroundings.

Emilie looked at him with a sly grin. She grabbed him by the collar with a fierce grip, hoisting him up so his head nearly hit the skylight. Then, without warning, she dropped him, sending him tumbling to the floor.

Mark shrieked as he fell at the mercy of gravity, terrified until he landed in a deep snowdrift, shocked into a fully alert state he had never felt, only ignited by the cold. His adrenaline spiked, his heart racing. A strange lucid mental state filled his head as he bolted to his feet, fire igniting in his palms.

Cold, but suddenly empowered, Mark bore his fists and briefly looked at the intense flames in his hands. This was real, not just his dazed state. The fire was real. That was all that mattered. In and out of his fingers, climbing his wrists and licking at his sleeves. This was his alone.

Sil stepped closer, bearing ice in his hands as he placed them on his hips smugly. "You've got good instincts," he analyzed as if this was some kind of lesson. "Can you feel that rush?" he goaded, bringing up the snow on the floor into a blizzard-like spiral that traveled across his hands. "Let it fuel you. Your body creates that adrenaline for a reason. Use it!"

Mark stood five paces from Sil, the fire on his hands singeing his sleeves, and he clenched his fist, wincing at the heat. The fire was starting to burn him, and he had to stop, consciously telling himself the fire couldn't hurt him. He wouldn't let it.

Trembling, his entire body shook, and his palms opened. His heart raced, and like Sil, the fire traveled across his hands whirling around him like a storm. The fire flowed through the air like unsettled water lashing out at the snowflakes that neared it, but at the same time, it calmed Mark, steadied his heart, and focused his Shadow.

"You actually have no concept of fighting, do you?" Sil mocked, spinning the snowflakes together like thread and compacting them into hard, dense, opaque ice. "Get used to it. The better you can use your Shadow, the better you'll fit in." Sil breathed of the cold, smiling grimly and using the Realm to cloud Mark's perceptions, tugging him into that dark world. "Refine your Shadow," Sil whispered through the darkness, "and practice!"

Taking hold of the ice in the air, Sil reeled his arm back and hurled it forward at Mark like a baseball. Mark stood shocked, readying himself and thinking maybe he could burn up the orb of solid ice, but he was distracted and amazed by the precision Sil showed with his Shadow.

Sil's wild, white hair whirled around him, his stance certain and golden eyes powerful. Mark didn't dodge until the last second, letting instinct take control, but the ice ball still struck him on the shoulder.

Giving a cry from the sudden impact, Mark lost all focus and the flames withered and vanished. The ice ball hit the floor, bouncing once dully against the white tile before Sil took control of it, causing it to crumble, and again, it became nothing more than snowflakes. Holding his left shoulder as the pain wore off, Mark glared at Sil. "Just stop it! I don't want to fight you!"

Sil laughed at him playfully, sending a flurry of his storm directly through Mark's footing, throwing off his balance and stance. "Are you getting angry yet?" he taunted, creating a new ball of ice.

Mark couldn't see a thing through the whiteout. He was getting cold and frustrated. Under no circumstances was Sil going to listen to him. "What are you trying to prove?" Mark shouted. "That you're the strongest here? What do you want?"

There was stark silence throughout the intense storm. Mark couldn't see Sil, and his panic rose. Mark's eyes flared crimson cherry, highly visible in the blizzard.

He let his heart open, let all his senses work together to feel into the tempest, and for only a second, he let his mind drift into his secret place. The Realm burst around him, black and all-encompassing, but for only a second as the wind blew over him.

It was quiet. He couldn't see Sil, but in the white-out, he knew exactly where he was. No human sense conveyed it to him. He just knew.

The fire exploded within his palm, then imploded, going volatile, and the crimson flames glowed brighter. Mark had never focused on one object harder in his life. The sight of the fire he created alone was enough to reassure his doubts. On instinct, using the adrenaline pulsing through him, Mark flung the tightly wound orb of fire, hurling it at Sil as hard as he could.

A fluster of fear and dread filled his heart, then it was overshadowed by an incredible elation, overconfidence, and power. The fear flowed from his secret place within the Realm, but it wasn't his own. It surrounded him.

The snow crackled, fire and ice trapped together in midair, before hitting the floor and shattering like glass.

"Mark, don't!" Emilie screamed, grabbing hold of his shoulders, but she was too late.

The fire had already consumed all the ice, evaporating, filling the room with steam. However, the initial blast struck

Sil in the chest. The whiteout cleared enough for Mark to see and he paled. Sil's clothes were on fire, and he was panicking.

The flames had taken over his shirt, and the unnatural fire clung to his skin, eating away. Collapsing to his knees, crying out, Sil tried to freeze the fire, but it wasn't working.

The bronze-colored energy field protecting the others vanished from Mark's side and he tensed, taken off guard as Ocie rushed out to him, taking his hands, and instantly enveloping them in water to put out the fire. "Mark!" She pled, "listen to me. You need to completely stop using your Shadow. Focus on me, okay?" She placed a hand on his face, startling him. Outside his control, his gaze locked onto her oceanic-blue eyes, and he was lost in them.

The fire died, and Ocie left him, hurrying to Sil with Emilie already at his side. Mark hesitated, his feet glued to the floor as his heart raced. The adrenaline held him fully alert and in a rush, but the crash was hitting him hard already.

Sil screamed, unable to pat out the searing flame. Mark stood petrified watching him panic, drop to the floor to attempt to pat out the fire, but Sil was unable to compose himself enough to freeze it.

"Sil!" Emilie yelled. She could only watch the fire take over his clothing.

Ocie grimaced on her knees, too late to prevent Sil from getting hurt. She grabbed his shoulder to hold him steady, but he writhed away from her touch. "Sil, you need to calm down. Hold still! I'm going to douse you with water." Her fingers nearly freezing as she contacted his skin, she placed a hand on his left cheek and tried to get him to look into her eyes.

Sil refused, pinning his eyes shut. For the few seconds Ocie coated his skin in water, and Mark winced. He had never been seriously burned in his life, he had no idea how much it hurt. But from the look on Sil's face, it was constant pain, too unbearable to function.

"You…" Emilie growled, turning her attention to Mark and storming over, stamping her feet, thoroughly enraged. "You moron. Idiot! Are you completely brainless? What in the world were you thinking? I ought to drag you up and throw you down so there's nothing you can do to save yourself!" Emilie ignored the fact that the elevator door was opening, but Mark saw it.

Keller burst into the room followed closely by men in light gray uniforms. They looked like police officers, and Mark's heart sank even lower. They gathered around Sil in a frenzy. "What on Earth happened in here?" Keller demanded, shouting directly into Ocie's face.

She didn't answer him, only briefly glancing at Mark long enough for Keller to know everything. Keller glared at Mark as Emilie drove him back with insults. "Separate them!" he yelled to his men.

Three men in uniforms rushed Mark and Emilie, causing him to panic. Rather than resisting, he pushed himself toward the man who took him by the arms and dragged him away from Emilie.

It took two men to restrain Emilie and pull her back as she bucked and kicked with her feet in the air. Mark's brain was dead as he let the man hold him firmly. In the silence of his heart, and the draining rush of adrenaline, he realized Emilie was unable to float these two men using her Shadow.

Finally, the elevator opened again and a woman entered the room. She wore the same uniform but loosely unbuttoned over an informal black dress. Mark's eyes locked on her, confused, but in awe as his vision blurred.

The woman carried a lightweight stretcher, and over her shoulder, she had a trauma kit with a first aid cross on it. But Mark's focus was on her long, strawberry-red, curly hair tied in a high ponytail.

"Not again!" she said, scarcely sparing a glance at Mark as she knelt down to Sil and tore away the remains of his shirt. "Can you stand, Sil?" she called down to him.

Sil's face contorted with intense pain, but he opened his

eyes and the woman got him to sit up. Sil winced and cried out when she urged him to stand, pulling him onto his feet, supporting him by his arms and back.

Sil could walk, but he was slow, wincing at every movement. Keller and the other men followed into the elevator, leaving the Shadows behind. The two men waited, refusing to release Emilie until the room cleared.

When the elevator door closed, silence overtook the whole space, and all eyes fell on Mark. Emilie glared at him, an unhampered anger raging inside her.

Painstakingly slow, all the Shadows moved to their beds, but Mark remained standing, too afraid to take a single step like any movement would trigger Emilie to attack him.

"Look..." Mark's breath quivered, attempting to reason with Emilie. "That was just an accident... I couldn't see him," he insisted, but Emilie's pent up rage drove her closer.

She dashed to the switch for the shield which would trap him on this side of the barrier with her. Slamming down on it, she flung herself off the wall like she was swimming and propelled herself at him. Mark could feel the bronze light behind him as if it was hot. It illuminated against his skin and he feared the moment he impacted the surface.

"I'm sorry!" Mark shrieked, his arms flying up to protect himself. He stumbled, forgetting—other than the intense pressure on his feet—he was still wearing skates.

He reeled backward, collapsing, and heard Kip shriek as he plummeted onto his spine. Mark knocked the wind out of himself and felt his shoulder blades throb from the fall. The pain worried him since he already had back problems, but not more than seeing Emilie rushing at him through a fog of red.

She crashed into the transparent ward, sending her flying and tumbling to the floor. Only then did Mark realize he had fallen through the bronze-red shield.

The Shadows sat shocked, staring at the sight in complete awe. Emilie sat up on the floor, shaking off her disorientation and the temporary canceling of her powers.

"What the…" she breathed, staring at Mark's rollerblades sticking out from the other side of the transparent curtain.

Mark scurried backwards, fully inside the energy field in case Emilie changed her mind, and decided to attack him. He saw the rage in her eyes die as she stood in amazement. Kip ran up to the shield with wide eyes. "Mark! How did you do that?"

Wincing from the fall, Mark got up, a sharp pain shooting down his back. "What?" He didn't know what they were surprised about, but he didn't doubt the look in Kip's eyes.

Curious, Mark reached out to touch the energy field, but his hand passed through it.

Amazed, Kip did the same, but it sent his hand flying back, firing electricity through his arm. Mark jumped when Kip winced and stepped back almost losing his balance on his skates.

His friend massaged his hand, used to the occasional sting. "Do you know what this means?" Kip whispered, his voice a little strained.

Mark shook his head, and the hopefulness in Kip's eyes struck him.

"You can defy the ASH! This shield can't hold you back!" he said, jumping with excitement. "Here!" He extended his hand just far enough to not touch the shield. "Pull me through."

Mark reached out reluctantly. It felt like nothing separated him from the others. He could still feel them like they were waiting within the Realm, hiding.

He grabbed Kip's hand through the shield, taking it firmly and yanked. Kip stumbled, passing through the energy field with ease. The boy gasped, utterly shocked as Mark steadied him. "I didn't feel a thing!" he declared. "Just contact with you makes it so the ASI doesn't work on me either!"

Emilie set her feet on the floor, and cautiously, each Shadow gathered closer, their minds in tandem with the

Realm, thinking only one thing, *the Exodus has come.* A powerful wave rushed over Mark in the Realm, and the phrase shook his core. But there was still doubt in their voices, a worry that this might not be the answer to the hopes they had only dreamed of for years.

Kip stared at Mark in surprise, grabbing his hand tighter, walking back through the shield toward the other Shadows. Mark protested in a few steps but let himself glide forward on his skates. While Kip still held onto his hand, Kip entered the Realm and pulled Mark with him.

Mark felt thrown into it, the darkness bursting around him, and Kip's immense form of light overpowered him. Shadows appeared like fiery pillars and moved closer, surrounding him and his fear rekindled as never before.

Feeling his worry and the crippling fear, Emilie floated nearer, gazing deeply into his form so he would feel her anger slip away, revealing only the strongest desire to escape and be free. Mark had never met another being with a more intense need for freedom, even within these walls. Emilie, beyond all others, wanted nothing more than to leave the ASH.

Emilie scrutinized Mark's fiery hand reaching toward her, blazing, warm and bright. Mark hesitated to meet her eyes, but in return for her change of heart, he offered her his confidence.

The fire flickered as he touched her hand, but when their Shadows combined, her will met his. Mark allowed her to see the freedom he had before now. He knew through the Realm that in her heart, she wanted it.

Emilie gasped at the visions Mark imparted to her. She stepped out toward the Shadows. *This is our ticket out of here. We have been waiting for this. You can share your power with us and help us escape.*

Wait! What are you talking about? Mark cried out through the blackness. *What's the Exodus?*

A softer Shadow neared him, gentler than Emilie, and bright as a star. Mark was slow to assess that this was Kip until the boy explained. *The Exodus is an event that happens every generation. Humans hate Shadows and try to imprison them, but a time always comes for us to be free. No one will be afraid of us anymore.*

Why? Mark yelled, a thousand fears consuming him. *Why does everyone hate Shadows? I still don't see why. If you guys are just people with powers, what's so dangerous?*

We're not dangerous, Kip assured graciously, *but it's something we can't control, humans are just threatened by us, they always have been.*

Feeling himself sinking, Mark couldn't move. It couldn't be that simple. There had to be a real reason the Shadows were stuck here, why he was stuck here. What had the Shadows done to be so hated? No one let him ask any questions, no one who had real answers, like Keller, or his mother.

Mark's form wavered in the airless space, doubts whispering in his mind. *Mark, the Exodus is here because of you.* Emilie smiled up to him, overjoyed. *I bet that was why your Shadow test was negative and you could hide for so long. Your power is to defy the ASH's technology.*

A Shadow touched his hand and Mark tensed until he saw it was Ocie. His heart relaxed, and he relayed all his fears to her without speaking. It calmed him, and he glanced around at the other Shadows as Emilie declared, *The Exodus is here at last!*

A stir of warmth resonated through the water enveloping his hand, and Mark could feel all these wonderful things in Ocie's heart, feeling the fullness of Emilie's hopes. This powerful hope enveloped all of them, and Mark knew this feeling had been growing for years. Nevertheless, there was a sorrow in Ocie's demeanor as if she knew something would break their hearts.

Emilie's Shadow brightened in the dark, and the other Shadows stretched their powers, strengthening themselves. It was glorious to see. *But we must keep it a secret.* Emilie leaned forward on the nonexistent floor of the Shadow

Realm.

Emilie's right. If the ASH finds out Mark is the Exodus, they will take him and make sure he never gets out. Elise said, looking at the other Shadows.

We'll have time to celebrate once we get out of here. Kip asked, *Shadows agreed?*

Agreed. The Shadows said together.

VI
FAULTS

A mixture of poor timing, a horrible choice, and a sudden spark of hope among the Shadows churned a bitter taste in Mark's stomach. He portrayed an air about him that he wanted to be left alone as he sat on his bed for the first time. Through the skylight in the center of the room, Mark could see evening drawing near, even though his horrible, terrible day had just begun.

Sil's frozen eyes and the look of hope in all the Shadows was all Mark could think about. He fretted over how seriously he had burned Sil, how he would react to him, how he would apologize, and—

He gave up. Letting these thoughts whirl about in his head only sickened him more. He tried to justify himself because Sil challenged him. Mark didn't know how to use this Shadow he had, and in the fullest sense, both of them were toying with fire.

Mark saw the flames burning away at Sil again. He dismissed the thought that anything that had happened was Sil's fault. Mark's power was fire, but he didn't know how to control it. He banished all thoughts of everything except he felt a little hungry, which was probably part of why he felt sick.

Leaning back into a borrowed pillow, he gazed at his hand. He assumed it would be blistered, especially with how much fire it had endured, but to his surprise it wasn't burned in the slightest. His fingers trembled a little bit, and with much effort, he caused dim and scattered flames to race across his skin.

Fire... in his hand.

It was deep red and entirely unnatural. It felt hot, but it didn't hurt. He didn't want to burn himself and he didn't. He gulped, listening to Keller had helped. He let the flames grow higher and hotter, engulfing his hand to his wrist in bright, cherry colored fire. It twisted around his fingers, climbing up into the air and wavering at his bidding.

He forced a breath to steady the spinning rock in his stomach. Just yesterday, it had been an accident, out of his control as he destroyed his computer. Now, it was like he had full control over it. But too late. He'd already hurt someone.

Despite how much he wanted to be alone and used a dark aura to deter the others, Ocie came to him without warning and took him by the hand. She said several things, but Mark didn't listen as she pulled him along, and her words flowed over him. She laughed. "Aren't you hungry at all?"

Mark came out of thought a little startled until he realized it was probably time for the evening meal. Ocie pulled him out of the room and into the elevator. He noticed her stifling her grin. "You're gripping that railing like you're holding on for dear life," she said.

Mark let go and took a step away from it. "Sorry," he replied. "I just get uncomfortable in elevators."

Ocie giggled, but tried to hide it as the doors opened, and Keller appeared on the other side. She left the elevator, turning back to Mark, saying, "Walk with us." Before Mark's eyes, Keller took Ocie's arm tightly and tenderly.

Mark drew his brows together and didn't budge, dumbstruck, and then he noticed Ocie's hidden grin. Keller met eyes with him. "Mark," he addressed in a strong authoritative voice, "I'm sure my daughter has introduced you to everyone, hasn't she?"

Mark's psyche cracked his brain open ten times over before he recognized Keller had pushed him forward by the shoulder. Ian Keller was Ocie's father. Mark remained silent as he walked with her and Keller down the hall, following closely.

Keller, in Mark's eyes, attempted to become personable. "I hope you understand, Mark, that you are here to learn to control your powers as every Shadow is. Unrefined Shadows can be very dangerous. And we don't want you hurting anyone," he assured. Mark gulped uncomfortably as his gut turned. Keller saw it and sighed. "Unfortunately, I was a little quick to put you in with the Shadows, and I didn't think how Silverstonarellena would react to you." He seemed apologetic in his tone.

They continued down the stairs when Keller spoke again. "Did you know, Mark, that you are the first new Shadow the ASH has received in five years?" He stated it as if it were an amazing fact.

Ocie took Mark's attention and explained. "That's because the generation of Shadows ended five years ago. Children stopped being born with Shadows, and generations usually last about fifty years." They continued down the hall after they reached the bottom of the stairs.

The passageways were lined with windows along one side. The sunlight beamed in on Mark's right, and doors to rooms were on his left. Mark noticed one door labeled "Infirmary" next to a reception area. He had a feeling Sil was in that room, and a sense of dread came over him at the notion the room held many memories of injuries and long sicknesses.

They took a turn in the hall and passed through double doors into a loud, spacious room which appeared to serve as a mess hall.

Keller spoke over the crowd. "You're about to meet

Kimberly. She works here as our main nurse in addition to being a fabulous cook. I'm sure she'll be pleased to meet you officially," he said with a hint of sarcasm and more meaning, which Mark didn't catch.

He could, however, manage in this state to acknowledge Keller was speaking about the woman he had seen earlier who had been so quick to care for Sil.

Keller left them as Ocie pulled Mark into the line to get their dinner, which flowed quickly in spite of being immensely long. Mark was thankful for the efficiency as he entered the room and the delicious scents worsened his hunger.

When he was closer to the front of the line, already with a plate and several items on it, he spied the woman managing the portions of food. Her curly red hair was still tied up in a high ponytail, and to Mark's surprise, now that he got a closer look, she had bright pink eyes. This was Kimberly.

As the line moved, Kimberly glanced up from the serving spoons directly into Mark's eyes, and she froze. He assumed her shock was from the fact she had never seen him before, but the look in her eyes said more. It was a mixture of amazement, shock, and grief all at once.

Kimberly took a hasty step back from the counter and her hand drifted over her mouth as she stared at him. Mark felt she was looking at him as if she saw someone entirely different, someone she loved, maybe someone she had lost.

Ocie instinctively patched things up for her. "Kimberly, this is Mark. He's the new Shadow."

The hand on Kimberly's mouth drifted over her heart. "It's nice to meet you," she said, burying her surprise and adding awkwardly, "Sorry, it's just you remind me of... someone I used to know."

"It's fine," Mark said only to get past her wide-eyed shock, which hadn't vanished yet. He and Ocie continued, and Mark looked to Ocie, asking, "What was with her?"

Ocie sighed a little. "A few months ago, Kimberly lost

someone she loved a lot. I suppose you remind her of him."
Ocie led Mark to a table among dozens in the room where
most of the Shadows from the room ate. Mark sat next to
Ocie, forcing Kip to scoot down, who was happy to see him
joining them.

Looking across the table, Mark stared at Emilie oddly
for a few seconds and noticed she was sitting with her feet
on a chair next to her. She gorged herself, gracelessly
stuffing in forkfuls of an odd-looking green veggie, which
Mark guessed was zucchini. She either loved it or was
simply compensating for her anger by overeating. But one
thing was clear, she was saving the seat next to her for
someone. Mark didn't have to guess who that was.

He looked around, bewildered. There were so many
Shadows. Indeed, the youngest must have been around five
years old, and the oldest were adults. But there were so
many, easily a hundred Shadows in this room if not more.
Looking at the door, Mark noticed a uniformed man held it
open. He thought for a moment the man was one of the
officers or guards he had seen earlier, but as he watched
longer, he saw the man was holding the door for a Shadow.

As the Shadow entered with slow, smooth footsteps,
Mark grimaced and gulped. It was Silverstonarellena. From
the distance, Mark could easily see a white gauze bandage
on the side of Sil's neck and face. Mark said nothing, but he
watched Sil, thinking frantically about how he was going to
apologize, or say anything, so Sil knew he hadn't meant to
hurt him.

Sil traveled through the line, heavy-footed, gaining the
gazes of everyone along the way. Kimberly tried to smile,
asking, "Are you holding up all right, Sil?" He simply turned
her a cold shoulder and continued to the place Emilie was
saving. Sil ate silently after adding a layer of frost over his
food to cool it down. Silence overtook the table and soon it
spread through the mess hall.

Mark noted the bandages were only in places where Sil
had received more severe burns, and the rest of the burns

were cleaned, open, and oozing a little. Mark had a hard time looking at it, but it was equally difficult to tear his gaze away. Emilie slid a napkin to Sil across the table, but he pushed it back at her.

Very briefly, Sil's golden eyes flared at Mark for staring at him, and Mark cowered his gaze into his half empty plate. The mess of Sil's white hair was tied back, and Emilie commented under the chatter that it looked like Kimberly fought to ponytail it.

Sil snapped, "Emilie, it was gauze, not a haircut." She didn't even seem fazed by the harsh tone of his voice.

By not letting herself be intimidated by him, Emilie cozied up to him like he was her protection. Mark assumed the two of them had played off each other for years, but they didn't have any kind of friendship. Mark's fear overwhelmed him, and he panicked. He had to apologize somehow.

Even so, he couldn't make a single sound as he watched him eat. Sil's slow, fluid movements terrorized Mark, but he knew he would regret any attempt to grovel.

"I'm so sorry!" Mark got out in a brash second breath he had intended to say in the first, which was why it was so hoarse in the second one. Sil's cat-like eyes locked onto him abhorrently, but Mark still forced himself to add in a choking whisper, "Please, I didn't mean to hurt you..."

Regret seemed to freeze Mark's soul like Sil's Shadow as he watched Sil bolt up, raising his hands as fists. Mark flinched and closed his eyes as Sil slammed them down onto the table, blasting ice over everyone's meal.

In addition to frying all Mark's senses with fear, Sil screamed out, "You keep your mouth shut around me! Get it through your head that the only way I'll ever forgive you is if you get a hold of that blasted Shadow of yours!" His golden eyes burned into Mark's, paralyzing his heart.

Right about bloody now, Mark wished he could just die, and that his petty soul would fly out of him and leave this place forever. The color drained from his face as the room fell silent. The whole table was covered in ice, and there was a pile of snow all over him. Mark sat unmoving, staring into his lap ashamed.

On instinct, the Shadows filled the room with chatter, knowing the silence was likely to beckon Sil's anger on them, and make Mark feel worse. Sil sat down frustrated, and the Shadows around Mark watched him as Sil spread a layer of icy frost over his burns before he continued eating, ignoring Mark's very being. The ice on the table retracted back into Sil's hands, then vanished, and Sil proceeded to chill his own meal, to eat it practically frozen.

Mark put his hands in his lap, seeing that Sil had done the same thing to his own meal when he blasted ice all over the table. Mark slid his chair back from the table and got up to get away.

⌒◍⌒

Kimberly watched Mark closely as he left the room, and only turned her gaze away when Keller spoke to her, assuring, "He'll be in the hall. He's not going anywhere."

They sat at a table away from the majority of the other Shadows. Kimberly reluctantly acknowledged Keller. "Who exactly is he?" she asked, still as concerned as before.

Keller wore reading glasses and browsed through papers strewn across the table. "Marcus Ezra Halo," he stated as if he had read it, "born November 6, 2015, age fourteen, Shadow Fire. Emilie Meyvise is his cousin. Apparently, they have the same birthday. That's about all I know for sure about him, at least all that matters."

Kimberly's countenance stiffened as Keller paused, and in return, Keller sighed heavily. "I know all those details mean a lot to you, but Kimberly, you need to let go," he replied, his tone growing warmer as if in warning a close friend.

Hesitantly, Kimberly folded her hands under the table. "But they're so much alike," she insisted. "What if it's him?"

66

Keller again sighed, thoughtfully removing his glasses, with a stern aura. "I have thought this. It occurred to me the moment I saw him. He's got the same fire in his eyes, and the red patches in his hair, but they're not nearly the same person. Think about it. He has a family. He's lived with that family all his life, and even if it is him and his memories of the Shadows are somehow gone, how does that explain how he has a family he's known all his life?" Keller started to stack the papers. "What I'm worried about now is finding out how Mark has hidden from the ASH so far and why his powers have never surfaced until now."

"But they even look alike!" Kimberly pled, her eyes flaring as her tone became brash. "Like, it could be dyed, and it's not hard for a Shadow to change their eye color. What color are his eyes without his Shadow?"

"Stop!" Keller snapped. "I know what you're feeling, Kimberly, but you have to let go and accept that he's gone. He's never coming back, and Mark is not him."

Kimberly cringed, fighting off what Keller knew were tears, but in fighting them, she got up, and like Mark, left in such a way that made her look as if she were going after him. As she crossed the center of the room, Sil abruptly stood from his seat calling out a loud word, "Keller!"

Sighing heavily, Keller stood as well. "What is it, Sil?"

Sil's golden eyes sparked with his intent. "I would like permission to go outside so that I can feed and check on my hawk."

Nodding, though still quite frustrated, Keller affirmed and signaled one of the ASOs to accompany Sil as he snagged up the last of the meat portion on his plate in his hand and took it out of the room.

⁊◑ᨈ

Sil and the ASO turned in the hall toward a short staircase leading up to a door which was left unlocked most of the time and Shadows often used it to go outside. Upon exiting, Sil and the guard turned the corner into the courtyard where Sil looked to the sky.

He had the ASO unlock a supply closet in which the Shadows kept many belongings for outdoor use. This included Sil's leather arm guard he took out of the closet and strapped to his arm. In his mind, Sil called to the air while he was still fastening the arm guard. He only waited a few seconds before, a large golden-brown hawk came from the clouds and landed directly on the leather guard.

Sil embraced the force of the large bird's landing and as it did, he took the time to switch hands with the meat he had snagged. The Red-Tailed Hawk tucked its feathers behind its back and began to preen itself on Sil's arm. With his fingertips, he stroked the gorgeous bird's breast, but the animal smelled what he had in his hand and paid more attention to the food than Sil's touch which it seemed to enjoy.

"Hungry, Winter?" he spoke to the bird. He let her have the pieces, one by one, and spoiled her. Like Emilie, she was something he genuinely cared for.

As she scarfed down the last two or three pieces, Sil placed them in his hand where she was perched, and with only his other hand, tried to fasten a shoulder rest across his torso. Fortunately, the ASO aided where he could in fastening the straps. Sil mostly had it covered but he thanked the guard without the normal scowl he provided to everyone else and paid more attention to the hawk as she tore into the food.

Winter was a large Red-Tailed Hawk. Without her tail feathers and head, her body was larger than Sil's shoulder from his neck to almost his elbow. He had developed a deep connection with Winter, and when he was around her, his dark demeanor often completely vanished. As Winter finished the food, she climbed his arm and onto his shoulder where she nestled herself.

Sil stroked her breast and smiled when she eyed his burns, knowing something was wrong with him. Reaching up, he brought a hand across her wing on the opposite side of him and laid a layer of ice on it. Winter reacted by preening to get the ice off but refrained when he frosted over her speckled breast as well. She enjoyed it, and Sil loved both his ice and his hawk.

Winter was wild, and Sil had befriended her with his powers. It hadn't been that she was injured, or he had saved her, or that he had used his powers on her. In fact, it had been quite the opposite. He felt Winter had saved him.

When Sil was seven, he and Kip had brawled, and like Mark, Kip accidentally overpowered him. Winter had come for him, to comfort and help him heal. Sil also considered that they had some sort of mental connection. He didn't know how to use it or how to explain it, and he never spoke of it to the others, but somehow, Sil knew he was connected to Winter and he could understand her.

Winter was a beautiful creature. He would never cage her, nor would he look for her if she didn't return. Sil believed this was what Winter wanted, to stay free but to always return. Winter wasn't a bird for show, she wouldn't obey a master. She was a free wild animal, and Sil had sworn to her he'd honor that.

Tenderly, Sil forced Winter in the one way she allowed him and laid her on her back in his arms with her claws tightly around his fingers. Her talons were very strong, and like this, Winter could easily slice off any of Sil's fingers and get away, but the fact that she didn't showed her devotion to him.

Sil strode farther out into the courtyard and let Winter up on his arm. Promptly, Winter took off from this position and flew above the courtyard. He watched until he couldn't see her anymore, then the ASO urged him to come back inside.

Sil kept the leather guards with him except for the shoulder guard because it was scratching against his burns. He had made the leather guards himself. Keller had provided him with the materials, and in his interest, he sewed them together.

He stepped into the ASH and down the halls, but not back to the mess hall. The ASO left him as he walked to the reception area and main entrance. Several times a day, when the Shadows where allowed to roam freely, these doors were left locked. For now, the Shadows were allowed to wander.

Sil retrieved a project he had started a few days ago. Drawing it up, he sat in the reception area to continue the work. Until now, he had been able to ignore the horrible stinging pangs throughout his chest. His shirt brushed against the burns, and the bandages were only adding to his discomfort.

As he focused on his hand project, the pain seemed to worsen. Things were going to change in the ASH. Sil knew that despite how inexperienced Mark was with any form of Shadows, he had already successfully reopened wounds in Sil's heart.

Sil's project was making a right-handed glove to hold Winter. It was supposed to be like the ones trainers used, but it was going to be smaller with thinner material. Winter wouldn't intentionally claw him, and Sil had no need to hold a leash. The glove would button up to his wrist to fit under the arm guard and the insides of Sil's fingers, except for the tip would be open so he could still create ice and thread it into Winter's feathers.

"What are you doing?" A devious voice asked from nearby.

Sil didn't even look up to greet Emilie's eyes as he threaded the thick needle through his leather material. "Working," he answered. "It's none of your business," he murmured, attempting to turn her away. But he, like all the others, knew nothing could turn Emilie away when she wanted attention.

Emilie placed a hand on Sil's shoulder. She knew it irritated him, but he did little to make her stop. "Most of us are in the room. You should probably—"

Sil flared his golden eyes at her, and she stopped. "Or you could stay out here all night..." she rambled, giving up.

Sil's focus returned to his work in the tight stitches of the glove. Emilie sighed. "Sometimes, Sil, even I wonder why you act that way…" she breathed.

Getting up stiffly, Sil met eyes with Emilie, and with a cold hand, he took a loose hold of her throat with only one finger. His skin nearly turned blue as he imparted ice onto Emilie's neck. "If I made you cold enough, you'd go numb, then slowly it would spread, and your heart would freeze, and even if your body is preserved in the ice, you won't come back to life when you're thawed, not with my ice."

A deep grin painted itself across her face as the color of Sil's fingers became the color of her neck. "I could get away, and you'll never hear the end of it from Keller if you kill another Shadow." She laughed in a low voice. "If you really intend to kill me, which I know you don't, you would have done it already. I haven't done enough to irritate you to make you kill me, and this is no circumstance for you to kill someone, not when Kip injured you, and not when Mark burned you. You reacted just enough, and you have no intent to kill. That's just who you are."

Sil drew his hand away from her, and a snowball formed in his fingers, which he proceeded to smash against her shoulder. Grabbing his work, he strode past her in a huff, frustrated for obvious reasons and with no desire to deal with Emilie any longer.

However, Emilie naturally floated alongside him down the hallway until they reached the stairs, and then she shot up above him and ahead to the room.

VII
KIMBERLY'S ADVICE

October 27, 2030

Sweating hard, Mark woke up suddenly in the morning. His consciousness bringing him out of a flaming nightmare. Opening his eyes, Mark held himself from jerking up to prevent the others from hearing him.

He hoped the room would be very dark when he glanced around and that it would be small and warm with no one else there. Alone in his own room. He had no such luck as he saw morning light streaming in from the skylight and the others were all still asleep.

He missed his own bed. This room was too cold, the mattress beneath him was springy and sank too low, and the blanket he'd been given was completely useless. Most of the bed articles had mysteriously appeared, either given to him by the Shadows—mostly Kip—or in the case of the bed, he'd woken up in it.

He kept his own room warm and dark, claustrophobic to some, but like a hug to him. How was he ever going to get back there? The Exodus? Somehow escaping this place? He just wanted to go home.

A quiet twinge in his mind made him freeze. His mother hadn't even hesitated to call the ASH and tell them he was a

Shadow. She hadn't shown the slightest pause in sending him off as quickly as possible. Why would she want to get rid of him?

Mark seethed silently. His dad hated Shadows, at least that was his perception. January Halo glowered at the thought and every mention of Shadows, on the news, on the Internet, and especially in his own house. Surely his dad would want him to have nothing to do with the Shadows.

Maybe in a few days when January caught wind of this, he'd find out what happened, what Marissa had done, and he'd come get his son. Mark prayed that could be possible. As much as his dad was always absentminded and introverted, surely, January would get him out of here. Maybe he just had to wait a few days, if he could survive.

As quietly as possible, he sat up and set his feet over the side of the bed. His breath trembling, he shuddered, holding his head in his hands for a few minutes. He was still in the ASH with the Shadows, and everything he had hoped to be a dream was reality.

Looking at each of the Shadows sleeping in the room on various bunks and beds, Mark glanced down at his feet to see his toes in contact with a pile of fresh clothes for him. Casual and somewhat dull, but clean, nonetheless.

Without making much noise, for he was quite light on his feet, he dressed in the bathroom. Sleep had done him good, but thinking of Sil made his fear resurface.

Tiptoeing across the room, Mark pushed the button for the elevator and left without waking anyone. He held on tightly to the railing, and with no one there to embarrass him with his fear, he exited promptly as the door opened.

From the hall windows, Mark saw from the balcony there was very little light touching the world and a clock he found in the hall stated it was nearly six o'clock in the morning. Across from him, the balcony overlooked the lobby and the front windows, and Mark leaned against the railing to watch as morning painted the horizon gold and the world became lighter.

He looked down to see a lit, round reflecting pool in front of the ASH with a fountain that accented the front courtyard. At the bottom of the hill the ASH stood atop, Mark saw the headlights of cars passing below, and the distant city lights. He was right outside a bustling town he, and he guessed they knew nothing about the ASH or the Shadows hidden within.

"Oh—I-I didn't know anyone was…" a feminine voice started, and Mark turned and looked through the darkness to see Kimberly coming down the hall with a cart of food. She startled a little, when she spotted him. "Oh… Mark…" She frowned.

Just his face disconcerted her, and she looked right through him. Not even seeing him, her thoughts were with the person she had lost that Ocie had told him about.

"Kimberly," Mark greeted her as brightly as he could.

"I was just… coming through to set up breakfast,"

"I see that," he murmured, masking the shakiness in his voice. He could easily see she was fretting over something and he pinched his arm to ask, "So, who do I remind you of?"

Kimberly grimaced, her knuckles on the cart turning white. "I'm sorry, Mark, I really don't want to talk about it…"

Mark sighed, still wanting to pry because he knew she didn't mean it. "Would you like me to help you?"

Hesitating again, Kimberly pushed the cart forward. "If you like," she said, her hands shaky on the cart's handle, and proceeded to open the elevator door to the room Mark had just come out of. When she stepped inside, Mark followed her, light-footed. Gulping, Kimberly mustered a smile and asked, "So, why are you awake at this hour?"

Mark eyed her with a little sarcastic smirk, and Kimberly forced a small laugh. "All about what happened to Sil?" she confirmed, and Mark nodded in response. The door opened, and Kimberly pushed the cart into the center of the room. "Do you see those handles on the wall over there?"

Kimberly asked, pointing them out to Mark.

Mark nodded when he saw them, and Kimberly instructed, "Pull on them." He did as told and out came long sturdy plastic slabs, which Mark found to be a table and two benches.

"The legs are underneath," Kimberly stated, and Mark reached underneath to pull out the supports for the table and the benches. Kimberly rolled the cart closer, and adopted a pleasant smile as she whispered, "I remember when Fliiy got in this room a few weeks ago." Mark met eyes with her briefly encouraging her to continue. "Her powers are really difficult for her to control, and they're more unrefined than even yours are. Twice already since she's been moved to this room, her powers have gotten out of control, and she's been taken out to be alone," Kimberly explained.

She took out a stack of eight bowls which she set on the table near the wall, "You're by far not the first one who's had a run-in with Sil. Last time Fliiy's powers went off, she was trying to be nice to him, to sort of get him out of that act of hatred he puts up for everyone.

"Sil threw ice at her, and she tried levitating it to stop it. Whatever she did triggered her powers to go nuts, and she had to be taken out of this room for a few hours until her powers calmed."

Mark took the second stack of bowls and set them next to the first. He listened while Kimberly set out a warm covered bowl. "Sil has always gotten into trouble. When his powers were unrefined while he was younger, he nearly stopped his own heart with ice like you nearly burn yourself with fire. He's fought with every Shadow in the ASH.

"He's dealt with more Shadow related problems than anyone here, and it's fair to say his powers are more refined than anyone's here. If he learned to control that temper, the ASH might even allow him to go home, but…We don't know who his parents are."

Mark's attention piqued hearing this. "He'd be allowed to go home?" he inquired with hope in his heart. Kimberly had the knowledge he desperately wanted.

She laid out the rest of the breakfast with a chipper, light step. "I'm sure Keller has told you at least once that unrefined Shadows are very dangerous, and it's very true. One of the main goals of the ASH is to contain unrefined Shadows and keep them from hurting people, and most Shadows here are unrefined.

"Another goal is bringing the Shadows together so the interaction with others of their kind to help them get used to their powers. Spend time in the Realm, that's probably how Sil has such an acute control over Frost."

Mark sat on the bench. He'd already spent countless hours in the Realm before he'd come here. It had been his safe place, and even still, he used the Realm. He was wary since he was no longer alone in there. "You seem to know a lot about Shadows." He kept his voice low to not wake the others.

Kimberly nodded with a sorrowful smile. "Well, that tends to happen when you've been here as long as I have," she whispered.

Mark accepted it and asked in return, "Are you a Shadow?"

Eyeing him long and hard, Kimberly's eyes grew a bit wide as she stared at him. Shrugging, she answered, "Sort of..." she whispered and then gulped before she continued, "I can use the Realm, but I can't use my Shadow anymore. For some reason, a while ago... probably before you were born, I woke up one day and my Shadow had gone completely dormant. I've been trying to find out why since before the ASH even came into existence.

"I used to be pretty powerful. I had refined powers, and then one day I just..." She hesitated, clearly hurt from the loss. "I came here. I'm helping Keller because I know something is wrong with me and my Shadow, and I have spent almost fifteen years trying to learn how to control it again."

Mark let off, starting to wonder how old Kimberly was.

She could have been in her late twenties, but he couldn't be sure. Kimberly had a look in her eyes as if she had seen eons. She had the eyes of someone old, but maybe that was her recent loss clouding her demeanor. Mark sighed, certain it was related to what made Kimberly so upset when she looked at his face. Restarting, Mark asked sensitively, "What is your Shadow called?"

Kimberly took hold of the cart's handles again, closing her eyes before answering. "Shadow Love. I was once able to briefly control people's minds," she explained. Kimberly gazed at Mark as the thoughts of her powers ran through his head several times, processing, and grasping it. She fought herself and stepped up to Mark. Forcing him to stand, Kimberly met Mark's eyes. "You want my advice?"

Mark nodded, and Kimberly's pink eyes flared. "Spend time in the Realm. Practice with your Shadow as much as possible without hurting anyone. Maybe have some of the other Shadows stick with you and help you," she suggested in a firm voice. "If you want to fix what's between you and Sil, try not to say anything to him today. Ignore him altogether if you have to. Sil will resolve his problem with you on his own, and there *will* come a time when he'll confront you again. Sil's slow to trust others and that makes him prudent. You'll just have to get used to him."

Kimberly laughed a little with a truly brilliant smile. "I could keep going," she joked, "all the dos and don'ts and precautionary advice about Sil," she mused and started pushing the cart back to the elevator.

When they were inside, she raised her voice. "Above all, don't come between him and the few things he cares about, like Winter, Emilie, or anything he sets his mind to. But he's not impossible to get through to."

The elevator opened and the two stepped out. Kimberly turned, her demeanor brightening. "Do you want to know the good news?" she offered. Mark nodded but stared beyond her at how the world was lightening, and a sparkle of pink set the sky ablaze. "After Fliiy came back from her room alone, Sil apologized to her and they made up. Now they're very close. I think Sil has a liking for her," she joked.

Mark chuckled but didn't find it as funny as Kimberly. He sighed and gathered courage to ask again as she started down the hallway without him. He gulped heavily. "Kimberly..." She turned to him, and he fought himself to continue, "You still haven't told me, and I'd like to know. Who do I remind you of?"

Kimberly gulped hard, fighting off tears. "Another Shadow," she whispered sorrowfully, "But he died several months ago. That's all you need to know..." She finished and solemnly continued down the hall leaving Mark and the sunrise behind.

He sighed heavily and grimaced. *How can I look so much like this person for Kimberly to cry just looking at me?*

"I'd listen to her," someone said from the open elevator door. Mark reeled around as a Shadow left the Realm and holding the elevator door open by her presence. Elise.

He tensed and jumped. "Just watch," he threatened, pointing at her. "You Shadows appearing out of nowhere like that is going to really freak me out." He turned toward the window, sulking. "What? Did you sneak into the elevator with us to eavesdrop?"

Elise affirmed from behind him. "Pretty much," she murmured.

Mark sighed and put his head to the window pane. "Could you hear my thoughts in the Realm too?"

Laughing, Elise denied the accusation. "It doesn't work that way. You'd have to be open in the Realm for me to hear it. I'd assume that means I missed a good one."

Mark mustered a false laugh at this, and Elise cut him off. "You really should listen to Kimberly. She's been around Shadows all her life. She once helped me solve my problem with Goran. Now, he and I are good friends." Her feet tapping lightly upon the stone, she joined him by the window. "So how did you sleep?"

Mark raised a brow, flaring his crimson eyes when he

shouldn't have. "With what happened yesterday, how do you think?"

"Thought so." Elise giggled slightly. "You should probably get down to the room before the Shadows wipe out all of breakfast. It tends to be a favorite around here."

Mark shrugged, but he couldn't help but think he had made a lot of progress so far. "Will you help me learn how to use my Shadow?" he asked. "So I can get out of here and back to my home."

Elise smiled warmly and placed a hand on his shoulder. "We all will," she assured, then joked, "but none of them are kind when it comes to those who are late for meals." Mark laughed easily as she urged him into the elevator and followed her back into the room. He felt pulled into the crowd as Elise dove in head first like water at the breakfast table.

It couldn't be said that the Shadows were bickering, but they were certainly competing and rushed to get through breakfast. Their actions were fast, somewhat greedy, and almost playful as they fought over remains with their forks and fingers.

By diving in, Elise snagged Mark the most difficult breakfast foods to obtain—that being bacon and a biscuit— then left it up to Mark to fend for himself for the rest.

Together with Mark, Elise pushed aside a few Shadows to make room for him. "So, Mark, next time you help Kimberly with breakfast, get breakfast for yourself before the others do," she suggested, then pointed out. "The first one who smells it, gets it." As she spoke, the last slice of bacon was torn to shreds by several quick hands.

Mark glanced across the room and noted that Sil was awake but hadn't gotten up from his bed. In fact, he sat alone, skipping breakfast and working on his hand project silently. Mark eyed it, seeing several pieces of leather stitched together in the vague disconnected shape of a leather glove.

Mark recalled that Kimberly advised not to come

between Sil and anything he cared about, and she included Emilie, anything he set his mind to, and Winter. Who was Winter?

A crackle of green energy flung bits of bacon and egg from a plate across the table into the faces of two other Shadows. "Fliiy, What the heck!" one of the boys blared.

Mark looked over and saw a little girl with a messy blonde ponytail shrink back ashamed. "Sorry..." she whispered, clenching her fists and containing her power. Mark's eyes lit up a little. Fliiy's power did get out of hand often. He frowned to himself, fairly certain he was in the same situation. At least there was hope, that much he was thankful for.

Kip wiggled in next to Mark, snickering. "What do you think?" he asked.

Mark knew what he was referring to. "All of you are completely out of your mind," he joked and Kip laughed at him.

VIII
SUN BREAKING THROUGH

Kip snagged up the remains of breakfast on his plate before it was stolen. "So, what would you like to do today?" he asked, offering Mark suggestions if he wanted.

Eating much slower than Kip, Mark shrugged. "I want to practice using my Shadow, so I can refine my powers like Keller suggests," he said. His thoughts stayed with Sil and the privileges Sil had, and yet Sil's temper kept him here.

"I can help you with that," Kip said with a small smile. "You don't actually believe that refining Shadows is something you can do quickly, do you?" He bit into a biscuit. "It takes years with lots of practice, and it's not something that can be done like exercise, and all Shadows work differently."

Kip lifted his hand and an immense light formed in his palm, hot but mostly bright. "It wasn't until I was five that my powers started surfacing. I was seven when I created my first light shot. It's taken me a very long time to hone my powers."

Mark listened and watched the light in Kip's hand. He finished off the remains of breakfast like a civilized human rather than a food crazed animal like the other teens and pushed his plate forward. "What is your Shadow exactly?"

Grinning, Kip got up. "Let me show you," he offered

and hurried away from the table. At that point, Mark got up as well and followed Kip into the center of the room where they had been skating yesterday. Kip picked a spot on the far side of the room as if to prevent anyone from getting hurt when he used his Shadow.

He adopted a stance, and briefly with his fingers, brushed his curly bangs out of his face. He thrust his right hand before him, and Mark could see light and energy drawing itself to Kip's hand in a spiral down his arms, through his veins with fire. A great light appeared in Kip's hand, and from it, a fine beam of light like a laser shot across the room at the wall.

Kip held it there with a proud smirk. "The walls are protected from powers like mine by the ASI; otherwise, this beam would slice through to the outside of the building."

Mark was in awe, most impressed by the extreme amount of light. "It's that strong?"

Kip nodded, simply glowing with happiness, and released the beam. It let off a substantial amount of force, enough to throw Kip back, but he was used to it and kept his balance.

Satisfied, Kip massaged his right hand from the return shock. "My Shadow controls the phase of plasma. Really, I'm just creating the same elements that power the sun and firing them in the form of a beam."

His eyes widening, Mark stared, amazed as the pulsing light from within Kip's veins receded under his skin. "How long has it taken for you to refine your powers?" he asked.

Kip smiled and shook his head. "Right, back to that," he mused. His hands sparked with light again. "When I was younger, I could only create light in my hands, but my Shadow has a unique tendency unlike any other Shadow. I guess you could say it performs well under stress. So, when I am pressed to use my Shadow, my powers advance dramatically in a few seconds, leveling up in a sense.

"Because of this, my powers can never be refined, because every time this happens, I start over knowing nothing about my powers. The last time that happened was when I was seven and I don't remember well what went through my mind to spark the advancement other than it was my turn to butt heads with Sil," he added as a joke.

Mark tried to laugh, but thinking about the appearance of Sil's burns made him otherwise frown. "So, you can't refine your powers at all."

Laughing hard, Kip hugged his sides. "All right, Mark, I want you to show off now. You've had enough talk," he mused and instructed at the same time. "Set something on fire for me!"

Mark stared blankly at Kip, then sighed and struggled to keep this focus on creating the fire. He summoned multiple thought patterns to do it, but he wasn't sure how, and the first thing he focused on was that his fire was not to burn himself. The temperature in Mark's hands increased suddenly until it sparked between him and Kip and Mark jumped, startled.

Kip snorted, absolutely tickled. "You just don't know where to focus. That's your problem." Taking Mark's hands which were cool since he had released his focus, Kip raised them to eye level, then letting go, he summoned light to his own hands. Mark again noticed the coils of energy and light flowing under Kip's skin and through his veins, lighting them.

"You see my veins are glowing?" he pointed out. "Your Shadow is in your heart, and it runs through your blood. Focus and think about that, and the Shadow in your heart will do the rest for you."

Nodding mindlessly, Mark took in what Kip said. If his Shadow was in his heart, how did it get there? How did one become a Shadow? He didn't have to think about it this time as his hands lit on fire easily and without burning him. His eyes widened, both excited and surprised at how effortless it really was. A broad smile appeared on his lips and he beamed happily at Kip.

The fire on his hands was deep red in color. It wasn't a

natural flame, and Mark felt no heat. He extinguished the fire on one hand and touched the other to feel it for himself and indeed the flame produced no heat and Mark wasn't being burned by it. Cautiously, he thought to instate heat to the flame, and as he touched it with his other hand, he could feel the fire, it was scalding, but the heat did not harm him.

"I wonder..." Mark whispered, immersed in the flames.

Kip smiled calmly. "Humor me," he murmured.

"I wonder if I can't be burned by anything. I feel this heat, it's really there. My hand is as hot as a burner on a stove, but it's not hurting me."

Again, Kip snickered. "Probably, it's just another way our Shadows are very alike. I can create heat as hot as the sun and it doesn't affect me, and I've never been burned by anything. Fire only burns me if I allow it to, and I can control it whether or not my nerves react to the fire with pain."

Mark's curiosity piqued while his hand was still on fire. "So, if I want to, I could use my fire to possibly seal up bleeding, like cauterization, and it won't hurt me if I have to do it to myself." He smiled, a little proud and incredibly excited. "I can't be affected by heat, and I can't be burned unless I want to." He reveled with the thoughts of this ability, and again, he met eyes with Kip. "That's incredible!"

Kip lit up his hand. "Now..." he murmured, "I can only create light in my hands, but can you set more of your body on fire?"

Mark outstretched his arm to find out and thought deeply on how to bring the fire up his arm. It was an effort, but it stretched up to his elbow where he stopped it at will. "How come you can only make light in your hands?" he asked, noticing the fire didn't burn his clothes which surprised him a little, but then he realized he didn't want to burn his clothes and that mental restriction had taken place subconsciously.

Shrugging, Kip ran a hand through his strawberry-red curls. "I don't know. It's just my Shadow, unique from all others, but because I can level my powers, I might be able to light up more of my body someday. I don't know what purpose it would serve, and I'm fine with just my hands."

Mark smiled, feeling a rise in confidence, and bemused by Kip. He looked over Kip where they stood. His hair was rather short, and its color was confusing for Mark to look at. Redder in color than fruit but not dyed, it was natural and even had a slightly pinkish hue to it.

His eyes reflected the color of the sun, and for the hour this morning, they were also slightly pink with gold and purple like the sky. Kip's eyes weren't human, Mark could see that. All of Kip's features appeared like a flaming sunset, bright and exquisite, a sight normally seen only once before it was painted over with black and indigo in the night. Kip's existence was a painting of the sky and the sun.

The red strand of hair fell between Mark's eyes and he sighed brushing it away with his fingertips, recognizing the irony of the situation. "What about other Shadows?" he asked. "Your Shadow is so complicated, and Sil's is too, but that's only two Shadows to fifteen others around me."

"Go ask them." Kip shoved him from behind. "We're not shy about showing off our powers. Using Shadows is equivalent here to asking someone how their day is. All we think about is our power."

Kip pushed Mark to the beds to sit and find another Shadow to talk to. The Shadows dispersed, helping themselves to any entertainment they had at their liberty. "That's odd," he remarked. "I'd think that would be a bad thing for Shadows to be seen for only their powers instead of the person they are."

Kip nodded and shrugged. "Shadows are different from humans," he stated as the two sat on Mark's bed. "Humans think about people and the person. Shadows think about powers and how they work. We have personalities just the same as humans but that's not the focus of who we are."

He gazed off at the others. "Sure, we care for each other's person, but in an introduction, we'd ask about the other's power before we ask about their personal interests aside from Shadows." Looking at Mark, Kip smiled. "We're just different, and we think differently," he said.

Mark shrugged as well and sighed, looking at the Shadows. He locked his eyes on Sage the Shadow Quill then looked to Kip. "What about him? Those quills on his body don't disappear, do they?"

Kip smiled, intrigued, and promptly called out, "Sage!" The Shadow with gray quills turned sharply from where he lounged in the room and came over. Kip grinned seeing Mark's utter embarrassment. "Sage, Mark wants to know about your Shadow," he stated as a broad question.

Sage beamed and sat on the floor. "What do you want to know?"

Mark gulped. "Can you make your quills disappear?"

Sage held out his arm, showing off the quills which grew out of the greater curves of his elbow, wrist, and on the back of his hand and forearm. As if they were his own fingers, he flexed them all to stand on end.

"Nope," he replied in a happy voice, "I have a Physical Shadow—as opposed to an Elemental Shadow—my Shadow is a part of my body permanently. Some Shadows like me can make it disappear, but that's another story." Before Mark's eyes, Sage grabbed hold of one of the quills and yanked it out like a strand of hair, wincing slightly, and gave it to him.

Hesitantly, Mark took the quill and looked at it. The quill was under five inches long and blue-gray in color. Sage smiled as Mark felt it at the point for its sharpness and along the shaft for its shape. Along the sides were two groves. If Mark broke it in half, it would have a sort of rounded T-shape.

Mark reached out to give it back, but Sage smiled and refused. "It's not like I can put it back on," he mused. Mark looked over Sage's appearance. He had quills everywhere! For fun, Sage frilled out all of them so their pointed ends were most potent, and Mark spied various places under Sage's shirt where the quills were flexing outward.

Sage's smile brightened. It was clear what Kip said about Shadows, and Mark asking about *his* Shadow was like asking someone about their hobby or profession with interest. "Sometimes, when I move too quickly, the quills come out and go flying," he stated.

Kip groaned sarcastically. "Sometimes, when that happens, you hit things that weren't meant to be punctured, like other Shadows."

Sage blushed, the color looked odd mixed among the blue-gray color of his quills. All the quills turned back, and he raised his arm to Mark. "Want to touch them?"

Mark hesitated but trusted that he wouldn't thrust the pointed ends at him. With all the ends turned down, the quills were like a smooth armor. Stroking them backward, Mark learned the painful way they grabbed his skin and he felt the points. "It's so real..." he murmured, "like they're really alive on you."

Sage snickered. "Of course, they're alive. They're part of me." Flexing them, he moved his arm back.

Mark leaned away and brushed the red-strike out of his face. "So, Kip..." he said, "would you say his powers are 'refined?'" he asked.

Kip eyed Sage humorously, and frowned playfully shaking his head, uttering, "Nah... you misfire too often."

Sage lunged at Kip angrily. "Hey!" He took offense. "Physical Shadows become refined quicker than Elemental Shadows, so I'm more refined than you," he replied, his quills fanning out.

Kip didn't reel away. "Yeah, but I'm older than you, and you started growing quills when you were ten. I've been able to use my powers much longer than you have," he countered.

"Wait a second!" Mark insisted, butting in. He looked to Sage, confused. "You couldn't use a Shadow until you were ten?"

Sage nodded floppily. "Late power appearance is common. It takes a while for a Shadow to work its way fully into the bloodstream, and for some Shadows, it's longer than others."

Mark tensed. "That's it!" he exclaimed and looked to Kip. "That's what happened to me. That's why I couldn't use my Shadow until now."

Kip didn't seem to be as shocked as Mark was. "It's common," he said. "What should be confusing is how you stayed out of the ASH until now."

Kip gestured across the room at Sil while he worked on the stitching to his glove. "Take Sil as a contrast example. He was able to use his Shadow soon after he was born, which caused complications while he was being taken to the ASH—from the stories I've heard—but not only that, he was able to use it well from early on. All Shadows are different. Sil's different from me. Sage's different from you, and the same goes for all Shadows in this room and in the ASH," he explained.

Mark contemplated this, not responding. Sil had been pretty much the center of his thoughts since he got here, but as he learned more, Sil was getting more interesting by the minute.

He could use his Shadow soon after he was born. He made it difficult for them to take him to the ASH. He nearly stopped his heart when he was younger, and he had a run-in with Kip that had changed him somehow.

Mark knew it wasn't his business since Sil probably didn't want him to know, but he had to get to the bottom of this.

Sage left, and Kip stayed by Mark's side. Mark set his hand on fire again and stared intently at it. "Kip, you and I have similar powers. Is there anyone else with the ability of fire?"

"I don't know. Seems like there would be now that you're here. It makes me feel just a bit less out of place." He lightly punched Mark in the should with a warm grin, but Mark didn't share in his revelry. He couldn't help but get the feeling there were a lot of secrets in the ASH that the Shadows simply wouldn't explain to him.

Mark lost track of time as Kip described wild stories about the Shadows he had grown up around. But the boy's curiosity silenced him and he got Mark tell him about what it was like outside, living normally and going to school, things Mark never thought would be fascinating to even people who were deprived of it.

Kip explained that Shadows learned what they wanted to at the pace they wanted, which tended to be rather quickly. They had a natural instinct to learn about the outside world and every bit of knowledge they could get their hands on.

Mark admitted he enjoyed learning, but he was rather average as humans went, and the Shadows ached for knowledge as soon as they could figure out how to read. They would learn everything they could get their hands on.

Kip learned to read much earlier than Mark, and he studied chemistry and physics in his spare time. Times like now, to learn more to control his Shadow.

Mark awed at the daunting subjects Kip was eager to learn, but it seemed quite normal for Shadows to pick up subjects with interest like Kip. Something that annoyed Mark was that Kip claimed he was any smarter than a normal human; he was just more eager. And he only read and studied what caught his eyes or pertained to his Shadow.

Mark glanced at the clock above the elevator and noted they had been talking long into the morning, and it was now almost midday. A few minutes later, the elevator opened, and Kimberly exited. "Sil, will you come with me? I'd like to change your bandages," she stated in a way that didn't seem like it was directed at Sil.

Begrudgingly, Sil put down his hand project, protecting the needle and the stitches from slipping and he left, shooting a hateful glance at Mark for staring at him. It was only a few short steps, but Sil intentionally prolonged them, so when he and Kimberly were gone, Mark exhaled a sigh of relief.

Sil clenched his fist tightly with ice forming over it as he followed Kimberly downstairs to the infirmary. They took the walk leisurely and Sil's thoughts wandered to Emilie. He honestly didn't know why those thoughts were present. She intrigued him, he guessed. She was powerful and interesting to him. She wasn't deterred by his act, and she seemed to genuinely be interested in him as well. He figured he was probably worried because she was much more volatile alone than when they were together.

They entered the infirmary silently and Sil scanned the room warily. The large, low bed against the wall was comfortable and still unmade, and the table-like bed, which he himself had spent time on stood in the center of the room crisp and neat. The room was divided by a half-wall separating the front of the room from the living area with a bookcase, box television, coffee table, and a couch he couldn't see from where he was. On the other side of the room, there was a kitchenette area and cabinets containing medicines, serums, and supplies.

Sil sat on the table-like bed and watched as Kimberly opened a cabinet to take out light gauze for his burns. "I keep expecting him to be here, excited to see me," he sighed, staring at the wrinkled sheets Kimberly often slept in, even still.

Kimberly paused in her motion. "Yeah… you're not the only one. Cesc is in denial that he's actually gone and keeps coming here to see him."

Sil looked at the floor and grimaced. "I remember when I first met him…" He cursed mildly. "He annoyed me, but he was kind and kept my mind off the pain."

Kimberly smiled, coming to him. "Now stop thinking about that. You're all healed up, and this is nothing compared to last time," she encouraged as she began unraveling the gauze.

Shaking his head, Sil batted her hand away at first and flared his eyes at her. "Don't talk to me like I'm a patient," he threatened. Kimberly reeled away holding her wrist and seeing how the ice was forming on it when Sil touched her. Sil closed his eyes to fight the grief. "He was my friend," Sil stated firmly. "I don't want to think of him as dead. I don't want to think of that time either. It's passed, it's over."

The ice relinquished from Kimberly and she lowered her hands to Sil cautiously. "Sil…" she said, "among the few people you would admit to being friends with, it makes me so happy you've chosen him."

Sil's eyes became cold and his skin appeared slightly blue. "Stop it! It's over!" he demanded. He lowered his hands only to let Kimberly clean his burns and re-bandage them. "I was trying to be pleasant, not nostalgic," he finished.

Kimberly fell silent before him. Conversation would do nothing to improve Sil's attitude. She did as he wanted and cleaned his burns without a word. She removed the gauze on the worst of the damage; however, Sil brushed away her hand, proceeding to lay a light layer of frost over the burns, cooling them and soothing them deeply.

When the layer of frost melted, Kimberly set a layer of medicine coated netting over the burns to help them heal, then set the new gauze and realized something she didn't point out.

The burns were warm. Kimberly hid a faint smile, underneath that cold exterior, somehow, Sil had a warm heart. He might have lacked the kindness, but Sil was still amazing to her.

"Would you like me to take a look at your other scars?" She offered gently, knowing Sil probably wouldn't and as she suspected he scowled. Sil's torso was sliced with old raised scars he'd been given when he was very young. She knew they still bothered him, but he'd never admit that.

As Kimberly finished, Sil got up of his own accord and headed back to the room, leaving her in the infirmary alone. Kimberly looked around the room as always and strode about in the living area.

Nostalgic, she sat on the floor in front of a CD player and pressed play on the disk. Soft classical music resonated from the old device. A tempest of hurt welled up inside her. She really couldn't let go.

In the bookshelf beside her, she gazed at all the books that *he* used to read to learn and entertain himself. Trembling, she reached out and took a book, opening it briefly, tears flowing over her eyes and she couldn't see to read. She gripped the book, crying, mourning, and missing the lost child of hers. "He loved reading!" she sobbed on the floor. "Why couldn't I save him?" she cried out on the floor hugging the book.

She felt a hand placed on her shoulder and she jumped, looking up, expecting it to be him or his ghost to comfort her, but it was Keller. Gently, he knelt with her on the floor and wrapped his arms around her as if she were a child. "Kimberly..." he whispered, "I told you, you have to let go."

Kimberly laid her head on his arm with tears in her eyes. "How can I?" she wheezed in a jumpy, uneven voice. "I promised him I wouldn't let him die!"

Keller grabbed her shoulders and turned her face to his. "Kimberly..." She tensed when she saw his face, he was already broken, and certainly not as impervious to the pain as she thought he was. "It's been almost ten months. You need to let go. He's gone." Keller's eyes were full of tears, but his voice remained strong as he embraced Kimberly in grief, which she would not forget.

IX
COMPETITION AND CLUES

Sil exited the elevator with fluid movements, not rigid like one would think ice to be. And upon his return he shoved a snowball into the face of a Shadow who zipped around the room using a power of some kind that allowed him to run fast. Sil timed it out, and the poor guy ran face first into a handful of snow.

"What a moron…" Sil sighed and continued walking across the room to his bed.

Mark felt a stir of panic in his heart when the boy hit the floor and Sil tread past him without a kindness in his being. Sil took up his hand project, minding the loose threads hanging from the material as he continued. He looked like he was in a good mood, as long as he was left alone.

For Sil to be pleasant meant everyone had to stay away from his bed and not make eye contact with him. Unfortunately, Mark didn't learn very fast, and he gazed at Sil from across the room like an idiot.

Mark didn't turn his gaze away when Sil found his gaze across the room. It took a ridiculously long second for him to jump and pretend to ignore Sil. Sil smirked at his cowardice, silently mocking him from across the room. From the way Sil abused everyone around him, Mark was pretty sure he enjoyed tormenting the Shadows.

Sil's eyes were burnt golden, and sometimes they flared into light blue, which sent a cold shiver up Mark's spine. Those were the two traits immediately evident to Mark. He was about as tall as Mark, but he was very thin which made him look taller. It only intimidated him more that Sil had dark eyes, deep like their color, and empty cheekbones.

Kip came up to Mark abruptly urging him to come. When Mark asked why, Kip only smiled wider. "They're unlocking doors. I'm ready for some fresh air. How about you?" He slapped his skates over his shoulder by the laces and took Mark by the arm to drag him along as Ocie had yesterday.

Everyone was scurrying out of the room, and somehow, they managed to squeeze all sixteen of them into the elevator. The tight space made him a little more comfortable in the elevator, but once it started moving the unease swirled in his gut. "I hate elevators," he murmured.

Kip eyed Mark oddly. "What?

Mark clenched the railing so hard, his knuckles turned white. "Nothing," he stared at the steel railing along the walls, not meeting eyes with Kip, and not focusing on the shuddering lift. If he had to keep using that elevator to leave and enter the room, he swore he was going to have a heart attack. Hurrying, they joined others in the hall.

Shadows ran down the stairwell and threw open the doors to the courtyard. There was another short flight up, about seven steps total. The top three stairs were scuffed and blackened and the very top one was cracked and weeds were peeking out through the fissures. It couldn't have just been wear from Shadows regularly using powers on this spot. And wasn't the ASH shielded from any damaging powers? What could have done this?

There was one thing clear, the blackness was from fire, and probably extremely hot coals that had been dropped there. Grabbing Kip's shirt gently, Mark pointed them out. "Who made these burns?" He was certain about the fire, and thought himself a bit of an expert on the hot coals, if not, he was getting a little too confident.

Kip looked down at them briefly, shrugging. "I'm not sure. They just appeared there a few months ago, and I wasn't around to see it happen."

Continuing, he took the steps, dismissing any ideas on why. There was a stone wall which blocked off Mark's immediate vision of the courtyard. Around the corner he was towered by the three-story building coated entirely by smooth white marble. A row of taller stairs led up a balcony overlooking the courtyard and the whole hill the ASH was set on.

Mark turned the corner of the wall which had blocked off his view and looked out at the courtyard, dumbstruck. Aside from the number of Shadows around him, Mark was overcome with the amazing sight before his eyes.

His eyes lifted, taking in the enormous coverage of the ASI. Above them, surrounding the entire courtyard was a ginger-bronze shield keeping the Shadows in what seemed to be a habitat where they could do what they wanted with their powers. The courtyard was huge, probably a quarter mile across, and the shield towered over it all.

Mark stopped walking to stare up at it, and Kip laughed at him. "The shield is invisible from the outside. The old Shadows worked together to make it that way," he explained, and Mark struggled to take it all in. "We can do what we like with our powers inside, and no one outside will see. It's part of Keller's plans to *refine* our Shadows."

Mark looked out at the rest of the courtyard. The circumference of the shield was a wide concrete sidewalk all around, and there were paths all through it. Gardens were patches all over from the edge of the patio and balcony. "Do the Shadows plant all these gardens?" he asked, in awe of the flowers and various other plants, things which would be out of season now.

Kip affirmed, nodding as he and Mark stepped to the sidewalk path. "Mostly Shadows with powers corresponding to growing and the plants." Kip thrust a hand out at one, stopping Mark from stepping on it. "But that one's a Shadow!"

Mark scurried away, now watching his every step and panicking. "Really?"

Laughing hysterically, Kip held his ribs. "No, I'm just messing with you." He pointed to a giant tree growing approximately in the center of the courtyard, but Mark could tell by looking it was off center. "But every tree other than that one, is a Shadow."

Mark gawked at the size of the tree and he knew instantly that the Shadows had grown it there to be tall and a symbol of their power as they grew stronger. "What kind of tree is that?" he wondered.

Shrugging, Kip smiled amused. "Who knows? Probably inspired by any tree the Shadows wanted it to be. If you find any Shadows talking to plants or tending the gardens, don't be shy to ask them," he suggested. On the path, a few Shadows skated by them at incredible speeds and Kip tore Mark out of the way before he was completely run over.

They continued walking into the center as Mark identified other things. There was a playground for the younger Shadows, a good deal of odd equipment for Shadows to improve physical strength and playing fields for general ballgames.

A shadow passed over him in the sky but right as he looked up a huge hawk swooped down. He dropped to the grass, its talons missing him by inches and he only perked up when he saw it land on the gloved arm of a white-haired Shadow. Sil smirked at him a little, but Mark averted his eyes, remembering Kimberly's advice to not interact with Sil today.

Kip took Mark's attention. "Let's make a clear place for you to practice."

Breaking into a light jog, Kip ran out into the open courtyard, leading Mark behind him, who followed. He chose a clear spot, and with a twinkle in his eyes, Kip turned about to Mark, mischievous and lighthearted as he raised a hand to the sky.

Within his arm, veins of energy lit up under his skin, rushing to his fingers and bursting like a small star within his hand. The bright light in his palm grew more intense, giving off heat that Mark could feel on his face until, suddenly, it burst from Kip's fingertips, traveling skyward toward the shield.

The shot was like a firework, discharging sparks on its way up until it dissipated into smoke and debris. Kip shrieked in pure excitement and his joy, loving every chance he got to do that was so pure to Mark. All he succeeded in doing was drawing three Shadows closer, who he ignored at first as he held the light in his hand closer to Mark. "Watch this!" he urged, raising his hand and firing another shot.

This one he aimed at the shield with the momentum and trajectory to impact it. The shot flew like a laser and struck the shield as a ball of fire. Sparks spiraled out upon the inside of the shield before the energy force suddenly changed to a golden color. With the contact of the foreign Shadow, the shield caused the shot to ricochet out across the courtyard and back to them at the same speed.

Beginning to panic, Mark frantically took a step back, hurrying to get out of the line of fire, which Kip stood in fearlessly. "Wait!" Kip reached out in front of him with both his hands. The veins in Kip's arms grew brighter as he mustered any extra energy he could. The extreme amount of heat welling within his arms caused new orbs of light to form in his palm, and the light in his hands flickered as he prepared to receive the shot.

To Mark's surprise, the beam of light which spiraled like a misfired firework directly at Kip, dissipated and burned off, leaving Kip panting as the light in his hands faded. "I'm not very good at that..." he admitted and found himself coughing once or twice.

Mark's eyes flared crimson as a spark of worry appeared in his demeanor. "You can't control it once it has left you?"

he wondered, more to confirm.

Kip nodded, still panting. "If I could, I could erase a lot of mistakes I've made."

The three Shadows drew nearer cautiously, and Mark could identify two of them as Elise and Rita, but the other one he hadn't met before. Elise applauded Kip in his efforts and joined them.

Mark eyed the Shadow who had come with Elise and Rita. The Shadow was male, but Mark's eyes drifted first to the Shadow's mauve colored skin. The color was first noticeable on his bare arms, but Mark realized the mauve was also all up his neck and jaw. Only his face and the palms of his hands were a pale tan.

Elise snickered, seeing Mark's expression, staring blankly, of course, neither Elise, nor the Shadow Mark was staring at, found it odd. "Mark this is Cesckim," she declared as she drew the two of them together. "He's two years older than you," she added calmly.

Cesckim thrust Mark a hand to shake and Mark could see that the palms of his hands were not mauve like the rest of him. "Shadow Mail, as in chain mail. Not snail mail," he introduced himself. "You can call me Cesc," he finished.

Mark hesitantly took his hand to shake and opened his mouth to introduce himself when he suddenly felt the uncomfortable, startling sensation of something other than Cesc's mauve skin touching his hand. Abruptly, he let go and abruptly a small green snake morphed, curling itself around his fingers. Mark shrieked, not because he was afraid, but because he never saw it coming, and the tiny creature was trying to attach itself to his arm as it seemed to grow bigger.

Cesc guffawed loudly as Mark flung it off him to the ground. The snake was the size of a boa constrictor now and it sat up, raising its head like a cobra as it turned brown and flattened its head into a hood like one.

That was when Mark figured it was a Shadow, but still, surely whatever ability that was, the Shadow could also produce the venom and the strength to go with it. Cesc's laugh became obnoxious as he watched the snake turn into a person.

"Mickey!" Elise scolded deafeningly. She stood over the young boy as he held his sides cackling. "Really! A prank?"

Cesc nodded playfully. "Hey, come on, what's a little fun?"

Elise shook her head. "But you always do this," she complained.

Cesc shrugged as he looked down at the child, Mickey, who turned himself into a dog and ran off. He shook his head, amused. "I hate shape-shifters. They drive me crazy. I never can tell if they're what they're portraying or not. That's Mickey, or Shadow Mix, he can literally turn into anything he wants, so you could say he's my prank buddy."

Mark held his own hand as the sensations of the scales was still present in his mind. "What's your Shadow then," he asked uneasily.

Cesc's smile broadened. "Invulnerability," he stated the long word effortlessly. "The mauve protects everything inside me from any form of injury. It dulls my sense of pain, but I don't mind," he explained.

Half-heartedly, Mark nodded. It was interesting, and he had honestly never imagined such a power could exist. "Can you make it disappear?" he asked curiously.

Cesc shook his head but smiled smugly. "I don't know of any Physical Shadow that can make their power disappear."

Mark shot a glance to Kip. "So, your Shadow is a Physical Shadow too?" he wondered aloud to Cesc. Nodding as if it wasn't significant, Cesc crossed his arms. Mark drew his eyebrows together. "If you and Sage are physical Shadows, Kip, what am I?"

Grimacing a little, Kip sighed. "I thought that was pretty clear to you. You're an Elemental Shadow, as am I. Our Shadows aren't a physical part of our body, and we have to summon them to use them. For Physical Shadows, the power is always there. There's no way to stop using it," he explained, though seeming a bit disappointed.

Kip patted his back suddenly, his smile returning. "But there's more than just Physical and Elemental Shadows. There're also Psychological Shadows, and those ones are really powerful! Abilities to control minds, manipulate chance and perception. I've never met any Psychological Shadows, but everyone knows about them. The most famous one is Shadow Hope. Keller told us it has appeared in this generation and we're still waiting for its powers to surface."

"What's so special about the power of Hope?" Mark asked, a little snark in his voice.

Laughing at him, Kip's innocence prevailed. "Shadow Hope isn't the power of Hope. It's a special kind of Psychological Shadow called an Orchestrator. There's only five known Orchestrators that I've heard of. And they have the ability to push events into place without even showing themselves. They orchestrate things, that's where the name comes from.

"Keller told us that an Orchestrator is always responsible for bringing about the Exodus, that's why everyone is keeping an eye out for Hope." Kip's cheer never died.

Elise cut in. "Aside from that, Mark, are you aware of any of the rumors going around about you?" she asked seeming a little concerned for him.

Mark tensed, puzzled to no end. "Rumors? What are you talking about. I just got here. How can there already be rumors?"

Rita spoke up, shaking her head. "You wouldn't understand them anyway," she put forward, cutting off Elise. "I know you're well aware Kimberly thinks you look like that Shadow who died nine months ago, but that's not the only thing the Shadows are guessing about you. See, no one can get how you stayed away from the ASH so long, unless you were here before and you just can't remember."

With his eyes widening, Mark said, "But that can't be possible. I've lived with my family all my life."

Blowing it off, Rita continued in her thick Scottish accent, "What if you only think that?" she suggested. Mark fell silent growing more confused by the second. "A few months ago, there was a Shadow here that no one saw often, and one day he came out here as if he were running from the ASH and somehow, he passed through the shield just like you did yesterday. There were many Shadows who saw it, but rumor has it that Shadow died hours later for an unknown reason. No one ever saw the body afterwards, not even Keller."

Elise cut her off. "You're making that sound like a ghost story! The basis of the rumor is clearly untrue, but some Shadows are guessing that somehow you faked your own death after your first attempt at escaping failed, and you've lost all memory of the ASH and now you have memories that you've been living with your family all this time. It can't be explained, and it's probably not true, but I thought you should hear them, so you can prove them wrong."

Mark looked at the ground, his heart beating faster. It did seem to fit and what if it was true? What if his own memories were false? "But..." he got out hoarsely, "I know I've been living with my family, just two days ago I was with them."

Elise shook her head. "Don't worry, Mark. The rumors are most likely false, but even I can't deny that I saw that Shadow escape months ago. I didn't see him die or anything, but I do know he passed through the shield like you did."

Grimacing, Mark tied his fingers together. "It gets deeper..." he whispered. Something was going on here, two Shadows now had been compared to his strange doppelganger, and a mystery as to how powerful Mark was had begun to unfold.

Rita suddenly laid a hand on Mark's shoulder. "Hey, do you see the track?" she jeered, pointing to the sidewalk which surrounded the courtyard.

Mark shrugged seeing the Shadows skating on it and muttered indifferently, "Yeah."

Excitedly, Rita knelt to tighten the laces on her skates. "Want to race?" she asked. Standing, she took a spin around him, circling him to entice, however, it was her accent that simply threw Mark off, almost unsure of what she was asking.

Mark tensed a little, comprehending her request and he sprung back from her. "No!" He reverted from his quick movements and sighed heavily, grumbling, "I-I'm in enough trouble with the Shadows as it is. I don't want to be in even more!"

Rita shrugged, disappointed. "But it'd be fun!"

Mark attempted to stand firm in his decision and crossed his arms over his chest. Rita smiled, unscathed in her humor by Mark's lack of it. She immediately looked to Elise, Kip, and Cesc. "What about you guys? Wanna race?" she asked.

They agreed promptly, laughing as they did. Kip pulled his hands into fists and raised them to about the height of his chin then faced Mark with a broad, puppy-like smile on his face. He didn't need to say anything. If Kip wanted him to do it, it made Mark infinitely more comfortable doing it. Mark succumbed, and Kip got him to fetch his skates, which all of them seemed to wear like normal shoes.

The sidewalk was like a highway with skaters, and Mark took the opportunity to put on his skates, tightening them as much as possible before getting up again. Kip offered him a hand, which he took, and it occurred to Mark that Kip claimed to be the same age as him and yet he was a lot smaller than him, very pale and underweight, and visibly weaker.

Of course, all Shadows were unique, but Kip was different than the others. Mark realized just how happy Kip was that he had a friend who had similar powers to him and would spend time with him where others would not.

They waited to step into the path until the Shadows skating along it had past and then lined up by twos parallel, except for Rita who started in the front. Faster than Mark imagined, more Shadows came up behind them seeing their

E. KATHRYN

stance and knowing immediately that they were preparing to race. Mark found himself starting in fourth place out of twelve, and he mused to himself. It was perfectly the same as when he raced in a video game with his sister just before all this nonsense happened.

Mark contemplated again what if that hadn't happened? What if it was a false memory, and he had indeed feigned his own death or something to escape from the ASH. He shook his head. The rumors couldn't be true. He dismissed them altogether. From beside him, Kip shouted, "Rules!" as everyone was in place.

Rita started. "One circuit!"

"No powers," Elise added from where she was positioned second place behind Rita, "unless it's to prevent you or someone else from falling!"

Cesc continued from third place, "To the spigot by the ASI." He pointed. Mark looked ahead of them and indeed saw a spigot where Cesc suggested. That was the finish line.

Mark tensed as he figured it was his turn, but he said nothing and Kip nudged him telling him that he didn't have to say anything by his expression only. In fact, no one behind Kip added any rules beyond that. There were enough. Mark's heart was already racing and they hadn't even started.

Rita shouted again to prepare, then everyone secured a stance. Mark tried to mimic the same position, but he gulped, confused at what he had gotten himself into. He was caught unprepared as Rita shouted a word that hardly sounded like *go,* and Mark was run over by the Shadow that was behind him. Struggling to get moving, Mark swerved unused to his skates as he stumbled to keep up with Kip, who was already ahead of him.

He tripped and stopped the fall unsteadily with his hands on the ground and Kip slowed considerably to help him if he needed it. Mark turned him down, and stood on his own, gaining his balance and finding his rhythm to increase his speed. Kip smiled and cheered triumphantly as Mark sped up by his side, and Kip had to increase his own speed to stay ahead of Mark.

Mark and Kip were now in sixth and seventh place with Kip ahead of Mark, but they were more working together than competing. The circuit was large enough that they would have plenty of time to catch up. Mark's footing became a pattern as he and Kip passed two Shadows who were walking together calmly in the late October air. The wind blew in Mark's face, holding his annoying bangs over his head for him, though they occasionally fell between his eyes and stayed there, pressed to his face with his speed.

In Mark's vigor, he passed Kip, who competed to stay in front of him though failed. As he surpassed him, despite his experience, skinny little Kip was no match for him. Mark was stronger. Losing his focus, Mark watched Kip's endurance, how he was constantly fighting the Shadows. He was smaller than them, and always weaker, but he wouldn't allow himself to be left behind.

Mark tensed abruptly, as he was saw Kip from behind. The little sunspot had gotten ahead of him. Mark groaned at his loss of attention and sped up again, focusing on his rhythm to pass Kip. He *was* stronger than Kip, but only when he was paying attention. Kip was quick and experienced, his movements smooth and premeditated, and his focus didn't ever seem to falter like Mark's did.

Mark felt his back aching from this activity, but even with the pain, he pressed himself harder to pass Kip and catch up with the others. Cesc gave him trouble as he caught up behind the mauve-skinned Shadow. He navigated to skate in front of him causing Mark to swerve, unbalanced.

Cesc wasn't even looking back to see Mark, and somehow, he knew that Cesc was using the Realm to know exactly what Mark's movements were. How had he known that? The Realm was a pulse in the back of his head, a quiet indicator of Shadows he had never been able to use because he'd never been around other Shadows. When he thought about it, he was able to sense the others' positions without even looking.

Mark could feel in his heart, the place Kip spoke about, something was guiding him forward to keep going, and a dark Shadow entered his soul and his demeanor. Mark's eyes became deep crimson in color and dark smoke of his fire... or something else, trailed behind him. Looking directly at Cesc's back, Mark whispered, "Stop," aloud, but softly.

Mark swerved to the right as Cesc abruptly halted, perfectly baffled as to why, and he even gathered others to see what was wrong. Cesc gazed at the others shrugging and gathering his senses gradually. Tensing, he continued racing forward with a loud swear. "That rat!"

"What!" Elise wondered as she had stopped to see what was wrong with Cesc.

Cesckim grumbled to pick up the pace. "He just used a Shadow on me!" he cursed.

Elise skated ahead of Cesc with a quicker pace. "Let's give him some grace. His powers are unrefined. It could have been an accident."

Kip came up behind hearing what Elise and Cesc had said. "But what did he do?" he wondered. "That was like mind control, it has nothing to do with fire."

Elise focused onward pensively. Cesc gained ground on them. "I don't know," she whispered. "A second Shadow?"

Tensing abruptly, Kip nearly tripped. "Impossible!" he swore. "There's no way for him to gain two Shadows!" Elise didn't respond after this and focused on racing forward. Kip followed closely, trying to put it out of his mind.

Mark continued accelerating and passed two more Shadows, who he didn't know or hadn't been introduced to, and soon he reached Rita, who was still in first place. Mark's demeanor grew dark again, and his eyes glazed over. "Teleport back!"

Abruptly, a flash of green mist surrounded Rita, and she suddenly vanished then reappeared some ways behind Mark. He wasn't exactly thinking about what he had done, but now he was in first place and that was all he was thinking about.

His back panged, but he ignored it for the sake of winning.

Suddenly, Rita reappeared in front of him, but now so closely that he almost tripped. "I'll have none of your tricks!" she swore in her thick accent.

Mark fought, racing at her side to get ahead of her again. He could see the spigot ahead of them now, vaguely just around the turn. It was then that he realized this second Shadow had the power of mind control, and he was the master over it.

Beaming happily, he strengthened his rhythm to go faster. This time, he mentally shot the beam without reaching his hand forward. "Stop, Rita."

Rita stopped at full speed and couldn't gather her thoughts fast enough to start back up. Mark passed her, unstoppable and leaving Rita behind to find her rhythm again.

Mark's eyes locked onto his goal. Nothing could stop him from redeeming himself from the mistakes and incompetence he had shown since he came here. He had to prove he wasn't weak. He wouldn't back down again. Rita teleported again, now right beside him. Mark tensed, startled by her sudden appearance and lost his balance. He fought to regain his rhythm, but he began to swerve.

Ahead of him, Mark spied Sil crossing. They weren't two yards apart when Mark lost control of himself to stop, react, or change course. Sil's golden eyes met with Mark's for half a second. He wore the leather strap over his shoulder with the rest on which Winter perched and the arm guard on his arm. He didn't have his hand-project with him. Mark and Sil tensed alike, gazing at each other simultaneously.

Mark couldn't regain his balance quick enough and found himself with a quick decision in falling. It would be more logical to fall to the right but that led into the energy field. He would pass through it and if he did, the entire ASH and Keller would learn he could lead the Shadows to escape. If he fell left it would be in front of Sil's path. He'd look like an idiot, but if he continued as he was, he would again collide with Sil and his life would be over.

Hastily, he closed his eyes, and fell to the left.

Mark's next sensation was that his back hurt terribly from the fall, but he stayed silent as he slowly opened his eyes.

Twelve Shadows looked over him concerned and confused. He figured he had indeed made a fool of himself. Abruptly, Mark heard Sil cackling at him, loudly and obnoxiously, but it didn't sound like Sil.

He spied that the gauze on Sil's face was gone, and so were the burns, and before Mark had even acknowledged the sight. Sil's facial features were blurring. "Wow!" said a voice that sounded completely different from Sil's resounded over him. "Are you that afraid of Sil?"

Mark cringed as Sil's white hair shortened in length and turned strawberry blonde. He grew shorter and his eyes turned from gold to gray.

"You again!" Mark swore angrily.

Mickey giggled like a little girl. It was just too much fun for him to prank Mark. He was ignorant, confused, and gullible, traits which made pranks work. Mickey looked like he was three years younger than Mark.

Confounded, Mark found Kip, desperate for an explanation but he blew Mark off. "Why don't you go torment somebody else?" Kip scolded Mickey

Before Mark's eyes, Mickey grew even smaller, got down onto the ground, grew fur, and turned into a puppy. The sight baffled Mark, and he couldn't believe that a power like his could be possible.

"Who won?" Mark asked timidly.

Kip gestured to the spigot as Rita was gliding over to it on her skates, passing it leisurely. "Rita always wins," he muttered. "You're actually the first one who's gotten close to beating her, however, you did cheat," he held out a hand to Mark.

Taking the hand, Mark stood up wincing with the pain in his back. He blushed, however, he had cheated by using a

Shadow. He groaned and massaged his temples. "What the heck did I do?"

Kip shrugged. "That was pretty bizarre. It was like some sort of mind control power..." he muttered with some effort, still panting.

"How?"

Kip shook his head unsure, and he changed the subject. "By the way, Mickey's Shadow is an example of a Physical Shadow that can disappear." He tied in Mark's interest, helping him ignore his confusion. "He literally turns his body into someone or something else, down to their Shadow, and genetics. He's let the ASH experiment on him a little, and they found that he is completely identical to the person he's mimicking, like fingerprints and blood type. But you noticed he looks younger than he is?"

Mark nodded.

"He's forgotten his real form, and he refers to a picture from when he was younger to mimic, he's actually seventeen when he looks twelve." Kip added in jesting, "And acts twelve..."

Mark was able to laugh a little, but not long. Out of nowhere a dark spike flew at him and missed him by only a hair. It scored Kip on the arm cutting him shallowly. Kip shrieked with a mild curse and Mark jumped back a pace. Mark looked behind him to see that it had been Sage who had misfired a quill at them. With his quills arched he apologized embarrassed.

Kip winced and looked at his hand and the blood coming from the cut. "Oh, the irony..." he whispered as Mark neared, concerned. "All right, Mister Cauterization," he mused and lit his hand brightly with heat hot enough to melt metal. He allowed his arm to be burned enough for it to close the cut, and it didn't seem to hurt at all.

Kip beamed, quite surprised. "That worked out well!"

Mark nodded exasperated and still a little winded from falling, his back ached a little more than he expected. "Told you." Even standing up straight hurt.

"Are you all right?" Kip asked, seeing his cringed face.

With a half-meant shrug, Mark winced. "My back is hurting."

Considerately, Kip laid a hand on Mark's shoulder. "Would you like to go back inside?" he suggested, offering Mark a little help in returning inside. Kip was calm and cheerful, but Mark began to see worry in his eyes, a little paranoia about what he had seen during the race. Just as the ASH's cold walls surrounded them, Mark could sense the fear in Kip's heart, revolving around that dark form, which had allowed Mark to trick Rita's mind and control it.

X

TOO PALE IN COMPARISON

Taking advantage of the open doors, Emilie wandered the halls of the ASH, floating almost aimlessly if it wasn't for her ever-present inclination to cause mischief. However, today it was Sil's absence that drove her to remain indoors even when it was her only chance to have a whole open space to feel the air all around her and the ground far beneath her.

Sil wasn't allowed to bring Winter inside, and she could tell it frustrated him, especially today because he had no desire to get out of bed.

He was in a mountain of pain. She could see it on his face when she returned to the room. He was awake, but had done his best to sleep in through the clamor of Shadows. He took no notice of her when she entered, focusing on his hand project and weathering the pain with restricted movements. She floated gracefully across the room to Sil's bed and extended a hand to gather his attention. "Here."

In her palm, he scrutinized a pair of red capsules, and took them but didn't fully trust them. "You stole those, didn't you?"

Emilie wrinkled her nose with a roguish grin. "It's just ibuprofen. It'll help."

Heaving a sigh, Sil set aside his hand project and reached over his shoulder towards his bedside table for the icy glass of water placed there. He winced at the motion, unable to twist that far so Emilie hastily grabbed it for him. He didn't even offer a thank you or an acknowledgement that she had helped him, coldly taking the medicine as his only gratitude.

"Has he gotten killed out there yet?" Sil asked, sinking back into his bed and heaving a slow breath. His right cheek felt like it was on fire still, and even holding his own ice to the burn didn't help much. Even now, the fire burned inside him. The burn would be with him for years if it even vanished at all.

Rising, Emilie placed herself upon Sil's bed, which she knew irritated him. "Shot at, run over, and knocked to the ground, but not dead yet." She chuckled.

Sil didn't react, the scowl still upon his lips. "What do you think of him?" he asked, breaking a silence between them.

Intrigued, she sat up and crossed her knees beneath her, excited and devious. "Apparently…" she murmured flirtatiously, "he's my cousin." Her eyes became tender. "His short comings are obvious, but he's more powerful in the Realm than he knows."

Sil nodded thoughtfully. "What do you sense in the Realm?"

Shaking her head, Emilie grimaced. "A lot of things," she stated. "Shadow Fire is unrefined, but he's got good instincts. He's a little slow, but that'll change." She leaned back against the wall and crossed her arms. "He has no clue what he has coming to him. Defiance of the ASH, Fire, Mind Control, maybe even Hope," she added.

Sil tensed and looked directly at Emilie with a cold golden glare. "What did you just say?"

Emilie smirked and flared her lightning green eyes back at Sil. "You heard me right. I think he's Shadow Hope!"

Shaking his head dismissively, Sil scoffed. "He can't

be."

Smiling ear-to-ear, Emilie taunted him. "Are you rejecting it because you know he's more powerful than you?"

Sil recoiled and leaned back on his bed. "More powerful, yes, more refined, definitely not. He's already screwed up, but he's got a lot more mistakes ahead of him."

Emilie hummed at this pleasantly. "Honestly, I think your Shadow is more powerful than his, even if he has more than one."

Eyeing her, Sil adopted a tone of mockery. "Is it flattery now?" he mused without a smile. "I liked it better when you pinned me down for attacking you."

Giggling, Emilie pulled up her legs to her lap, floating off the bed a little. "I was never afraid of you, and physically, I am a lot stronger than you or Mark."

A smile touched Sil's lips. "I'm impressed..." he murmured, brutal sarcasm in his tone. "I thought you could just manipulate gravity so that we weigh nothing." The smile didn't leave his face as he sat up and placed himself next to Emilie on the bed. "I have to admit, you're more persistent than most Shadows," he said.

Emilie grinned. "It is flattery now!" she responded in the tone of mockery. "Silverstonarellena..." she whispered pronouncing the word like a song. "You're more than you seem. More caring, more dedicated, more fastidious than all the others."

Sil's grin grew a little, and hesitantly he laid a hand on Emilie's knee. "You need to get out of the ASH, you, of all Shadows. You, are meant for the outside world because you're already freer than the rest of us." To exemplify this, he pushed her off the bed with his other arm, and she floated without gravity out into the air.

Abruptly the elevator doors opened and many of the Shadows entered into the cool air after having been active outside. Sil laid back on his bed, and Emilie floated around the room like they had never spoken to each other. With quiet disinterest in the other Shadows, Sil picked up his hand project and continued, focusing on each heavy stitch in the leather and excluding all else.

⁂

"I don't want to do this..." Mark insisted pointlessly.

Kip shook it off, ignoring him. "Mark, it will be fine. If anything, Kimberly will give you something for the pain."

Mark grimaced. He didn't want Kimberly staring at him like he was the devil or something. He got jitters just thinking about how she glared at him with that disturbed expression. But he succumbed and followed into the infirmary where Kip heralded Kimberly. It seemed at first sight that she had been expecting someone to be injured from outside and the only start she got was that it was Mark.

Kimberly's eyes scrutinized Mark. "What's wrong?"

Mark stared about the cozy room utterly distracted until she came to him and he gulped. Fighting off a horrid sense of déjà vu, he thought this place was familiar, but he couldn't pinpoint a time when he had been here before. He couldn't meet eyes with her and found himself looking at the floor. "My back hurts."

Kimberly offered him a smile that was priceless. "Would you like to sit down?"

Mark nodded and with Kimberly's gestures he took the seat in a rather comfortable chair between the two beds.

Kimberly leaned against the table-like bed. "You can go, Kip." She dismissed him. Mark wanted Kip to stay but he couldn't bring himself to say it with Kimberly gazing at him.

"Want to tell me about it?" she asked.

Mark focused more on the coarse gray carpet, ignoring all else. Now that he was sitting and not moving, the pain subsided. "I have a weak back," he murmured. "I've never been able to be very active because of it. The Shadows got me to race."

Kimberly smiled endearingly. "Did Kip overreact and

make you come here?"

Mark produced a nod.

She beamed now, showing her teeth. "Kip does that. He overreacts to every little thing. It's quite funny. He's always been like that."

Mark noted how she twirled one of the loose curls in her ponytail, awkwardly fiddling as she spoke of Kip. "I'm really surprised you two have hit it off so well. It makes me so happy to see Kip has friends," she explained but not without a hint of affection for Kip.

Nodding in a slow motion, Kimberly finally gestured him to stand. "I have no diagnosis for Shadows. So, it's probably exactly what you say it is. So, I *diagnose* you fell," she mused slightly.

Mark had fallen thrice now, on Sil, through the shield in the room, and today not twenty minutes ago when Mickey pranked him. Mark lost eye contact with her and sighed heavily. "I have," were the only words he could get out.

Kindly, Kimberly sat on the raised bed. "If you want, I can give you something for the pain."

Grimacing, Mark lost himself in the carpet again, unable to look at Kimberly. "Uh... I think I just need to rest," he muttered. He wasn't ever getting out of here, as far as the ASH was concerned, and unless he could refine his power, which Mark determined to be impossible, he would need a miracle before he left the perimeter of the shield.

Kip trembled, completely unsure how to feel about Mark. He was different for sure, but to have multiple Shadows wasn't something Kip had ever seen before.

Keller sat across from him in a lounge chair comfortably. "You make it sound like you think you have two Shadows, when you're talking about Mark, am I correct?"

Kip tensed but nodded bitterly.

Keller brought a hand to his chin, inhaling forcibly. "It's not only possible, Kip, but it's actually rather common," he explained in an understanding tone.

Curiously, Kip's interest piqued.

"However, the ASH's environment somewhat restricts Shadows from gaining multiple powers. It's one of the major side effects of the ASI."

Contemplating, Kip listened intently. "Are there any other Shadows you know with multiple powers?" he asked.

Keller grinned with a dimple. "Before the ASH, I knew several, but there were much fewer Shadows back then, and it was difficult for them to find each other. That's why the ASH exists, to bring you all together," he explained somewhat beside the point.

Accepting it, Kip nodded. He had heard that a million times, but nothing excused that this place was a prison. "How come Mark has two Shadows?" he asked, unable to explain it for himself. He knew so little about the outside world for its culture. He had read all about the world, but what Mark had lived through was completely foreign to him.

Keller sighed and gazed out the windows behind Kip. "Mark lived outside of the ASH's environment. It's possible he gained the Shadow on accident, and because he could never use his powers before now, he never knew. Or he gained it soon after he learned of his powers, possibly on the same day." Keller laid a hand on Kip's shoulder. "At this point, Mark and his powers are still a mystery to us, but if you could learn his Shadows and keep me informed, it would be very useful, Kip."

He fought himself from meeting eyes with Keller. He knew Mark could pass through the shield, but if Keller found out about that, they might not ever get out. "Um…" Kip stammered, "y-you know that Orchestrator that spawned in this generation?" he wondered tepidly. Keller took his hand off Kip's shoulder and nodded. Kip swallowed past the lump in his throat. "What if Mark is that Shadow? What if he's the Shadow who is able to use despair and hopelessness… to free us…"

Keller eyed Kip and raised a brow, a bit curious, "Shadow Hope?" he confirmed. Kip nodded. Keller merely shook his head. "I don't know. That's a farfetched guess, and it's very unlikely, but if he is, it might be time for the Shadows to leave this place," he murmured.

Kip's spine stiffened, and his hopes rose.

Keller saw it and smiled. "But until you or I can confirm that Mark is Shadow Hope, I don't want you getting any ideas," he mused.

Honestly, Kip felt comfortable around Keller. He was an odd man, short yes, but for someone who forced the Shadows to stay here, he was kind to them and readily helped them with their problems. Keller placed his hand on Kip's wrist as he spoke again. "Did you know… that even though it's common for Shadows to gain multiple powers, it is impossible for you to have been born with two Shadows?"

Kip shook his head. "No, I didn't."

Keller nodded. "No one has ever been able to understand why. Even Shadows with more than five powers were born with just one to start with," he explained and stood to lead Kip back down the hall.

Kip got up and followed along the long, curved corridor of the hallway back to see how Mark was since he left him. Now uneasy, Kip clasped his hands together. "Mr. Keller…" he said, "I hope Mark is the Shadow Hope. I'd love to see what the outside world is like, just for one day if I could."

"You *hope*?" Keller joked, but Kip's wish saddened him.

Kip stopped in his tracks abruptly and a hand drifted over his heart. "Mark?" he wondered aloud. Keller put his hand on Kip's shoulder, concerned. Kip's eyes were wide. "I just heard Mark in the Realm, but I'm not in the Realm. I shouldn't be able to hear him." Looking onward, Mark left the infirmary and immediately looked in the direction Kip stood. Kip hurried to him. "Did you just use the Realm—"

"—to locate you?" Mark cut him off. "I think I did… I suppose I'm getting the hang of the Realm-thing," he

E. KATHRYN

guessed.

Kip's eyebrows drew together. "Mark, no one can use the Realm like that," he insisted. "How did you do that?"

Mark shrugged, mildly stunned. "I don't know. I entered the Realm for a second. I could see all the Shadows around me in the Realm, and that was it."

Putting his palm to his face, Kip grimaced. Mark's power and the vastness of it increased every minute. Keller helped hide Kip's mild frustration, and his smile brightened. "Why don't you boys come with me?"

Hesitantly, the two followed Keller back to the reception area.

"Mark, you've likely been able to use the Realm from a very young age, like all Shadows, but until recently, you've never actually entered it and turned invisible. Most of the Shadows learn how to do that together because the purpose of invisibility like this is not to hide, but rather, to share an intimate bond with the Shadows nearest to you," Keller explained in a clear voice as he led them back down the hall. "It is a gift of unity." Keller knew an abundance about the Shadows and it was evident he had amassed this knowledge over many years. If anyone was cut out for this work, while not being one of the Shadows, it was Keller.

At this point, Mark could see the entirety of the ASH's property for himself and awed at how large it was. On the second floor was a balcony that cut off and the ceiling was two stories above them. There was a large, round check-in desk which seemed to be there for another purpose unrelated to Shadows.

There was a waiting area and seating, and to the far corner toward the doors leading out, which were normally locked, there was a dimly lit hallway. With the lights off, Mark couldn't see farther into the room ahead. Keller took them into the corner room and hit a light before inviting the two boys inside.

As Mark and Kip stepped inside, they learned it was a coffee room. Mark tried to keep his nose from wrinkling up as the pungent smell of coffee strongly enveloped the room. His mother drank coffee, but he rather disliked the smell and the taste.

Keller entered behind them and gestured to the large chairs around a low coffee table. "Thirsty?" he asked.

Immediately, Kip's face shirked. "I don't like coffee," he replied.

"Me neither." Mark found himself relieved that since Kip felt the same way as him, he could also admit he didn't like it.

Keller laughed at the both of them, amused. "I can easily prepare something else." Kip and Mark glanced at each other apprehensively, unsure what to expect whether hot, cold, soft, or hard. It didn't take long for Keller to set two steaming mugs in front of the boys.

Mark gazed into the mug seeing an opaque light brown liquid that looked mysteriously like coffee, however, it didn't smell like coffee. He drew his eyebrows together and looked at Keller skeptically.

Keller merely chuckled at him. "It's not coffee," he assured. "It's just tea with milk."

Mark looked to Kip seeing he had about the same expression toward the coffee-looking-tea. Hesitantly, Mark lifted the hot mug, using his Shadow to embrace the searing temperature. Daring himself, he tasted it.

At first, he was surprised that he hadn't at least jumped from the incredible temperature of the boiling water, but he could only think about what he had sipped. Finding he enjoyed the sweet, robust flavor, he began drinking it eagerly, wanting to drink it all at the temperature it was.

Kip gazed at Mark slightly confused, but likewise cautiously, he sipped the tea and found in the same way as Mark that the taste was delicate.

Keller sat with them smiling and looking between the two. Keller had prepared himself a coffee, and the smell was very prominent to Mark as Keller sipped it more leisurely. Keller probably couldn't take the extreme heat like he could, and thus he drank slower.

Kip's curls frayed about his cheeks and he fought them to stay out of his face. His eyes flared to nearly white from yellow every time he took a sip of the tea. Mark on the other hand simply sat back and sank into the mug.

"Two Shadows of Fire..." Keller muttered. At this point, both of them met his eyes, and Keller could merely blush. "You two are friends? I can't think of a better combination."

Mark and Kip glanced at each other again as Keller spoke. He turned his attention to Mark in a firm though kind voice. "Do you know your powers are a lot stronger than many of the other Shadows here, Mark?"

Hesitantly, Mark thought to deny it. He certainly couldn't agree. He had only been a Shadow for a day now.

Keller's eyes twinkled, apparently seeing his apprehension. "However, with that power, it is also more dangerous."

Studying the floor, Mark gulped.

Kip's back stiffened and at Keller's prompt, he inhaled sharply, garnering Mark's attention. "Earlier today when you used that mind control Shadow, I theorized that you have a second Shadow." Kip paused, hesitating when Mark searched his face for his motives in telling him this.

His eyes grew tender and his hands cupped the warm ceramic mug. "I've never seen another Shadow with two powers like you, but Mr. Keller says it's common for Shadows outside the ASH... I'm just lost, I guess..." he whispered.

Mark set his mug on the table. "I am too, Kip," he murmured. "But I think all I need is practice, and I can make this work. I'll figure out how to use my Shadow. I know I can do this. It gets easier each time." Before Keller, Mark was afraid to say it, but through the Realm he sent his thoughts to Kip, expressing how much he wanted to help the Shadows escape.

Kip started as he heard it, and shocked, he looked to

Keller.

Keller tried to empathize with Mark with a gruff assurance. "It takes time."

"I don't care!" Mark raised his voice, bringing his hand down on the table. He didn't strike it very harshly, but suddenly his hand combusted on the table, and abruptly Mark jumped up and got away, startled. Regretting the action, Mark fell silent and extinguished his own flames.

Keller eyed Mark admonishingly. "It takes time," he repeated. "Normally if a Shadow did that to me, I'd segregate them, but because your Shadow is so incredibly unrefined, I'll let this one pass."

Hesitantly, Keller got up and glanced in Mark's mug to see it was empty. He stepped to Mark and laid a hand on his shoulder. "Use your Shadow a lot, become accustomed to using it under stress, and you'll learn fast." He gestured for Mark and Kip to leave the room with him. Kip drank the last sips of his tea quickly and got up to follow.

XI
A Lost Child

In an attempt to ease the pain in his back, Mark collapsed onto his new bed and sulked, letting everything wash over him. He hated this place. He could only name one good thing that had come to him here, and that was Kip. Still, it was awkward. Kip was very ignorant.

Mark's eyes followed Kip as he was addressed by Sage with an apology for misfiring, but Mark didn't want to pay attention.

He didn't know what to think, if he was different or he was meant to be normal. He didn't know what was going to become of his powers, or what he would have done with his life if he were not a Shadow. All he had to him two days ago were school and video games. All he cared about were the stats, the adrenaline, the playful screaming, the aspects of video games, which were completely useless in real life.

Despairing, Mark buried his head under his pillow and gave up. It was useless. He'd never get out of here. He'd be stuck with these people for the rest of his life with powers that would never become refined. Who was he kidding? He had powers. He could light his hands on fire. That was not normal.

Mark heaved a sigh as he watched Kip. Overthinking everything, Mark found himself pitying the Shadows who had been trapped in this place for their entire lives. He stared at Kip mindlessly as he sat on his bed with what looked like a big textbook.

Mark guessed the text had something to do with Kip's Shadow since he was glancing at his hand every few lines and creating bright lights which experimented with various purposes that came to Kip's mind.

Not only was Mark unable to understand Shadows, but he felt like he would never understand Kip. The boy was creative and bright, kind and active, friendly and compassionate. It was entirely unfair that Kip was lost from the world. However, Mark felt he could tell by looking at Kip and through the Realm, that there was a lot more to Kip that even he didn't know, and maybe no one did.

Sitting upright starkly, Mark mimicked Kip, crossing his legs and sitting very still. While Kip had a book, Mark had nothing but his thoughts, and acquired a meditative posture. It relaxed him, soothed his worry, and he found himself closing his eyes.

In the darkness through his eyelids, he could see the Realm, black and magnificent. Even without entering it, he stretched his mind out through the Realm, feeling each of the Shadows around him and even the Shadows beyond them.

The whole ASH shimmered with the colored lights of over a hundred Shadows living within it. Even the cold marble walls glittered with a bright cyan light from Shadows feeding their power into it. Outside the ASH, Mark could see the ASI shield covering the whole property, but it wasn't ginger-bronze.

Within the Realm, it glowed cyan, the same as the walls. It was the same power. It was all the same Shadow that controlled the ASI. Mark's brows knitted together as he recognized it. A Shadow was responsible for keeping the Shadows imprisoned here.

He opened his eyes slightly and frowned. Who could have done this? He thought the Shadows all worked together. They all thought the same, didn't they? How could one of their own be willing to work with Keller to keep them locked up?

Catching sight of someone near him, Mark looked up and gasped. Sil was standing over him, watching him closely. Scrambling back onto his bed so fast, he slammed his bruised shoulder into the wall, Mark barely took note of the perplexed expression upon Sil's brow.

"I've never seen someone learn how to do that so quickly."

"D-do what?" Mark stammered, still very nervous even though Sil remained calm with only a miniscule hint of that icy demeanor.

Sil bent down a little, nearing Mark, uncomfortably close to his face. "You've known you are a Shadow for all of forty-eight hours, and you already know how to use the Realm without entering it?"

Gulping, Mark eased his way upright, letting himself be in Sil's presence without being afraid. "It's always been there," he whispered. "I've always been able to feel it. I just didn't know what it was, and I never saw any Shadows."

Rising, Sil crossed his arms. "Ocie taught me how to stretch my range in the Realm, but the ASI blocks me from reaching much farther than the shield..." Pausing, Sil closed his eyes and grimaced. "But your range is huge!"

"How do you know?" Mark asked, ever cautious.

Hesitating, Sil bit his lip, and gradually, he gestured beside Mark. "May I?"

Flustering, Mark tensed when he realized Sil wanted to sit on his bed. Pressing his lips together, Mark managed a very slight nod, and Sil sat.

"You've never felt the restrictions of the ASI like I have." Sil spoke a little faster than Mark expected. He sounded slightly accusative, a little jealous maybe, but not in an intimidating way. "You've had fourteen years, completely free, to expand your range in the Realm, whether you knew it or not, and even here, the ASI can't hold back your ability to see all the Shadows beyond the ASH."

"But what is it good for?" Mark puzzled, not sure if he should be flattered by Sil or continuously worried.

The hint of a smile appeared on his lips. "Oh, so much! If I could just get free of the ASH, I could find Shadows anywhere in the world. I could communicate with them through the Realm, without even entering it. That's telepathic communication, don't you get that? It's a whole new level of achieving that unity Ocie always talks about."

Mark frowned and folded his hands in his lap. "That's just another power to keep track of. What do you mean 'unity?'"

His eyes growing tender, Sil gazed off from Mark. He contemplated silently, then heaved a sharp breath. "Come into the Realm with me."

"What?" Mark gasped a little too promptly, but Sil didn't wait for him. Pulling his legs up onto Mark's bed and crossing them so they sat beside each other identically, Sil vanished into the Realm.

Mark groaned, shooting a nervous look to Kip who was watching with equal skepticism from across the room. Rolling his eyes, Mark summoned the familiar feeling, relaxed, focused his breathing and closed his eyes.

Instantly upon entering the Realm, Mark felt very cold and flustered at how close he stood to Sil. His icy form spread a cold aura all across the Realm. It surrounded Mark and enveloped him in a bright light. Sil conveyed only cool calmness with nothing to intimidate Mark, only peace, and Mark accepted the cold, letting his own fire dim slightly.

Sil walked into the Realm, and he led Mark to a quiet place deeper inside. Lower in the plane of reality, Sil's Shadow closed in ever so gently, and the aura came to rest over Mark's mind. A shimmer of ice sparked before his eyes, and its light burst.

At first, Mark was terrified, but when the Shadow

imparted a string of feelings to him, he could only be mystified. These feelings belonged to Sil, who willingly shared them. Sil not only had an extremely refined Shadow, but in the Realm, he was even more powerful, able to impart his own memories, and take from other's memories to see for himself.

Mark watched with eager anticipation as the vision in the Realm brightened and became clearer. A blinding light offered a view of green as a portal formed into the real world. It smelled like early summer, a part of the memory that Sil's Shadow imparted to him.

Every sensation of heat or cold, scent and sight was given to Mark's mind. He was outside in the courtyard many years in the past as it was revealed to him. The grass was a vibrant green, the sky was true blue, all seemed normal. But to Mark, it was too vivid to be his own memory. He perceived he was actually there.

Mark entered the memory of his own accord and all at once the Realm disappeared behind him. Trembling, Mark stumbled through, feeling gravity take hold of his feet, and he whirled around as the dark world vanished behind him, not sure how he was going to get out.

He looked around seeing the ASH. There was hardly any difference from the courtyard he had seen today, with the same amount of Shadows if not a little less. He couldn't recognize all their faces, but those he did, he found appeared much younger.

Stepping upon the sidewalk, he was abruptly plowed over by a seven-year-old running into his legs. Even in his memories, he was still just as clumsy. As he hit the grass, he hesitated to get up, surprised he could interact with Shadows in this memory. It was difficult to get up, and though his body did feel like his own, it felt lighter. He stumbled about until he realized in this memory, in whatever year this took place, his body was years younger.

He spotted Kimberly across the field and to his surprise she appeared to be exactly the same age she was now. It seemed odd to him, but not outside the realm of possibilities. She was leading around a young Shadow, a boy, the same apparent age as Mark. The Shadow was ginger, and very scrawny. From the distance, Mark could learn little to nothing about him—other than figuring this was the Shadow he reminded Kimberly of so much.

"That's the Recluse," a young voice pointed out seeing Mark staring.

Mark looked down and nearly jumped seeing the child's wild white hair and golden eyes burning directly into his. "The Recluse?" he repeated.

A young version of Sil sat on the grass, surrounded by a light blue frost and playing with toys on his own. He nodded, seeming grumpy but not as irritable as he seemed in real life. "He never comes outside, except with Kimberly," he explained.

The Reclusive Shadow was a frail child, with long, outgrown red hair, clinging to a black bag he had strapped over his shoulder. He could barely stand as he ventured into the grassy field, testing his limits and savoring the faintest freedom. Mark wanted to get closer. He wanted to learn more about him, but Sil's memory didn't permit him, so he stayed.

"You are Sil, right?" he made sure, looking over the little boy before him.

Sil eyed him flaring his eyes an icy blue. "Are you stupid?" he mocked and threw a little snow at him which was out of place in the summer.

Mark used fire to melt the snow instantly. "Who is that guy over there?" he asked.

The wild-haired child scoffed, "I don't know his name. I think he's sick."

"Sick with what?" Mark pressed his luck, warily.

Shrugging, Sil leaned back in the cold grass contently. "Maybe it's because he's ginger," he mocked softly.

Smirking, Mark sat down with him. He somehow managed a broad smile on his face even though he knew Sil was quite hostile to everyone. "What do you have against gingers? That's just rude."

With a scoff, Sil pushed him away, using a literal wall of ice which Mark playfully tried to get around. "Weak redheads, they're everywhere. Like that guy over there. He thinks he's so tough!" he pointed across the field, and Mark turned to see over his shoulder.

Over the distance, he saw Kip. The boy was so small at this age, but he happily played with his new Shadow. Mark remembered Kip had told him he couldn't use his Shadow fully until he was about six or seven. *Was that right?*

Now Kip easily fired off shots into the shield above, playfully enjoying himself as he fought back against his little prison. The beams of light were like bright lasers, capable of slicing through everything they touched. Mark could feel it in Sil's memory, Kip's cockiness enraged him.

Mark grimaced, Kip wasn't cocky. Not by a long shot. Kip was the nicest, gentlest, meekest person he had met so far. Kip showed off a little, but it never came off as haughty.

Paling, Mark realized there had been a change in Kip. He and Sil had gotten in a fight before. *Oh no...* he groaned. He knew what was going to happen.

The younger Sil got up out of the grass, disregarding Mark as if he wasn't there. *No!* Mark wanted to cry out, *you're not going to attack Kip! You can't do that to him!*

This was a memory. Nothing could be changed.

Just as Sil had done to Mark, he instigated a fight with Kip, convincing the young boy he wasn't as powerful as he thought he was. While practicing, his Shadow was good, but Kip was too unrefined to hold a candle to Sil, and Sil proved to him that he had no control over his Shadow, shaking his confidence.

Why is fighting the way you refine a Shadow? That's wrong!

The memory took its course.

Sil tried to hit Kip. Kimberly had to abandon her child to stop the fight until Keller and the ASOs arrived but nothing could stop Sil. Mark wanted to dive in there himself, he wanted to protect Kip, but for some reason, he couldn't make his body do anything. He could only stare with the other onlooking Shadows.

"I am as powerful as you!" Kip screamed suddenly. "You can't treat me like I'm less than you!" His face was red with tears, barely bruised by Sil. Kimberly raced up behind him, not Sil.

Mark tensed, something changed. In a second, Sil was no longer an aggressor. Kip was furious, and even in such a tiny form, he wasn't helpless. This was what Sil wanted. As always, Sil had a firm purpose in the fights he picked. Not to terrorize or beat down Shadows, but to push them, teach them, and encourage them to refine their Shadows.

This was never a good idea. Kip might not have been more refined or more powerful than Sil, but Mark could see easily. Kip was a thousand times more volatile than Sil.

Pushed to the edge, Kip was sobbing. In the same position Mark had found himself in, Kip hadn't lost his fight with Sil. Out of rage, he stood as victor. A fine beam of light zapped across the courtyard, horizontal with the ground. An unbreakable vector, singeing the air, and directed at Sil.

The glistening gold burned into Mark's eyes. The beam struck Sil in the shoulder, unstoppable and flying undisturbed until it ricocheted against the shield. One after another, Kip shot three quick blasts, each piercing Sil like a blade and passing through his torso.

Mark felt like his heart stopped. That was a seven-year-old child he'd just seen get impaled three times. That was what unrefined Shadows were capable of. That was why they were dangerous. Sil knew this better than most.

Kip collapsed to the dirt crying, barely realizing what he had done as Sil fell back, as good as dead. Mark couldn't believe his eyes as Kimberly rushed to Sil, and Keller grabbed Kip, whisking the child off to a detention room while Sil was taken to the infirmary.

How on Earth did you survive that! Mark pled, not sure

if Sil could hear him now. He watched the child as he was carried off, barely breathing, but not bleeding quite as much as Mark suspected. Surely it had been the heat of Kip's shot that had burned the wounds and cauterized them to some degree.

The next thing Mark saw was blackness, Sil's memory was bloody and dark, painful and long. And then suddenly, he saw a bright light and infinite seconds later he woke up. Sil opened his eyes to the fluorescent lights of the infirmary and the eyes of a small boy watching him.

Sil was too weak to move, to even clearly see the boy near him. He wasn't as innocent as Kip, but he had that wide, sweet smile. The Recluse had his long hair tied back neatly, and he sat on the lower bed in the infirmary. Brandishing a wet washcloth, the boy kindly dabbed it across Sil's forehead until Kimberly arrived.

"He's waking up."

"You shouldn't bother him."

Faint noises. Shuffling. And then blackness once more.

The passage back to the Realm was given to Mark, and upon entering the Realm, he returned to the real world. As soon as Mark ceased to see the black void of the Realm, he faced Sil's eyes gazing into his own. Unspoken, Sil simply looked away from Mark and whispered, "Thank you," before turning away and leaving.

Kip leapt to his side and gaped. "Are you all right?" he asked, his voice cracking. "What happened?"

Mark watched Sil's fluid movements, now understanding. "Sil's never shown that to anyone..." he breathed, "but... he showed it to me." Mark stared bewildered by the knowledge he now had.

XII
INSECURITY OF FALLACY

Emilie couldn't stand the afternoons sitting around in her bed. She spent most of her time listening to loud music through headphones off the computer in the back room. The computer seemed like the only way to the outside world, and Emilie, most of all, valued that the ASH gave them the freedom to use it.

Now, she had a name: Hellen Meyvise. Taking advantage of the ASH's gift, Emilie knew how to learn using a computer and how to *search*.

She knew her mother existed and that this woman had given her up. With all her soul, Emilie wanted her mother to know that *she* existed, and she wanted to be found. With years of searching on her own, Emilie had finally learned her mother's name and she released all of her talents on the name.

Nothing stood in her way now that the first major barrier had been passed. The Internet gave her access to know everything about her mother. She could see what she liked, who she was before Emilie was born, and most importantly, where she lived. A part of Emilie hated this woman for letting her go. Emilie had a free spirit that would kill her, and she knew it.

The enclosing walls drove Emilie mad. If she never got out of the ASH, she was sure that someday she would do something terribly rash and someone would get hurt. She wanted her free spirit to bring out the best in her, and this prison merely amplified her worst.

Emilie had attempted to hack into the ASH's system countless times to disable the ASI in order to free the Shadows, but it was beyond her. She had succeeded in messing with the security system and the cameras once, but this only tightened security in hindsight.

She didn't enjoy herself as she learned of her mother. A burning anger welled inside her, becoming more and more volatile the longer she was alone.

She kept at it until dinnertime when a poor Shadow came to inform her. She regretted it, but that didn't stop her from mauling the Shadow as she had Mark when he first arrived. It did make her question her motives.

Out of all the Shadows, she was the freest. Nothing bound her to the ground and she—more or less—did whatever she wanted. But still, she was unsure what exactly she was trying to escape from. She hated the ASH, of course. But what on the outside did she truly want, if she indeed hated her mother as much as she thought she did?

There was a great excitement in the hall on the way down to dinner, and Mark couldn't help but gaze at Sil with a new understanding of him. Just because Sil had shown him his memory of the Recluse didn't change the fact Sil was still angry at him for burning him.

Mark figured a little news had made it around the ASH. Quietly through the Realm, they knew their hope for the Exodus was coming soon, and Mark was greeted with smiles. In the halls, Keller walked beside the Shadows, blissfully oblivious to the excitement as he worked his way towards Sil.

Keller spoke in a friendly manner. "How is your project coming along?"

Sil's expression remained neutral. "I'm almost done," he muttered, disinterested in humoring Keller. In spite of the civil conversation Mark and Kip had shared with Keller, he couldn't help but feel the muted disdain Sil had for the man.

Watching Sil, Mark couldn't help but remember the young, lonely Sil he saw in the memory. Sil was more than alone in the Shadows, he was a child who had never seen his parents or the outside world. Sil was so close to leaving the ASH and his anger was misunderstood. It was so confusing. Why didn't all the Shadows envy Sil?

Keller continued, his voice seeming to grate on Sil's nerves. "You know, Winter has been at our doors all day. Why didn't you go outside today?" he wondered as if trying to empathize with Sil.

With a snide smirk, Sil merely spat, "We have doors?"

Abruptly, only a second later, Keller grabbed Sil's arm and forced him to look into his eyes. When Mark caught sight of Sil's face through the whirl, the icy Shadow glared at Keller with smug satisfaction.

Keller's shoulders arched, enraged, as he signaled two ASOs to come over to him. "I warned you!"

Mark's heart dropped as he watched this happen. The two guards hurried over, taking Sil by the arms, holding his hands behind his back while Keller clenched his fists. "The next time I hear you say that, it'll be the detention room."

Keller's gaze slowly became tender and his voice softened. "Sil, I built this place to bring the Shadows together, to harness your abilities, and to not abuse them. Your powers far exceed the others, and you know it, but I need you above all to not lose hope. A time will come, and when it does our doors will be open forever."

Sil arrogantly snickered at Keller's plan despite how the ASOs restrained him. He smirked haughtily and froze his arms. The guards held tighter despite the cold, which was what Sil wanted. The ice formed over their hands freezing them to him. Suddenly, before Mark's eyes, Sil spread his arms out, spraying ice over the two guards. With ample opportunity to spring free, Sil ducked and dashed out, vanishing into the Realm as he assimilated with the other Shadows.

"Stop him!" Keller shouted for more ASOs. Sil was already gone. There were enough Shadows in the hall that they could never find him by his shadow on the floor. No one could see Sil, but Mark could feel him in the Realm, laughing.

Sil reappeared in the line for food without any further trouble, even when Keller saw him. Mark found a seat among the Shadows, hiding his amusement when Sil sat alone at the end of one of the far tables.

Angering Keller put Sil in a good mood, but Mark did not dare to attempt to straighten things out with Sil now. Kip plopped down next to Mark, and smiled at him. None of their voices could be heard over the talk and chatter filled and overwhelmed the room.

At the very least, he was thankful that dinner didn't include the sour taste of his worry and guilt. He sat back in his chair restlessly touching the soft point of his left ear and sighed cheerfully. To his great surprise this day had gone well.

He had learned a lot about the Shadows, and he felt a great deal more comfortable around these people. As much as he wanted to be home, and for things to be normal, figuring out how to use his Shadow had been the most fun he had had outside of video games in months.

Still, his mind lingered on the thoughts of the Exodus, and the spark of hope in the Shadows. Maybe they were getting at something when they talked about Shadow Hope. Mark didn't want to think about it, but he got the feeling he was under the veil of some kind of destiny.

Hope was an *Orchestrator,* after all. Maybe it had some kind of control over outcomes and it was using him as a means to an end. He didn't know if he felt violated by that thought. He did like the idea of having the power to get out of here within himself.

They had to come up with a plan of sorts soon. Emilie had seemed so keen on getting out, and yet she had barely shown herself today. She wanted the Exodus to happen, and it was clear enough to Mark that she liked to use Sil. So why wasn't she trying to use Mark.

Maybe Emilie was Shadow Hope. Maybe she had a hand in all this. Mark frowned over his dinner and slumped in the hardbacked chair. He wanted to be home so badly, but now he was too curious. More was going on behind the scenes in the ASH, things that affected him, the Shadows, Shadow Hope and maybe even the Recluse.

He had gotten a feel for his surroundings now, if he played it safe, maybe he wouldn't screw up anymore. He had Kip to show him around, and he guessed Sil was on his side now, or at least not trying to kill him. Sil had gone through something terrible because of a Shadow of Fire. All at once he didn't blame Sil for hating him.

As they had last night, Kimberly and Keller sat near to each other and oversaw the Shadows. Keller watched Sil closely to make sure he wasn't doing anything mischievous. He looked to Kimberly, murmuring, "How has your day gone, concerning Mark…"

Kimberly grimaced, lying, "Fine."

Keller acknowledged she had no desire to talk about it, but he pushed the conversation. "Mark has two Shadows. I and a few Shadows are under the impression that Mark is Shadow Hope. No one is sure, but it's stirring the Shadows." Keller looked back to Sil. "Even Sil isn't one to act up like that."

"Mark is changing everything around here…" Kimberly murmured. "What if it is time for the Shadows to be free?"

Keller shook his head. "Not until we find Hope. We've

been searching for that Shadow for almost twenty years. You were the one who told me how important Hope is. Until I can confirm Mark is Shadow Hope, the Shadows must stay within the ASH."

Protesting, Kimberly's tone doubted Keller. "But have you forgotten why? Hope is a leader in the Shadows, not the turning factor," she insisted. "Hope can lead the Shadows where you can't, and there's multiple Shadows at play each time the Exodus has occurred. Even if Mark's not Hope, he's still as much a part of this as any of them are."

Eyeing her, Keller smirked. "And exactly how many times have you seen the Exodus happen?"

Kimberly fell silent, and looking down at her plate, she muttered softly, "Three times…"

Scoffing, Keller did the math in is head piecing together just how old Kimberly was. "When do you plan on sharing your vast knowledge?"

Pushing herself, Kimberly folded her hands together. "I can only help so much without my Shadows."

Seeing her distress, Keller finally let off and let her eat. She had stood by him in the early development of the ASH. She was among the first to come to the ASH, and unlike many Shadows, she needed a home and she came willingly.

She knew better than most Shadows, the need they had for a home, and what the world was like for Shadows outside the ASH. Humans rejected them, and she had constantly been in hiding. She believed at least by doing this, some families would long desperately to see their children, the Shadows, again.

Kimberly believed in Keller's goal, but frankly his motives were growing increasingly impulsive. He was blind of how the Shadows felt. Early on, many Shadows supported him. Twenty years of this had changed the man. She was starting to doubt him.

It was only a matter of time before Mark would take matters into his own hands, or worse would happen.

⊰◑⊱

Emilie expected to see Sil in the lobby, working on his project as always, but when he wasn't there, she stopped. Her feet touched the floor, and she sank against the crescent shaped desk. As inviting as the entire lobby appeared, it felt dark. Sil was in pain, she tried to remind herself. He didn't want her to bother him right now.

She had skipped dinner, stealthily using the Realm to slip out without anyone noticing. She had a lot of freedom to roam the ASH, but she still couldn't get beyond the ASI. The fading autumn light accentuated the burning glow of the reddish shield surrounding the windows. She never felt so trapped. With Sil's absence and the taste of the outside world that Mark gave her, her skin crawled.

She was hungry, but wouldn't admit that to herself, either gorging herself or skipping meals altogether when she felt lost like this. Her knees gave out, and she floated down allowing a subtle gravity to bind her to the stone. She didn't want to be alone right now. She couldn't let herself assimilate with the blinded and mindlessly optimistic Shadows. Even Sil was being affected by the hope that Mark had brought into the ASH.

Emilie was sickened by it, scooting into the deep darkness under the desk to hide. She just wanted to be free, convincing herself that was all she needed. If she could feel miles of air on all sides of her, she wouldn't need anyone else. She wouldn't need to feel tied to Sil. She wouldn't need to feel loved by someone, by her mother.

Why did she even care about Hellen? It wasn't like the woman cared about her. Emilie been given up the moment she was born. She never wanted to see that woman. If anything, she wanted to mess with Hellen's life, to get under her skin and then reveal herself to be her long-lost daughter.

Emilie cringed, her face burning as she bit back tears. She didn't care. She didn't care about anything. But a part of her did. A part of her wanted to spend every waking moment with Sil and leave any idea of family behind. Another part of her wanted to face her mother, look her in the eyes and ask, *why?*

Emilie couldn't stop the tears now, thankful for only the darkness in which she could cut herself off from the Realm and prying eyes to cry. She didn't know any other place she could have such privacy. It was hard enough just to make sure the only thing the Shadows ever saw of her was that she didn't care.

"Are you all right?" a voice asked, his feet shuffling closer.

Emilie's hopes rose, seeing him near. It was Sil, she was sure of it. He had sensed her distress, and he did care. Mark's crimson eyes illuminated the darkness and Emilie glowered. "Of course..." she groaned.

He tensed when he saw her, clearly not expecting to see her, as strong willed as she was, as uncaring as she was, hiding to cry. Emilie scoffed at him. The idiot didn't have enough mind about him to leave her alone. The others would have known better, but he didn't even know her.

"What's wrong?" he asked.

Hastily, she dried her face with her jacket to hide her tears and her bright red face, making sure all Mark would be able to see of her was the glow of her lightning green eyes. She was a monster in the darkness. She would eat him alive if he got closer. He ignored every impulse inside him that might have made him afraid of Sil and drew nearer.

Staring at him indignantly, Emilie eyed Mark with thoughts swirling in her mind, and aura in her posture to drive him away. Mark, however, ignored it, mostly oblivious.

Mark confused Emilie beyond all else. He saw Shadows differently than anyone. He might have been a Shadow, but he thought like a human.

Emilie attempted to dry her face skittishly, knowing Mark was trying to empathize with her as a human would. "Just stop." Shadows wouldn't understand, so why would a human be able to? "You don't get it!" Growing increasingly more uncomfortable by the second, no snide look could get him to leave her alone. "Things can't stay like this..." her tears returned as she tried to explain, "The Exodus can never come!"

Emilie found herself making the mistake of meeting eyes with Mark, and suddenly, at his crimson eyes, she froze in fear. Even with the kind, calm flames flickering within Mark's irises, even in the fear he wielded, Emilie found a strength and peace while gazing at them. Only perfection could hold those traits in one body.

Her shoulders sank and her whole body drooped closer to the floor in despair. "I could never be good enough... not after spending the day cyber-stalking my mom!"

Stepping out on a limb, Mark reached out and brought an arm around her shoulders. She writhed uncomfortably under his arm, but he held her tightly as he whispered, "If you wanted to know about your mom, you could have asked me."

Emilie tensed, feeling Mark's embrace around her shot a shiver up her spine. Mark... cared for her? Emilie's heart beat faster. She hadn't known him for a day, and she had done everything in her power to come off as cruel toward him. How could Mark show her kindness now?

"But..." Emilie insisted, "She gave me up. She doesn't care. Why would she? Why would you! You can be human. There's no way you could understand both humans and Shadows unless you were somehow a perfect being. Why don't you get how..." she struggled for a word, "unnatural you are?"

Mark smirked a little sarcastically, only to assure her. "I got that much."

Emilie ignored him as she grappled over how he could act this way after the way she had treated him. "I just don't get you..."

Emilie shifted under the dark desk and caught Mark looking her over. She drew her coat tighter to hide her skimpy pink camisole which delved well below her collarbone. Her clothes were in disarray, and it didn't help that her cheeks were red and puffy.

Mark averted his eyes, the crimson glow of his eyes disappearing for a moment. "You don't know me, but if it helps, Emilie, I'm your cousin. Your mom is my aunt, and I can tell you. I know she didn't want to let you go, and that ever since she lost you, she hasn't been the same. That's how my mom talks about her anyway. Listen, I'll do anything for you, I'll tell you anything. I care for you like this because you are a part of my family."

Mark moved out into the light on his knees, the cherry shimmer sparkling when he locked his eyes on her. "Now, I admit, I don't know you that well... but because you are my cousin... I love you."

Emilie froze completely, shocked to hear him say that. Admittedly, Mark didn't know her well enough to say that, but his reason for saying it was solid. And, frankly, right now, Emilie was the only family Mark had. "I just don't get you, Mark," she whispered, adopting a pleased smile.

A bit of color appeared in Mark's face as he blushed. With his hands still on her shoulders, he briefly wrapped his arms around her, and embraced her firmly. Emilie sank lower, her Shadow dying inside her as her guard lowered. He scooted a little closer refusing to let go until she pushed away, and she never did. Emilie's heart steadied, and she laid her head on Mark's shoulder, relaxed. Sil could never comfort her like this.

"What are you two doing down here?" a sweet voice came. Mark jump up and hit his head on the desk's underside from around the circle, Kimberly showed herself.

Mark took his arm off Emilie and leapt to his feet. "Emilie was upset," he said shakily. "I only wanted to help." He adopted a serious stiffened tone when Kimberly appeared before him.

Kimberly laughed, only a touch of the wariness she usually had around Mark showing. "It's all right, Mark," she assured and stepped into the desk area. Turning her attention to Emilie, she observed her state and looked back at Mark, smiling. "I think you've done enough."

Mark nodded, a little scatterbrained, and he stepped out of the desk area to head to his room, but not without looking back as Kimberly helped Emilie up and walked with her. Mark took the stairs and was out of sight by the time Kimberly spoke to Emilie. "I'm assuming you didn't tell him."

Emilie looked away from Kimberly grimly. "He wouldn't get it anyway."

Kimberly stopped outside the infirmary door. "Come with me."

Emilie's feet left the ground, floating. "Why?" she beckoned, adopting a sitting position in midair.

With a sly grin, Kimberly gestured Emilie inside. "Let's talk in private," she invited. Easily enough, Emilie entered the room with a cautious air as she flew in. Once inside, Kimberly sat on the larger of the two beds in the infirmary. "Tell me, what do you think of Mark?" she asked.

Emilie smirked, amused. "Are you kidding!"

Kimberly's eyes remained firm. "I'm not kidding, Emilie. You can see Shadows' abilities before they can see themselves. How is Mark different from the other Shadows?"

Floating higher, Emilie's humor vanished. "I don't believe you're asking me this..." Hesitating, she floated airlessly to the higher bed and sat. "Kimberly..." she whispered desperately, as if a little scared, "you know that power is unrefined. I'm bound to make mistakes... but..." she stammered, distressed in her voice, "the way Mark spoke to me earlier, I'm as sure as I can be..."

With a terrified expression, Emilie met eyes with Kimberly. "I don't know how else to interpret it." She couldn't deny it. "Kimberly... Mark is Shadow Hope. He has to be!"

Kimberly looked down as well. "I see..." She grimaced.

"Then it's only a matter of time." Kimberly stood and stepped over to the kitchenette across the room. "Hope will show itself in a few days inevitably, then I can prove to Keller that it's time for the Shadows to be free."

Kimberly came back to Emilie with a slip of paper and took Emilie's shoulders tightly. "Please, Emilie, convince Mark that he's Shadow Hope, and try to get Hope to show itself. Will you do that for me?"

Emilie crossed her arms, contemplating. "Sure thing." Thinking aloud she murmured, "But... what if I were to trick him into using Hope?"

Kimberly perked up. "How so?"

Shrugging, Emilie leaned back in the air. "Maybe... sneak up on him..." she posed. "Maybe Hope will react, and—"

Kimberly shook her head. "It won't work. Hope is a being of the Realm. It would hear your thoughts and protect Mark without even revealing itself to him or you. There're only five Orchestrators that I know of, and what Keller doesn't realize is that Hope isn't the only one who's chosen a wielder. It's not the only one we have to find. This is the first time in over five hundred years that all five of them are alive at once. The Shadows need a leader. Keller can't lead the Shadows as a human."

Emilie eyed Kimberly and floated toward her. What Kimberly said infuriated her. Emilie was independent. The idea that her freedom depended on someone to lord over her was outrageous. A devious smile appeared on her lips as she leered over Kimberly and uttered, "Bug off!" in a whisper then flew over to the door.

"And you are aware..." Kimberly broke in before she left. "Of the risk you are at by using your Shadow too strenuously. Just because gravity doesn't affect anything you touch doesn't mean it doesn't have an effect on you. If ever you were unable to use your Shadow, you know you don't have the strength in your legs enough to walk, or worse, what if you are flying and you fall."

Emilie shot back at Kimberly, "What?"

Kimberly's expression remained calm. She saw right through Emilie's defenses. "You've never walked in your life. It's always feigned because gravity doesn't affect you, your legs are too weak to walk." Kimberly met eyes deeply with Emilie in consequence. "While you rely on your Shadow for all your strength, your real muscles are never used. Without your Shadow, lifting a cup would be a struggle, much less walking, or throwing people around like you do."

Emilie grinned with all her teeth and spat, "Then I will never stop using my Shadow, and I'll find a way to become stronger so my Shadow is unaffected by anything!"

Not feeling in the slightest bit cocky, Emilie made it crystal clear getting her to stop using her Shadow was a lost cause. At least she had learned the truth about Mark's Shadow.

Emilie still hung in Kimberly's face as she stood. "Here." Kimberly thrust the small piece of paper at her. She took it and looked it over. "It's the recipe you asked for, that is, for when you are free," Kimberly said.

Emilie read it and sank lower. "You really want to see the Shadows freed..." She grimaced. Kimberly knew what Emilie wanted, and with this motivation, Emilie admitted to herself she couldn't resist. "I'll do it..." She succumbed. "A love like that...has to be sincere." Looking into Kimberly's eyes, Emilie's brow became softer. "I'm sorry, Kimberly, you of all people should have my trust, considering your past..."

Kimberly smiled and cheerfully laid a hand on Emilie. "And you have my trust,"

Emilie beamed, and taking the recipe, she flew off, exiting the infirmary promptly and flying up to the room where she should have been as soon as dinner ended. The Shadows were already preparing themselves for the evening comfortably, and to them the day was ending, but for Emilie the night was just beginning.

Adopting a standing position, Emilie pretended to walk toward the computer room in the back. With a look, she begged Sil to come with her, but he raised his hand project, dismissively. Emilie took a glance at Mark, but didn't let him notice, and she silently stepped into the back room only lit by the light of the computer.

Emilie put her feet on the ground, and deliberately, she relinquished her power over gravity. Her legs gave out and she sank to the floor, her knees snapping against the hard marble.

Wincing, she was sure she had bruised her knees, and she reinstated her power, biting down on her lip.

"She's right..." she whispered. "We do need a little help..."

XIII
DECEIT IN DARKNESS

The elevator did open when he summoned it, and that surprised him. He expected this room to be a cell, but in fact, he was allowed to roam the halls at night. The solid stone floors were freezing on Mark's feet, but he remedied the cold with a smoldering flame in his hand.

It was so strange knowing the intense feeling of imprisonment many of the Shadows suffered even when they had most of this facility open to them. Mark still didn't exactly feel trapped, just homesick.

Making his way downstairs, Mark strode toward the lobby. For some reason, he felt safest there, like it was truly a home, unlike the mass bedroom he had to sleep in like some overwhelming summer camp. He could be alone down here, under the open sky of the huge windows overlooking the town of Culpeper. The night was clear, and the moon was bright, shining into the old building.

The abandoned reception desk stood out like the ghost of what this facility used to house. The remnants of a metal detector stood at the door, and an old movie camera sat in a glass box upon the round desk. It was once a Library of Congress dedicated to preserving movies, now this was all that had survived.

Stepping past the lounge seating in the middle of the room, Mark tried the front door, the only door he had seen that didn't lead to the courtyard. It shimmered when he touched it. A bronze glow protested when his fingers latched around the door handle. The ASI prevented the Shadows from even touching the door, but Mark could, and he tested his luck. The doorknob clicked, but it wouldn't budge, locked securely.

He sighed, he could destroy the locks if he wanted. It would be easy. He thought better of it, keeping his cover for the Shadows. He clenched his fists, letting the fire warm him. He'd get out; he knew he would. He'd see his family again. He was sure of it, and he wasn't going to let a single locked door get in his way.

A little tiredly, he yawned and stepped back into the lounge, finding a seat near the window. He didn't want to sleep now that he was thinking of home. His mind raced with how his family was doing. What did his mother think of him? How could she hate Shadows so much she'd be so quick to turn him over to the ASH? It seemed ridiculous that she'd do this to him willingly.

None of this would have happened if his father had been around to stop her, to make her think this through just a bit longer. Mark sulked under the window. January either hated Shadows or was completely afraid of them, and Mark only gathered that much because of how the man would shut him down at every question about Shadows. January was absent-minded, all he cared about was work and being as far away from his family as possible.

Mark admitted to himself he had a level of resentment for January. Why would he even get married or have kids if he didn't want a family? Mark did know one thing; his dad would have stopped Marissa, made her think this through a little harder, and then Mark would be subject to hiding his powers from the world rather than learning to use them here.

Mark didn't know which outcome was worse.

He shivered a little and let the flames in his hands grow hotter, soon to the point of combusting. He realized that small red flames were tickling upon the surface of his skin, and his sleeves remained unburned. They were getting easier to control, a soft, dim light to keep him warm, and an asset he was sure he would come to appreciate. Looking out at the hill on which the ASH stood, Mark sighed to himself, convinced no matter when the Shadows escaped, he was going to be here a long time.

Mark determined to not let this place break his spirit. Even if he would be here forever, he would refine his Shadow. He would have perfect control over it, like Sil did. In the darkness of the midnight lobby, Mark's hands burst into flame, a relaxed action, not sparked by an ounce of rage inside him. If emotion controlled his powers, then the Shadow controlled him, and he would never leave.

It came easily, the crimson conflagration bringing light to the air around him like an evil force. It trickled up his sleeves, latching onto the fabric, but he wouldn't let the fire burn it. Spreading out his hand, he set the floor on fire. The cold stone which couldn't sustain a fire on its own lit up with a warm red. The ASI protested as Mark burned through it. He caused no damage to the building, he wouldn't dare, but he could, if he wanted to. That was the most empowering thought.

"You're kidding, right?" A voice startled him, and in the instant he whirled around, all the fire vanished.

Sil sat in one of the lobby chairs on the far wall, having left the Realm. Mark's face burned with the realization that Sil had been spying on him. "You figured out how to use the Realm without entering it, you can set stuff on fire without burning it, and the ASI has no effect on you... I mean, what's your deal? How come you're accomplishing what took me fourteen years to hone!"

Mark pinched his arm nervously, refusing to meet eyes with Sil's golden gaze. It glowed in the darkness from across the room, a dull shimmer which Mark's own crimson eyes reflected. "Maybe… it's because I didn't grow up in the ASH. I never had the ASI holding me back in the first place."

"I'll say," Sil complained, crossing his legs and reclining. He seemed content, a little too content, but one thing was clear in his stance, he was as restless as Mark was. He heaved a long sigh, a cold breath fogging around his lips. "Get me out of here… whatever it takes. We have to get the Shadows out of here."

Pressing his lips together, Mark gave a slight nod. He took a cautious step forward, testing his luck with Sil. "What's the plan?" Now completely determined, Mark walked right up to Sil. "Let's get out of here tomorrow!"

"Tomorrow?" Sil fretted. "You want to break down the entire ASH tomorrow? Good luck with that!"

"No!" Mark defended himself then hesitated, faltering and crashing. The high of escape now fading.

"You need a plan," Sil insisted quietly.

"I've got a plan!" Emilie's voice interrupted, and Mark nearly jumped clear out of his skin when she came out of the Realm. Clearly, Sil knew Emilie was beside him, and they sat uncomfortably close, staring at Mark, who wasn't open enough into the secret world to know they had both been watching him.

"Both of you!" Mark shrieked causing his crazy cousin to laugh.

Emilie floated upward when she giggled, barely subjecting herself to making contact with the sofa. "Mark, I've been trying to get out of here all my life! Trust me, I've got a plan." Crossing her arms confidently, she leaned against Sil's shoulder, annoying him a little, which Mark could see in his eyes. "We could steal one of the ASH's vans. They have a couple big fifteen-passengers. I'm sure I can figure out how to drive it."

Mark raised an eyebrow, fairly certain Emilie had never been in a car in her life. Equally doubtful, Sil rolled his eyes. "I suggest Elise should drive. She's the oldest, and the tallest. You wouldn't have any experience driving?" he asked, directing a cold eye at Mark.

Shaking his head promptly, Mark chuckled a little, "Nope." Finding the seat facing them, Mark sat, rubbing his arms because it was still very cold. "Where are we going to go? I don't know the area. None of us do."

Sil had a quick answer for this. "We'll go south. North is into the city area, and we'll get caught too quickly, but south of here it's all forest. We can ditch the van at night, get into the trees and hide in the Realm until they lose our trail."

Pressing his lips together, Mark frowned at the idea of going farther away from home, but he nodded. The plan made sense. "We have to stick together," he whispered, directing this toward Emilie. "For a couple Shadows, at least in our room, there's going to be a huge temptation to just run, but we have to stick together to protect each other."

Smirking, Emilie scoffed. "We are all Shadows," she mocked, still refusing to touch the sofa as she floated weightlessly. "If we get caught... I'm gonna fly. There's no way I'm coming back here."

Sil nudged her shoulder firmly. "It'll work."

Mark nodded eagerly. "You've got me now! You'll get out of here for good, and I'll introduce you to my aunt," he offered, hoping that was enough incentive for her to stick around. His eyes gave away his worry, and Sil glared at him only worsening that fear.

As if knowing what he was thinking, Sil flared his eyes blue at Mark. "The last Shadow to pass through the shield died."

Emilie took the words out of Sil's mouth. "If you can take us through safely, it won't be terribly difficult with all our powers to get away."

"Shouldn't you be asleep," another voice appeared. They all looked to see a figure with long dark hair. The three panicked, and Mark rose to his feet when he saw both Sil and Emilie immediately obtain defensive stances, as if ready to fight. The figure came into the light of the room, allowing

Mark to make out Kimberly's face, but this only worsened their terror. She had heard everything.

Kimberly should've gone home at eight o'clock, but she stared at the three wayward children with understanding, loving eyes. "If you want your plan to work, you're going to have to get some sleep." Her warning struck them, and Mark gazed between Sil and Emilie at the woman.

"Take a small group," Kimberly advised. "Keller will be too crazy trying to find you and I can help get the rest of the Shadows to freedom. Think you can keep yourselves from getting caught?"

Sil and Emilie looked to each other with wide eyes. Nonetheless, they nodded, standing between Mark, their one ticket out, and Keller's most trusted friend.

Kimberly smiled a little at their confidence. "Go to bed." She gestured toward the hall. "I'll give you a head start."

October 28, 2030

Morning came to the ASH on Mark's third day. He managed to speak to Sil without getting hurt. But Emilie, on the other hand, did her best to stay away from Mark for some reason. When Mark tried to ask her what was wrong this time, she said, "Pack your things. Room 13-15 will be abandoned tonight."

Mark was a little numb at the thought of being the single key for their escape, the tool that Emilie hoped to use to get her freedom. Breakfast was boring, lunch was bland, and he couldn't wait to get outside. The fresh air was nice. It was a crisp October day, but unlike up north where all the trees had already turned, there was still a lot of green clinging to the trees here.

Mark had been to Virginia before, a long time ago to visit some caves in the mountains. He didn't know where Culpeper was in comparison to Luray where the caverns were. That trip had been a nice family vacation, a camping trip with their close friends, and nothing like this nightmare.

The golden bronze shield hung over him like a dying sun. He wanted to destroy it, to just get it all over with, but he was sure Keller had some fail safe that would get in the way. Kimberly's advice kept rolling around in his head. "Take a small group." It felt like abandoning the Shadows to run away, and something deep inside him didn't want to leave anyone behind.

Sil spoke with Elise, filling her in on the plan and Mark only knew this because Sil flashed his eyes at him and a tone shot through him in the Realm, conveying everything Sil had said. It was disorienting, and Mark felt like Sil had punched him. Afterwards, Elise probably told Ocie softly, wanting her along for her wisdom and the strength in her Shadow. Finally, and despite Sil's urgings, Mark wanted to tell Kip, to get him to freedom.

Sil warned him, but he wouldn't listen. Sil thought Kip was weak and useless, he'd slow them down and be a nuisance. For a moment, Mark really hated Sil and all his utilitarian beliefs. Even after all Sil had shown him, Mark was certain Sil only saw Shadows as tools, the people and their powers.

Despondent, he sat down on the sidewalk, watching Sil prowl the courtyard to terrorize the younger Shadows. He chuckled a bit. Sil did this every day, didn't he? Suddenly, the ice Shadow wasn't quite so terrifying when he saw Sil casually bullying ten-year-olds, and mischievously gifting snowballs to the kids who were soaking up the last semblance of mild autumn.

Otherwise, the kids seemed completely normal, rarely using their powers like the older Shadows did.

His eyes followed Sil as he knelt by the edge of the barrier, getting very close to the shield and risking touching it to peer out into the grass only inches outside the ASI. Mark pressed his lips together, painfully aware that shield would have no effect on him if he were there. If Sil knew they were planning an escape, why would he risk getting so close to the edge now?

Mark didn't realize it at first, until he noticed Sil digging in the grass, rooting around the edge as if he was trying to dig a hole under the imaginary fence. Mark didn't have to dig to figure the ASI went deep into the ground to prevent something like that.

Sil patted the grass drawing it away to expose a little gravel that had been stamped down and he selected a few rocks. Mark watched a little more closely, curious as Sil counted stones in his palm and stared out of the barrier. Cautiously, he selected one, weighed it in his hand, then threw it at the shield at a gauged strength.

The stone didn't ricochet, unaffected by Shadows and the shield, and it passed through, flying a good distance into the grassy field.

Mark perked up to see where it landed. The sun was gentle and warm for late October, and he was completely unused to the mild weather in Virginia, but he was thankful for the sunlight, allowing him to spy something moving and squirming in the grass. About five feet from the shield, a snake reacted to the small stone which had been thrown at it. The black snake coiled and constricted, confused and eyeing up the direction from which the stone had appeared.

It didn't leave, it just watched, flustering when Sil threw another stone. Mark tensed and it only occurred to him then that maybe, from outside the ASI, the Shadows were invisible to the world. The creature had no clue how the loose gravel had appeared.

Suddenly, a large bird of prey swooped in from the sky, landing squarely on the snake's head and taking advantage of its distraction. Sil smiled and sat back from his crouched position to watch his hawk kill a quick meal. He seemed genuinely pleased and gave a quiet call, just loud enough for the bird to hear. Mark barely caught his voice, only seeing his lips moving.

The hawk swooped low in the direction of Sil's voice, trusting the empty void as she flew into the barrier. He received her on his right arm, embracing her weight and now really smiling. He smoothed her feathers and frosted them, savoring his time with her since he was leaving soon and he didn't know when he'd see her again.

Mark's eyes grew tender to realize all that Sil had done, was just to stay goodbye to his pet and companion. Sil had a deep connection to animals, Mark could see that, coaxing them and understanding them well enough to lure a harmless black snake to become his bird's dinner. There was something charming about it, if not a little morbid.

Gazing off, Mark's eyes drifted from Sil and Winter to the expanse of the courtyard and the scampering young Shadows. The young ones played with each other much like Mark's sister June. Laughing and crying, screaming and squealing, having true fun with no conflict. Their innocence struck him, and he was almost terrified to upset the haven these children had.

In spite of how the ASH was a prison, and how these kids had been stripped from their families, this place was still safe. They *could* learn to refine their Shadows here, and it was safe to make mistakes.

The boys wrestled around the yard and the girls played among the grass, some gentle, others wild, with no distinction based on gender. The microcosm created by the ASH created a beautiful environment for the Shadows, not like friends with separate families, but miniature sibling dynamics, unparalleled loyalty

They were so innocent and completely pure, and while he watched them, he overheard what he could have sworn was singing. Their song seemed hopeful, but it seemed powerful as if they used their Shadow instead of voices. Mark could hear the lyrics from far off, but in his heart, he felt them and their meaning in the same way he felt his Shadow in his heart when he used it.

"*A day comes with sorrows and joys,*" the first line harmonized with the Shadows. "*Light of day, Shadow of hope. When darkness falls on us, we will have hope, when Shadows fall on us, we will remember.*" The song built without rhyme, and without a need for poetic structure. *"Come now, rest, day meets night, you can rest in hope, you can rest in the Shadow of our Trust."*

How could the Shadows be so happy in this prison? Mark counted the beats of his heart as he saw how desperately the Shadows needed to be free. Tripping in a step, Mark realized he was backing away, hastily turning and running away into the ASH.

Hurriedly Mark made his way down the stairs and stopped in the hall. A temptation in him pushed him toward the lobby, but in the middle of the day there were a handful of Shadows lounging there quietly. He needed to be alone.

Panting from the terror growing in his heart, Mark finally released all the pent-up anger he had been pushing down. A combination of rage and fear spun in his stomach, and the fear he had determined to hide from his heart had finally reappeared. Why on Earth was this the way Shadows were treated? They were people, children, innocents. They didn't deserve this.

Mark paid little attention to his surroundings, not the few Shadows who saw him nor the flickering scarlet flames trailing from his hands. Continuing down the hall, Mark gazed into his hands, terrified.

He collided with someone, slamming face first into Emilie. Impulsively, he pushed her aside, and ran past her. What good did the ASH do but stop these people from fully controlling their Shadows. Keller was a hypocrite, admitting openly that the ASI kept Shadows from gaining more powers. It was stopping them from growing stronger. The flames in his hands burned hotter. He was so frustrated he was ready to burn the ASH down right now.

Glancing to his left, Mark realized he stood directly beside the sliding door to the infirmary. His heart was like a burning lump in his chest as he turned toward it. This was the secret Keller was keeping, the reason the ASH existed at all. This was where their precious Recluse had lived, and probably where he died. An impulsive rage driving him,

Mark stepped up to the door and slid it aside.

He hit a light in the room, illuminating the pair of beds, the shelves of quick medical equipment, and the tiny living area in the back of the room under a small window. Mark jumped, startled, gazing down at his hands upon the light switch, seeing the flickering light at his fingertips blazing hotter than ever. He could barely feel the heat, he knew in his mind it would sear anything it touched, but as a perception, he couldn't feel the heat as pain.

Mark's eyes widened as he stared into the flames, his breathing accelerated, and his heartbeat raced in his chest. In the middle of the room, Mark fell to his knees, his hands trembling under the fire. He let out a low growl in frustration uttering out, "Why!?"

In the silence, nothing responded to his plea, which was heard by no one. Mark's hands blazed hotter as he looked up through the incredibly small window. "What did I do to deserve this!?" he shouted holding his flaming hands to his heart. "Why me!?" he cried.

The glass was a beacon of hope, the only natural light that entered the room under the sterile fluorescent lightbulbs. It must have been unbearable for the Recluse, the reason he had been crazy enough to escape alone. Mark wished he could have met him, to know what he had been going through, what had empowered him to run when he had been so weak.

Mark looked at his flaming hand again, and his anger grew. Swinging his arm up at the ceiling, he released the fire, destroying a ceiling panel so that it fell, filling the room with smoke. Mark watched it, burning with his fire until the flame sustained itself and turned golden like real fire. Figuring it out, Mark balled up the flames so that their intensity grew into an orb which he threw at another ceiling tile so it too fell to the floor.

"I have a life!" Mark insisted. "Why do I have to care about the Shadows? Why am I one of them?" He didn't deny in the slightest that he did care about the Shadows. They were *people* imprisoned for no crimes, *racism,* simply because these people were different. In Mark's mind, he saw all of them, all the names he had learned, the friendships he had built, and so many Shadows with their powers living ignorant of the world outside.

Kip, Mark thought as tears scorched down his cheeks. The boy was the same age as him. They were so similar, and yet Kip had never seen the places Mark had been, like the caverns that couldn't be more than an hour from here. Much less left the walls of the ASH. Kip would likely give anything to leave the ASH.

"But what can *I* do?" Mark demanded sending off another blast of fire.

As another ceiling panel fell, Mark found that the room was filled with smoke, and through the fog, he could no longer see the door. He was breathing it, but not even smoke could harm him! Mark heard the door open, but through the thick smoke he couldn't see who it was.

His hands glowed in the opacity of the cloud, unaware of who had entered or who had disturbed his solitude; the first he had received since he had arrived.

"Mark?" Emilie's voice came through the smoke, and he could vaguely see her silhouette in the doorframe.

The smoke forced her to stay low to the floor, and she neared enough for Mark to see her covering her mouth with her shirt. She scanned the room, unable to see him and Mark drew back. The flames on his hands and the bright color of his eyes drew her to him like a beacon. He just wanted to be alone. Why couldn't he have that? Another ceiling tile fell and she jumped back, slamming into the wall behind her and crashing into the low infirmary bed.

Extending his hand, Mark controlled the smoke, drawing it into his palm to clear the room. Only the burning panels on the floor with fire he wasn't focusing on continued spewing smoke into the air of the tight enclosed space.

"Emilie! Are you okay?" He rushed over at her, seeing her rubbing her head.

Dazed, Emilie lifted her eyes and hesitated when she saw Mark's face so close to her. Mark didn't have to use the Realm to read everything on her face. His eyes, their intense crimson glow; it paralyzed her.

Abruptly, she scurried back into the corner of the bed, kicking him away with her weak, flimsy legs. "Don't touch me!" she shouted.

Mark tensed, stepping back with his hands still outstretched to hold her. Silence filled his heart as he despaired and looked down to the floor where the blackened panels laid. Mark's heart sank, and he turned away from Emilie as the smoke cleared away.

Bumping into the other bed, Mark sat on the sterile surface, devastated by her reaction to him. That was pure fear. He crumpled up the white sheet under his fists and shuddered. If he was supposed to be able to get the Shadows out of here, how could he have scared one of them like this? Emilie was the strongest Shadow Mark had met other than Sil. She didn't scare easily.

Gasping, Emilie floated up and flew across the distance to him. "I'm sorry, I'm sorry, Mark, I—"

"Just don't," Mark snapped, brushing her hand away. Gulping down his fear, he turned his faced away. "If you're scared of me, why would any of the Shadows trust me?"

Tensing, Emilie's lightning green eyes flared. "Mark!" She raised her voice, reeling forward in the air.

Mark turned away and stumbled toward the window. Even though her footsteps wouldn't make any sound anyway, Mark knew Emilie was still there. He could feel her nervousness in the Realm, he could feel how conflicted she was.

She stammered, choking on her words until finally, she bellowed out, loud across the room, "You're Shadow Hope!"

Stopping, Mark fully faced her and stared silently, his eyes flared, piercing deep into her heart. "What?"

Emilie flew over to Mark hastily. "You are the Exodus of the Shadows!" she revealed taking his hands. "You, Mark, that's why you're here. You are meant to free us!" Circling him in the air while holding his hands, Emilie urged him, "I don't know how else to say it… you're perfect…"

Mark seized Emilie's wrist sending her off through the air in her weightlessness. "I'm not anything special!" he insisted, walking toward the open area of the room. "I'm a normal person. I have a normal life, and let's face it." he spread his arms out and shrugged. "I'd much rather be playing video games right now, than thinking about breaking a bunch of people out of prison!"

Emilie floated down to him. "But you can free us. You already have the power, Mark. Please!"

Mark seized her by the shoulders. "Emilie!" he shouted at her, flaring his deep crimson eyes. "Just because I'm a Shadow doesn't mean I am anything like you!"

Emilie tried hard to turn her face and look away, but his eyes pierced her thoughts and scared her to the bone. "You're one of us. You're my… family, both Shadows and blood…" she pleaded. "If you accepted it, this wouldn't be so hard!"

Mark released her and again strode away to the window. "Don't try to convince me…" he whispered.

Emilie floated up to the ceiling, still too petrified to will herself away. Mark only looked back once more, his eyes burning into her heart as he finished softly through the Realm. *Just go… just leave me alone.*

Mark looked around the room seeing the charred ceiling panels and blackened burned patches on almost every surface. Mark stepped into the back room and collapsed onto the low sofa beneath the window. He buried his face in his hands, putting out the flames with stray tears while he gazed with coal-like eyes through his fingers.

With his anger growing in his heart, Mark gazed down at his hands. "The more I use this power, the more it's going to consume me…" he whispered, distraught. He held his shoulders. "This isn't fair!" His mind returned to his family. What would they think of him if he ever saw them again?

Looking forward again, Mark watched his eyes flare in his reflection from the old TV set. He was one of them, but no matter how many times he acknowledged the fact, the harder it became for him to accept it. Mark vanished into the Realm. He was enveloped instantly by the darkness. Without a sense of space and matter, his form floated in the endless void. He was brighter than when he last saw his fiery form traveling deeper into the emptiness.

Mark...

A voice echoed from the blackness into his mind. He didn't hear it; he felt the creature's power and wisdom. Mark looked around the Realm for the Shadow who had addressed him, but he could neither see nor feel another's presence. Looking in all directions, Mark heard it again, sweet, gentle, but strong.

Mark...

Thinking broadly, Mark searched his heart for the way to confront the being calling out to him. *Here I am.*

Silence returned, long and disarming and Mark began to see the creature whom he was speaking to. An air of reverence flowed out from Mark's heart as the form of the entity became visible. It was dark, flowing with violet garments, and dark hair of ghostly shadows blacker than in the real world. Mark couldn't see its face because meeting eyes with this Shadow was too high an honor for even him.

Mark fell deeper into the Realm so far below the creature before it said anything more to him. The Shadow held compassion for him, knowing his mistakes, his short comings, everything about him so that he could find no excuse.

I am the Shadow Trust, it spoke with a voice unlike any Mark had heard. It wasn't masculine or feminine, not in a language that could be uttered, but in thoughts, caring feelings, which Mark understood in his heart.

The Shadow Trust gave Mark comfort with a tone in the Realm, *I am the one who gave you this gift, for the price of your service. I feel the bitterness in your heart, and I know your sorrow.*

Mark panicked, feeling the presence of the Shadow in his heart working through his senses and helping him. Mark forced himself to look at the creature, and desperately, he whispered, *What do you want with me?*

The creature's utter supremacy restricted Mark from denying it anything. He gazed down at Mark, reprimanding him with the very air he breathed. An intense shame filled his heart, complete unworthiness and he lowered his gaze.

That feeling was immediately replaced with forgiveness and the being came down to him in his lowly state. *Throughout this Generation of Shadows, I have seen the suffering of my children. I have heard their cries. I have listened to their pleas,* he explained gracefully.

Mark's mind clouded with the pain all Shadows felt, but they suppressed this heartache to live in the ASH. Mark could feel as this being did for his children. The Shadow Trust took Mark's gaze firmly so that Mark peered into his eyes seeing they were deep indigo with power. Mark possessed eyes with similar power, but not nearly as authoritative as this being.

So, now, I have decided the day for them to be freed from their prison, not merely from the ASH but from the world that holds them back. For I have made them for a greater purpose... the Shadow echoed understandings of this to Mark, so he could not question.

Therefore, the Shadow lowered itself deep into the Realm, so Mark could see it more fully, *in order to make the world see this purpose, I have chosen you, to take them out and confront those who restrict you.* The creature allowed Mark to look upon him and see the pain in its eyes while its Shadows were suppressed.

Mark lost eye contact with the Shadow Trust, lost in this world and the world of the Shadows. *But...* he protested, *who am I to do this! You kept me hidden from the Shadows until now. Why do you pull me up now and demand my best? My Shadow is so unrefined. I have no status to you. Why*

would you lower yourself to beg help from someone like me?
The Shadow Trust raised itself far above Mark. *I do not stoop. Who was it who chose and designed all Shadows?* The Shadow took the form of fire, a blazing pillar, growing larger than the Realm could contain enveloping Mark fully. *Who made your heart to wait until now? Who made your Shadow to amount to more than you even know?* Mark hid his face as the voice echoed all around him, terrified by the fortitude the Shadow possessed over him. *Did not I? I am the Shadow, the creature which chose you, and raised you up according to my purposes!*

Mark grasped his heart, drunk on the feelings stirring in him welling and overflowing from him. *Mark...* the Shadow whispered to comfort his fear, *I have already given you the power to do all I ask. If I had not, I would not have chosen you. If you trust me to give you strength, I will guide you to succeed.*

The creature raised Mark up in the Realm to a place of high status. *Mark... go and never forget that you are a Shadow, therefore I am with you to guide you wherever you are!* The creature drifted away and into the darkness of the Realm, vanishing from him.

Mark left the Realm staring into the light from the window above him. His eyes glowed with an enchanting cherry which now seemed... less violent, less terrifying, and more powerful. He panted, his body trembled, and stray tears trailed his face. It wasn't sorrow, it wasn't frustration, it was a mixture of gentle things: peace, strength, hope, love, and of course trust.

Mark glanced to his left at the door and sighed. He knew what he had to do. He could do this. He still had a hint of reluctance but he was determined now. He knew now that if and when his own strength failed, he only needed Trust.

XIV
ESCAPE!

Kip stood up from his bed to fasten the last button of a burgundy vest he was wearing. "What do you think?" he beckoned to Mark, sitting next to him with a glazed look on his face.

Half-focused, Mark proceeded to look him over. Kip was wearing a high collared vest with gold trim and buttons, which possessed a slightly Asiatic appearance. Also, Kip fastened around his waist a sturdy belt with a long strip of matching fabric with gold trim attached to it, which flowed to his ankles.

Kip stepped around the proximity of his bed, "Elise just finished making it for me." Excitedly, he fanned out the waist cape.

Mark drew his eyebrows together. "Why?" he wondered.

Kip's shoulders fell. "Because I think it matches my hair," he joked lightheartedly. "Why do you think? Because it's cool!"

Shrugging, Mark chuckled as he gazed emptily around the room. "It looks pink," he mocked gently, only wanting to come off as a touch sarcastic. It was getting dark out, and the skylight emitted the grayest light into the room that was already completely white.

Overreacting, Kip's hands ignited with a bright light. "Hey, take that back. It's burgundy!"

Mark gave a laugh. "Kimberly told me you overreact a lot…" he mused.

Eyeing Mark anxiously, Kip plopped onto the side of the bed, pinning down the cape under him. Sighing. Kip grimaced. "What else did she tell you?"

Tensing, Mark met eyes with Kip gravely.

Kip smiled weakly. "Kimberly raised me pretty closely to her when I was young. I don't remember much, but I know she's always been really worried for me, like she has some expectation for me that she's afraid I won't be able to uphold…"

Kip smirked, still cheerfully. "I'm not weak, I just feel like she's always been protective of me, even from a distance."

Mark placed a hand on his new friend's shoulder. "Is something wrong?" he asked, concerned.

Hesitantly, Kip lost eye contact with Mark. Silently he folded his hands in his lap, whispering, "I like her. I feel like she used to care a lot more before…" he trailed off, hiding the truth.

Abruptly, the elevator doors opened, and the blood drained from Mark's face as Keller entered the room. Immediately, fear shrouded Mark's mind in a cloud as he thought of the possibility that Keller knew of their plan to escape. Mark reverted, not wishing to reveal it to him by his poor judgment in fear and he turned away preventing Keller from reading his intentions in his face.

"Ocie, can you come with me?" he called firmly to his daughter.

Ocie came toward him without hesitation. "Yes, sir," she answered surely, but not without a bit of disrespect in her proper choice of words.

Mark got up from Kip's bed and hurried over to her, any fear he had of Keller blocked out by madness. "Ocie, what's going on?"

Ocie gave a sad smile to him. "It's all right. He's my father. I'm sure he just wants to talk." Her sweet voice was overwhelmingly kind, but it couldn't mask the sorrow behind her eyes.

She seemed so confident, but Mark couldn't help but see how sad she was. She knew what was going on, what the Shadows already knew. She placed her hand on Mark's arm and he heard a rustle in the Realm, quietly assuring him.

"Wait..." Mark whispered, stepping out after her. "Wait!" The elevator doors closed on them. Mark's eyes widened as Ocie smiled warmly and waved goodbye while large wholehearted tears streamed down her face. "No!" Mark called when he could no longer see her.

Suddenly, Mark turned to Sil and Emilie, "Did you know that was going to happen?"

Sil and Emilie glanced at each other befuddled, but that was all the confirmation Mark needed. "Ocie didn't know anything about the plan, right?" he shouted.

"Keep your voice down!" Elise urged.

Mark shook his head, adamantly. "She was supposed to come with us, right? Was she planning to distract Keller?"

Sil contemplated the situation with a curled finger under his chin. "It could be. She's very strong in the Realm. It's probably better that she stays behind because she can keep Keller busy."

Mark seethed. The Shadows remained silent, every one of them completely unaware of the escape plan they had concocted. He didn't want to leave anyone behind, especially Ocie. She was such a strong Shadow, invaluable to the group, the one who kept them the most unified.

Cracking his knuckles, Mark pushed past his anger. "It's time to stop sitting here waiting for something to happen! This is it."

Emilie stepped out. "He's right! Now is our best opening. Keller will be distracted by Ocie. We can't let this chance go!"

From her bed in the corner, Rita crossed her arms. "Easy

for you to say. You've been planning an escape all your life!"

Lightening his heart, Mark came closer to Rita. "That's it, Rita. You can teleport us out of the ASH."

Rita scoffed at this. "Oh, aye!" she mocked in her thick accent getting up from her bed. "So how do you suppose we get past the ASOs if we all walk out there? The doors are all closed! Have you planned that one out!"

Mark stepped closer to her. "We don't need to! I can defy the ASH! This is our ticket out of here. Are you going to take it?" Mark felt a chill run down his spine and jumped as Sil got behind him.

The ice Shadow gazed deeply into Rita's heart as he coldly stated, "Rita, Mark is our ticket, and you are the key. We can't do this without you!" he stated firmly in an intimidating manner.

Mark flustered. Sil was backing him up. Rather than cowering, Mark figured he should stand up straight and remain firm.

Behind him, Sil flared his eyes at Rita nearly threatening her until she gulped and lost eye contact with the both of them. Abruptly, she teleported and reappeared in the center of the room.

Rita smirked, proud and spunky. "Well… let's do it!"

Emilie zipped over to stand next to her with a wide smile. Sil laid a hand on Mark's shoulder, briefly signifying affinity between them before he joined Emilie in the center of the room.

Mark watched as the Shadows gravitated to the center. Elise, Fliiy, Goran, and Sage, each cautiously neared the group. Fliiy joined hands with Rita, who took hands with Emilie until the Shadows formed a circle in the center of the room. All the Shadows gazed at Mark curiously waiting for only him now.

Kip smiled and urged him closer. Mark gulped, taking a step toward them. Now was the time for the Shadows to be free. They had waited so long for this moment and Mark was ready to give it to them.

Am I ready for this? Mark asked himself.

He took hands between Kip and Fliiy and sighed, breathing firmly before he started using his Shadow. The room darkened as Mark intertwined himself with the powers of those around him, everyone's: Sil's, Rita's, Fliiy's, Emilie's until his mind held no distinction over which Shadow was truly his.

Using Rita's Shadow, Mark allowed himself into the power and before they could comprehend, the green mist of the power of teleportation surrounded them and abruptly they vanished.

Light of the outside shone brightly and stunned the Shadows. It took an agonizing moment for their eyes to adjust. The sky was overcast, and a light rain misted the courtyard where they had appeared still inside of the ASI. Tripping up on the mud, he dashed toward the shield with the others who followed with equal disorientation.

Mark paused staring at the bronze-gold shield covering them from the outside world. He did think twice, all the stories about a Shadow who had passed through the shield months ago and that this Shadow died.

Unsure of the outcome, Mark pushed himself through the shield first. It felt like he had touched nothing and stepped forward without obstruction. But he did feel something in the instant he pushed through, strange memories pouring into him.

He learned fast that for the other Shadows, he had to consciously extend his power to them for them to pass through. Kip hesitated on the opposite side, watching Mark as he pulled the others through one by one.

Cloaked in a film of bronze-ginger light, Mark's hand came through the shield directed at him. "Hey, take my hand!" Mark urged Kip, who took it hesitantly and then let himself be pulled through the shield.

Kip felt immediate discomfort as the shield passed through his body. A sharp sting shot through him the moment he reached the other side. Kip's chest imploded and he cried out, falling to his knees outside the shield. Mark felt his gut turn inside out as he watched this happen and in a fit of panic he dropped to the gravel. Kip gripped his sides and his chest as he fought to inhale.

"What's wrong!?" Mark yelled, grasping Kip's shoulder.

Kip struggled to stand up, his shoes slipping in the gravel and suddenly he fell into coughing, agony painted on his face. "My whole chest's burning up," he whispered breathlessly.

Mark helped the last few Shadows through the shield but they were more reluctant, seeing Kip on the other side, coughing painfully, and struggling to breathe. Mark took Kip's right arm and hoisted it up over his shoulders. "We can't stop now."

Gripping his throat, Kip struggled to recollect himself and run with Mark. Their group rushed into one of the fifteen-passenger vans, one of them was locked, the other wasn't and each Shadow selected seats with Elise behind the wheel and Emilie in the passenger's seat. Mark pulled Kip into the middle seat and squished himself into the corner by the window. Sil filled the aisle seat, remarkably composed.

Kip laid his head against the back of the seat and panted shallowly to weather the pain. Mark kept his arm around him to help him keep his head up. "What is it?" he called into his face as Elise started the van, finding the keys already in the ignition.

Kip's fingers pawed loosely at his throat. "I can't breathe..." he wheezed. "It hurts to breathe!"

Mark grimaced, gazing away from Kip. Maybe he was wrong to try and free the Shadows, maybe to pass through the shield was what killed that Shadow. But then, why weren't the others affected the way Kip was?

Elise got into the driver's seat and put on a seatbelt, glancing about nervously as the fearsome engine hummed. She knew about as much about driving a car as the rest of them did, nothing except what she could glean from books.

It was beyond Mark how she was the best choice just because she was tallest. Mark was legitimately surprised she knew how to put the car in reverse without them ramming directly into the bushes in front of them.

She backed out slowly, watching her corners, and keeping a wary eye on the ASH's slick stone walls, then when she was certain she was clear, she shoved her foot on the gas. The vehicle accelerated faster than she expected, running over a curb as she acclimated herself to the van's limits. Mark could tell she could barely reach the pedals with her toes, but with her Shadow, she extended her reach with an unearthly elasticity.

The dark clouds hung low in the sky as the van sped down the road from the ASH. Thunder rumbled in the distance, and their fear rose as they reached the gates. Mark could see cameras on high, and face recognition programmed to every Shadow in the ASH, apart from that, a fortified gate blocked their exit.

He spied a single man guarding the gate in a tiny tollbooth which pathetically protected the poor man from the elements. He was human, and Mark was thankful for that.

As they neared the gate at racing speeds, swerving towards the bottom of the hill, the Shadows began to panic. Mark, however, kept himself calm. Sitting forward in his seat, he extended a hand before him, a dark mist enveloping his being and spreading out to the guard. He closed his eyes, breathing in a quiet whisper, "Open the gate."

The man had only half-noticed the van barreling towards him when his hand involuntarily opened the gate. It moaned as it slid on its rails into the fence around the property. It wasn't moving fast enough, and Mark's heart trembled and pounded in his chest, fearing they would hit it if it didn't move faster.

Elise increased their speed as their fear of the gate grew more potent. "Hang on tight!" she shouted.

Suddenly, the driver's seat window shattered, and Elise screamed, swerving the vehicle before they broke through the gates, scraping along the side of the van as it skimmed past the narrow opening. She prevented the van from overcorrecting and suddenly the realization struck the Shadows. They were no longer on the ASH's property. They were free!

✦

Alarms blared throughout the ASH, alerting Keller who was walking alongside his daughter solemnly. He cursed aloud as he heard it. ASOs flooded the halls and hurriedly made their way to the balconies overlooking the ASH to see the last seconds of the gray van disappearing down the road.

"What is this!" Keller shouted to one of the ASOs passing in the hall. Keller saw with his own eyes that the gate was broken open; although unable to see the van now, he knew immediately what it meant. "No!" he shouted, leaving Ocie.

Grabbing a guard's arm, he demanded, "Watch my daughter!" as he ran down the hall to the security camera room throwing aside the curtain and hastily finding the camera for 13-15.

Before his eyes, the Shadows were still in the room together and a sigh of relief passed over him until he spotted the date displayed in the corner of the screen. Yesterday's date. "Someone manipulated the data!" he exclaimed, dashing out of the small space he sprinted to see for himself.

As he reached 13-15, Kimberly came his way in the halls and followed him down into the room. As soon as the elevator opened, their eyes widened in fear. Keller stepped into the empty bedroom with heavy feet. "How?" He gasped. "How did they do this?!"

Kimberly didn't leave the elevator, her hands clasped over her mouth. "No…" she whispered as eyes welled up. "Kip!" Keller looked to her eyes, stunned. "Kip is with them!" she cried.

Keller gulped knowing the gravity of the situation, "He's

not going to last very long out there…"

Kimberly ran to Keller, pleading with him, "We have to find them, please." Tears streamed over her face. "I won't lose Kip too! Not after what happened last time! I can't lose Kip too!"

Keller reached out and embraced Kimberly. "We'll get them… We'll find them."

✥

As the van barreled down the road away from the ASH, Emilie white-knuckled the passenger's seat armrest next to Elise. Something wasn't right. Elise seemed to be struggling to keep her eyes open.

Elise gripped the wheel so hard that her wrists were shaking. "Emilie?"

Emilie looked to her directly, but Elise kept her eyes on the road, only repeating, "Emilie!"

Reaching over, Emilie touched Elise's shoulder, feeling her shaking. From the arm next to the window, Elise strained herself to pull something out of her skin and showed Emilie.

"A dart!" Emilie exclaimed.

Elise's head fell forward as she struggled to stay awake. "Take the wheel," she begged. "Take the wheel…"

Floating up in the car, Emilie's head hit the roof of the van before she got her hands on the steering wheel, weightlessly slipping into Elise's place. Sil rushed forward, grabbing Elise and dragging her into the back seat with him as she dozed away.

The van's side tires slipped off the side of the lane, and Emilie overcorrected, fighting to keep the swerving vehicle on the road. Luckily it had slowed, giving her a moment to get her bearings before reinstating the gas gently. She couldn't freak out and didn't dare slow down because they'd be in a weak spot when the ASOs caught up with them.

Her hands steadied as she got the hang of it. She exhaled forcibly and sped up a little. "Is everyone all right?" she asked, glancing back at the Shadows.

They were scared, unaware of where their escape would lead them. Sil held Elise securely. Mark's arm was still tightly wrapped around Kip, whose eyes were closed and his breathing was rapid, but he seemed to have lost consciousness.

Even in her brief glance, she sensed Sil's unease despite how collected he appeared on the outside. His warm eyes reassured her, and that was all she needed.

Sirens from behind them caused the Shadows to startle and Emilie found herself slowing down. Emilie knew what it meant and caught herself hyperventilating in fear. "What are we going to do?" she cried out, spying flashing blue lights in the rearview mirrors.

Mark looked back, the state vehicle drawing nearer behind them. Thinking fast, Mark looked through the Shadows to Rita. He touched Emilie's shoulder suddenly. "Pull over," he advised her. Emilie pushed the brake, listening to what was going on behind her.

"Rita, I need you to get rid of that cop. The rest of us will hide in the Realm." Mark instructed, taking the initiative.

"My pleasure!" She grinned evilly when she realized what Mark was asking her to do and teleported away. Emilie stopped the van, and they all vanished. In the Realm, Emilie floated out of the van through the broken window to be ready if Rita needed help.

Behind them, the state vehicle stopped several paces away and the officer got out, walking cautiously over to the large van. The man swore as he looked through the shattered window and saw no one was inside.

Emilie saw Rita appear several yards behind the cop car, dusting the green mist off herself before she screamed out haplessly, "Hello!" Her strong accent echoed down the road, beckoning. "Can you help me?"

The cop walked away from the fifteen-passenger van toward her. "Who are you?" the officer asked.

Rita held her hands behind her back. "Just a Scot who's a long way from home..." she pleaded, shifting then running her fingers through her coal red hair.

The officer hurried to her. "You're from... Scotland?" he puzzled.

Rita nodded with a smile then eyed the man with her enchanting green eyes. Emilie had to keep from laughing when Rita said, "You should be careful. Don't ya know of the dangerous people who've escaped their prison?"

Emilie heard the officer's radio in his car already blaring with warnings about the Shadows. "Oh aye, of course, you have," Rita said.

The man extended a hand worriedly. "Stay right here," he instructed, watching her cautiously while he walked to his car to listen to the police broadcast about the Shadows.

Rita teleported over to the car adopting a casual posture, as Emilie hovered in the Realm some distance above her. The word Shadow was heard on the radio, loud, clear, and ominous. "Fifteen people escaped from a prison, fifteen powerful people, who share one thing in common..."

A shudder rippled through the man's body when Rita appeared. "I told you to stay put."

Rita teleported back before the man's eyes. Emilie cackled as the man screamed and Rita teleported around erratically. Rita vanished from him teleporting back into the van and Emilie dove in the window. "Let's go?" Rita inquired with an urgent brow.

Mark looked flustered with a disapproving glare, glancing out at the cop who stood on, perplexed. Rolling her eyes, Emilie watched Rita lay her hands on the seat of the van and dreamily she inhaled. "It's time for us to be free."

Abruptly, a hazy green mist surrounded them. It was cool and calm, but the Shadows felt Rita's raw power. It was ravenous but joyous to be unbound. This was her true uninhibited power.

The mist blew through them like a strong wind, enchanting everything around it. The gust became violent, then with a small abrupt explosion of Shadows, the entire van vanished, teleported away.

⁓◐᷾

Keller returned to the security camera room with Kimberly. "There's no way for the Shadows to get to this room. It's outside the ASI. Someone must have helped them," he rambled, waking the computers by shaking a mouse.

Kimberly's heart dropped as she heard this. She wanted the Shadows to escape. She honestly wanted them to be free, but she had been too hasty in encouraging them. It hadn't occurred to her that Kip would be with them.

She told Mark to take a small group. She assumed that meant the strongest Shadows, not the weakest. It hadn't even crossed her mind that after all these years, Kip might still be affected by this.

"Keller…" she whispered. She had been wrong. Hesitant to do so, Kimberly prepared to tell Keller the truth.

"It's gonna be all right," Keller assured her. "If we can find them fast enough, Kip will be fine!"

Kimberly held her shoulders. "Are we being reminded…" Tears rolled down her cheeks. "First Mark! He has the same face and the same powers. He can pass through the ASI too!" she cried, despairing. "And now Kip…"

"You act as if he's already dead." Keller grimaced, guiding Kimberly away from the camera room. Keller trailed off to stray her thoughts. "Do you remember that Scottish Shadow I knew so many years ago, that one we could never find?" he asked gently.

Kimberly shook her head, and Keller smiled, leading her down the hall hand in hand. "That pipsqueak could never do anything right. Sometimes I think about him, wondering if he's still alive and out there somewhere. But then, I remember he was like Kip, and I wonder if he somehow found the cure we were never able to make. That's the hope I have, that someday we can cure the Shadows of this disease!"

XV
THE COST OF FREEDOM

The mist cleared over them abruptly like a dust cloud, and the overcast sky of Virginia had vanished. A bright golden sun hung low and glared in through the front windshield of the van.

Mark shielded his eyes, startled at how brilliant it was. The Shadows neared the windows on all sides as slowly the fact that they were nowhere near the ASH finally sank in.

They were free. They had successfully escaped. But all their friends were still trapped. Mark opened the door of the van cautiously, feeling the cool dewy air hit his face as his eyes adjusted to the light. The ground was uncomfortably dry and gravelly, all dust and no grass, and barely thirty feet from the van, the world seemed to end over the edge of a cliff.

Emilie flew up out of the driver's side door, and Mark whirled about just in time to see her shoot a hundred feet into the sky. Mark smiled. She didn't even hesitate. Sil laid Elise down in the passenger seat and jumped down to the dusty ground. He stepped out with Mark, following the Shadows as they slowly assembled around the edge of the crag.

"The Grand Canyon!" Mark breathed almost in a

whisper, realizing where they were.

"Rita, you're a genius!" Sil said, finding Rita's big smile among the crowd of Shadows.

Mark's heart grew tender. He'd never heard Sil compliment anyone before. Maybe freedom was what Sil needed to shed that cold persona.

Rita shrugged with a great big grin. "I've always wanted to come here. It was the top of my bucket list."

Emilie dropped out of the sky, hitting the dust a little harder than she anticipated as if she had allowed gravity to let her fall. Panting hard, Emilie laughed hysterically. "It just goes on for miles!" Sil hastily knelt down to her where she collapsed, wordlessly checking to see if she was all right. Tears of joy flowed from her eyes, and she rubbed her face to ineffectively stifle them. "We're free... we're free! I can fly as high as I want!"

When Sil touched her shoulder, she suddenly threw her arms around him and floated up, crying and laughing as she spun around him. Immediately the tension among the Shadows broke and smiles formed upon all their faces. Mark couldn't help but share in their happiness as a special kind of euphoria he'd never experienced before washed over his heart.

It was so worth it.

Abruptly, their celebrating was broken and Mark hurried back to the sound of Kip coughing. He clung to the back of the driver's seat, holding himself up. He gagged on something deep in his chest, and his cough sounded like there was something in his throat he couldn't get up.

"Kip! Kip... how are you doing?" Mark asked, climbing into the van to be with him.

Getting a brief chance to breathe, Kip pinned his eyes shut, grasping his other hand tightly over his ribs. "I'm okay..." he lied, wheezing.

"You're not," Mark fretted, taking Kip's arm to help him stay upright as he fell into another fit of coughing.

Rita teleported into what little space was unoccupied

between the two front seats. "As far as I know, he's always had really strong allergies. I guess the ASH shielded him from that."

Mark nodded shakily. "That sounds likely. I just hope he'll be all right…"

Kip's coughing finally relented, and he let himself fall against the back of the bench, panting. His labored breathing was painful to listen to, and it sounded like his lungs were filling up. Mark couldn't do anything for him, and feeling helpless only made him more worried for his friend.

"I… just need to rest," Kip insisted breathily, barely keeping his eyes open long enough to look up at Mark.

"No way!" someone exclaimed, and Rita perked up, teleporting instantly to the back of the van where the other Shadows had opened the back hatch.

Mark patted Kip's curly red hair to gather his consciousness a little. "I'll be right back. Try to stay awake."

Kip managed a nod as Mark left, rushing around the van to see what was wrong.

Mark's eyes widened, and he stepped back shocked. In a compartment in the back of the van, the Shadows had found a stocked supply of water bottles, two tents, and food. He gazed in awe of it all. "We have a helper?" he mused, seeing there was plenty for several days.

Mark immediately grabbed a water bottle and started around the van. "Emilie," he called, gathering her attention to the ground, "find out what all is here and get some Shadows to work on setting up those tents."

Emilie nodded slightly, giving Mark the opportunity to return to Kip, gently helping him to sit up.

Kip's breaths were rickety and trembling, and he was unable to control himself while Mark held him upright. "Here." He opened the water and held it to Kip's mouth. "Drink up." Upon feeling the water on his lips Kip accepted it and Mark helped him take several long guzzles.

Kip panted, becoming more cognitive. "More," he pleaded when Mark tried to take the bottle away. Heaving steadily, Kip's starlit eyes opened fully, and he asked, "Where are we?"

Mark let go of his friend and sat next to him on the bench. "Rita teleported us to safety," he revealed. "We're a long way from the ASH." Kip gave a weak nod. Hugging his ribs, Kip summoned the strength to lean forward on his own and tried to get up.

Mark stopped him. "How are you feeling?"

Sighing, Kip inhaled deeply, wincing as his face told the truth he tried to hide. There was a piercing pain in his lungs he was struggling to ignore. "Better," he lied again.

Mark gently laid a firm hand on Kip's head, ruffling his wild hair with a weak smile. "I want you to stay right here, and don't do anything. Just try to get some rest." He didn't wait for any kind of affirmation. "I'm gonna help them set up the tents. That much I've got a little experience in." He winked.

ꙴ◖ꙴ

Among the supplies, Rita found instructions on how to turn the back row of the van into a bed. So, while the boys cooperated to assemble the pair of tents, she took responsibility for this, even though it was mostly out of curiosity.

Climbing up into the back hatch of the van, she spotted a lever indicated within the instruction pamphlet. On the side of the row, and jammed quite hard, Rita tried to pull it, but it didn't move. When she got her fingers around it, she wasn't totally sure if it was broken or just old. Putting her back into it, she pulled even harder, but it wouldn't budge.

"What are you doing?" Kip's voice suddenly appeared from the other side of the bench.

Containing her surprise, Rita jumped up to her knees. "I'm trying to turn this row into a bed. Shouldn't you be resting?"

Kip shrugged, laying his chin and arms across the back

of the seat. "I'm feeling a little better, at least. I need to focus on something else."

Grasping the lever once more, Rita wedged her foot against the wall of the van to get a better angle and pulled it with all her might. Suddenly, it gave way and flung open, and with Kip's weight on the seat back, it fell. Reactively, Rita teleported a few paces outside of the van, leaving Kip to fall.

Chuckling nervously, Kip raised himself off the flat foam. "Wow, you okay?"

Teleporting closer, Rita sat down onto the bed. "Fine, you?" she asked, worried for Kip's health and how he was already protecting his ribs.

Kip turned about and plopped down onto the mattress pad, smiling a little as his breathing became noticeable again. "I still can't believe we're actually here," he whispered, closing his eyes, letting himself relax.

Rita smirked, her eyes growing tender. He was so content. Even with how much pain he seemed to be in, he was all too happy to be free with the others.

She was sure it must hurt for him to not be able to run around with the others. Kip deserved this just as much as they did, and small, pure, and kind little Kip would savor every freedom this world had to offer.

She gazed out at Mark setting up the tent with Sil close at his side. Even from this distance, she could see how his back stiffened whenever Sil got close to him.

Kip laughed brightly like a little bell. "We actually did it!"

While he laid on his back, his breathing became hoarser and in the light from outside streaming in, Rita found dark patches growing under Kip's eyes as he grew paler. Kip attempted to rest, and Rita reached out to lay her hand on his forehead.

She drew her brows together. "You're running a fever," she whispered.

Kip coughed a few times and crumpled up onto his side.

Rita drew closer to him, laying her hand on his shoulders. "Tell me, Kip, what hurts?" she beckoned.

Kip's hand covered his mouth as he coughed, and he groaned from the pain in his chest which was ever prevalent. It felt as if his chest was being pressed in, and his ribs ached as if they had been smashed like glass. His head throbbed, and his stomach hurt.

"Talk to me, Kip. Hey, stay awake, okay." Rita couldn't tell what was really hurting him. But he had a hand over his ribs and it seemed like every cough felt like being shattered into tiny pieces.

He let out a short answer which was muffled but it was enough for Rita to hear. Coughing, Kip brought his hand over his breastbone, and Rita's eyes widened.

A dark stream of blood dripped from his lips as he hoarsely cried out, "My heart..."

Rita teleported out of the van instantly. "Mark!" she shouted getting his attention, "Kip's coughing up blood!"

Mark tensed. "What!?" He kicked up dust as he ran, climbing into the back of the van to see for himself. Kip coughed several more times smearing the blood on the side of his face in the process. Mark forced Kip's face upward at him. "Kip, look at me!"

Kip opened his eyes dazedly reaching up to wipe the blood from his face. With his hand above him, he saw blood along the heel of his thumb, deliriously aware of it as he promised in a whisper, "I'll be all right."

Mark reached behind Kip's neck as Rita came up behind him with a pillow from the stash of supplies and a blanket. He gritted his teeth. "This complicates things. Passing through the shield injured him." He looked to Rita as they situated Kip comfortably. "If his lungs are filling with blood, there's not much we can do to help him..."

"Keep his head elevated," someone instructed. Both Mark and Rita turned on their heels to see Elise behind them from the passenger seat of the van. Elise supported herself very carefully, unsure of her own strength as she awoke from the sedative. Dizzily, Elise sat forward but didn't get up. "Make him drink a lot of water and keep him cool. That'll help with the fever."

Rita teleported to the front of the van to help Elise. "We thought you'd be out longer…"

Elise shook off her fatigue. "What's important is that we all stay safe."

Mark nodded from within Elise's view. "Kip already drank half a water bottle and that helped him for a while."

"Let's not take any chances…" she acknowledged, reverting to resting since she was still under the effects of the dart.

Affirming as much, Rita teleported to Kip's side, "I'll keep an eye on him."

Mark pressed his lips together, his crimson eyes growing darker and he left them. Rita followed him with her eyes as he returned to the tent he had been constructing. As much as Rita was happy to be there for Kip, she kept the urge to stretch the limits of her power quiet in her heart.

She wanted to explore. She had always dreamed of visiting this place. And here she was, confining herself to take care of someone she was sure would be fine if she left for a few minutes. Kip had already mostly passed out, one hand hugging his ribs and the other putting pressure on the bridge of his nose.

Inhaling sharply, she filled herself with the cold desert air of freedom. It could wait. She had all the time in the world to find her way back to her family.

✿

Mark came alongside Sage and a few other Shadows to scan the edge of the cliffs for firewood. He had built a fire before, but wasn't the outdoorsy type, and neither was his father. But it occurred to him that with his Shadow, building a fire was going to be the easiest thing he had done all day.

He arranged the sticks on the ground next to the van,

surrounded them with rocks and exposed dusty soil so it couldn't spread, then lit his hands on fire. He wasn't really sure how to best go about making a fire that would keep going for hours, so he stuck his hands into the midst of them, burning the wood with the hottest flame he could produce.

The red flames latched onto the variety of mossy and dry sticks, turning a bright yellow when the fire sustained itself without his Shadow. He smiled at his hands when he realized how easy it was. His first day had been a mess but now he felt like he truly had a handle on his flames. He had refined it, at least to some extent.

After this, the Shadows broke into the food they had found in the van. Underneath a pile of bread rolls was an ice pack which still seemed to be cold, and under that were several packages of hotdogs. Mark puzzled over the sight of it. Kimberly had known they were planning an escape, but had she really put the effort into getting them food ahead of time. It was suspicious, even if it was helpful.

As the light dwindled, the Shadows lit up, and around the fire while roasting their dinner, Mark watched their joys overflow. He sat down near the fire with a broad smile as they chanted in song. *"Come now, rest, day meets night, you can rest in hope, you can rest in the Shadow of our Trust."*

Mark understood now, their Trust was the Shadow Trust, the being who had confronted Mark with his commission. Whoever Trust was, another Shadow, or a deity, Mark was thankful for him. Without a little guidance they never would have gotten this far.

His eyes glazed over as the Shadows stayed up late into the night, singing around the fire, and even Kip perked up. The boy appeared from the van with Rita guiding him and a warm blanket draped around his shoulders.

It made Mark happy to see Kip was feeling better and had enough energy to join the Shadows around the fire. Kip even had enough breath to sing and chant with them the words of their verse, and he didn't cough. Mark hoped what was wrong with Kip was allergies like Rita had suggested and Kip had once again overreacted as Kimberly said he always did. But the blood… that was real, even if it had only been once.

Mark slipped off into the crackling flames, the wood they gathered disintegrating before his eyes. Trust was such a powerful thing, and Mark couldn't quiet the fear that the Shadows had no reason to fully trust him yet. Sil and Emilie had put a lot on him with his power to pass through the shield, but it didn't feel like they trusted him. As far as he was concerned, he was just a tool to them, especially Emilie, who had clearly been trying to escape the ASH all her life.

He didn't eat and slipped off to the tents in an attempt to find some time alone. The pair of tents had been set up away from the fire, and each were large enough to sleep five. They were incredibly dark inside, but they held warmth nicely especially in the cold October air in the desert. There were multiple mattress pads provided and blankets but not enough sleeping bags, so they were required to share in the cases of the mattress pads. Mark slipped away early so that he could get a hold of a sleeping bag before they were all taken.

Lighting his hand on fire to warm the air gradually, Mark carefully stepped inside the tent and right onto a hard ankle beneath the dark blankets. "Taken!" a voice declared as the Shadow's legs curled up under the sleeping bag. Mark jumped back startled. The sleeping bag opened and Rita sat up laughing at him.

Mark fell back onto the floor of the tent. "T-there's two tents. Didn't we agree this is the guys' tent?"

Rita guffawed happily. "I've slept in that room with nearly half guys and half girls. No one came to that conclusion."

"That's messed up!" Mark shivered, putting out the flame on his hand as he sat on the empty mattress pad.

Merely smiling at him, Rita sat up fully with her hands in her lap and mocked him with a sly grin in her emerald eyes. "Ya worried about sleeping next to a girl?"

Mark grimaced, gritting his teeth together. She was

comfortable, but he couldn't help but feel awkward. "There's nothing wrong with that..." he whispered. Did the Shadows really have no concept of separating the genders? There was no way they could be this innocent to the point of perfect platonic cooperation, and no romantic relationships among them that Mark could see.

Mark sighed and opened another sleeping bag, poking it first to make sure. It was located on the far side of the tent in hopes that he wouldn't have to sleep next to a girl. Rita chortled at him some more for his peculiar behavior. Mark smirked with that thought, *his* peculiar behavior, everything about the Shadows was peculiar. He was normal!

"Ya know what we need?" Rita wondered loudly in the tent.

"Two rooms in 13-15?" he muttered under his breath.

Laughing, Rita mused, "I heard that, we need a prank, ya know, to take everyone off the edge."

Bursting into laughter, Mark mocked her in return. "Wait, this is what the Shadows look like when they're on edge?"

Rita pressed her lips together in the darkness and rolled her eyes, which were the only glowing things Mark could see in the dark. "I should have said, to take you off the edge..."

Calming down and wiping away some tears, Mark sighed contently. "Any suggestions?"

"Are you telling me you've never pranked anyone before?" Rita gasped raising exaggerated brows.

Mark shrugged to himself, though Rita couldn't see. "Of course, I have, but that is a terrible idea."

Rita again chortled. "What are you supposed to do with powers when you're surrounded by your friends? Obviously, you cannae fight them with your powers. Ya prank them! Are ya too chicken?"

Flustering, Mark's crimson eyes flickered in the dark. "It's not that, it's just I'd prefer to not get my head lopped off by Emilie or Sil." He laid inside the sleeping bag flat on his back and heaved a sigh as he stared at the roof of the tent. Everything felt weird, but he didn't actually mind being near Rita. She seemed like one of the saner of the bunch.

"What's wrong?" Rita asked quietly.

Mark's hands rose over his chest as he inhaled. "Is it weird that I feel like a tool, like I'm just being used right now?"

"Probably not." Rita hummed, rolling onto her side under the silky fabric of the sleeping bag. "If anything, you and I are in the same boat. It doesn't feel... bad, does it?"

Mark closed his eyes in the darkness. "No."

Rita was the only reason they had made it out this far without getting caught or arrested, she was the tool of their escape as he had been. It didn't feel wrong, it just felt impersonal. If a Shadow was just an object inside him, something he was born with or chosen for, why didn't it feel like a part of him?

It still didn't feel real to know that his Shadow was flowing in his veins, a real, physical, measurable part of his blood. He had refined his Shadow because he had put his mind to it, it wasn't hard. It could have been because he was an elemental Shadow that made it easy, but everything he had learned jumbled together. Nothing made sense.

His Shadow had been dormant all this time, like Kip had told him, it took time to work its way through his body. But Trust had forced his heart to wait. It wasn't a physical thing like other Shadows, Kip or Sage. Another Shadow had caused his power to remain dormant. It was like Trust had full control over this thing.

Maybe it was another power, maybe it was a unique thing Trust could do. Mark felt his mind drifting off, but he didn't feel tired. He looked over in the dim light and realized Rita had fallen asleep. Where was Trust in all this? If he was a Shadow like the others or some kind of ethereal entity. All he knew was those words Trust had said to him.

Who made your heart to wait until now?

XVI
WAIT

October 29, 2030

Other Shadows shuffled into the tent quietly, but Mark laid awake, feigning sleep through the noise. Through the weariness of night, Mark discovered that Sage had fallen asleep in the sleeping bag right beside him and he learned the painful way, not to roll too far in that direction.

Mark also accidentally discovered that Sil and Emilie were sharing a mattress pad and to disturb them meant a snowball to the face. It disturbed him that they were sleeping together but he knew they were fully clothed and tried to keep all other thoughts out of his mind.

He couldn't make himself fall asleep, that phrase still stuck in his head. He had been forced to wait. Someone had made him wait. Trust had intervened when he was very young to hide the truth of his Shadow and prevent him from getting his powers until now. He couldn't make himself believe that Trust was a god, not after all the Shadows he had met. Trust was a person, a person who had been messing with him all his life.

He wanted to have a little respect for the man, whoever he was. He was obviously very powerful, communicating with him through the ASI and over a distance probably.

Mark assumed his power to disregard the ASI was Trust still pulling the strings. The Shadow was something within Mark's heart, and he felt a little violated to realize Trust had touched his Shadow.

Mark sat up in his little pallet restlessly, clenching a hand over his heart. He couldn't tell if he felt sick, had a horrible case of heartburn, or was just hungry from skipping dinner. It was almost like he could feel it in there. His Shadow was like a rock in his chest, making it harder to breathe. His hands started to sizzle, the warmth causing him to sweat in the tight space of the tent.

He cringed, and when he moved his hands away from his breastbone, he felt an incredible weight lifted off his chest. Opening his eyes abruptly, he tensed. The tent was dark and crowded but it was nothing compared to the intense blackness within his hands. He was holding a blackhole, and the singularity was his Shadow.

Now that word was more than a formless silhouette on the ground, this was where the Shadows got their name. It was so black is devoured all light, making the tent feel like it was bathed in light compared to the thing in his hand. He was holding his own Shadow.

Frantically, he threw it away, pushing it through the air where it hung by itself. Mark's heart raced, and he held his hand before him, making sure he didn't wake the others as he tried to light his hand on fire. He focused with all his might, but he could only feel a slight warmth, and he was sure that was just the blood rushing to extremities from his surge of adrenaline.

His eyes widened but he knew they didn't flare, he was sure the brightness in his red eyes had dimmed. He didn't have Fire anymore, he couldn't use his powers. He had gotten rid of it! A wave of relief washed over him, when this was over, he could go home.

Looking up to the black orb above him, floating aimlessly in the top tent poles, it wasn't going away. Keeping quiet, he reached up to take it and the Shadow stuck to his hand despite being intangible. To his senses, it felt like air, like he was grasping nothing, but in his heart, in his gut, he knew it was powerful.

Sliding the zipper away from the ground as soundlessly as possible, Mark looked over his shoulder at the dimly lit tent where the Shadows still slept soundly. The cool night air flooded the space and Mark stuck his hand out to release the Shadow and let it float away. It left his hand, but it didn't leave. Under the starlight it was easier to see and he felt like it was alive, like it was sentient, and it was looking at him.

He felt like it wanted to ask him, *why do you want to get rid of me?* Or, *don't you have a job to do?*

He closed the zipper and left it outside, hoping to now be able to fall asleep, and to take whatever tomorrow had in store for him. It would be easier without his Shadow to worry about, and he'd be able to relax without the nagging thoughts of Trust's tampering. He closed his eyes in the sleeping bag, feeling comfortable and cool.

Suddenly, a stir in his heart spiraled inside him, like his blood was a whirlpool and he felt incredibly dizzy. A hot flash rippled across his skin and he gasped. His hand grasped at his chest as he panted and he could once again feel it in there. The Shadow wasn't blocked by corporeal boundaries, and it was back. When he opened his eyes, he could see the cherry glow against his skin.

His fingertips burst into flame at his command. He groaned. It was a part of him. It always would be.

Sitting up, Mark now felt like this tent was too hot, and he kicked off the blanket. Sleeping was a lost cause, and how could he with a trickster like this residing in his chest? It wanted to torment him. It wanted to be a pain. Curiously, Mark's gaze turned to the others sleeping in his tent, undisturbed by all his movement.

Emilie and Sil slept very close to each other, Rita laid on her chest, and Sage laid on his side with his quill-covered back facing Mark. Getting to his knees, Mark pushed his luck. None of them had awoken so far, maybe they wouldn't stir if he tried to leave. However, as he grasped the zipper, he got an idea and stopped.

Carefully, without disturbing anyone, he reached over Sage to Rita, and very lightly, he touched her back. Right over her heart, Mark closed his eyes and felt her Shadow. Like his own, it was easy to feel, and just as easy to grasp. Rita sighed audibly when the dark orb attached to Mark's hand, but she didn't stir.

His heart charged inside him like a war horse, but he had done it. It would come back to her so he wasn't really afraid, but what was making him panic was the idea of using it. He cringed, not really sure what he was doing, but he cleared his mind and he pressed the Shadow over his heart.

Immediately his head filled with images, each one like a doorway. Every place he had ever been in his entire life, even locations inches apart were all doors in his mind and it completely overwhelmed him. He flustered but he forced himself to think of the campfire outside. A doorway appeared in his head and he grabbed it, his eyes flashing with green and when the light cleared, he was outside.

A stream of smoke rose from the dying embers of the fire he had built. He trembled, his whole body shaking but he had done it. He had used Rita's Shadow. Rita would kill him if she found out. Hurriedly he reached into his heart and took out Rita's Shadow, casting it away, the black orb danced across the dusty ground, meandering leisurely back to its wielder.

Mark watched it go, knowing its way to Rita without any help. He shivered, as much as this ability was amazing, he never wanted to teleport by himself again. With so many options given to him, he could have accidentally ended up anywhere. His control over her Shadow was completely unrefined, and he knew how dangerous his experiment had been. He was so lucky to have made it first try.

He exhaled forcibly, steadying his breathing as he got his thoughts into a usable order. Maybe this was what Trust had done to him, maybe Trust had taken his Shadow like this, and given it back to him, maybe back in February when his mother had mentioned the tachycardia fit. It made sense the more he thought about it. It had taken a little time for his Shadow to work through his blood, and then at the least opportune moment, he figured out how to use fire. That was it.

This power wasn't unique to him, he was pretty sure about that. Maybe to all Shadows their power was something that could be taken, if only gently and with good intentions. Mark was sure if Rita had felt a thing, she would have awoken and stopped him.

He heard the zipper moving and tensed. Maybe she had woken up when she felt her Shadow return. Maybe she knew what he had done. He vanished into the Realm. It was dark enough out that he wouldn't cast a shadow on the ground. He was perfectly hidden when she emerged, but it wasn't Rita, it was Emilie.

Mark watched his cousin exit the tent groggily and float over the dusty ground to the van where five of the other Shadows were sleeping. He had no idea what time it was, but he could see the faintest light on the horizon, so it had to be getting close to morning.

Emilie sprawled out on the cold roof of the van, stretching out and resting under the open sky. Mark left the Realm when he was certain she couldn't see him from this angle, and he smiled a little. Of course, she wanted to sleep under the stars. She wanted to be free. She wanted to be able to fly away at any moment. It was fascinating to be able to see her desires so easily. It was those sadistic impulses she had that kept him guessing.

Mark wanted to know what drove her. What was so incredible about flying? When almost a half hour passed, and more light appeared over the canyon, Mark was pretty sure she had fallen asleep. His curiosity got the better of him. There was still time.

Careful to not make any noise, Mark stepped lightly across the rocky ground, taking a glance at the open tent flap. Heavy fog enveloped their camp near the cliffs, making it impossible to see anything below the edge. The only sound Mark could note was the distant birds in the crevasses far below. Even in the wide white out, Mark could still see her figure, enjoying the sting of the cold air as she slept soundly.

She was in heaven right now, Mark could tell.

Using a tire as his first step, Mark climbed onto the roof of the van, and with all his reach, he hoisted himself up where Emilie lay. She didn't stir when his weight jostled the suspension of the van and remained completely content even when Mark was so close, he could feel her breath. With gentle fingertips, Mark stretched out to her, and ever-so carefully, touched her breastbone.

With another glance over his shoulder, he kept a wary eye on the tent flap, making sure no one was waking up. He stepped down, keeping his steps quiet until he got some distance between himself and the van.

As the light grew, the blackness of a Shadow became even more intense. This one was different. While Mark's Shadow felt like a rock, this one was pure light. It was like air, like the wind blowing in his face. It was freedom incarnate.

Hesitantly, he pressed the Shadow over his heart and took it for himself. It wasn't an immediate rush like Rita's Shadow. It was much easier. He still felt gravity's power over him, but he had to think about it for a moment, to tell himself that gravity couldn't control him. This Shadow was a little harder to get a hold of, and he was almost sure its entity didn't want him messing with it.

His feet lifted off the ground. When he realized his own weightlessness, he panicked and stopped using the Shadow. Falling to his knees, he grasped his chest, panting violently. Now that was terrifying. For just a second, he could have floated away or worse, fallen, and even an inch into the air was like a mile. He didn't know how she did it. She had absolutely no fear of falling.

The van door opened suddenly and Mark's heart sank into his stomach. The whole van jostled as someone got out and surely it would wake Emilie. Elise appeared and shuffled over to the fire pit tiredly. She plopped down by the embers and yawned, only looking up when she spotted him.

"Oh Mark, you're up early." She smiled across the fog, genuinely kind. "Think you could wake up the fire?" she asked, shivering a little.

"Y-yes!" Mark stammered, his heart beating a million miles a minute, but he forced himself to go to her.

On his way, he grabbed a few twigs off the ground and a single branch that would burn for a while. When he bent down, he felt gravity wane, and he tripped, clinging to the ground as he waited for his body to steady.

He had to get rid of Shadow Feather, but he couldn't let Elise figure out what he had done. Kneeling by the ashes, he arranged the sticks into a little tower and lit his hands to get the fire going. Emilie gave a loud contented sigh like a princess waking up from a century's nap. She was oblivious, but she wouldn't be for long.

She woke up leisurely as the light grew and seemed quite pleasant as she sat up and stared over the canyon for a few minutes. Mark's heart ran rampant with her every movement, and before he could do anything more than light the fire, the other Shadows were already waking up.

Emilie set her legs over the side of the van and pushed herself off, gliding nonchalantly to the dirt. Mark gulped but let out a sigh of relief to see she still had some control over her power, or at least the remnants of it in her blood. She walked with a spring in her weightless step to the back of the van in search of food, and to her delight she found the supply of nonperishable food including canned vegetables and fruits, jerky, and a good snowball fight's worth of dinner rolls, which she helped herself to.

Mark bit his nails, but felt his spirit leaving his body when Elise elbowed him. "What's got you so worked up? You're looking pale."

"Nothing," he said hastily.

Elise gave a knowing glare. "Don't worry about anything. We have food for a few days. We'll figure it out."

Emilie took a handful of the dried meat with her and strode over to the edge of the crag but about ten feet from the edge she stopped, almost suspicious, then she looked back at the drearily awakening camp and smiled. She took a deep breath then ran and jumped off the edge of the cliff, ready to fly over the world.

Mark's whole being imploded, the world rushed around him and he burst to his feet. He couldn't speak, he couldn't yell after her, he could only scream.

"Whoa!" Elise gasped, rising with him.

"Sh-she jumped!" Mark stammered helplessly, pushing himself to run after her.

"She'll be back," Elise assured confidently, "She's probably just going out to enjoy herself."

Shaking his head furiously, Mark ripped Shadow Feather out of his heart. "She won't. She can't fly!" He exclaimed holding out the black, smoky, wavering orb. The Realm declared it to Elise. She knew what he had done.

"Is that..." Her whole demeanor darkened.

Mark didn't answer and pushed past her, running with all his might. His feet couldn't get good traction, he couldn't run very fast, and then the Shadow left his hand. It moved of its own accord, flying away then circling back and impacting his chest like a bullet.

Gravity lost its hold on him as Emilie's Shadow took control, and before he reached the edge of the cliff he was flying.

He could barely hear the Shadows behind him screaming at the sight. There was only one voice he heard—Emilie screaming in terror as she fell to her death. Mark didn't have a clue how to use her Shadow, but it made him fly fast, pushing him faster than gravity tugged, faster than Emilie was falling to grab her.

Feet away from sharp rocks, Mark touched her and slowed her fall so they landed with a soft tumble. Mark's back ached but he could barely acknowledge it. Emilie sat up slowly only five feet away from him. She met eyes with him, shocked and speechless, then she looked down at her legs. Very slowly, she tried to get up, she tried to move, but her thin legs couldn't lift her body.

Mark's eyes widened in terror when he realized what he was seeing. Emilie's legs were too emaciated to carry her body. Without her Shadow, she wasn't just grounded, she was completely unable to walk. Frantically, he took out Shadow Feather again and held it to her. "I-I'm so sorry!"

The Shadow left his hand faster than either of the two Shadows had moved before and it bonded with Emilie's heart like a rush of wind. She floated up as soon as she could, rising off the ground. Her green eyes sparked as fury filled her being.

Mark sank to the ground and she glared over him menacingly. She didn't have to be physically strong. She could still pulverize him. He had done this. He had almost killed her. The ravine they'd landed in was incredibly dark, but the fog wasn't as heavy, and racing river rapids were faintly visible in the distance. Mark's skin felt stretched and pinned and his fingers trembled as he tried to raise himself up.

She fumed, floating up over him when he moved, but she didn't wait for him to stand. She didn't raise a finger against him, she just left. Shooting up like a rocket, she zipped up and out of the canyon leaving him behind. Mark collapsed into the rusty red stone. He deserved it. He had done this to her. She had every right to get her revenge.

He bit down the tears welling in his eyes. Like with Sil, apologizing would only make everything worse. A shimmering green mist flashed before him but he didn't move when Rita appeared.

"Mark... are you okay?" she asked.

He didn't answer, too terrified to own up for what he'd done. She stared at him, completely unaware of what he'd done to her this morning. He had tampered with their Shadows, in spite of how violated it made him feel to know Trust had done it to him, he was dumb enough to do it to someone else. He was wrong, but owning up would only make them angry at him.

Rita gave a sigh and touched his shoulder, teleporting him back up to the camp in a quiet instant. Mark wished that instant had been an eternity for when they reached the top, at the edge of the crag, he had to face the Shadows.

They were all awake now, all staring at him, and rightfully judging him. Emilie floated by Sil, her ankle at Sil's shoulder. Her lightning green eyes sparked with mad hatred that was already barely contained. Elise rushed to Mark's side at the cliff, and Rita stepped back from him.

"What... happened?" she asked confused.

Mark's head drooped, his hands dug into the dust ashamed, and he refused to meet eyes with anyone. "I took Emilie's Shadow." He could barely summon his voice, but he wouldn't allow himself to sugarcoat it as much as he wanted to lie.

"How?" Elise gawked. "What were you thinking?"

Mark clenched up a handful of dirt. "Like this," he paused and with an open hand he touched his breastbone to remove his own Shadow again. It was easy, but this time he didn't feel like a huge rock had been lifted from his chest.

Gasps rippled through the onlooking Shadows. "You could have killed her!" Elise yelled. The anger came through, the anger he deserved.

Mark pressed his lips together and placed his Shadow in his heart. "I found out Shadows are connected to their wielders, they come back if you remove them. I was going to give it back, but... you woke up before I..." There was no use making excuses.

Rita flustered. "How do you know that? You've only known about the Shadows for four days now, and you've already discovered something even we don't know about?"

Emilie swooped in and shoved Rita aside, almost throwing her to the ground. She charged and toppled into him so that they both clattered to the dusty ground. Unwilling to hesitate, she grabbed Mark by the collar and slammed him into the ground. "I'll kill you for this!" she roared.

Mark disregarded his aching back, everything hurt, his head hit the hard ground and she shoved him down again. The hollow silence afterward rattled Mark's psyche. Emilie froze, her lightning green eyes cold for a spell, until she looked back down at his eyes and all the rage in her being flooded over him. "You monster," she seethed.

She lifted him up, causing him to float into the air and she forced him to his feet. "Do you even know what my Shadow means to me?" She howled, "You saw my legs. I need my Shadow! I can't walk without it! How in the world are you dumb enough to take my Shadow from me!? Who gave you the right to touch it!?"

"Mark," a Shadow behind him addressed him and his spine stiffened. His feet on the ground quivered but Emilie turned him around to face Silverstonarellena and meet him in the eyes. Before Mark acknowledged it was him, he was struck to the ground receiving a fist to the jaw.

Mark cried out in pain as he impacted the ground. He couldn't get up, all his limbs trembling as Sil stood over him glaring his golden eyes down upon him. He deserved this. The bruise on his face didn't even hurt, nor did the ground under his scraped elbows.

"Let's see how you like it when I throw you off the cliff, but this time there won't be anyone coming down to save you." Emilie yelled, dropping her foot onto his back and kicking him. She didn't really have the strength to hurt him, but with her powers over gravity, he felt like a ton of bricks had slammed into his already weak back.

"Emilie..." Sil whispered coldly, forcing her to pause and glare at him astonished. "Shut your mouth." he snapped making her feel smaller than a hummingbird.

Breathing frantically, Mark tried to get up but Sil grabbed him by the collar and raised him up to his feet. "Do you have any idea why the humans fear us?" He threatened, receiving only a terrified silence from Mark. "It's because they think we do things like that! Don't mess with other people's Shadows. It's a part of them, an incredibly personal part of each one of us! You can't just take that away and use it as you want!"

Mark pushed himself out of Sil's grip in a bold move. "What if I did it for another reason? What if I took someone's Shadow to help them?" he burst, standing up to Sil. *What am I doing?* He didn't think anything through as he gained a stance and stood firm.

Sil crossed his arms and eyed him, glancing only once to the Shadows gathering around them and staring. An intrigued smile touched his face. "All right, Mark, how could you help someone by taking their Shadow?"

Mark tensed, seeing the offensive nature of his argument. Thinking on his feet, he let words fall out of his mouth "I could…" he hesitated and found Rita's gaze as she stepped back partly scared of Sil. "I could take Fliiy's Shadow when it goes crazy. That would stop it!"

Fliiy flustered among the Shadows, watching the argument and covered her mouth. "How do you know about that?"

"I'm right!"

Sil reeled closer to Mark. "You put Emilie in serious danger! How on Earth does that compare? What if you hadn't gotten to her on time?"

"Then I'd take a different Shadow and use that!" He shouted, not really thinking it through when out of nowhere, Mark was struck again by Sil's frozen fist causing him to fall back to the ground. Annoyed, Mark sprang back to his feet and lit his hands on fire. "Stop that!"

Sil's eyes flared cyan, intrigued by the sight of Mark's fire. "Ah… so you're prepared to make the same mistake again? You really have no shame."

Mark bore his fire readily, feeling much more confident using it than last time. "I would never hurt someone intentionally." He swore, "And I won't let you keep bullying me into thinking I can't use my Shadow right."

Growling, Sil formed a fist in his left hand while his right froze over imparting ice to the ground and making it slippery. "You're not doing a great job convincing me," he sneered spitefully. A gust of wind thrust at them blowing about Sil's braided and wild hair in his face as he jolted forward at Mark.

Waiting for his vision to clear, Sil hesitated when Mark appeared through the snow. Mark's arms were held up before him, blocking the blow. "I'm not falling for that again!" Mark insisted, pushing Sil off him, "I want you to see Trust!" he shouted into Sil's face firmly.

The fire in his hands wavered, he questioned everything he was doing. Trust had manipulated him to some extent, toyed with his Shadow, and forced him into this position. "I'm not asking you to trust me," Mark panted, staring at his own fire as Sil stood on, shocked. "I've already messed up too many times for you to actually trust me. But we're still out here, we made it this far, and I know I didn't do it alone, I had you, Rita, Emilie, and Trust. The ability to pass through the shield is not mine, I'm not the one in charge. Trust is pulling the strings here, just like Shadow Hope!"

Sil's eyes flared and widened, almost weakened by the words. Mark didn't know the first thing about Shadow Hope, but he was certain that was what startled Sil. The ice Shadow glowered, the air around him growing colder. The Shadows watched in amazement as Mark was actually standing up to him. At this, Sil flustered and sprang at Mark, beating him down with an icy fist.

Mark hit the ground again, his cheek bone bruised and his fire had dissipated, but he didn't lose eye contact with Sil. Glaring at him, Mark raised himself to his feet with some effort. "Our lives are not in our own control. I still want to make things right with you, but what's important right now is putting our trust in the one who brought us out."

Sil smirked, attempting to maintain his attention on Mark while his mind spiraled with whatever visions possessed him. "You still just want me to forget what you did to Emilie!" Sil spat angrily, freezing his fists and going at Mark violently.

"Because Trust did the same thing to me! I'm not going to apologize over and over because I know you won't listen!" With his fire igniting again, Mark's hands met with Sil's suddenly. Sil cried out in fear as Mark's fire melted the layer of ice coating his hands, and he retracted his fist to make sure he wasn't burned, and to his surprise he was uninjured. Mark's crimson eyes came into his view, startling him, and he jumped back only to feel Mark reaching out and getting close to touching his heart.

Sil stumbled back, his lips trembling when he realized what Mark was trying to do. "If you touch my Shadow, I'll end you!" he warned, his voice cracking with dry rage.

Skittish on his feet and wavering with his fire, Mark gritted his teeth. "That's what you're trying to do, and you're failing!" he taunted.

Sil's anger sparked and he reeled forward at Mark with a frozen fist only to feel Mark grab his wrist. Sil met eyes with Mark, fully terrified but again his vision blurred and his eyes glazed over. Mark forced Sil's fist downward while his opposite hand plunged smoothly to touch Sil's heart.

Sil's heart imploded, mystified, as he lost all ability to control ice and he fell to his knees overwhelmed. Looking up to Mark, Sil's eyes became desperate, a look which he had never seen in him. Mark clutched his Shadow with two hands over his heart. Sil's head fell in despair, exasperated and panting. He breathed one word, only Mark heard.

"Zachary..."

Mark tensed hearing Sil say it and he knelt down in front of the ice Shadow. "What did you say?"

Sil's golden eyes died down to a poor yellow. "I'm

E. KATHRYN

sorry… I never got to tell you the truth." he nearly cried.

Mark laid his hand on Sil's shoulder. "What does that mean?" he asked but received no answer. Mark's heart pounded, *Zachary,* he thought, *what if…* what if that was the name of the person Mark was always being compared to? Was Zachary the Shadow who died in the ASH?

Sighing heavily, Mark grimaced, looking into Sil's Shadow. In it, Mark could see heartache, dear loss, and the true feelings of Sil's heart. Whoever the Recluse Shadow was, Sil had been close friends with him. Calmly, Mark held the Shadow before him. "I do want you to trust me, Sil. I want you to be able to place your Shadow in my hands and trust that everything is going to turn out all right."

Sil looked drearily into Mark's eyes and tried to reach out and take his Shadow, but his fingers passed through it. He despaired. "I can't," he gasped, "I've never been able to believe in anyone. Why should I have to? I have perfect control over my Shadow. Why should I trust you to use it?"

Mark gently took Sil's hand, using the Realm to impart feelings and instructions on how Sil could take his Shadow back. "I won't have to learn to use it," he whispered as Sil's hand gripped and held the Shadow in the same way Mark had. "I'll just trust you to use it when I need you," he assured kindly pushing Sil's hand to touch his heart and return his Shadow there.

XVII
DISCOVERING TRUTH

Sick to his stomach, Kip hugged his sides near the campfire. He barely clutched a blanket around his shoulders while his whole chest was in pain.

Mark plopped down on the dusty ground, disgruntled, and he poked at the fire still shaking from the fight. "How are you feeling?" he asked to distract himself.

Kip drew the blanket closer and gritted his teeth. Mark could see it when Kip refused to answer, it was all he could do to not think about the pain. "I can't believe I didn't get to see what you did to Sil! That was incredible!"

Mark smiled slightly. "You needed the extra sleep… but I'm impressed you slept through all that screaming."

From the extra sleep, and tossing and turning on the mattress pad, Kip's curly red hair stood on end while his eyes mimicked the color of the sun to a light yellow with blue tint. "Are you hurt at all?" he wondered, gesturing towards Mark's trembling hands.

Laughing it off, Mark nudged Kip with a gentle fist on his shoulder. "Hey, you're sick. I'm the one who's supposed to be worried for you!" Mark guessed his own hair was a little crazy from sleep last night, but there was little he could do out here.

Kip nodded but pressed his lips together with a bitter taste in his mouth. Kip was weathering quite a lot of pain, and Mark could tell just breathing was agony when Kip hugged his ribs like he was about to burst. The morning light combined with the firelight allowed Mark to see Kip was deathly pale.

Kip gripped his stomach and suddenly coughed until he gagged and lost the contents of his stomach. Bursting to his feet, Mark rushed to help Kip, to hold him upright, and to keep his hair out of his face as he threw up. Kip should've been lying down right now, not pretending he was okay or putting himself out in this cold. When Kip finished, Mark took his arms and dragged him gently back into the van to make him rest on the mattress pad.

"It's dangerous if he keeps that up..." Elise's voice appeared behind him, standing in the doorway with her arms crossed.

"What can we do though? We can't take him to a hospital, and certainly not back to the ASH." Tying her fingers together, Elise uneasily led Mark back to the fire with heavy thoughts. "We need to get him some help. There has to be people out there who sympathize with Shadows, who would hide us, especially on this side of the country. Kip has always been weaker than the rest of us, and I don't know how long it could take for him to adjust if it is strong allergies or something like that."

Mark grimaced, comprehending the danger. This wasn't some kind of environmental allergic reaction, something was wrong with Kip's lungs. Mark didn't have to be a doctor to see that. "What do you know about him and Kimberly?" he asked, out on a limb.

"What do you mean? Their relationship? Well..." Elise recalled, a little startled by Mark's forwardness. "I'm not that much older than him, but I remember when he was young, he spent most of his time with Kimberly instead of other Shadows. And Kimberly spent most of her time in the infirmary, caring for you-know-who."

Mark guessed it was the Recluse she was referring to.

"So that's where Kip spent most of his time too. Kip's always been slow to get used to people, and often makes bad decisions because of it, like picking a fight with Sil, for example." Elise's eyes grew tender gazing down at Kip's pale face. "He's been slow in about everything, come to think of it, from walking and reading, to his Shadow and all his relationships. I think you're the closest friend he's had."

Mark considered the part about Kip being slow to read after having learned he was so quick to pick up daunting subjects such as chemistry and physics. Elise interrupted his train of thought. "By the way, where did Rita get off to? She disappeared after your little outburst."

Mark shrugged, a touch of guilt in his eyes. "I don't know. Might have gotten scared off by Sil."

Elise disagreed, knitting her brows together. "No, it's not like her to run away, at least, I don't think so."

Mark raised his chin in a half nod. "I'll look for her. You'll stay with Kip?"

Elise gave him a calm smile and left the van to check on the other Shadows who were making no use of their time. Mark breathed in deeply, contented by his surroundings as he opened his mind in the Realm to look for Rita. He already had an idea of where she might be, based on the images he'd seen when he took her Shadow, but he wanted to confirm before he ran off looking.

The Realm declared to him where Rita was, as he had used it to find Kip before, and as he suspected, she was down in the canyon. Mark looked over the edge of the cliffs cautiously, but he could see no immediate sign of her.

He skirted the edge for about thirty feet and found a steep path to get down into the ravine. The trail couldn't have been more than two feet wide, and its edge led to certain death. Watching his every step as if it could be his last, Mark only had the Realm to assure him he wasn't walking himself into a dead-end or going the wrong way.

Mark reached a point where the path against the wall

became too narrow to traverse any farther, but there was another ledge about eight feet below him. It seemed wide enough for him to feel safe jumping. Getting down as low as he could, Mark hesitantly eased himself over the edge. His ankles buckled when he landed, unprepared for the impact, but the ledge was wide enough and he recovered more or less unscathed.

Panting, Mark paused to steady his breathing and get his bearings. The ledge was only wide for another three feet, and what could be called a path, was only six inches at an angle as it became narrower to the point where Mark's back was pressed against the wall. He took it slow, inching his way sideways.

Rocks crumbled under his feet, and suddenly his left foot slipped. Hastily, Mark grasped at the slick wall behind him, but it was no use. He was falling. His right calf scraped the ledge, but before he could cry out, he saw Rita's face. Green mist flashed around him and he landed on his feet.

"Are you off your head?!" Rita shrieked at him.

Mark's heartbeat accelerated like a war drum. If Rita hadn't teleported him, he would've fallen to his death. He looked around confused. They were much closer to the bottom of the ravine, about fifty feet above the rushing water. However, as soon as he acknowledged in his mind that he was alive, he gaped trying to translate in his mind what Rita had said in her thick accent.

Rita stepped away from him and sat on the deep red stone of the crag. "I cannae understand how it's so easy for you to make a fool out of yourself." She gazed out at the canyon.

Mark sat with her, just to assure himself he wasn't falling. "They're looking for you up there." He panted.

"Ach aye," Rita mocked, "I suppose they've already forgotten how you tried to murder Emilie!"

Feeling another pang of guilt, Mark shrank, his back hit the stone wall behind him and he sighed nervously. "Rita... I took your Shadow too."

She tensed a little, her knuckles stiffening upon the ground, and she looked away from him. Mark could feel the anger radiating off her like Emilie. She had every right to be furious with him and to throw him off the side of the cliff.

"I don't mind."

Mark felt his heart stop. Rita's eyes grew tender, and that anger he thought he had felt was gone. She stared longingly into the abyss without a negative feeling in the world. "I mean." She chuckled suddenly. "You still shouldn't have done it!" Her warm smile lifted Mark's heart like a playful child. "I guess, I haven't been able to really use my Shadow for four years, and out here, for the first time, I have total freedom!"

She smirked and punched his shoulder lightly, not enough to actually hurt, so Mark let her do it without flinching. "So ya used my Shadow, obviously ya didn't go anywhere, and ya gave it right back, so I don't mind."

Able to smile a little, Mark took another hit and rubbed his shoulder. "How come that accent is so strong? In the ASH, wouldn't you have lost your accent by now?"

"Why do you think..." she ignored him gazing off endlessly with all her focus on the scenery.

Mark regretted his words. It was probably rude to suggest she should have lost a part of herself. As frazzled as he had been the day he had met her, he did know she had only been in the ASH a few years. Rita had her own reasons for wanting to be free, and like Mark, he was sure she had a family. "You must be really enjoying this. I'm guessing you've had this place in mind for a while, so escaping here was your first thought... right?"

Rita lowered her veil of sarcasm. "And how would you know that?"

Brushing the red strike out of his face, Mark gave a little smile. "Lucky guess..." He lied, the images he had seen still rolling about in his head like flashes of light. "Have you always wanted to come here?"

Rita hesitated and stared off into the ravine. Her ember-red hair blew in the wind on the ledge, and as Mark gazed at her, and for a moment she was the most peaceful person in the world. He had never seen a tumultuous storm of a person so satiated in his life. "I came here to see this place..." she muttered to the wind. "I mean, from my homeland... because I was sick of the oppression I was getting as a Shadow. We were locked inside those walls, no matter what we wanted to think of it."

Meeting eyes with Mark, Rita grimly explained, "In Scotland, the Shadows are free, but only from our point of view, we hide from everyone else. That's why I came here! I wanted to see more than our six walls. A few years ago, I came here to see the world I had only heard about. America and all its wonders. I had seen enough mountains, but the idea of an inside-out mountain intrigued me so that's why I'm here. But when I arrived, the ASH caught me, and I've been stuck there ever since."

Mark listened considerately, beginning to understand. "How old were you?" he asked.

Rita grinned evilly with all her teeth. "I would have never been caught if I were this age!" she spat. "I was only ten. That's how they caught me so easily," she admitted.

Mark couldn't imagine being a ten-year-old so fed up with their own situation they had the audacity to leave home forever. "I get you can teleport... but traveling by yourself from your homeland at ten... that's crazy!"

Rita nodded, soullessly staring at the rock formations to hide any hint of emotion. "I know... but that's a mistake I'm living with."

"Why don't you go back now?"

Rita shrugged. "I did, found my family and several of my friends who were Shadows, but... something stopped me from going to see them. Besides, you Shadows here would be sitting ducks without me, and I felt a little dutiful to you. Until the Shadows here are free, I have to stay with you."

Pensively, Mark continued questioning her. "Don't you miss them?" he asked. "I've only been gone from my family for a few days and all I can think about is going back to them."

Rita gave him a smile. "I'm staying for the same reason you're not asking me to take you to them right now. The Shadows must be free, and you know as well as I do that we have to stay together for that to happen. They can't do this without you, or without me, or Kip, or Elise, or Emilie, or even Sil!"

Standing abruptly, Rita looked up. "I think we've wasted enough time down here," she muttered.

Mark remained seated, thinking. What if he asked Rita to take him home right now? She could do it if he asked her to. Mark stood dizzily, ignoring the steep fall below him. "Rita... Take us to my home!"

Rita drew her eyebrows together. "What? But the Shadows—"

"—all the Shadows!" Mark asserted, allowing Rita to understand. "My mom kept me hidden from the ASH for fourteen years, would never turn us away. We could easily hide there!"

Rita tensed, figuring it out. "Are you sure?"

Mark nodded. "Kip needs to get out of the elements. Elise thinks we need somewhere to hide too."

Nodding, Rita barely touched Mark's arm when the green mist rushed all around them to bring them up. To Mark's surprise, when the mist faded, they were at the top of the crag staring at the camp. Mark remained a little startled as he realized how fast Rita's ability was and how well she could control it.

His head whipping around back to Rita, Mark regained his orientation of the world only a little ridiculously. "Will you tell Elise to get everyone to pack up?" he asked. "I want to check on Kip,"

Rita nodded promptly and vanished, showing up elsewhere in the camp. Gulping, Mark walked back to the van and to Kip. In the back row where it extended into a bed, Kip slept. Mark could hear his troubled breathing from the front of the van and climbed through to the back to touch Kip's forehead and feel his fever.

Mark closed his eyes. He used his Shadow to feel the heat and the temperature. He guessed Kip's fever was close to one hundred four degrees Fahrenheit, if not on the dot. Mark liked the idea that his guess was more accurate than humanly possible, and that he had used his Shadow to take Kip's temperature.

Fliiy meditated in the front row in the Realm and showed herself to Mark. Somewhere in the back of his mind he already knew she was there, and he wasn't startled when she materialized. Climbing back, Fliiy's gaze grew tender to look down on Kip. "He was crying a little while ago, and said everything hurt... but it's good he's asleep..."

Mark's eyes fixated on Kip. He could tell Kip was not actually asleep, and in fact, he was using the Realm to bury his consciousness from the pain. Mark gathered that Fliiy had no clue he was able to feel it when Shadows reached out through the Realm, and thus no idea how deeply Kip had buried himself. They were on entirely different levels of the secret world and Fliiy wasn't as skilled as Mark seemed to be.

Mark hesitated to call out through the Realm knowing Kip's fever was getting too high and it could be dangerous. Perhaps he could lower the fever, but that would mean he'd need Sil's help. It took seconds for a response and Mark's head whipped around to meet the cold. Mark's psyche panicked, warning himself to be cautious but he ignored it, gulping down his worry to say, "I need you to lower Kip's fever."

In the doorway, Sil's cat-like eyes flared at him. He seemed appalled that Mark would still speak to him, especially through the Realm. Mark straightened his back. He wouldn't put up with anymore of Sil's threats. He wouldn't be intimidated. Slow and silent, Sil moved to the back of the cramped van. By that time, Fliiy had returned to the front to give Sil space. With a gentle frost, Sil laid a hand on Kip's forehead.

Mark knew well enough that Kip's body needed to stay warm, but his head had to remain cool. Maybe the fever was helping Kip fight, but he was completely incapacitated by it, and they needed to move.

When Sil finished, Mark felt Kip's forehead again, then at his cheek, his skin was cool, but Mark could feel deeper and determined his temperature was normal. However, Mark's hand drifted down to Kip's neck and the temperature increased. Feeling closer on Kip's chest he found he was still running a fever, a little lower than before.

Sil stared down at Kip coldly. "After what Kip did to me... I didn't think I'd do him any favors again," he muttered staring down at Kip. "But then... Kip and I have a common friend... and sometimes I forget to take into account that some people have lost as much as I have."

Gradually, Sil met eyes with Mark, flaring his eyes cyan. "I'm sorry..." Sil forced out. Mark tensed as he heard it. Sil lost eye contact with Mark immediately after and reverted to fiddling with and undoing one of his braids.

Not sure what to think, Mark gave a fake laugh, raising an eyebrow to gracelessly smirk. "Are you feeling all right?"

"It comes down to this." Sil glared at him, his cold certain eyes smashing Mark's false humor into the dirt. "I was cold. I acted too quickly. I was being defensive, and it was altogether too soon for me to try and teach you anything about the Shadows. Kip taught you more than I was ever able to," he blurted out with as much sincerity as he could convey.

Mark reeled back, startled but piecing things together. Sil had been trying to teach him something; he knew that much. To his surprise, his silence uncharacteristically forced Sil to speak again. "So... I'm sorry for that..."

Quiet for a time, and staring away from Kip, Mark took this in with heavy breaths. "I forgive you." It was his only logical response. Sil visibly relaxed, warming Mark's heart to know he hadn't put his foot in his mouth. "I get it. I know you were just trying to teach me. But I stepped into your space."

Sil bit his lip. Opening his mouth, he inhaled sharply only to be interrupted.

"But I do have one question..."

Becoming expectant, Sil warily opened up to him with a nod. Mark gulped before he asked with some skepticism. "Who is Zachary?" Immediately, Sil froze, but his eyes became sorrowful. Mark pushed himself to plead with Sil for the answer. "I know there's another Shadow who's like me, and everyone's telling me how much I look like him, but no one's said who he is."

After this remark, Sil gave a little smile, something Mark had never seen up close before. "I think you have it all mixed up..."

Mark saw it in Sil's eyes and through the Realm. Looking down at Kip, Mark sighed. He was no closer to the answer. "You're Zachary..."

Sil leaned back and smiled. "My real name is Zachary André Addison... it never really occurred to me until you took my Shadow this morning. I've always known I was so much more powerful than other Shadows, but when you took it, the first thoughts that came to me were 'What if I'm not a Shadow' and 'Who would I be without it?'"

Addison, he knew that name all too well. Could it be, Mark thought, the neighbors who had a Shadow long ago. "So... where did Silverstonarellena come from?" he asked diverting his thoughts.

Enjoyably, Sil threw his hands behind his head. "It was just a nickname at first, a lot of Shadows made up or changed their names. My name didn't fit my Shadow so I made it up and started introducing myself as Sil instead of Zack."

Mark pressed his luck. "But then... how did I remind you of your real name?"

"You didn't. I..." he hesitated, "I have an ability to reach into minds. All my life, I've been able to look into people and see their thoughts, fears, shortcomings, and hopes. But for some reason, I've been able to see visions of my family, and a lot of the time I don't understand them. I have full control over my ice, but this power has full control over me."

Mark's heart flustered. "Your family? How detailed are these visions? Do you know who they are?" he blurted out, getting a little too excited.

Sil paused, startled by Mark's eagerness. "I don't know a lot. I know I have two sisters, and a younger brother—"

Mark could barely contain his excitement. "Your sisters, are they twins, and your brother is about a year old?"

Sil's eyes flared. "How do you know that," he whispered, a little scared.

A bright smile covered Mark's face feeling affirmed in everything. "The Addisons are friends of my family." Mark's eyes widened, amazed. "I don't believe it, all this time I've known them and I've known you, and the whole time you—"

Sil faltered. "No way!" he gawked.

Mark's smile widened. "Your father and mine have been best friends for longer than I can remember. Your sisters babysit my sister all the time. And I always felt like the odd one out when our families visited because there was no one my age!" he cackled. "Because you're here!"

Sil couldn't believe it himself. "I've had the visions for years, but without outside information, I've never fully understood them. I… I think I've even seen you before," he muttered, "probably only once and very vague, but I don't know how I even get the visions. Here, I have to be near the person to reach into their mind. I'm not sure how I'm able to see my family when I've never met them before."

Mark nodded. "Who cares about that..." he got out. "Think about it, your Shadow makes you psychic! Think how you could use that to help the Shadows!"

Contemplating this, Sil scratched his head. "The moment you took my Shadow, I saw my mother." He finished undoing the one braid he was fiddling with, brushed it out with his fingers then undoing another. Mark couldn't help but stare at the long strands of smooth white hair which appeared cleaner and less messy than the rest of Sil's hair.

Sil noticed Mark looking and he smiled, giving another little laugh. "I know... this is crazy." He ruffled his fingers through his ice-white hair and brushing out another braid with his fingertips. His hair had many braids matting and tangling it up, and it was probably much longer than what Mark was seeing.

Mark shrugged, trying not to seem against Sil in any way even if it was just the state of his hair. Sil smirked, his eyes twinkling. "C'mon, don't deny that the first thing you did when you had a quiet moment in 13-15 was fix your hair!"

Realizing he had, Mark drew his brows together. It was the first time he saw his crimson eyes. "How did you know?"

Sil gestured to his temple with a smile. "Psychic, remember..."

"What an invasion of privacy..." he joked.

Shrugging, Sil levitated a large snowflake, being as playful as Mark. "It's my power. I should be allowed to use it. After all, restricting these things is how the ASH came to be."

"You have a point."

Sil reached up and tried to brush his fingers through his hair only to get it further tangled. "Then we see the same..." he muttered, "and you won't think anything of it when I go try to brush this stuff..."

Immediately confused, Mark stared at Sil positively baffled as he left the van. "Wait... what?"

Sil waved him off from outside the van, *I'll be close by,* he assured through Mark's mind and in the Realm. The silent voice in Mark's head made him jump clear out of his seat. This was what Sil had told him about, telepathy between them, using the Realm. Sil really was so much stronger outside of the ASI.

Mark felt a certain touch about Sil, something that he hadn't seen in him until now. Sil had literally reached into Mark's heart to send the simple phrase but by doing that he connected himself with Mark and allowed him to feel his heart in return.

Sil was passionate, subtle, he didn't need relationships, he wanted deeper roots and connections in the Shadows. Friendship was too small an achievement for him, even family was too small. What Sil wanted was to be a literal part of the Shadows, vital to the system. For who would dismiss their arm as a friend leaves, and who would give up their eye where a family loses hope? Sil was a vital part in a body of Shadows, not physically dismissible under any circumstances.

Mark considered how the Shadows were united. Ocie had repeated *we are all Shadows* like a mantra. As he spent more and more time in the Realm, he learned how interconnected all the Shadows were. As a Shadow himself, Mark began to understand how he also was a vital piece in the Shadows. As without Rita, they would be stranded, without Sil they would be lost, but without Mark they would be trapped.

As Mark watched the Shadows pack up their camp in minutes, Kip awoke and sat up as he heard the Shadows loading the tents into the van. Mark knew eventually the bench where Kip laid would have to be up-righted into a seat and not a bed for them to all fit in so it was good he was awake. He seemed a little surprised to find Mark was still with him but he was unable to express it as a sudden crack in his ribs forced him to double over.

Mark laid a hand on his back as he winced, seething at the pain. "How are you feeling?" Mark asked.

Kip had already heard the question a million times, and he didn't answer. What was there to answer? It was obviously too much pain to respond but he still tried "We're leaving?" Filling his lungs felt like sucking in sand.

"We'll have a better chance at hiding where I live. My mom could never turn us away, and we'll be able to find out what's wrong with you," Mark rambled, helping Kip sit up as the mattress pad was adjusted into a seat.

Sighing, Kip cleared his throat. "I'll be okay..." he tried to assure.

Mark shook his head. "No, you need help. You're—"

"Hey!" Elise said suddenly coming into the van, "have you seen Sil? He's missing."

"He said he'd be close by. Did you check the cliffs?" he asked in return.

Elise drew her brows together. "But... why?"

Hearing a tone in the Realm, Mark gazed out at the canyon at the prompt and gestured. "It's all right... There he is now."

Looking over the horizon, Elise hurried out of the van freezing only when she saw him. Mark also got out of the van following all the Shadows who were now staring in the direction of the crag. Struggling, Kip turned in the van to gaze and gasped a little at the glare of the light over the canyon behind Sil's back.

Every braid the Shadows knew of, every tangle and collected mat, was gone. Sil stood surely with the blue sky behind him, his white hair was long past his waist, and smooth save a few strands of ice-white, which flew freely.

Uneasily, Sil smoothed a few shorter strands over his head—too uneven to be called bangs—and pulled the length of his hair over his shoulder twisting it to keep it from tangling. Joining the Shadows, Sil looked about to see if there was anything he could help with. Finding otherwise, he headed over to the van to get in, only once looking back to gesture them all in.

Pleasantly surprised, all fourteen Shadows, save Kip who was already there, scurried into the van. Once inside and Rita was ready, the green mist surrounded the whole vehicle and they vanished without a trace.

XVIII
SURPRISING ARRIVALS

October 30, 2030

As hastily as possible, Keller's hand thrust at the ringing phone. "Any luck there?" he asked spitting into the receiver.

"No, sir, they're gone," the response of one of his men came regretfully.

"So, they *were* there!" he chanted excitedly. He listened for a few moments and didn't respond while he received more bad news. "All right..." he whispered. "Thanks for the report, please keep looking." Hanging up without another word, Keller reeled back in the desk chair surrounded by security screens, hopelessly.

Reaching out, Keller sipped a cup of coffee. It was too early in the morning for him to function fully, but the Shadows' last location had been discovered and he was forced to take calls even in this state. Sighing, he waited behind the dark curtain for more calls when suddenly the curtain opened and Kimberly peered in at him.

When Keller's eyes adjusted to the light, he could immediately make out Kimberly's tear stained face. A little shocked, Keller stood. "Really?" he raised a discouraged brow. "This is tearing you apart that much?" he wondered as he held her shoulders.

Kimberly embraced him as Keller pulled her into his arms. "Any luck?" she asked.

Keller whispered to not incite any of her emotions. "They were in Arizona yesterday morning. But Rita's with them and they left before anyone got there."

Despairing, Kimberly's tears revived. "I wouldn't be able to live with myself if anything happens to Kip..."

Holding her tightly, Keller shushed her. "We'll find them," he patted her curly hair. "Just trust me."

Kimberly nodded gravely and released Keller. "What did we do wrong? When did the Shadows hate us this much?"

Keller sat and heaved a broken sigh, but the phone rang again and he raced to pick it up. "Where are they?"

Kimberly's hope rose as Keller quieted himself and listened carefully. His hand scrambled to write down notes and Kimberly leaned over, realizing he was jotting down an address.

Acknowledging, Keller's tone remained firm. "Do not engage them. Don't let them know you're there. Keep a perimeter, and wait 'til I get there!" he ordered and hung up. Kimberly's eyes met with Keller as he stood, grabbing the note. "They're in New York. I think Mark's trying to hide with his family. Are you coming with me or not?" Not waiting for an answer, he darted out of the camera room toward the loading bay.

⁑◉⁑

Among the dusty jars of tea, Marissa thought of her husband. Between the large container of Ceylon and the nearly depleted Mason jar of Sencha, January collected teas here and there, drinking it in the morning as his first ritual. Everything January did was habit. He never deviated, and he had been battling bouts of depression since before June was born.

His nine-to-five job consumed his days, and Marissa couldn't remember a time when he came home with any energy. He had only one friend who gave him the motivation to spend time with Mark. In the single week she had known January would be away for work, the most unspeakable thing had happened. Marissa still didn't know how to tell him what happened to Mark.

The empty side of the bed was unbelievably cold this morning and lying there in the early hours left her shivering. All warmth had left the house, and even her playful six-year-old had fallen quiet with Mark's absence. June was oblivious, of course, she had seen the men come and take Mark, but it could have been an issue with school as far as she was concerned. Marissa bundled it up, keeping it quiet to her entire neighborhood that Mark was gone.

In staring at those lonely tea jars, sipping her coffee and overthinking how she would tell her husband, Marissa slammed her fist on the table. With the kitchen table chair scooting out from behind her loudly, Marissa stormed toward her cupboards with the first look of determination in her eyes in five days. Mark wasn't coming back, and January wasn't going anywhere. It was time to get her life back together.

Rattling her pans, she found a heavy-bottom skillet, flour, milk, baking powder, eggs, and a touch of butter. June slept in undisturbed usually, so even when she began loudly mixing together these ingredients into a batter, her daughter still didn't appear until the pancakes were bubbling on the griddle.

"Pancakes?" June's singsong little voice chirruped from the dining room.

Adopting her fakest smile, Marissa brightened up when her daughter waddled in groggily. "Hey, June-bug, first batch will be done in a minute!" Her six-year-old sat at the kitchen table, laying her head on the surface, and nearly falling back to sleep.

Marissa flipped a pancake, her creeping thoughts sneaking forward and beginning to worry again. She pushed these thoughts back. It was time to move on. With two large pancakes ready, she started the next batch and set a plate in front of June with syrup and a fork. "June, I need to talk to you about something."

The young girl dug into her breakfast eagerly, not a *thank you* on her lips as she devoured the pancakes. "Is Mark coming back today?" she asked.

Taken off guard, Marissa swallowed back her terror. "Listen to me…" she forced out, keeping her tone level, "Mark's gone away, and he's not coming back for a while, okay?"

"Yeah, he is," June blared, not an ounce of uncertainty in her voice. "I figured he was just staying at Gary's until Dad gets back, but he wouldn't tell me anything other than he'd be coming by today."

"W-what? Mark has talked to you? How?"

June stuffed her mouth with pancakes and shrugged. "I'm not a tattletale!" she gloated, happily protecting her big brother.

"June," Marissa reprimanded gently, now standing over her daughter and sliding the plate out of her reach. "Telling lies is not going to help anyone. How did Mark talk to you?"

Shirking down in the kitchen chair, June left the sticky fork on the surface of the table and gazed up through her lashes with big puppy-eyes. "The latch on my window is broken. Mark uses it to sneak in and out," she blurted, now reaching for her pancakes desperate to finish them off.

Marissa grumbled and pushed the plate closer to her baby girl, more conflicted than frustrated. She had to get that window fixed. It wasn't like she didn't already know Mark occasionally snuck out. She had to change her attitude. Mark was gone. He wouldn't be coming back. He should never come back. None of the children ever did.

Smelling something burning, Marissa's thoughts turned to what Mark had said. He had created fire. Perhaps that was fitting, he had always been drawn to warmth. His red streaks were hint enough. Part of her had always known he was probably a Shadow even though he had tested negatively when he was born. Something was burning. Her pancakes were burning.

Scrambling to take the pan off the stove, Marissa flipped the pancakes to reveal a charred black disk. She gripped the oven door and groaned as she stared down at them. She was so distracted. There was no escaping it now. Her son was a Shadow, and he was lost to her forever. Somewhere in the world, he would grow around his own kind, he'd move on, mature, and as an adult, he would be completely and unimaginably different from any preconceived vision she'd ever have of him.

Quieting her emotions, she muted the sounds around her to the point where she only recognized the doorbell rang when June burst up shrieking, "It's Mark!"

Rubbing her face, Marissa straightened herself, certain it was most likely her neighbor checking in on her after her silence. It was a tight knit community, gossip got around, and Marissa could easily get tangled in it no matter how hard she fought to avoid rumors. All she could fret over was how she was going to tell January when he returned.

June answered the door, throwing it aside so the doorknob slammed into the patched spot on the wall adjacent. It wasn't Mark. It was Arianne Addison, right? Marissa paid all her attention to June, at her unfettered excitement when she was scooped up into the air, screaming for joy.

"Hey, June-bug!" His voice sounded like his father's. She thought it was January at first, but she stopped dead in her paces when she saw him in the doorway. Tall and dark, but still gangly and young, he was growing up too fast, and despite her nightmares, she didn't want to let him go so soon. When he stood there, blushing, she could never have been more grateful.

"Mark?" Her voice could barely escape her lungs.

Mark brushed the red strike out of his face nervously. "Hi, Mom." He dulled the confidence he had acquired, weighed down by the knowledge that this wouldn't be easy for his mother.

Two Shadows stood at either shoulder, hovering close behind him, and one with silver hair and glittering golden eyes glared at her with a deep frown. Marissa remained stunned, her mouth hanging open. "Mark, wha—how... what are you doing here?"

Mark stepped inside the threshold of the door onto the old beige carpet. He was her son, the same boy under her roof as four days ago, but the gentle confidence in his eyes startled her. He looked right into her eyes, not faltering for a second, nearly as tall as she was, and giving her a long hypnotic view into his glowing crimson gaze. "We need a place to stay."

"Wait!" She held him at the door, preventing him from taking another step toward her and pushing June far out of his reach. "You're a Shadow. You're supposed to be at the ASH!"

Flustering a bit, Mark seemed to rise up over her, "I can't come home? Mom, we only need a place to hide. Please, my friend is sick."

Marissa tensed, wide-eyed as she scanned the faces of the Shadows standing behind him. Every cell in her body screamed to let him go, to push him out, to let the ASH deal with this. They'd take care of him. That's what they promised. However, surrounding those cells was blood, and her heart told her to protect her family. She could not refuse her own son.

With a heavy side step, she moved out of his way from the door. "All right, explain yourself!"

At the moment of permission, Mark rushed in with a boy sporting long white hair and a girl whose feet didn't touch the ground behind him. Marissa tensed when she saw the white-haired Shadow was carrying a younger boy who appeared unconscious.

Eleven Shadows filed in behind them, and by the time the unconscious child was laid on the couch, there were fifteen Shadows in her living room. Mark knelt beside the couch, stroking the sick boy's bangs over his forehead where they had been glued with sticky sweat. His sickly skin was pale and clammy, and his breathing rattled hoarse and audible.

June jumped up and down excitedly as the Shadows came into the house, innocently unsure of what to make of all Mark's new friends. "Wait!" Marissa cried out with a kitten's voice as she watched June run about excitedly. Mark didn't acknowledge her, all his attention on Kip. "Why? How did this happen?"

Mark gulped and rose up from the floor to face his mother. "Right when we left the ASH, Kip collapsed. He's having trouble breathing, and he coughed up some blood. I didn't know what else to do. We couldn't take him to a hospital and you cared for me when I had asthma, so you have to know how to help."

Marissa neared the sick Shadow warily. "Mark, that was years ago." Regardless of her feelings, she still knelt beside Kip.

"There has to be something you can do to help him," Mark pleaded,

Feeling Kip's forehead, Marissa assessed the fever. "I could try giving him something small to break the fever, and lessen the pain, but I don't know if it'll help in the long run..."

Mark grimaced. "Anything you think can help, please." Marissa nodded, meeting eyes with him but Mark hastily threw his arms around her. "I missed you..."

Marissa was hesitant to accept his embrace but couldn't help herself. No one could ever take him away from her, as much as she told herself to let go, they couldn't stop her from loving him. "I missed you too..." She breathed onto his shoulder. "I'm glad you're back."

Taking a pass outside to check and double check that

everyone was inside, Sil peeked around the small front yard of the suburban home. In spite of how enclosing the walls of the ASH felt, there was still something very confining about the sectioned land, each portioned out equally.

A shadow passed over him, and upon looking up, a bird swooped down from the sky. Given just enough time to recognize her, Sil raised his arm to receive the hawk.

"Winter?" The hawk's talons dug into his arm and now more than ever he wished he had his leather project to protect himself. "How did you know where I am?" he whispered into her silky feathers, stroking them with the tips of his fingers.

It made no sense. She had no scent to follow, and she had traveled well over four hundred miles. He made out her markings, observing her cold blue eyes, and confirmed this was his hawk. He couldn't believe it.

Winter protested to his handling, and flapped her wings madly, prompting Sil to release her. Smiling to the sky, Sil watched her fly off, knowing she would always come for him. That still didn't answer how she had found him or how she had traveled such a distance. Returning inside begrudgingly, Sil eased himself into the commotion of Shadows hovering around the sofa.

Marissa rushed from a linen closet with a large fluffy blanket and laid it over Kip while Elise dabbed his forehead with a damp cloth. Kip shuddered, in too much pain to otherwise react. He had been positioned on his side to make it easier for him to cough, but right now, he was panting hard, fighting to get oxygen in his lungs.

Sil pulled his long hair over his shoulder, uneasy, and not used to its length. Out of nowhere, June abruptly threw her arms around his waist in an odd hug, startling Sil, who stood there placidly, too panicked to move. Nobody touched him, nobody got near him, but this little girl didn't know him, and for the first time he felt truly frozen.

"There, the last one," June said with her arms wrapped around him. "I've hugged all of you." She released him and then ran over to Fliiy and Elise.

Shivering, Sil glared over the Shadows protectively, like his hawk as they all quietly made themselves at home, seating themselves and falling silent. Marissa focused on Kip at Mark's request, but she glanced sideways up at Sil, distracted.

"Mark..." she addressed warily.

Mark felt Kip's forehead again to guess accurately at the temperature. His eyes were red and startlingly bright, paralyzing her with their mystifying aura. Marissa stared down at her hands which were trembling. How was this her son? In five days, he was completely different. "Mark... what happened?"

Mark attention fixated on the Shadows, making a silent count of them to be sure they were all here and safe. "I told you. He collapsed as soon as we left the ASH."

"No, I mean to you. What's going on?"

With his eyes becoming tender, Mark sighed. "I guess I found out who I was..." His eyes flared bright cherry, and anxiously he brushed the red strike out of his face.

"How?" she protested. "It's only been a few days and you're not even the same person. Look how you've changed!"

"This is who I've always been." Mark stood up to her, flaring his eyes brighter so the tiny red flames licked at his lashes. "But this," he pointed at the Shadows gathered about in the living room, "right here is where I'm called to be." Adopting a coarse voice with his mother was uncomfortable for him. She could see it behind his stance. He was just as terrified as she was.

Kneeling again, Mark forced himself to continue in the midst of fretting over Kip. "You have to face it sometime... but I believe in the Shadows. I can free them. They need me, and we need you."

Grimacing, Marissa tried to turn away without much success. "You're dangerous," she whispered. "The Shadows are dangerous, and I've already lost too much because of them..."

Tensing, Mark gathered his courage and turned to her. "What's that supposed to mean?" His tone didn't help her to open to him, and she cowered into herself. All she could think was what she had been told. The Shadows were dangerous, uncontrollable, unpredictable, and that was why they were taken away. That was what she believed, what her husband believed.

Somehow, she felt warm again, even as she told herself the Shadows had taken away her son, the warmth that was lost in her life finally returned. Startled, she saw the golden glow and realized he was holding his hand out toward her. His hand radiated heat, smoldering like an element until he caused his fingers to crackle into small flickering flames. He brandished them, in full control of their wavering movement and temperature.

Uncannily close to the fire, Marissa leaned away uneasily. "Do you see?" he whispered, showing conflagration to her like it was a gift. "This is my Shadow."

Marissa felt her nose sting and her face tighten as the tears welled up inside her. "Fire... somehow that makes sense... I saw how you were different, and I feared that maybe it had been something I'd done that made you like this."

Extinguishing the flame, he saw a tear fall from his mother's cheek. Mark frantically reached out to put an arm around her. "You had nothing to do with this. I promise, but we still need your help."

Marissa shook her head. "No, Mark..." she forced herself to speak. "I saw how you were different. I knew you were a Shadow, but I didn't want you to turn out anything like—" she stopped short, abruptly, wiping her eyes dry. "I don't know how I'll ever explain it to you..."

Mark's crimson gaze remained firm. "You don't have to... What's important now is finding out what's wrong with Kip, and helping the Shadows stay hidden until I can come up with a plan..." His eyes drifted to the Shadows.

Hesitating, Marissa ground her teeth. "I…" she whispered then met his gaze again, without fear of Mark's red eyes. "I think I might have kept an inhaler for you in emergencies, but it's probably really old now…"

Giving a smile, Mark stood. "Anything you think could help."

XIX
NEW EXODUS

Turning his attention to the Shadows, Mark sent them a brief urge in the Realm for Elise, Emilie, Sil, and Rita to follow him as he stepped back through the house to his room.

Upon entering, Mark couldn't help but tense, seeing his room was cleaned up to the point where his possessions were no longer where he kept them. Had his mom organized his room out of guilt and grief like this was a mourning shrine to the loss of her son?

Thinking that was the case, Mark grimaced, trying to ignore the fact his mom had been fighting for the last few days to forget that he existed. The Shadows entered and without a word, Mark vanished into the Realm to be absolutely sure they couldn't be eavesdropped upon. The Shadows entered the Realm soon after him.

It's not safe here, Mark declared as soon as all of them could hear.

But... Emilie protested. *You heard her, she won't turn us in. She's your mother!*

Mark sent a tone of denial in the Realm. *I know my own mother better than you. She's hiding something from me. I was wrong to think it was safe here, but we'll stay here long enough for Kip to get the medicine,* he insisted firmly, assuming some authority in this situation.

Elise cringed, Mark could feel it in her presence but only Emilie had the guts to respond. *What if she doesn't though, and she can't help Kip at all!*

Even for Mark it was a stretch. He knew as well as any that he hadn't had an asthma attack since he was eight, and asthma wasn't even what Kip was dealing with. *We'll wait...* he decided. *If Kip receives any medicine for his lungs, we'll stay for the night, if not...*

Rita affirmed the suggestion, *I'll teleport us all to safety.*

Mark's form of fire knelt in thought, *in any case... it may be wise if we just—*

Mark! A voice in the Realm screamed to him.

Mark tensed, recognizing the tones in the Realm. *Ocie?*

The Shadows looked between each other, sending feelings of confusion and doubt. *What about her?* Elise wondered.

I heard... Ocie? Mark insisted.

Don't panic! Ocie's voice came again, *your range in the Realm is much farther than theirs. You can hear me, they can't.*

Mark looked around frantically, and before the Shadows, he appeared as if he was spinning in circles. Mark felt her presence, but not close to him, even though she was growing closer.

Have faith in yourself, Mark. The Shadow will guide you. Ocie's voice assured. *You've finally discovered the leader in yourself, and I commend you.*

Mark scowled to the Shadows who watched in horror. *You're not Ocie!* he insisted, *Show yourself!*

Ocie's voice laughed, appearing for the other Shadows. *You'll understand soon, Mark. I am Shadow Hope, and I've come here to point you in the right direction. Fate has almost come upon the Shadows like the rushing water, and with Trust, I am responsible for triggering this once: NOVA LIBERANTI!*

The Shadows stood back, shocked, overwhelmed, as this form of blue fluid light covered them all. *the New Exodus!* she declared, holding out her hand to Mark. *You are the Exodus of the Shadows, wielder of my power, and Hope for all of us. You will not fail me, Mark, as fate would have arrived upon you!*

Mark's eyes widened as flaming orbs, which he couldn't control. Like everything else in his life, his path was being chosen for him, and he accepted it. Mark clenched his fist and left the Realm, he knew what needed to be done, he didn't need to be told further but as the Shadows left the Realm he tensed again. Their faces, Elise, Emilie, Sil, and Rita, they were shocked, in fear of him.

Inhaling to speak, Mark was cut off by none other than Sil. "Mark... you were just named by Shadow Hope! The Exodus, it's you!" Sil's face filled with fear and awe at the same time. Mark saw in his heart that Sil feared how he had treated Mark could have affected the Exodus.

Elise gulped in disbelief. "You're..." She could only stare at him. "Mark, you're the third most powerful Shadow in the world!"

Growing shocked himself, Mark stepped back and tripped, sitting on his bed. "Third..." he whispered. "Who else is there?"

Crossing her arms, Emilie seemed to be the only one not scared of Mark. "Trust... obviously, Love, then Hope," she revealed, meeting eyes with him. "I've had my suspicions for a while. I've known you were Shadow Hope, but I wasn't sure until now."

Again, Mark met Emilie's gaze. "Love?" he whispered, overwhelmed. Mark felt his hands shaking, "But that would mean... Kimberly!" scanning the Shadows' perplexed faces, he insisted, "Kimberly is Shadow Love! She told me herself! But she's working with Keller. What's going on?"

The present Shadows gawked, as confused as he was. "She's a Shadow?"

Mark nearly shrieked, "Of course, she is. Can you not

feel it in the Realm!" he yelled at them. "Why is Kimberly helping Keller?"

Rita crossed her arms. "Isn't it obvious?" she muttered. "They're lovers!"

"That's preposterous!" Elise burst. "Are you not able to see the age gap between them?"

Rita's spitfire nature took hold of her. "She and Keller raised that Recluse of a Shadow from birth. They're practically his parents if they aren't actually. They're close and they love each other."

Mark clenched his fists, forming fire in them. "Who is the Recluse?" he burst, cursing and standing up to them. "I'm sick of fighting for the answers. Who was this guy and why does everyone think he's me? But more importantly, why would the second most powerful Shadow help Keller imprison the Shadows?" The strength in his voice silenced the Shadows, so he could gain no answer.

Frustrated, Mark collapsed again. "If I'm so powerful..." he whispered, "why wasn't I like the rest of you?"

Emilie stepped forward unsteadily but fell to her knees taking Mark's shoulder. "Trust sent you, Mark. He protected you from Keller, to hide you long enough for your power to grow, and you are the Exodus!" she pleaded. "You are our deliverer!"

Brushing off her hands, Mark stood. "If I'm so special, why not bring me up with the Shadows? Why separate me all my life?" Staggering back from her, Mark tore himself away from them, brokenhearted. *Why,* he thought, ages of worry consuming him. *If I needed to be there for them, why wasn't I taken to the ASH when I was born?*

Running from his own room, he hurried to find a place to be alone, to enter the Realm, and to get his thoughts together. The instant he stepped into the hall, Mark felt a draft, cold seeping across the beige carpet which he assumed Sil had caused, but he knew this was different. The front door was open.

A lie concocted in his head, praying that his mother hadn't answered it. But maybe she had, maybe she had called them, and maybe she wanted him gone. Before he could come around the corner, Rita teleported in front of him, throwing him to the floor.

Exclaiming, Mark reeled up with flaming eyes alit as a uniformed officer grabbed Rita's arms and shoved her down beside him. Mark's heart dropped when he saw her face hit the floor, her terrified eyes filling with a bright glint of green. Just as she was preparing to teleport, the man shoved his hand down on her back and with his free hand he pressed the end of some kind of gun into her shoulder.

Rita gave a small shriek when he pulled the trigger, but it took another second for Mark to realize she hadn't been injured by it. He spied a small needle on the end of the gun that had penetrated her skin and injected her with something. Mark hadn't any time to get up by the time another officer held him down as well, with a hand on his aching back. Mark barely yelped when he felt a similar needle stab into him, and then he was released.

Springing to her feet, her eyes wild with anger, Rita tried to grab Mark and teleport away, but she laid her fingers on Mark's shirt and froze.

"Impossible!" she breathed, shocked. "I can't—how! I can't teleport!"

A stir of panic in his limbs, Mark took hold of both her arms, assessing in his heart. He felt his Shadow, being sure that this power, whatever was stopping her from using her Shadow, was the same as the ASI. He didn't dare light his hands on fire to reveal to the officers that he could still use his Shadow, but he conveyed quietly through the Realm that he still had his power. The ASI still couldn't touch him.

Rita's eyes softened, watching as the six or so ASOs flooded into the back room of the house to neutralize all the Shadows back there. "Stop them..." she whimpered.

Abruptly, the two of them were yanked apart, restrained firmly, and Mark felt his feet being dragged towards the door. Marissa stood against the wall, panting horrified as she found his gaze. She had let them in. Through the door, taking no notice of Marissa pinned to the wall, Kimberly rushed in scarcely taking a glance at the other Shadows around when her eyes locked solely on Kip.

She slid on her knees in the carpet, falling beside him. "Kip! Can you hear me?" she called into his face frantically, touching his cheek, and feeling how hot his skin was. Gently, she reached under his neck to lift his head and he let out an extremely hoarse breath. Tensing, Kimberly ground her teeth with unease. "Ian!" she called.

The man of short stature, Ian Keller, entered Mark's house, building a rage in Mark so unquenchable that he forgot every instinct in him to hide. Mark ignited his hands and burned the two men dragging him and Rita outside.

With all his might, he pushed through them, stumbling as he grabbed Keller's coat to pull him away from Kip. "Leave him alone! Don't touch him!"

Keller tensed, seeing his crimson eyes shining only briefly before Mark grabbed his collar. "Mark, wait!" he insisted desperately. "You don't understand the full consequences of what you've done!"

Mark glanced briefly to Kip and Kimberly. "Why should I? You imprisoned him, all of them, all their lives! Why shouldn't I just burn you to a crisp now?"

"Mark!" Kimberly screamed, garnering his attention. "Kip is dying!"

Mark hesitated, and Keller bat his hands away from his collar.

Kimberly merely pled with him. "Kip can't survive outside of the ASH. Without the ASI, Kip's problems will come back and he'll die! We need to get him home now!"

Mark stepped back, shocked, in fear for his friend's life. Kimberly, elevated Kip's torso to help him breathe. "I've already lost too much. I can't lose Kip too…" she whispered. "Kip is more dear to me than you can comprehend, Mark. Almost more than—" she stopped herself, unwilling to speak his name.

Tears drifted over Kimberly's cheeks. "You know why he's dead, Mark... because he was just like Kip. Passing through the shield didn't kill him. Being unprotected by the shield is what killed him! And Kip's not the only one. There are many others!" Kimberly burst up at Mark. "Neither of us can be selfish when there's too much at risk!"

"Enough!" Keller screamed, swiping his hand through the air, and immediately taking Kip in his arms, caring for the boy as much as Kimberly. "I will not argue with you. I will simply do what needs to be done!"

Mark's rage built inside him, and his heart pounded faster, Keller left the house, and Mark ran after him finding that the Shadows were surrounded. "Keller!" Mark shrieked in fury.

Keller ignored him long enough to get Kip in the van he had brought to take the Shadows back. "Mark, give it up!" he insisted. "You have to return if you want Kip to live!"

Mark seethed at the threat and the Shadows clamored behind him angrily, unable to use or control their powers. Mark heard them. He heard them all. They were infuriated that Kip was being used as a lure to get them back, and it was working. Mark's fists tightened as his anger grew more and more, no hate, his emotions were fueling his Shadow allowing the flames to flourish evermore.

"I can't convince you to get in the van, Mark," Keller seethed, pausing at the open door of the fifteen-passenger van, "but you have to understand, none of you are safe out here." He gestured into the vehicle, but it wasn't to urge the Shadows to come willingly. It was to someone inside, prompting them to come out.

Mark's eyes widened, all the rage stirring inside him to the point where he feared he'd burst, but then, someone stepped out of the van at Keller's behest. In a blue dress below her knees, her long brunette hair tied back loosely, Mark's terror culminated when Ocie appeared. His eyes dashing between father and daughter, Mark's voice cracked. "You're... with him!"

Ocie hurried out toward the Shadows, leaving them shocked and hardly able to protest with their assailants when they saw her. The ASOs surrounded them and let Ocie enter their midst. "Mark, please believe me. The ASH is not a prison; it's a safe haven. Outside of the ASH, Shadows like Kip die, and the rest of us are ostracized. We always had to hide. Shadows can be themselves in the ASH. They don't have to worry about hurting people or breaking things when they're still learning their powers. It's there to keep us safe!"

Furious, Mark let the flames return to his palms, a well of anger inside him bubbling over. "What about the Exodus! This isn't living. The Shadows aren't free."

Nodding cautiously, like she was taming a beast, Ocie neared him warily. "It will come, and when it does, humans will come to trust us, then we'll be free. Do you understand that?"

Trust, that was the name of the Shadow who had come to Mark. Somehow, he knew she was right, but he couldn't shake the feeling, looking into Sil's Shadow, getting to know Emilie's soul, they were trapped.

Mark held himself up, nonetheless by himself, and breathed in his insanity to the phrase. "I am the Exodus of the Shadows! *Nova Liberanti,* the one who will deliver the Shadows!" he declared. There was no denying it now. He had to trust the power he knew he had been given.

Ocie jumped back, shocked at the sudden power in his voice. "Mark, listen to me! Not like this! It can't happen like this!"

Somewhere in his destiny, right now, Mark saw his future, somewhere high, lifted alone, without his closest friends to guide him, having made this one decision, and spoken this one phrase. Mark's cherry eyes ignited with flames, licking about his hair and in his red strikes the same. "LET... MY PEOPLE... GO!"

Exodus, he thought, it was appropriate. Only one phrase

held its meaning. Maybe it was his place, the Moses he was meant to become, to lead his people into their promised land, conquering it as their own.

Fire trailed from his fingers, licking up his sleeves and igniting through his heart as if his blood were gasoline. Letting his fire loose, Mark felt a warning in his heart, remembering how he had hurt Sil. The blaze spread all around him, pushing the Shadows back toward the house and forcing Keller back. Ocie however stood firm, even when the crimson tongues caught hold of her dress.

"Mark, don't—" the voices of Shadows clamoring behind him echoed somewhere in his mind, but he ignored them. Allowing his own conflagration to burst, Mark pushed them back, holding his ground, and determined to stay. Kip needed help, Mark acknowledged that, but none of the Shadows were suffering. Right now, they were free.

Catching a glimmer of blue through the blaze, Mark watched Ocie shroud herself in water. Steam rose off her ward as Mark pressed his flames down over her, but she stepped through it, nearing him in spite of it. Her water enveloped every strand of fire and put it out, surviving through it even when he directed all his flames at her.

"Mark!" Sil burst beside him, keeping low to the ground underneath the heat. He laid his hands on the pavement and ice shot out from his palms. Coating the grass and gravel and latching onto Ocie's water like food. Her shield froze in seconds giving Mark the opening to swoop in and slam his fists onto the icy film.

It fell down on top of Ocie before shattering and sending her to the ground under its weight. Mark hesitated when he saw her under the ice, his flames dying down when Sil took his side. Ocie moaned a little as she sat up from the icy rubble. Mark spied a little blood on her head where the ice had struck her. "Mark..." She grimaced, dazed and frustrated. "You're just going to have to learn patience."

Feeling struck, Mark felt his feet freeze to the ground, staring at the blood upon her brow he couldn't move. He had done that, with Sil's help but it was his fault. With the fire dying away, Keller rushed to his daughter's side, helping her out of the ice and toward the van to keep her safe. "This is exactly what I warned you about. Unrefined Shadows are dangerous. You have to hone them in a safe environment!"

"Shut up!" Mark screamed at Keller. "It's your fault she's here. It's your fault the Shadows are unrefined in the first place. How can you even try to speak to us now?"

Keller let Ocie sit before he glanced back at Mark with a vehement glare. Mark tensed at the flash of blue in Keller's old eyes. He had never seen the man angry. Clenching his fists, Keller stomped across the pavement at Mark, each heavy footstep resounding through the ground. Mark's heart welled up with fear as Keller walked right up to him. "I've had enough of you!" he muttered, soft and threatening.

Abruptly, Keller grasped Mark's arm tightly, manhandling him like a child. "If you are *Nova Liberanti*, then that's all the more reason to keep you with the Shadows! You're coming back to the ASH!"

"No!" Mark couldn't scream loud enough, fire weaving about from his palms as he flailed. "The Shadows will be free now! Shadow Trust told me!"

"You don't have the slightest clue under god who Shadow Trust is!" Keller blared, dragging him toward the van in spite of the fire coming off Mark's hands.

"And you do?" Mark shrieked, but he realized Keller's sleeves weren't catching fire. Panic rose in Mark's heart as he dug his heels into the concrete. "How am I not burning you?"

Keller finally gave up and released him, throwing him down to the pavement. "Because I am a Shadow too!" he bellowed. The Shadows froze in terror. Keller held his hand forward and showed them as a cyan mist flowed from his palm. "I am Shadow Inhibitor, the first Shadow! How have you not gotten that yet? I created the ASH because, apart from each other, the Shadows are disjointed and unrefined. Only together can you achieve your powers' full potential!

The Shadows have to stay together!"

Mark's wide eyes faded to mahogany. "What..." Keller's whole Shadow was devoted solely to inhibiting the Shadows.

Keller ran closer to Mark. "If you listen, I can save Kip!" he pleaded. "But we have to go back to the ASH!"

"Shut up!" Mark screamed again bashing away Keller as he tried to hoist him to his feet again. This was the Shadow he was meant to defy. Keller's Shadow Inhibitor didn't work on him, and he wasn't sure Keller knew that for certain yet.

Mark scurried back on his knees away from the cyan mist in Keller's hands. Mark rose, finding his footing even though his entire being was tense. Tremors ripped through his bones so fearsomely that once more his fist lit into bright crimson flames.

Mark's rage grew only more fervent as his eyes burst into gleaming cherry, and the fire stretched all the way up his arms. Mark was almost sure he gained another red strike between his nose as he screamed, lashing forward. If not, he certainly gained a few gray hairs for how his anger dulled his senses.

Mark's fists flew around Keller wildly. "This is your fault!" he screamed. "Not just the ASH, not the truth, not the Shadows, it's your fault!" Keller ran, it was all he could do to keep himself safe from potential burns. Mark was feral and uncoordinated, rage locking him into this spellbound state of pure violence.

Keller formed the cyan mist around his hands again to defend himself. The old man appeared out of practice, as if once he had fought for the Shadows, but he hadn't used his Shadow in defense in too many years to count. Mark was much stronger than him. Throwing fire at Keller, Mark could not help but cringe when he realized he was burning himself.

Blisters were appearing on his knuckles, and the tremors rippling through him never subsided. Keller wasn't as strong as him—he could do it. He could take down Keller and free the Shadows.

Keeping his distance for as long as he could, Keller was slow, prudent, and stayed defensive. Mark might have been younger, faster, and stronger, but Keller was far more trained in fighting and more refined in his Shadow.

Making only one motion against him, Keller hooked his foot under Mark's ankle, tripping him and kicking his leg in the back of the knee. It looked effortless, but Mark howled in pain. His leg wasn't broken, was it?

His knees knocked against the concrete the instant Mark felt Keller grasp his arm to keep him from scraping himself, and with his other hand, Keller spread cyan mist about his hand. Mark couldn't react, it happened too fast. Keller's hand swooped in, trailing with light, and he touched Mark's forehead gently. In one last semblance of confidence, Mark was certain Inhibitor would have no effect on him.

Mark's spine stiffened. He was immune to the ASI and the injection form of the inhibition, but in its raw form, Mark felt it racing through his veins. Mark's eyes briefly flared with cyan then died down to dark brown, almost black as his Shadow was completely inhibited in a second and more so, Keller took control of another piece of Mark.

It took no effort for Keller. With the brief contact he stole Mark's power and his very consciousness. Mark collapsed lankly with nothing in him to fight as his consciousness escaped. Keller snuffed out the cyan light in his hands and turned his attention back to the Shadows. "I won't take any more of your arguments, get in the van now!" Keller ordered them.

A few officers responded to the order and took Mark's unconscious form into the van, followed by a few who cautiously moved toward the crowded group of shivering Shadows. Gritting his teeth, Sil took a step closer to Keller. He couldn't abandon Mark, and regretfully he made the decision to take the lead here.

With sorrowful eyes, he sent a tone into the Realm, only focusing on Emilie's eyes. She couldn't walk and knelt on the ground with her scrawny legs under her. There was so much devastation in her eyes, but she couldn't find her voice as Sil knelt with her to carry her himself. Sil and Emilie were the last two Shadows to give up freedom, and seeing them walk willingly to the ASH destroyed the Shadows' hope.

XX
DISCOVERING HOPE

A gurney was ready at the door when they arrived in the last light of the evening. Kimberly rode in the front with Kip in her arms safe, having stolen the blanket from Mark's house, which was wrapped around him like a baby. He hadn't stirred, too weak to awaken at all, a fever raging like she had never seen. As they pulled to a stop, she just prayed they had enough time.

One of Keller's staff opened the door for her, but she personally carried Kip to the gurney, and laid him on it. At his side constantly, she took him into the ASH with very little help. Being inside the ASI's barrier wasn't going to help him at this point. He needed Inhibitor in his blood. She did receive some help in moving him into the small infirmary bed, but the moment his back hit the firm cushion, he coughed. His mouth welled up with blood, and he choked.

"He's aspirating it!" Kimberly panicked, guiding the other nurse to turn him on his side. Kimberly had her hand in some medical expertise, especially after caring for the Recluse until nine months ago. However, she felt very out of practice and it was difficult sinking back into these stressful fits. She had seen them many times before.

Kip gagged, blood bubbling in his throat and on his side,

blood drained from his mouth onto the white pillow. "That's it, Kip." Kimberly soothed, stroking his curls over his forehead and humming, "get it out."

Kip didn't have the strength to cough it all out, his breathing was so faint. And it was loud, hoarse to the point it could be heard across the room. She only left him to fetch an IV tube and a bag of light blue fluid. Déjà vu struck her, remembering all the silent hours, just listening to *his* breathing, making sure it was still there.

She let the nurse sterilize a section of Kip's skin on his arm, and she placed the intravenous needle herself. "Once his Shadow is inhibited, the fit will slow down. Hopefully, we caught it in time, or this is going to be a long night." Hanging the IV bag, Kimberly fretted over Kip. "I've got it," she assured the nurse gently.

Fetching a stethoscope which was always close at hand, Kimberly didn't watch her helper leave. Placing the cold metal inside Kip's unbuttoned vest, she listened quietly. His raspy breathing could be heard by the most untrained ear, but she understood from what she heard, Kip's lungs were saturated. They were full of blood, welling with it, expelling the Shadow in his veins.

He hadn't been coughing much already, she could tell, there were no scars yet, once his lungs cleared, they would heal. Tenderly, she set aside the stethoscope and cleaned the blood off his lips.

The bleeding was normal, and this was nothing like the most extreme case she had dealt with. Kip moved a little when she touched his lips. He didn't shift at all or cringe, he closed his mouth briefly, swallowing some of the blood and continuing to breathe through his mouth.

Finally, Kip coughed voluntarily, not quite conscious, but delirious enough to force it. More blood came up, and Kimberly found herself patting his back, wishing he had the strength to sit up on his own. She could remember hours of this, sitting at *his* side, holding him up while he gagged on it. She cleaned Kip's pillow as much as she could, this was already going to be a long, sleepless night, waiting for Kip's lungs to clear, and praying he could get Inhibitor in his system fast enough to heal his lungs.

The door slid open to the side and Keller appeared, overwhelmed and keeping his panic away from Kip for as long as he could. "How's he doing?"

Kimberly threw away another bloodied tissue. "He's stable. I haven't put him on oxygen yet."

Keller leaned against the wall for support and rubbed his face. "How's he taking Inhibitor? No negative reactions, right?"

Nodding aimlessly, Kimberly sighed, rubbing Kip's back lovingly as he drooled blood. "So far so good. He's never been on it before, so he has no immunity and we shouldn't have to use a very high dosage."

Blinking tiredly, Keller found the ability to sink down into the Recluse's bed. "I sent all the Shadows to their rooms. Mark is segregated from them." He sent her a look for her approval, but Kimberly made no response, her dull eyes locked onto Kip's pained face. Distraught, Keller lost the ability to look at her. "Mark got me to reveal my identity tonight… after all I did to cover it up, blocking myself out of the Realm. The plan was to never let them know I was one of them."

Grumbling, Kimberly supported herself against the higher bed, frustrated. "And what did that accomplish?" she snapped, startling her partner. "None of them trust you."

"They already didn't trust me when I built the ASH!" Keller rose, "If they knew who I was, what Shadows who came here in the beginning would have protested, bringing them up to not know I was Shadow Inhibitor kept them from being afraid of me."

"It's too late for that!" Kimberly yelled down at him. "After what you did tonight? You knocked Mark out by touching him! Now they know you could do that to any of them! They have every reason to be afraid of you! None of them know what Inhibitor is for, and how much good it does. It's just a prison to them!"

Gritting his teeth, Keller paced into the kitchenette area of the infirmary. "So, what do you propose we do?"

Kimberly clenched her fists upon the bed railing over Kip. "Take down the ASI! Let them see the outside world. Let them know this isn't a prison and that the ASI protects very specific Shadows, not all of them."

Keller stopped pacing, all the pent-up aggravation inside him splitting him apart. "Kimberly... don't you think I would have thought of this?" He belittled her. "I can't risk it! And I understand, I really do, the Shadows need to be free, but all I want is to keep them safe."

Kimberly's confidence in his motives had been destroyed. She glared at him like he was the devil himself, letting his belittling words be the death of him.

Heaving a sigh, Keller finally built the courage to meet her gaze. "Mark is Shadow Hope, isn't he?"

Grimacing, Kimberly formed a tight fist around the cold bar. "I'm sorry, Keller... but you're wrong..."

"Then who is?" he demanded.

Her eyes flaring pink, Kimberly tried to remain firm. "I've known the identity of Hope since the birth of its wielder, and I've watched her all her life, growing and maturing. I don't know how you could have become so blind to not see her right under your roof."

Drawing his brows, Keller seethed. "Regardless, Hope didn't help the Shadows escape. Even with Mark's defiance of my power, if the Shadows were planning to escape, we would have known about it in the Realm!"

Kimberly's gaze fell to the floor while Keller faced her sternly. Keller crossed his arms, bearing over her. "Unless, the surveillance data was corrupted..." Kimberly tensed trying to lose eye contact with him, Keller nodded and grinned. "I knew it..." he lost his voice. "It was you. Why! Why would you help them escape, and you knew Kip was with them!"

Kimberly held her shoulders. "I didn't think. I was too hasty, and I didn't realize he'd be in so much danger."

"Dad?" Ocie's voice came from the open doorway, roaming the halls freely while the other Shadows remained locked in their rooms. "Is everything all right?" she fretted, her attention on the blood around Kip's face. "How's Kip doing?"

"He'll be fine," Keller groaned, his tone softening. "What about you? How's that scratch?"

He spread out an arm toward her and she floated into his arms, hiding a touch of grief. "Just a bump. It's not the first time I've run in with Sil." She found Kimberly's eyes, seeing the sorrow in them, and Kimberly turned away, inadvertently admitting to the girl that she had lost faith in Keller. Ocie nuzzled closer to her father before standing back and looking him in the eye as an equal. "What do you want to do?"

Keller awed at the maturity in his daughter, the inspiration she was to all the Shadows and the hope she still had. "I need you to convince the Shadows..." he stopped himself, unwilling to use his daughter to meet his ends. "I need you to give them hope... if Mark's not Shadow Hope. I need you to let them know I'm not here to hurt them."

"I know, Dad," she whispered, a sparkle of blue in her oceanic eyes. "I'll tell them." Her brunette tresses bounced behind her as she turned and left, settling the uneasiness in Keller's stomach.

"She's Shadow Hope," Keller whispered, parental love in his eyes, even if it was weak.

Kimberly frowned behind him. "Took you long enough..."

Whirling about, Keller met eyes with her shocked. "You're telling me that my daughter is an Orchestrator!"

"Only the most powerful one out there next to Trust," Kimberly snapped, letting go of the bed railing and rushing at Keller. "And Shadow Love," she threatened.

"Please!" Keller scoffed, "your Shadow has been dormant for over twenty years. Are you really going to try to use it now?" Even though he stood shorter than her by about half a head, he stood up to her with cyan eyes. "Do you think I look up to you or something for your powers. It's good none of the Shadows ever figured out about your past or they'd be more scared of you than they are of me!"

"That's not true!" she roared, mostly trying to convince herself. "I'm trying to become who I was meant to be!" Swiping her hand to the side, a bright magenta light and flicker of flame trailed her hand.

Keller stepped back, startled when he saw it. "How? You can't use any of your Shadows."

Kimberly's excitement welled up inside her to see the magenta aura in her hands. "You and I are both liars, and because you've sheltered and hid away the Shadows, it will be your downfall and theirs. Don't you see the damage you've caused by hiding the truth from them."

Holding out her hand to him, a dark mist, much like Mark's surrounded her fingertips. She tested it, holding up her true power to use it on him. "Forget everything I told you about my past and the Shadows I've had contact with. All you will know me as is your assistant and the one who raised and cared for our son before he died."

Keller fell to the floor. "Kimberly, stop this!" he screamed unable to use his own Shadow, seeing just how powerful she was. "You know the risk, if the ASI doesn't protect them, they'll die!" he warned her as if in his last effort. "Think of Kip!" he begged. The dark mist surrounded him, covering him in darkness, both destroying and altering his memory of her entirely.

Kimberly watched coldly, as Keller fell unconscious while his mind recovered from the tampering. It would be a while before he awoke again. Turning to Kip, Kimberly assumed her true form, having finally brought the powers of Shadow Love out of dormancy. "There's still the business of Hope... and I can't exactly allow Ocie to die with her destiny in place."

Kimberly used Love's powers, a Shadow she hadn't used in twenty years to retake her true appearance, the magenta coat of a cardinal covering her, and her long overdress skirt flowing out behind her.

October 31, 2030

Clinging to sleep, Kip savored the warm bed covers, sinking deeper into it even when he felt himself being jostled and moved. He couldn't open his eyes, too exhausted to even try. The cold air felt fabulous in his throat and helped his lungs to open, but it wasn't long before he acknowledged the feeling of the air in the enclosed elevator. With a needle in his arm, he recognized the smell of his bedroom, and the sounds of the Shadows around him.

Two or three sets of hands moved him from the gurney into his own bed, and what were indistinguishably Kimberly's hands tucked him in to let him sleep. "Listen, guys," Kimberly's voice soothed his ears, calming his nerves, "he needs to keep this IV in for at least another two hours. Please don't mess with it." Kip could hear her footsteps trailing away.

"Where's Mark?" Sil demanded, an anger in his voice that Kip had heard so many times before. Kip managed to open his eyes a peek, and dazedly looked about the room. The Shadows were restless, unable to stay seated in their beds as they were told when Kimberly came down to them.

Kimberly stood outside the elevator solemnly, her bitter frown visible from across the room. "Keller put him in a detention room."

"What did Keller do to him?" Rita shrieked, jumping forward and only now getting her ability to teleport back.

"Don't worry about him," Kimberly insisted, levelheaded and mechanical. "Keller just inhibited his life functions. That's what his Shadow does, inhibits Shadows primarily, but if he wants, he can inhibit everything. I'm sure Mark will be fine. He's probably waking up now."

"How could you be on his side?" The Scottish Shadow rushed toward Kimberly, finding it awkward to walk the distance when she could have teleported.

Kimberly didn't bother explaining and scurried into the elevator, locking their access to it promptly. Kip moaned and shifted, finding the strength to draw the covers up closer to his neck. He was cold, but he liked the feeling of the fresh, crisp air on his face. It was helping.

"Kip, are you okay? Can you hear me?" Elise's voice pled, rushing to kneel by his bed and wake him. Already mostly awake, Kip's eyes opened a crack, and he groaned. He tried to inhale voluntarily and to fill his lungs, but the muscles in his chest protested and he coughed. Elise, Rita, and Sil crowded him with more coming, and they all reeled when they saw the blood on his lips.

"How do you feel?" Elise asked.

Hugging his blanket, and loving his own bed, Kip created a fake and forced smile accompanied by a thumbs-up. "Better..." his hoarse voice croaked. He coughed again, now attempting with all his strength to raise his torso and get the blood out of his lungs. "What'd I miss?" he got out softly.

"Apparently, Keller is a Shadow," Elise answered promptly, followed by Sil's snark.

"And Ocie has been snitching to him this whole time!"

Kip raised his eyes to Sil, a little shocked by how close he was. He still had a little fear that Sil was about to turn a cold shoulder to him, and he couldn't rationally explain the change in Sil.

Managing to sit up with Rita's hands guiding him, he gagged again, blood filled his mouth and he got a good long look at the tube attached to his arm. With his eyes, he followed up the line to the IV drip standing by his bed. The blue fluid filled the plastic, sending Keller's power directly into his blood, affecting the element in Kip's heart and neutralizing his Shadow.

Giving it a little thought, Kip looked at his hand making the effort to create a soft light. It was his Shadow's simplest form, but he still couldn't summon it. "Don't worry." Sil's voice broke into his thoughts. "It'll wear off, most of us have our powers back already. I just got mine back first by touching Mark."

"Which is unfair!" Rita blared. "I was right there beside him when they injected me with Inhibitor."

Kip let his hand fall, with half a mind to lie back. He was so exhausted, with a bitter taste in his mouth, his stomach felt queasy. Elise sat on his bed with him, allowing him to lay his head on her shoulder, panting slightly. "Where's Emilie?" His voice caught, and he coughed a few more times, coating his palm with blood.

Kneeling, Sil crossed his arms, drawing his brows. "Who knows where the great infiltrator got off to. She went into the Realm while we were still in the van. I didn't say anything, and she probably gave the ASOs the slip when we arrived."

"She could be all the way in Scotland by now," Rita groaned, also taking a seat on the floor. "It's not like she'll come back. At least one of us got free."

Kip could see the irritation in Sil's eyes, the jealousy. His closest friend had abandoned him, leaving him in the ASH, and it wasn't like her to form any sort of plan to free him. She was selfish; she always had been, and it wasn't hard to see the resentment Sil felt. "So, what now?" Kip asked, coughing painfully.

"What do you mean, 'what now?'" Sil snapped, sulking. "Nothing! Everything goes back to normal…" Crossing his arms, Kip sank back into his bed, resting on his side and waiting for sleep to come over him again. Everything was uncomfortable, not just breathing, but being back in this room, his home, their prison.

Emilie loved being a pain in Keller's side, and the man had devised many ways of subduing her. As it was, there was little hope that she could get free. And she wasn't. Among the confusion of the evening, and Kimberly's desperation to save Kip's life, Emilie had slipped in behind Keller, following him as he carried Mark to a detention cell alone.

Knowing Keller was a Shadow made it hard for her to hide her presence from him in the Realm, but she used that invisibility to hide in the darkest corner of the evenly lit, white room. With the ASI on all sides of the room, the dead silence in the Realm encroaching on her, the only other presence near her was Mark. The hard, stone floor couldn't have been comfortable, but Mark was left there unconscious, curled up and unmoving.

He groaned, fighting off the effects of Inhibitor, and pushing himself to regain some semblance of consciousness. Mark dreamt deeply, pulling his knees up to his chest.

What if none of this had happened? What if he'd never discovered his Shadow five days ago? What if he didn't have the power to defy the ASH and he had fallen in line like the rest of the Shadows?

In the end it was all a knotted mess that made him feel like a failure, not just on his own part, but on the Shadows', who promised to guide him. In a day, he had been transformed into a creature who was no longer human, in another, he formed relationships with similar beings he was beginning to love, and in the third, he had committed the greatest blunder of all.

Mark formed a fist, stretching out his arm on the floor where he laid. His anger grew as he pressed his fist on the floor trying to get up, but he didn't have the will. What was his future supposed to be if trying to escape led to this?

"I can't..." Mark whispered coarsely, drawing himself up on uncoordinated feet.

Emilie tensed behind him, watching him as he got up and ran forward at the door. Igniting his hands instantly,

Mark banged his fists on the door and the fire on his hands spread over the white stone repelled merely by its surface temperature. The ASI protecting the wall sparked golden-bronze and dissipated, burning away like paper.

"Keller!" Mark screamed up at the mirror on the door, knowing it was a window. "If you can hear me…" he shouted only briefly, contemplating his words. "Let my people go!" Banging his fists on the door again, he repeated, "Let them go! Free the Shadows!" he begged, sinking to the floor as he couldn't even burn through the thick stone.

Hesitating, Emilie sighed and left the Realm. She was stuck in there like Mark and she might as well show herself. She approached him and laid her hands on his shoulders to comfort him. Tensing a little, Mark jumped and whirled about, but he extinguished the fire on his hands to gently touch hers, accepting the embrace. "It's all right…" She held her hands over his chest, consoling him silently.

Mark felt her fingers press over his heart and he allowed her as she discovered in the Realm how to take his Shadow from him. Meeting eyes with her, Mark felt his Shadow leave him in Emilie's hands. While still embracing him around his shoulders, Emilie held Mark's Shadow before their eyes.

"It's so heavy…" Emilie whispered, somewhat distraught. "It's like I'm holding your heart… but it's heavy and cold…" Gazing then into Mark's eyes, Emilie frowned. "I didn't realize when you took my Shadow what a burden it must have been to even hold my heart in your hands. I can only imagine what it felt like."

Mark whirled about and embraced Emilie which forced his Shadow to return to him. "You are light, Emilie, so different from any Shadow. Your Shadow is an easy burden while mine is like a weight on my chest. You're full of emotion and life. I can't let the ASH keep that from you."

Emilie smiled as Mark released her and knelt on the floor, staring at him for a while. Until now, she had never thought of wanting family, but seeing Mark before her, her cousin, made her realize how she badly needed it. "Will you promise me something, Mark?"

Hesitating, Mark nodded, dulling the color of his eyes from crimson. Emilie clenched a hand over her heart. "When all this is over... can you and I always be together?" she asked, knowing Mark could probably never live up to the task.

All his despair clouded the room, tears in the corners of his eyes, and Emilie's heart softened. For one time in her life, she never felt so comfortable with a person to reach out and touch his cheek.

Mark shuddered at her touch, gravitating into it and grasping the back of her palm. Emilie floated up and drew her arms around him. "I believe in you, you hear me!" she whispered at his ear, holding him tightly. "We're gonna get out of here!" He nodded within her embrace, trembling and holding back tears.

Abruptly, they heard a rattling sound at the locked door and they thrust apart from each other. Mark jumped to his feet, keeping his eyes on the door while Emilie went into the Realm. The first thing he noticed was a key card in the dainty hands of Ocie Keller, then he saw her face, determined and soft as the day he had met her.

"What do you want?" Mark growled at her, quelling the flames already forming in his palms.

Ocie seemed startled, taking a glance about the rest of the room then her shoulders dropped. "Emilie... I know you're in here. You might as well come out." She slammed the door shut, pocketing the key card securely before Emilie left the Realm. "Do you know why the ASH was built?" she muttered wearily before flashing her blue eyes at him.

Mark clenched his fists tighter, still shaking with rage, but he stood and nodded grimly without a word.

Ocie pressed her lips together and frowned. She shook her head slightly and strode deeper into the room. "My father grew up in a Shadow settlement west of here, a close-knit community where the Shadows all lived and worked together. They never really had much, but he saw how the Shadows could do so much more when they came together.

"He created the ASI to protect that settlement, to give them a safe place to grow and focus on their powers, and from the stories he told me, there were some especially powerful Shadows living there.

"Unfortunately, some of them saw what the ASI was capable of and feared it was a way to trap the Shadows. This panic caused them to scatter, no one trusted each other, and many Shadows left and went into hiding. He acted fast, and with a handful of Shadows rallying with him, he fought to preserve the Shadows' unity, keeping them together.

"He was rash, and the settlement was destroyed within the ASI. With the Shadows who stayed beside him, and the few who reluctantly stayed, he built the ASH, and moved them here, a building that can't be damaged no matter what battles go on inside it.

"But that wasn't the only reason the ASH was built, and you know it. My father's best friend was like Kip, dying! And he didn't support my Dad. After his home was destroyed, his best friend disappeared, and probably died soon after!" Ocie's tone rose harshly.

"It wasn't until five years later that he learned his Shadow could have saved his friend! And that was through the Recluse! The Shadow that he raised like a son, a boy who urged my dad to use him to find a cure! A boy so smart, he helped Dad come up with the medicine that saved Kip's life last night!"

Taken aback, Mark's footing quivered at the sound of Ocie screaming. Tears welled in Ocie's eyes as she stood up to Mark, fully believing and trusting in her father. "I have watched my dad suffer. He just wanted to heal him, and after fourteen years, he still died, and then you come along, identical to him, and fighting to destroy everything my dad created! Yes, my dad has made mistakes, and yes... the Shadows must be free. But he can't accept that this coincides with the Exodus."

Tears streaming, Ocie covered her eyes, desperately trying to hold Mark's gaze. "I know you're *Nova Liberanti!* I know the Shadows have to be free! But please! Don't destroy the ASH! He's not ready to let it go!"

Gulping hard, Mark's hands felt cold for the first time in a while, the fire completely dead inside him. "Okay..." He panted, his heart raging in his chest. "Okay!" He shook off the wariness. "All right, what do you want to do?" He startled her, causing her to stare red-faced across the pale white room in surprise. Mark remained firmed, adapting his plan. "You're Shadow Hope, aren't you? You know what has to happen. Just tell me!"

Tearfully, Ocie's eyes shimmered and she managed a slight nod. "The shield..." she whispered. "That's what scares the Shadows. My dad needs to know it's not necessary for the Shadows to be safe. The walls are protected by the ASI. That can stay. That's all we need."

"Are you seriously—" Emilie gaped, her feet hovering off the floor. "I've been trying to hack into the shield forever. Are you telling me you know how to disable it?"

Chuckling, Ocie shook her head, drying away the last of her tears. "Not a clue."

Able to laugh as well, Mark ignited his hand in scarlet flames. "I think I have an idea of how to deal with it." Inhaling sharply, he put out the flames and looked to Emilie with a grin. "I'll go to the courtyard. You go to all the rooms and let the Shadows out. This is still their home, but they need to know it's not a prison. Sound good?"

With only the slightest hint of reluctance in her eyes, Emilie forgot about her need to escape and fly away. She nodded. "Got it!"

"What would you have me do?" Ocie asked.

Reaching out, Mark dropped a warm hand on her shoulder. "Stand by me." His assurance filled his soul with confidence, an excitement he had never known before. "You've given the Shadows hope. I need to give them their freedom."

"All right!" Emilie cheered, taking to the air, "Let's do this!" She couldn't wait for Ocie to open the door, tempted to take the key card out of her hand until the locks released and she zipped out like a comet, entering the Realm as she flew.

The shadows were long as the morning light streamed in the front window, and Mark could easily see the dark figure across the balcony as Emilie disappeared above them. Entering the Realm was just about pointless. In this light, it was impossible to hide. ASOs were in the halls, and thus far they hadn't been noticed.

"Get in the Realm!" Ocie snapped, grabbing Mark's hand tightly.

"They'll see my shadow," he protested.

"Just do it! I have clearance to be in the halls right now. You're supposed to be locked up." She winked, gently assuring him. He finally complied, and she let go of his hand. The Realm seemed different. He felt like he could see the light of morning, but he was mystified by all the light coming from Ocie's watery form, glistening, spreading hope everywhere she walked. Mark followed her closely, keeping himself in her shadow.

She rushed straight to the courtyard, passing two ASOs on the way, neither of whom spoke to her. She unlocked the door to the courtyard with her key, pushing it open to a flood of frigid October air. Mark left the Realm on the stairs. There was no one outside to catch him. At least, he was pretty sure. She didn't react when she saw he had reappeared, but looked up over the huge stone building and sent a powerful tone through the Realm.

She called the Shadows, and Mark knew when he heard her voice in his head, that they had all been able to hear the wave she sent out. She was incredibly powerful in the Realm, more experienced than Mark felt he would ever be. Taking his hand once more, Ocie dragged him along to the middle of the courtyard under the huge oak tree. They waited, and gradually, the confused Shadows appeared, streaming out of the small opening.

With the ASI still functioning, the courtyard was a dead end for them and vaguely, Mark could hear the outnumbered ASOs struggling to grab each of the Shadows. Mark stood as surely as he could, putting his hope in Ocie and his trust where it belonged. To the Shadows entering the courtyard, he looked strong. A powerful Shadow meant to save them, the perfect Shadow.

Mark couldn't hide his fears when he saw Kip in the little doorway. Rita supported him because he could barely stand on his own, and she had teleported him outside, carrying the IV stand with her. Mark panicked a little before the Shadows spread out enough to get close to him.

"Kip's going to be okay, right?" he murmured to Ocie.

She nodded surely. "He'll have to stay here, but my father will take care of him."

Still nervous, Mark winced hard, letting go of Ocie's hand as well as his fear. He didn't want to hurt Kip, but he wanted to know the secrets of the Shadows. He wanted to know who the Recluse was, and the reason why his mother grieved the Shadows. It was a vast ocean before him of questions and secrets that was dark like the Shadows and red like fears, and in the red sea was the gateway to freedom.

Mark gulped, hoping no one was looking as he swallowed down the last of his fears, accepting what was to come. "I'm ready," he said to fully convince himself.

Ocie laid her soft hand on his arm, hearing him and seeing his fears. "We are all Shadows," she whispered surely. Meaning together, as one, unified and perfect, the Shadow supported Mark. They did more than that—they believed in him.

On his right, Sil stepped closer to him, and from behind him in the air, Emilie readily watched after him. A calmness filled Mark, and in his heart, he felt the truth—this was his family, right here, whether it was in the past, present, or future, he would always be with them. Around him, many of the Shadows were unaware of what was going on, some were afraid, some were excited, but all of them trusted Mark.

Uncomfortably, Mark's hands formed into fists and he closed his eyes, stretching his Shadow and his power in the Realm. Mark wasn't fully sure what he had done but as he opened his eyes he saw before him ten billion futures and pasts, Shadows from all generations in his grasp. Mark's crimson eyes flared to bright cherry as they caught fire, he opened his fist, igniting his hand in scarlet flames.

He didn't know what else to do but rely on his Shadow, the instincts in his heart that told him to raise the fire above him and let it fly. He looked up to the ginger-bronze shield surrounding the courtyard and the alizarin star shooting up to meet with the oppressive power. Mark's eyes flashed in the second before it happened, but he tensed, jumping several paces back, startled as his fire impacted the shield.

Light burst in a wave horizontally over all the sky and the shield melted around them, stars fell from heaven sparkling with cyan and orange and giving off scents and sounds as they sprinkled on the Shadows. For a second, the sky went dark and the ward around the ASH exploded, sending bursts of flames throughout all the circuits sending the ASI through the walls.

The ground trembled as the explosions came from the ASH, destroying its upper level. Cyan mist burst from the veins in the ground and between the floors which conveyed Shadow Inhibitor, and they flew into the sky in spirals until the cloud of cyan light rushed into the ASH in a fine stream where it vanished. The falling stars touched the ground, and silence was all the Shadows could feel.

Above them, the Shadows could see blue clouds, untainted by the ginger-bronze color of the shield. They felt the sun, they heard the breeze, they breathed of freedom. Mark smiled to the sky at the sound of rejoicing in the Shadows. First, crying out through the Realm in their happiness and then with their voices. They sang about the joy in their hearts. Mark could not even fully comprehend the unity of the Shadows as they walked out of the boundaries freely.

Kimberly appeared from the ASH brandishing a crowbar loosely in her hand and a little smirk on her face as she declared with many other Shadows to Mark, "You did it!"

Mark turned to her and his eyes widened seeing the crowbar. "What did you do?" he puzzled, a little amused by Kimberly's grin.

Her smile brightened. Just gazing a Mark brought her joy. To her, it was almost like her lost child was alive and triumphant. "I got my powers back!" she said, happily extending an open hand in front of her and displaying the dark mist she had used on Keller.

Mark tensed seeing it. He could feel its power and how it worked by looking at it. "Mind control!"

Seeming embarrassed, Kimberly let out an exaggerated sigh. "I tried using it on Keller to get control of all the doors, but after I knocked him out, he woke up too fast... so I just..." she hesitated tapping the crowbar in her hand. "He won't remember me for a while," she snickered.

"You did what!" Ocie wailed, fury stirring in her as she rushed inside to find her father.

"I see now..." he muttered and gently touched his heart, removing a dark orb from it. If Trust had given him the ability to defy the ASH, and Hope had named him *Nova Liberanti*, then the only one left was Love. "My second Shadow... It's not mine, it's yours."

Mark held out the black orb to her as Sil stepped closer to Mark puzzling, "If that Shadow isn't yours, how did you get it?" Sil asked.

Kimberly took it with a smile. "You are its vessel," she revealed calmly. "My powers were dormant, like yours Mark, but Shadow Love can never become dormant, so it came to you until you could activate my powers and return it to me."

Perplexed, Mark stepped back drawing his brows together. "I don't understand..." he gulped a little worriedly.

Kimberly gave a little laugh. "You will, eventually. But it's not just me. Can't you feel it? You've activated powers in many Shadows around you, even in yourself. Can you even begin to understand how powerful you are in the Realm?"

Mark shied away. "I have yet to understand a lot of things apparently…" he whispered, but then his eyes turned to Sil, Kip, and Emilie. "But first things first. You all have families out there. If there's anything I can do to help you find them, that's what I'll do next." Mark immediately looked to Emilie "You're my cousin so you can come home with me to meet your mom." He turned next to Sil. "And your family lives close to mine."

With this, Emilie smiled warmly. "Then let's go home," she suggested.

Nodding, Mark accepted this readily, home. He was going home. Sending a declaration in the Realm just as he had seen Ocie do, Mark called out, and a second later Rita teleported to his side. Mark laughed a little when she appeared. "Would you do me the favor of teleporting us back to New York?"

Rita poised herself with her hands on her hips, blaring in her thick Scottish accent, "I dinnae leave ya in that canyon. I cannae leave ya here!" At this the Shadows around her cackled brightly.

XXI
BRAIDED

Dropping to his knees, Kip collapsed in the grass, rolling onto his back and smiling at the blue sky far above. He wasn't safe unprotected by the shield, but he didn't care. The intense blue of the sky, untainted by bronze, overwhelmed all his senses.

A dark figure peered over him, and he beamed to himself like a little fallen star. "I can't leave…" he gasped up to Mark, barely able to find his breath.

Mark sat with him, throwing himself into the grass beside Kip, sighing peacefully. "Kimberly will be here to take care of you."

Nodding aimlessly, Kip closed his eyes. The warmth of the sun was almost nonexistent in the October air. "I'm going to find my family. It might take a while. I can't begin to know who they are, but I'll find them."

Sitting up quickly, Mark fretted over his friend even now. "Don't you know your last name? Wouldn't that be a good start?"

Chuckling, Kip shook his head without opening his eyes, "Not a clue. But I'm okay. I've got the Shadows after all."

"Are you sure you'll be okay?"

Pawing at the needle in his arm, Kip hummed quietly. The IV was like a ball and chain to his prison, but he didn't mind as long as it helped him recover. He didn't need to say anything, just having Mark beside him for a moment, too thankful to ruin the feeling. He was far from free, but the Shadows around him were finally released from the oppressive nature of the ASI.

Mark reluctantly rose to his knees when the Shadows gathered around him. Emilie and Sil both procured bags full of their few belongings, and Rita sat on the ground with a smile. "Ready to go?"

Sil had his leather projects fastened to his wrist and shoulder, and his hawk perched on his arm, but he didn't seem to have many possessions. Whereas, Emilie bundled up what clothes she wanted in a pillowcase. "Two hours ago!" she blared excitedly. "I would've left already if I had a single clue how to get there myself."

Rita chortled. "That's what ya have me for. I just need a memory or a picture in my head."

Mark patted Kip's shoulder. He didn't want to leave him like this, especially knowing without the ASI he was at a greater risk. He tried to stand and leave, but it was hard.

"Don't worry, Mark." Ocie approached, coming from the ASH. "I'll make sure he gets inside, and my dad can keep an eye on him."

A bitter taste welled in his mouth when Ocie knelt in the damp grass. No part of him could trust Keller, but Ocie put her faith in her father, and it was uncomfortable letting this go. Kip was in the ASH's hands, and Mark feared it would be a while before Kip was truly free. He forced himself to comply and trust Ocie, but rising to his feet was still like raising a mountain.

Rita nudged him playfully and offered him her hand. "And you'll still have me to drag ya around if ya wanna come back here."

Ocie neared Emilie with a slightly authoritative smile. "Be safe, okay." She grasped Emilie's shoulders and gave her a hug, in spite of how Emilie's gravity protested. With Emilie in her arms, she reached out to Sil, just touching the back of his hand to convey the same advice.

Realizing he was already holding Rita's hand, Mark tensed a little, the present warmth feeling startlingly natural. She held tightly when she offered her hand out to Emilie, and by extension Sil. Her power moved through them simply, like a low electricity, and with a snarky smile, Rita wrinkled her nose at Ocie. "Bye-bye. I'll be back later... or not. Who knows!"

A blast of green mist and a glimpse in the Realm flashed before Mark's eyes, and with the feeling of Rita's hand still within his own, Ocie vanished, and the front walkway of his home appeared. Everything was the same, and yet home couldn't feel more different. From the sidewalk, there were muddy scuffs along the ground, the lawn was ripped up, and Mark could still tell where he stood when he fought Ocie.

The spinning rock appeared in his gut again, and he couldn't compel his legs to move forward. Rita seemed to see it and squeezed his hand. "What's wrong?"

He gulped down his nerves. "She let them in yesterday. She got rid of me the moment she figured out I was a Shadow." He clenched Rita's hand tightly, reluctant to push himself onward. "I just... don't know how she'll feel about this."

Rita gave him a firm nudge with her fist in the shoulder. "If it makes ya feel any better, I'm still procrastinating about going back home. I ran away. I'm nae sure they even think I'm alive."

"I'll go with you, if you want," Mark offered, attempting to get out of facing his own family.

Snickering, Rita pushed him from behind. "Only if you do this, right now! And you cannae forget, I'm here for you!"

Able to smile weakly as his feet gave way for about three steps, Mark nudged her back playfully. "Fine, fine." There was something admittedly nice about having a friend who could flee at any moment and take him with her. In the uncertainty, he liked how sure Rita was in her Shadow.

Getting close enough to the door to grasp the doorknob was incredibly difficult, but without knocking he turned it and prayed. The house was clean in spite of all that had happened, diffused light streamed in through the curtains, and all was quiet. It wasn't particularly early in the morning, and yesterday, his mother had been out and about, so Mark found it peculiar that she didn't rush out at the sound.

Sil sent Winter to fly off into the sky, not daring to take her indoors as he and Emilie stepped in behind him. They glanced about awkwardly, and Mark felt every one of his footsteps resonating through the carpet despite how light-footed he was.

It was odd since the door was unlocked, but no one was moving in the house. A little deeper in the hall, Mark heard the TV on in June's room, and he figured his little sister was already up playing video games and had been since the unholy hours.

"Stay here…" he murmured to the Shadows.

With an unruly step, Mark brushed his bangs out of his face, the horrid red strand blocking his view in the dark hall. He slipped back to his parents' bedroom, listening through the sound of roaring engines in June's racing game for any sign of his mother. The door was opened a crack, darkness between the hall and the master bedroom intermingling and making it very hard for Mark to see.

He pushed the door gently, and it didn't make a single sound. Gulping hard, Mark parted his lips, "M-mom?"

A shuddering sob resounded from the bed sheets, and Mark's face drained of color. Marissa laid tangled up in the sheets with a snowstorm of tissues. Crying through the night, she had closed herself off, and hearing his voice was unreal. She bolted up, not sure what to believe until she looked on his face and saw those crimson glowing eyes.

"Mark?" she addressed him, her voice crackly and heartbroken. There was an emptiness in her arms, she cradled her own blankets as if it were a child she was grieving. Ever so slightly, she raised her arms, beckoning him closer without words. Mark knew in the tiniest movements, she was desperate to hold her baby again.

Running, Mark hurled himself at the bed, throwing his arms around his mother and tightening to let her cry. She whimpered at his strength, but even when he tried to talk, to figure out how she had possibly chosen to let him go in the first place, she shushed him.

"Not yet!" she stopped him from pulling away. "I just want to hold you a little longer."

The silence grated on Mark's psyche like sandpaper, self-conscious of the Shadows alone in the living room or likely eavesdropping. He wanted to say something, but every time words came to his lips, they vanished. Something in his mother's shaking hands, and her shuddering breath was undeniable. Mark wasn't just her child returned to her, he was something more. Just being there for her wasn't enough.

Gradually, she let herself be happy. She fought to dry her tears, but she wouldn't let go of him. "I'm sorry," she got out among the blubbering, "I'm sorry for protecting you."

"What?" Mark gasped in the darkness. He fought to pull away to look into his mother's eyes when she spoke.

"I should have never hidden the truth from you," she breathed. "I always suspected you were a Shadow. I kept you from your own kind, from... learning about who you were. And I want you to know, I never let you go to get rid of you. I was afraid, and I didn't want you to hurt someone on accident."

Trying to accept this, Mark faked a smile. "Too late for that," he chuckled. "It took an hour for me to hurt Sil." He was lucky he hadn't done worse to Sil, and that the ice Shadow was now his friend.

"How did you get back?" Marissa asked, the words between them seeming to be enough for her, but Mark knew it wasn't.

Relaxed about it, Mark drifted away, seated on the side of her bed to avoid the awkwardness, "Rita, she teleported me, Sil, and Emilie here. They're waiting in the living room."

Her eyes growing worried, Marissa rose a little, gathering some of the spent tissues to throw them away. "Just three of them? What happened to the others, and the one who was sick. Are they okay?"

Mark helped her, switching on the bedside lamp and pulling her wastebasket closer. "They're fine. Most of them are still at the ASH and they're going to start looking for their families, but Sil and Emilie both have families up here." He gathered up a few of the white tissues as he spoke and tossed them away.

They heard an elated scream coming from the living room and both Mark and his mother's shoulders arched, assessing for a moment that it was June. Chuckling, Mark drew away. "Well, June-bug found them. Can I get some breakfast going for everyone?"

Marissa nodded, brief and emotionless, masking all else. Mark took the prompt, hurrying out to the hall, but turning on the light in his mom's room before he left. June caught his eye almost immediately. She raced around the three Shadows and her brown eyes twinkled when she spied her brother coming from the dark hallway.

She lunged at him, jumping into the air and nearly strangling him as she wrapped her arms around his neck. Mark let out a shriek as she slid off, but he made an effort to kneel to give her a proper hug. Acutely reminded of how much his back was aching, he tried to smile despite the pain. "It's good to see you too, June-bug!"

"Why do you keep leaving?" she pleaded, whining innocently.

Ruffling her messy brown hair, Mark stood slowly. "I'm not going anywhere now. You're stuck with me."

Not in the least disappointed, she scurried over to the Shadows and latched on to Sil. Mark stifled a cackling laugh at the look on Sil's face when June threw her arms around him. He was completely unsure what to do with himself, his arms hovering above the six-year-old confused and unwilling to touch her.

"You guys hungry?" Mark asked the girls.

Emilie dropped her pillowcase on the floor and imposed herself on the sofa, floating over to it. "Of course. I haven't eaten a full meal in three days other than some bread rolls," she complained as she tucked her skinny legs up to her chest.

Rita moved to join her, but Sil stood awkwardly in the middle of the room with a six-year-old attached to his waist. Mark left them, scouring the kitchen for breakfast until he acknowledged this was the first time he'd been alone in days. In the fridge, he discovered a roll of sausage and a half-depleted selection of brown eggs. He wasn't a great cook, but breakfast was his forte.

He couldn't be alone anymore with the Shadows near and the Realm so loud in his ears. It wasn't just a quiet place he'd seep into in his sleep anymore. It was a communication device that the Shadows abused. Sil had been right too, he was so much stronger outside of the ASH, his presence constantly in the back of Mark's mind.

Rattling the pans in the bottom cupboard to get two big ones, Mark set them upon the stove, fretting. As he emptied the roll of sausage into the smaller pan and began to beat up the rest of the eggs, he felt his heart flip-flopping and all his fear spinning around in his head. He didn't want to be alone but listening to the Realm didn't help.

"How'd it go?" Rita appeared abruptly in the corner of his eye.

Scrambling back into the corner of the kitchen, Mark slammed himself into the counter. "W-why do you gotta sneak up on me?"

"Sorry, Sil just said he can sense how freaked out you are."

Sighing, Mark rubbed his face and returned to the stove. "I'm fine. I just psyched myself out. I was expecting the worst and it…" he hesitated, losing himself in the browning breakfast sausage.

"That's good, I suppose," Rita hummed and stepped back, finding herself leaning against the kitchen table. Silence enveloped the room as her eyes wandered, watching Mark cook, picking out the various dusty decorations on the walls, and the tins of tea on the kitchen table.

Mark glanced back at her as she picked up one of the tea tins and shook it gently. She laughed. "Darjeeling, this stuff used to be my favorite."

Mark acquired a sideways smile. "Yeah, that's my dad's favorite. He gets it from international shops in the city."

She set the cylindrical tin down. "What city? Is it anything like Culpeper?"

Chuckling, Mark shook his head. "Nope, New York City. It's like fifty miles away."

"That's where we are!" Rita gawked. "Why didn't you tell me we were so close?"

"I assumed you knew. I said New York, didn't I?"

"You did," Rita hummed. "I just didn't realize you lived so close."

"Fifty miles is not close," he murmured before he realized how relative that was for someone who could teleport literally anywhere she wanted.

Rita beamed, an ecstasy burning through her rosy cheeks. "I've seen pictures and heard stories of the big cities."

"You could go explore there, if you like," Mark suggested, turning back from the stove to see how excited she was. "I can tell you're dying to get out there. You've got the whole world now. What are you going to do with it?"

Able to laugh, Rita sat on the table. "I suppose I should make a list. I definitely want to check out NYC. I can already check the Grand Canyon off my list, but it would be great to go back there too."

"I could give you some suggestions for Brooklyn if you want. That's where my dad works. But he's in Colorado right now for some business thing." Mark awkwardly shoved the sizzling meat across the pan, trying not to presume to know what she wanted.

"You could come with me."

Mark's eyes widened, scared to turn around because of the tone in her voice. Why would she suggest that? She knew he had family here. He couldn't just leave. But then, it occurred to him that Rita could be anywhere at any time. He could forget about the hours of travel itself. They could be there instantly, without an adult to drive them or traffic to worry about.

He reluctantly found her emerald eyes, content and warm, a smile on her freckled cheeks that invited him to adventure. "Not now, obviously," she amended, "but maybe after Sil and Emilie are with their families. Once you get a chance to settle down with your own family, make sense?"

Her accent seemed to lighten around him, the thick Scottish tones became easier to understand, and Mark admitted, he liked it. The little touch of her foreign nature pervading her posture and her power. It was fitting. But he was still confused that someone with the power to be so distant would want to stay close to him of all people.

"Sure," he forced, just to get it out, then returned his attention to the pans. He got the eggs going, certain they wouldn't take long.

"Can I help?" Rita offered abruptly, teleporting to his side rather than walking the short distance.

"Plates?" He finally succeeded in not jumping out of his shoes when she teleported, and he pointed to the cupboard above the corner. Rita had to stretch up on her toes to the shelf, and as she came down with six plates, she stumbled a little, nudging Mark again. He laughed and nudged her back.

With little instruction, Rita took the plates out to the small dining room table, and Mark followed her with the pans hot off the stove. "Food's ready," he declared as they came into view of the living room.

He stopped short when he saw the Shadows. June had managed to drag Sil to the floor where he compliantly allowed her to play with his long, ice-white hair. "June!" Mark gawked. "What are you doing?"

June shot up to her feet holding the last two inches of Sil's hair woven into a snake-like braid. "What does it look like!" She tied off the end of the braid with a little blue elastic and placed it over Sil's shoulder caringly. "There you go."

Sil tolerated her, but Mark could tell by the look in his eyes as he ran his fingers along the braid that he liked it. Scoffing at his sister's perpetually snarky attitude, Mark put his hands on his hips. "You can't just braid a guy's hair!"

She stood up to him, despite their age gap, she fully understood her only sibling and loved getting under his skin. "Can and did! Just look at his hair. It's over two feet long and perfect!"

Sil gently took June's hands off him and rose, sweetly patting her shoulder before muttering, "Relax, you don't have to defend me." He shot a piercing golden glare at Mark.

Forcing himself to let it go, Mark scoffed at Sil dismissively, but as he turned, he spied his mother finally approaching from the hall. "Is something burning?" she muttered, scanning the room and expecting to see smoke.

Rita stepped up beside Mark without a teleport and nudged him in the side again, jeeringly. "Just breakfast," she assured for him, simultaneously jabbing at Mark's fire Shadow.

"Ah." She nodded, seeing the hot food set on the dining room table. "Remind me your name?"

Straightening her back, she adopted a beaming smile. "Rita, Shadow Teleport."

Emilie flitted through the air over Mark's head towards the food, selfishly digging in, but June beat her to the chase. "And what about her?" Marissa asked, gesturing to the girl with her feet high in the air while she loaded up her plate.

Mark chuckled at the touch of sarcasm in his mom's voice and scurried over to drag Emilie to the floor. "This..." he hummed, finding it surprisingly easy to pull her through the air now that she had food, "is Emilie Meyvise!"

Her jaw dropping open, Marissa gaped at Emilie, assessing her up and down before covering her mouth. "Meyvise? That's im—you're Hellen's daughter!"

Stubbornly, Emilie kept her feet off the floor, but a bitterness appeared in her face. Mark saw it and let his cousin go, allowing her to sink slightly. As much as he didn't want to pry, the Realm declared that Emilie was incredibly hesitant to meet her mother, and she had a touch of resentment in her stance.

"Well, say something," Marissa pled abruptly, just happy to meet her niece.

Emilie's eyes flashed, a dangerous look that startled Mark's mother. "Who is she to you?"

A little startled, Marissa forced, "She's my sister. I was pregnant with Mark the same time she was pregnant with you." She seemed a little more taken aback by the need to relive that nine-months of her life, than to justify her relationship with her sister. Being pregnant together was the only positive memory Mark had ever heard about his aunt.

Sil inched his way toward the table, his braid dangling over his chest and his shoulder arched awkwardly with the new weight. He took a seat with a starkly straight back and when he attempted to help himself to food, June rushed around the table to sit beside him. The faintest smile appeared on Sil's lips when she did this, and Mark tried not to ruin how adorable it was that his sister had latched on to the Shadow he had been so terrified of.

Joining them on the opposite side of the table, Mark cleared his throat. "Do you want to go see your family today?" he offered a bit too excitedly. Rita appeared in the seat beside him, and once more, she scared the wits out of him. Why couldn't she just walk?

Sil swallowed anxiously, and with much debate inside himself, he mustered softly, "No." Cringing a little, Sil refused to meet eyes with Mark's surprised expression. "I have no idea what I'm going to say. I want some time to think it over."

"Fair enough," Mark shrugged, serving up his plate.

At last, Marissa took the head of the table, but she didn't fill a plate. "Do you have any clue who your parents are?" she wondered flatly, not terribly confident in receiving an answer.

In the midst of a half-nod, Sil was interrupted by Mark's overzealous nature. "He's Zachary Addison. We found out he has a—" Sil kicked Mark in the shin under the table impossibly hard, and Mark winced with an open mouth, feeling as if he had been stabbed in the leg with an ice pick. Effectively shut up, he had to check to make sure Sil hadn't shredded his leg.

Marissa hardly took note of the violence under the table. "Oh, wow, Arianne too..." her eyes fell tender, missing the brief instant Sil seemed surprised by her reaction. She nodded to herself slowly, contemplating the information. "I can't say you look a lot like them," she mused based on his hair and eyes, "but Arianne did have a Shadow who'd be about your age."

Mark watched Sil acutely, pausing in between bites to see Sil's eyes flare to cyan. A stir of enthusiasm in his posture, Sil's lips parted in anticipation, no one could be sure, but he had hope. He was getting excited, Mark could tell.

"I'm going to have to call the Addisons to see if you could come over," Marissa rambled, massaging her temple, "and I'm going to have to call Jan."

Mark's limbs stiffened. In an instant, his appetite was gone. His back ached like he had been struck again. "When is—" he cleared his throat, "when is Dad coming home?"

Stumbling, Marissa got up from the table and headed toward the kitchen. "He was supposed to get back later this week. In all this craziness, I still haven't got the chance to talk to him." She stopped at the coffee pot, tiredly setting it to brew since she filled it the night before on habit.

Mark crossed his arms over his chest and collapsed against the back of his chair, groaning. His mother was right. In all this craziness, he had hardly gotten a moment to think about all the stresses with his father. Between the fried laptop, the Shadow thing, and all of January's ticks, Mark had put all of it out of his mind.

"What's wrong?" Rita wondered, a little startled by Mark's sour attitude.

Heaving a sigh, Mark seethed. "Nothing... my dad's just not all there." The disdain in his voice shocked everyone at the table except June, who obliviously combined her eggs and sausage on her plate.

Marissa returned with a cup of coffee after several uncomfortable minutes. "January has very little memory of his life before he married me." She stirred the mug as she sat at the table, cautiously sipping the black coffee and ignoring the heat.

That's an understatement, Mark thought. His dad had no memory of anything before he was eighteen, no family, no homes, and a twinge of an accent in his voice, which had all but diminished. He was distant, just trying to take care of his family, and primarily working himself to death in Brooklyn.

Still Mark grimaced. Sometimes he wished he could rely on his father for everything from homework to moral support, but he was never there. Sometimes he wondered why his mother even married the amnesiac. Even though everyone in the household knew about it, no one talked about it like this, leaving both Mark and his mom in unspoken frustration.

Marissa pressed her lips together, now refusing to call January altogether. "Your father will be coming home soon enough. We'll tell him then..."

"Are you sure that's a good idea?" Mark asked.

Marissa shook her head. "Probably not."

June finished off her plate and picked it up, responsibly taking it away and offering to take Sil's with her, but not Emilie's or anyone else's.

"June," Marissa reprimanded her lovingly, "why don't you take everyone's plates to the dishwasher?"

The girl grumbled but complied. In spite of her spunk, she was ultimately far more good-natured than Mark was.

Mark spotted Sil jittering nervously. Even being cryokinetic, Sil was visibly shivering, unsettled with the knowledge that very soon he would be meeting his family for the first time. He had changed since Mark first met him. He had lowered his guard, and seeing him nervous was an entirely new trait.

Mark caught Sil ritualistically pulling his white braid over his shoulder and proceed to fiddle with it. Suddenly, Sil jumped, realizing what he was doing. He had just fully brushed his hair out, if he started braiding again his hair would look exactly as it had. The change in Sil desired clean, well-kempt hair, not a mass of poorly weaved braids.

"What?" Mark muttered seeing his fiddling.

Sil ran his fingers back through the long white spider silk to unweave the braid as he grumbled, "Breaking the habit... it's hard," he admitted.

Mark knitted his brows together. "So, you braid your hair when you're nervous?"

Sil shrugged. "Nervous, cold, hot, irritated, injured... I actually think I started because of Kimberly soon after my run in with Kip. It's sort of a coping mechanism." He smoothed out the spindly strands on the end of the tassel.

With breakfast cleaned up, the five of them moved to the couch, already trying to make themselves at home which was easier when June went straight for the video game console. Mark caught himself inhaling to comment along the lines of the odd possibility of Sil getting cold, but his thought was stopped as he noticed June eyeing Sil up. "Why is your hair so long?" she asked out of nowhere.

Sil tensed a little and eyed her in return, confused.

"'Cause I never cut it," he stated flatly in a somewhat raised voice, "What's wrong with it?"

June grinned a little sadistically. "Mark doesn't like cutting his hair either, but Mom makes him keep it short…"

Mark felt the need to scratch his head while his little sister spoke of him. It was true. He protested, ardently, whenever his mother insisted his thick black ocean found itself too long. It was on his neck now, and his bangs had gotten long. It wouldn't be long before his mother started hounding him about it, especially with this conversation. She heard everything. Nothing escaped her ears.

June giggled seeing Mark fretting. "And he gets more red strikes when he's stressed!" she added gleefully to irritate him.

"I do not!" Mark snapped predictably.

June nodded eagerly. "Yes, you do! Last July you didn't have the one on top of your head. It's from our trip to Luray. We had to stay in a hotel, and you freaked out whenever you had to go in the elevator!"

Mark's eyes widened as did the Shadows'. "Shut up, June!" he hoarsely demanded trying to hide his fear of elevators from everyone. It wasn't a fear… he just didn't feel safe.

Sil chuckled in his low mocking laugh. "I bet there's a story behind every red strike…" he mused intrigued and relying on the historian for an explanation. Mark sank into the couch, embarrassed, but Sil laughed, the smile warming his heart and allowing Mark to lighten up.

He was able to seep into conversation to help June set up a game and to show Sil how to use the controller so he could play with her. Sil was terrible at it, of course, but he seemed to like playing with June. Rita plopped onto the couch next to Mark and he perked up, glancing around to point out, "Where's Emilie?"

"Spreading her wings," Sil mused, half-focused on June's game. "Does she not have the right to use her powers?" Forfeiting the game, he turned to Mark. "She's been waiting all her life to have the freedom to fly wherever she wants. She'll be back when she wants to."

"When did she leave?" Mark asked, worried on instinct but not sure why.

"Obviously, you weren't paying attention," Sil jabbed at him. "Don't think about it too hard. She can handle herself."

Mark tried not to scoff. Emilie had scrawny legs and had been sheltered all her life. How on Earth could she handle herself other than running away?

"I should go," Rita murmured from beside him, a darkness in her voice as she forced herself to entertain the thoughts of facing her family again.

Mark's crimson eyes flashed with panic. No part of him wanted her to leave, apart from being quick transportation back to the ASH and Kip, he liked having her around. Also, she was the only one keeping him from freaking out in the presence of his own mother. He wanted to protest, but all he choked out was "Why?"

Hugging her arm, Rita pinched herself. "Emilie is taking advantage of her powers. She's doing what she's always wanted. I need to talk to my family. I need to at least let them know I'm okay. I mean, I'm not like the other Shadows. I've been gone four years; they must think I'm dead."

Seething inside, Mark gritted his teeth. She had a fair point, Sil and Emilie had every reason to be nervous to meet their families, but Rita already knew hers.

"I'll come back," she promised, "and there's always the Realm. You can talk to me in there if you want me to teleport over."

Still wanting to cling to her, Mark frowned, but nodded. She had every right to get out there and be free. He couldn't hold her down, just like Sil wouldn't hold Emilie back. "Be safe, okay?"

Smirking, Rita nodded, "Of course, and I'll be back to let you know how it goes!"

Even beside each other on the couch, Mark felt her drifting away. Sil seeming perfectly content to watch them from the floor in front of the small TV with June. His mother had drifted off with her coffee cup, and once more, Mark felt uncomfortable being alone. He needed to be with the Shadows, to use his Shadow, and to refine it. Even outside the ASH, he knew how important that was.

One last time, Rita nudged him in the side, elbowing him nice and hard, before she instated her power and teleported from the couch, leaving him behind. All at once, Mark felt it was wrong that they had left the ASH. Keller had been right in some ways. In spite of the last few days, fighting to get out, Mark wanted to go back.

XXII
FAMILY

November 1, 2030

"Press Start" blinked like a heartbeat across the screen, bright and revitalizing. It was welcoming, but Mark wasn't sure if he wanted to sink into it. The controller felt uncomfortable in his hands, even though it had only been a few days. He put on his over-ear headset, and quietly connected them to the TV in his room, never feeling more awkward in his life.

Beside him on an air mattress, Sil had been given space in the cramped, dark bedroom, where he slept soundly. Mark had had people spend the night before, mostly Gary, but it was beyond unnerving to have Sil in his room. The ice Shadow made the air frigid to compensate for the way Mark's dark blinds intensified the heat in the tiny room.

Mark wished he could have been asleep right now, but between being too nervous, and unusually cold, his unsettled stomach woke him before the dawn. It wasn't the first time he had gotten up to game this early. When he had his laptop, he would occasionally stay online all night until his mom caught onto that.

He logged in to check who was online first, maybe a few international players, but it was unlikely Gary was up right now. None of the friends' icons were lit, and he resolved to just play a mind-numbing first-person shooter with the com-generated firefight settings on extreme. The waves of NPCs to battle would keep him busy, and within his headphones, he could keep the volume up as high as he wanted.

For an hour, all he cared about was making sure he didn't miss an ammo drop as he fought the mindless waves of weak grunts and drones that were no match for his maxed-out character.

Round after round, he saw nothing and heard nothing real. It was easier to sink back into than he expected, and after his time in the ASH, none of his habits had been broken. He wasn't happy though, far from it. He still had to face his father, to show him the destroyed laptop, and to tell him he was a Shadow. With as quickly his mom had sent him away, he didn't want to think about how his dad would react.

Abruptly, Mark spotted a dark figure sitting up in the middle of the room and he jumped, pausing his game and shifting back on his bed to see Sil awake. Unfortunately, Sil's hearing must have been keener than he expected. Sil scratched his head tiredly through the loose strands falling free from his braid, which had migrated around his neck like a rope.

"Oh, sorry!" Mark apologized too quickly. "Was I too loud?" he asked with the big headphones around his neck.

Sil shook his head, partially aware of how crazy his hair had become through the night. He attempted to smooth it down, but the effort did little. "What time is it?" he groaned, trying to find some light through the windows.

Mark checked the time by hitting a button on his control so that the numbers displayed on the TV. "Six fifty-five."

"What are you doing up?" Sil asked, still rubbing his face.

"Couldn't sleep," he said in short.

"Same," Sil forced, staring about the dark room at the vague silhouettes of the closet door and the dresser.

Mark closed out of the game but left the TV on for the light. "Are you nervous about today?"

Sil stared into his lap, forming an intricate snowflake in his hands. He didn't have to say anything for Mark to know he was. Warily, he knitted his fingers together around the snowflake, fretting inside. "What if they don't recognize me?" A thousand fears whirled about in his head. "I've seen them in visions. I know I'll recognize them, but I don't know how I'm going to convince them it's me."

His fingers were shaking a little, and even in the darkness, Mark could see it. "I just keep thinking about what your mom said yesterday, about..." he swallowed hard, struggling to get the words out, "...how I don't look like them."

Mark forced a chuckle to lighten the air. "That's just your white hair." Somehow, Sil looked up to meet eyes with him and Mark made himself be serious. "You look like your dad. You've got his eyes, his scowl, and you're taller than me, so you've probably got his height."

Hope so strong and young appeared in Sil's face, he lit up at the description. "You're sure?"

Nodding firmly, Mark set his feet over the side of his bed. "I've known Mr. Addison all my life, and when you first said your name was Addison, I saw it instantly. And if your dad doesn't recognize you, your mom definitely will."

"Why?" Sil insisted a little despondently.

"Because mothers are psychic!"

Sil laughed, utterly perplexed by how serious Mark said it. "Really?" He raised a brow.

"I'm dead serious. Once my mom has had some coffee, she can read my mind from across the room. I can't get anything past her!"

Able to smile, Sil pulled his braid over his shoulder. "I wish I had known them all this time, and had real parents, not just Keller and Kimberly, and the Shadows."

Mark fell silent, letting their uncomfortable first-impressions dissolve away. Sil was far from impervious and soulless, refining his Shadow so young was a mask to live up to an unattainable desire. The Shadows were never enough for Sil. All he wanted was his family. At least, that was what Mark could guess right now. His knowledge of Sil's heart evolved with every hour, but he had a feeling he'd never fully understand him. For the time being, that was okay.

∽◑∾

As morning arrived, Sil started his day by retying his braid as neatly as possible then heading outside to call down his hawk. He sensed Mark spying on him through the front window, but he clung to Winter, cradling her in his arms and spreading a light frost over her wings as he turned back.

"Is it all right if I bring her inside?" he asked Marissa in the doorway. The woman nodded, standing aside as Sil entered, allowing the huge bird to climb up on his shoulder and perch there. He told himself he was ready, but he was certain no amount of mental preparedness would settle the knot in his stomach.

The morning inched by, and Sil panicked inside when he heard Marissa giving the Addisons a call. She didn't tell them the truth, only mentioning that Mark was coming by with June, and that he had some friends with him. The half-truth made his nervousness worse. He skipped breakfast, and he waited on the couch for Marissa to get June ready to leave. Emilie seemed to already be part of the family, terrorizing June and startling Marissa with how flippantly she floated around, using her Shadow.

She barely touched the ground for more than a few seconds at a time and was often close to the ceiling. Sil leaned back into the couch with his pet, stroking her feathers as she tolerated his affection. Meanwhile Mark, inhaling breakfast across from Sil, seemed to be enjoying the nervousness wrought across Sil's face.

June got together warm clothes, a coat, and a bike helmet and scrambled out the kitchen door into the garage.

Chomping at the bit to leave, June pushed the Shadows along, urging them to follow, and Marissa waved them off at the door. Sil was a little surprised that Marissa seemed so relaxed to let her two children out into the street. He wasn't sure how long the walk was, but the idea of a six-year-old with only her big brother as a chaperone to walk alone, worried him.

Mark pointed out the house when it came into view, only a few blocks from the Halo's, and as they drew nearer, Sil's anxiety grew more and more. June happily pedaled along in her little purple bike along the sidewalk, taking no note of her brother walking behind her, and Emilie flying up by Sil's shoulder.

He could barely walk forward without Emilie holding his arm and pushing him along and kept a fiddling finger underneath the edge of his arm guard. He was very thankful for Emilie. She was always there for him, either as the object of his irritation or a nice presence to be around. Whether through violence or calm words, Emilie was his closest friend.

Sil stopped in his tracks when he could make out the green front door and stared at the house for a few moments. The siding of the house was sky blue, with a small concrete porch. It had gardens all around, and one very large bush at the end of the driveway, which was bright red from the cold season. Also, Sil noted the garage door was sitting open displaying a set of family's bikes. He didn't know why but that calmed him some as if the family's openness was evident in this.

Mark pushed Sil ahead of the group, nudging him to step up the front porch. He dragged his feet, paralyzed at the metal door. He wasn't worried. He tried to tell himself to calm down, but he couldn't formulate any thoughts other than terror.

He nervously pulled his long braid over his shoulder, draping the snake-like rope in front of him. Inhaling deeply, he raised his hand as it clenched into a fist. He hesitated once more, and then knocked.

A dog barked almost the instant Sil's fist hit the door. Winter took off for the sky, and Sil jumped back into Mark, shuddering at the sound, but he didn't move as much as he wanted to. The dog was a puppy, he could tell just by hearing it as it barked on and on, until finally someone hushed it. A man opened the door, to greet June and Mark, but when he saw Sil, he stopped.

He stared, perplexed, and caught off guard, then he finally spoke softly. "Can I help you?"

His eyes widen and petrified, Sil felt his heart stop and twist up in his chest. That was his father! He swallowed hard, past the lump in his throat. "Are you Mr. Addison?"

The man frowned nervously. "I am." He spotted Mark and June standing behind the white-haired young man and relaxed slightly.

"André, are you going to just stand there or let Mark and June in?" a woman called from the powder room at the entry of the hall.

André hesitated a moment, then stepped aside out of the doorway, gesturing for them to come in. June hurried into the house and quickly found an almost-two-year-old child playing on the floor in the kitchen.

Mr. Addison stared at the three strange teenagers as they entered his house, a wondering expression on his face. "Mark..." he eyed the boy skeptically, "who are your friends?"

Sil glared at Mark hatefully, making his golden eyes flare icy blue, but he still said nothing. Mark swallowed, seeing Sil's ire made him act rashly.

"This is Sil, he—"

Sil elbowed Mark in the side harshly, silencing Mark who hugged his ribs, wincing.

Sil met eyes with Mr. Addison, hiding the flare of his golden eyes to not scare him. "Where is Mrs. Addison?" At this point, Sil lost sight of anything he had rehearsed in his head.

The man turned a skeptical downward glare at him and stepped away toward the hall. "Arianne..." he said, but the next few things he said were indistinct to the Shadows. Sil had a moment to glance about the room to get a bearing on his surroundings. The living room, dining room, and kitchen were open in a large, welcoming home, and to the right of the door was a staircase and balcony overlooking the expanse of the white interior. Sil could vaguely see bedroom doors in the halls upstairs, but his gaze was called away as a woman approached him.

She carried an overflowing basket of laundry hot out of the dryer which she plopped down on the living room sofa, offering Sil only a sideways glance. "Who are you?" she asked sharply as she began to fold the laundry.

The three simple words struck at Sil like a mountain of ice landing on top of him. The disdain in her voice terrified him and it became clear that starting by asking for her was a bad idea. Now he wanted Mark to talk for him, but he had already shut the poor idiot up. "My name is... Silverstonarellena," the words felt thick in his mouth like honey. On a whim he found himself adding, "Shadow Frost."

The two adults perked up, staring directly at him with glaring, brutal gazes. It hurt, Sil wanted to shirk back, but Mark stayed behind him, holding him firm. He didn't know why that comforted him. Arianne and André stood fast. It felt like they towered over him, and revealing he was a Shadow made them terrified. He could see it in their faces and feel it in his heart, they were sizing him up to push him out, to lock the doors, and call the police.

Sil blew through half-closed lips, forcing his heart to stop racing. He didn't know anything about them, he couldn't assume so much. "But..." speaking now was painful, "My real name is... Zachary."

He closed his eyes and winced just as Arianne tensed, dropping the piece of laundry back into the basket. Sil flinched as she looked him over, at his long white hair, his golden eyes, and the scars on his face. Hurriedly, she took two steps closer to him, hesitating and debating in her heart as Sil leaned away.

She turned her gaze to his right hand, watching as he clenched it shut and faintly blue ice spread across it. Abruptly, she lunged at him, grabbing his wrist and pulling it up to her face. The woman stared deeply into his pale fingers. She tugged him closer, and with a forceful but gentle grip, she guided his hand toward her heart.

Sil yanked away terrified, but her vise-like hand tightened on his. She wouldn't release him no matter how hard he fought, but she closed her eyes when a rush of cold from his Shadow flowed through her.

"When you were a baby, you did this to me..." she said quietly.

André jumped forward. "Aria, you mean, it's the same feeling?" Sil took the opportunity to draw back and stopped using his Shadow, but Arianne held his wrist firm.

"Do it again, freeze your hand." Arianne demanded eagerly, startling Sil, but he complied, so that it turned blue with frost. "Yes..." she whispered exhilarated. "A winter breeze. It's exactly the same feeling!"

Sil wrenched his hand away, pulling back abruptly, but before he could ask, or say a single word, André took him by the shoulders, shocked disbelief in his face. His eyes dashed about Sil's features, his Shadow traits, his sharp chin and cheeks, and dark brow. Sil's thoughts scattered back to what Marissa had said, he didn't look anything like the Addisons. This fear made him doubt every hope in André's eyes.

"Zachary!" André got out in a cracking voice, though mostly breath before he tightly thrust his arms around Sil, embracing him to never let him go again. "My son!"

Sil trembled as the touch of another restrained him. He didn't want anything to touch him or hold him back, but then André's words ripped through him, ringing through his head, and he let go of every emotion he hid in his heart, letting it pour out. This was his father holding tightly to the son he had lost. He had a family, a mother and a father who had both missed him and recognized him instantly, and he had a home.

His hands trembled, drifting up to clench around his father's back and hold him as long as he could. The burns on his chest and face stung as they pressed against his father's body, but that pain was worth every second to simply hold his father in his arms. It wasn't agony that pained Sil's skin, it was joy! Joy, writhing throughout his being! Joy, overflowing through his eyes as tears! Joy, that stung his face as the tears dripped down along his burns.

André, his father, guided his shoulders suddenly to stare into his face which was level with his own, and he laughed, still disbelieving that his son had returned. His father released him and directed Sil to his mother embracing her as well, renewing the joy from the pain of his burns.

He froze his lips as he kissed his mother on her cheeks and froze his hands while they were wrapped around her. Then a new feeling came over him, a feeling he had never felt before, even among the Shadows, one that made his heart feel as if it were going to explode, releasing emotions he had never felt, the feeling of being whole!

"Girls! Come down here!" André shouted suddenly. Before Sil could jump away skittishly, a pair of girls scurried out from their room and nearly threw themselves over the balcony to see the open foyer. Sil's eyes fixated on them, a pair of fair-faced girls with icy blonde hair, not white like his own, but close enough.

They rushed down the stairs to their father as André placed his big hands on the back of Sil's shoulders, presenting him. "Marlo... Marie, this is your brother, Zachary."

Sil couldn't tell Marlo from Marie, and it occurred to him that Mark had mentioned they were twins. He tried to smile at them, but it was impossible.

One of the girls raised an eyebrow. "You mean, he's a Shadow?" she said as if Sil's existence was a story shared fondly through the family.

Uneasily, he made himself respond. "I am... I'm Shadow Frost, I can..." He hesitated at the sight of their wide eyes. "...make ice and control it." He thought to demonstrate with a little snowflake, one of the intricate ones he loved to form, but somehow it felt like his Shadow was completely out of his control.

"How old are you?" the other one asked, stepping on her sister's foot.

"Fourteen," he answered easily, and his sister nodded as if another detail from the story had been confirmed.

"Mark," André puzzled, staring at the awkward boy in the doorway. Sil laughed at Mark's complacent posture in the foyer, unsure whether to step in or keep his mouth shut. He perked up when addressed. "How did you find him? He was taken to the ASH. How did you know?"

Mark managed a kind, innocent smile that Sil found himself admiring. As much as Sil liked to think Mark was an idiot, he was really just kind and a little naïve. "I found out I'm a Shadow too. They took me to the ASH, and I met Sil there. It took a while, but he told me his real name, and when I heard his last name was Addison, I knew instantly!"

André grinned warmly and gestured Mark over, giving him a brisk smack on the back. "We have you to thank for this then." Mark gasped at the pain and reeled over again giving Sil a good and honest laugh. Mark was totally winded as he glared at Sil, flaring his crimson eyes.

Arianne somehow had the emotional satisfaction to continue folding her pile of laundry. "So, when did your name get changed to Sil?"

Blushing, Sil drew closer to her, imposing himself on the sofa and quietly inviting Emilie to drift alongside him. "I-well... I made it up. I got everyone to call me Sil instead of Zack or something."

"Well," Arianne grinned, her cheeks turning red like his as she placed a folded shirt upon the couch beside him, "would you like us to call you Sil?"

Waiting for Emilie to float down to him, Sil's spine stiffened and on impulse he shook his head, "No... I... I'm home now. I want my real name."

"That's fine," André murmured, taking his wife in his arm lovingly, "Zack sounds good."

"It'll take a while for me to get used to it." Sil provided a fake smile. "But I'd like that."

"Who's this young lady, Mark?" Arianne said referring to Emilie and inviting Mark to join them in spite of not having a clue what to do with himself.

He flustered, and brushed the scarlet strand out of his face, "Oh, uh... this is my cousin, Emilie Meyvise."

"It's nice to meet you Emilie," André said, holding out a hand to shake.

Emilie leaned forward, smiling wryly, clearly offended by any advances at human contact, "You can call me Feather. It's nice to meet you too." She shook André's hand with a fierce grip. Sil began to think with this, she was either very defensive about any man touching, or she was just a bit racist about humans.

"Are you okay?" André addressed, noticing how Sil reverted to his normal sulking expression. The man didn't know any better yet, and Sil did his best to mask the need to avoid emotional contact.

"I'm fine," he insisted in a lie, stretching his luck. He was overwhelmed, but when he looked at his father's face, the man's frosty graying hair, his deep-set blue eyes, he was taken off guard. It was his own face he was gazing at, older, matured, and without a doubt, he knew Mark was right. "I'm fine," he whispered again, his fear slowly melting away in the truest sense. Breath fell heavy from his lips as he looked from his father to his mother. No Shadows, no craziness, no need to be the strongest, no need to seem together in his life.

"I'm home."

✍◈✍

After a relaxing first meal with his family, Sil followed André up the stairs and along the balcony into a small guest bedroom. It took very little for them to offer for him to stay indefinitely, and Sil was quietly grateful. The room was larger than Mark's, obviously smaller than what he was used to, but he didn't need the kind of space he had in the ASH.

The room had a small desk under a single window facing the backyard. A closet door stood along the far wall, and a dresser in the back-right corner both containing random stored things of no interest. But in the center of the room was a twin sized bed, made with a dark teal bedspread. It was to be *his* bed.

The bare walls were also painted teal, almost matching the bed spread, and every accent of the room from the bed frame, the doorknobs, and the dresser handles were gold. With the light off, the room seemed very dull, but when André switched on the light it became very homey and open. Sil liked the space. It was clean, smelled like a candle, and the window overlooking the backyard was a blessing he never thought he would have.

He stepped across the carpeted floor to peer out and savor the view. They had a big yard with an old playset close to the back door, but farther out there was a fence surrounding the whole yard, and a smaller fence made of wire surrounding a small shed too tiny for tools. "What's that?" he asked his father.

André checked to make sure the bed had sheets on it. "What's what?"

"The little shed out there."

"Oh." André shrugged it off and joined him. "That's our chicken coop. We don't have a lot of chickens right now, but we'll get more in the spring."

"Oh, dear." Sil mused to himself, "I have a hawk. I'm going to have to keep her away from those chickens."

André chuckled with a little forced humor. "Yeah, we've had some problems with hawks. But having chickens means free eggs, free-range food, and of course, endless fun for the puppy."

Sil smiled, only having gotten a glimpse of the dog at first, but now he saw it scampering around the fenced yard, sniffing around and digging holes in the mud. "What's its name?"

Nudging him in the shoulder, André urged him out. "Mango, why don't you come meet her?"

Nodding eagerly, Sil didn't have to be tugged along, he was practically leading his father down the stairs. André only guided him to the backyard, setting him free in the muddy space. The puppy galloped at the sight of the new person, happy to meet anyone, and she threw herself into Sil, wagging her whole butt with excitement.

Sil got down on his knees, petting the dog all over. He had never seen a dog in real life, so sheltered he was shocked at how soft her fur was and how enthusiastic a puppy could be. André stood over him chuckling. "She's a lab mix, we're not sure with what, but we're guessing it's pit-bull. She's tough as nails, and she's got a hard head!"

Letting Mango lick his face, Sil practically hugged the dog just to keep her under control. "How old is she?"

"Let's see, I think we got her in March, so..." he counted the months on his fingers. "Eight months?" he muttered unsurely.

Sil already loved her, and he thought he was going to love all the animals. Animals were easier than people. They didn't complain, and their needs were simple.

"Since you're here," André broke into his thoughts, "would you like to help the twins with chicken chores. I know they'd love to get out of it."

"Sure," Sil declared without hesitation. He scanned the yard, staring toward the far side of the fenced yard. There were a few trees on the property, mostly oaks from what he could tell, but they were mostly at the far side of the yard where the fence ended and a small planted forest marked the end of the land. From the thick trunked oak, a wide swing swayed under a low branch.

Sil only spotted it because he could sense in the Realm that a Shadow was over there hiding. "Hey... can I have a minute?" he asked, still petting Mango vigorously.

André gave a nod and stepped to the backdoor, noticing how his wife gazed at their eldest son through the glass. Sil rose and let Mango prance about his ankles, following him along to the swing. Dodging muddy spots along the way, he made out the shape of Emilie's shadow under the wood of the swing, which seemingly swayed of its own free will.

Nonchalantly, he wobbled the ropes, and nudged her shoulder even though she remained invisible. "You okay?"

She blinked out of the Realm like a flame and grimaced, moving over for him to join her. Only one foot touched the ground, but she didn't need it to manipulate gravity to move the swing. Their shoulders nestled against each other naturally, and Sil quickly discovered how cold she was. No coat, no sturdy shoes, just a gray jacket from the ASH, bland and useless.

"I'm freaking out, okay," she admitted suddenly. "I mean, I'm happy for you. You got your family! But I'm going to have to go meet mine, and I don't know what's going to happen!"

"Don't be scared," he assured, taking her hand in his own securely. "I was just as freaked out as you are, but it's going to be okay. Trust me."

She leaned against his shoulder, hiding her fear but clinging to him. "I don't really care what people think of us as Shadows. I know who I am, as you know who you are."

Breathing deeply, Sil pushed the swing, letting go of his anxiety. "Who am I?" he asked the wind. "I don't know if I feel acceptance or release. I've been accepted into my family as one of them, but still I feel like I'm leaving something behind." He waited a moment for her to meet his gaze. "Leaving behind my real home, the Shadows, and you."

Emilie hummed. "I'm not going anywhere. I don't care where my mom lives, or if you think I'm too loud, I'll always be here." She rose a little, wanting to fly away. "But things are changing. The ASH was never my home. It's the Shadows who are my home, and not even my blood can change that." She nudged his shoulder playfully. "You're changing too, and I think I like it."

Sil fell silent for a moment and contemplated as if waiting for Emilie to continue but when she let the silence flourish, he vanished into the Realm. Emilie still felt him near, holding her hand, her head supported on his shoulder, and it took no other prompt for her to follow.

While sitting on a ghostly version of the swing which glowed with white smoke in the dark world, she sat up and leaned away from him. He rose and began to walk away leisurely. In the Realm, his icy form sparkled in the dark, and he couldn't feel his long white hair dangling over his shoulder, just what felt like a huge snowflake mounted on his head.

Are you upset? she asked through his thoughts.

Sil's form emanated the cold frustration Emilie was always so used to. *I'm beginning to question if the Recluse Shadow actually died, or if something very bad happened to him.*

Emilie put her luminous, light yellow hands on her hips. She really was like a star in the Realm, and she glowed like one as well. *You do?* she asked through the Realm.

Do I what?

Emilie chuckled, a sound similar to the wind blowing through trees. *We're in the Realm. I hear everything you're thinking. You like me, don't you?*

Sil sputtered a moment disbelieving she had actually asked that. *I think you spend way too much time in here. You seem to like a part of me, and I don't think it's good for you…*

In the Realm, it was easier to be honest. Emilie gazed off into the emptiness. *I like you for you, all your quirks and bad behaviors.* She mused, joking a bit then she waited a moment, thinking to herself, *but why does that seem so hard for you?*

Sil's icy form shimmered and rippled in the dark. He came a little closer to her floating in the Realm. *Do you love me?*

Emilie turned her head quickly to him. *What?* She had heard perfectly fine; she just didn't comprehend his question.

Do you trust me? he continued. *Don't worry about tomorrow, think about today.*

Emilie frowned. *What do you mean? "Do I love you?" "Do I trust you?" What do you want me to do?*

Sil stretched his icy Shadow, surrounding himself and Emilie with ice. He came very close to her then scooped her up in his arms. *Give me your Shadow.* He said slowly and kindly, remembering what Mark had done to him and how everything in his power was entrusted to Mark.

What? she said quietly in his arms.

Do you trust me? he said again.

Emilie hesitated, then she placed a glowing hand at her heart and took her Shadow in her luminous fingers, *yes,* she said surely. She gave him the Shadow and they flew into the sky though the Realm. Drifting off into their freedom, Sil felt his new ties holding him back, but he knew Emilie, she needed this.

XXIII
ONLY ASHES REMAIN

A scowl brushed itself across Mark's face like every line drawn onto paper. Waiting for Gary to come online was going to drive him nuts. He needed to get away from the TV. The Realm and the sounds coming from it rang in his ears making it difficult for him to concentrate.

He didn't want to concentrate, he wanted to relax, to come to grips with his thoughts but he could hear every Shadow within a three-mile radius of his home. His mind wandered to the shattered laptop that was buried in his closet, wishing he could sink into playing games online with Gary, yet it somehow didn't seem right.

Whatever sleep he had gotten last night had left him with an image in his head, like a calming fantasy to help him understand his new reality but getting it on paper to see it again was proving difficult. It was a younger version of himself, something of an alternate universe.

The child had long, out grown, lank hair about his shoulders. He reached upward into the air and fire came from his hands. In his dream, he thought it had been him, but now that he thought of it, he knew it wasn't. The dream was his imagination creating the Recluse while he wrestled with his questions about who he could possibly be.

The graphite didn't seem to be agreeing with him. It had been a long time since he had tried to produce a half-decent drawing. The shading was weird, so was the anatomy of the figure, and he drew the boy standing up to a cherry tree with a burning hand and pointed elf ears longer than any Shadow he'd met so far.

Now he was just getting silly, adding ridiculous things to the drawing. He blew his bangs out of his face, but the red strike fell between his eyes, and he tried to brush it over his head and back into his obsidian ocean.

He pulled what little obedient hair he had behind his ears, touching the ends lightly. He compared his drawing to the shape he felt but then remembered. He had those pointed ears too, subtle and hidden under his wild black hair but the sign had always been there.

Nearly knocking over his desk chair, he burst to his feet and ran over to the mirror by his bed. Shadows had pointed ears. Surely before his crimson eyes, his ears both curved to a dull point. "How could I not have noticed this before?" he breathed.

He ran out of his room, bolting down the hallway to find his mother in the kitchen getting dinner ready. "Mom!" his voice cracked, and she eyed him, afraid of the look of desperation on Mark's face.

"Are you okay?" she asked worriedly, setting her preparations to make sure nothing was wrong.

Hastily, Mark brushed his ebony black hair behind his ears with shaky fingers, exposing his pointed ears. "Please don't tell me you knew about this?" he demanded shocked.

His mother flustered a little getting a good look at them, but she merely stammered, astonished by his reaction. "You're saying you didn't?"

Mark's heart dropped hearing this. "Shadows have pointed ears! You would have known about this. So if you knew I was a Shadow, why wouldn't you tell me?" Disbelief rippled through his limbs. Somehow his Shadow must have hidden it from him until after he discovered he was a

Shadow, but how was it even possible to hide his own body part from him?

Marissa brushed a finger under her chin nervously. "You know why. Shadows are taken away at birth, why would I want to be sure it was true?"

Mark shook his head denying it all. "You were pretty quick to get rid of me when you did know for sure." He took a step closer. "Why? Why did you call the ASH?"

She faltered, trying to come up with some sort of excuse. "Everything changed..." she whispered, fighting herself, "I saw you use the Realm back in February. I was afraid something was wrong with you, and Shadows were to blame."

Mark's mind scrambled for some kind of explanation for this. February, what had happened in February? Just before he went to the ASH, Marissa had said she found him on the floor with tachycardia, an increased heart rate. He pressed his lips together. "What happened?" he found himself saying aloud.

Crossing her arms, Marissa stepped back into the kitchen, with a drawn brow. "Nine months ago, I thought you were having a heart attack. You have no history of heart issues at all. I thought you were dying. And by the time your father called an ambulance, your heart rate was getting back down to normal and you were exhausted."

Mark quivered, finding himself pinching his arm. Nine months ago, the Recluse died. Was there any connection? He had no memory of the event, probably because of the intense stress. He couldn't even remember being in the hospital.

Why did it feel like he had some connection to the Recluse when he had never met him? The dying Shadow looked just like him except for bright red hair, he could pass through the ASI just like the Recluse could, and when the Recluse died, Mark's heart had started racing. It was as if he had some distant connection with the Recluse's heart his Shadow had only felt once. Maybe it was his Shadow that connected them, maybe Shadow Fire had belonged to the

Recluse, and when he died it had come to Mark. Was that possible? It couldn't be. He had been born with Shadow Fire, right?

He pressed his lips together, irritated. "What are you hiding from me?"

Marissa leaned against the counter and closed her eyes, inhaling her senses to deal with this. She frowned. "Why do you assume I'm hiding something from you?"

"Because you know more about Shadows than I do!" Mark yelled, slamming his hands on the other side of the counter. "Are you a Shadow?" he demanded.

Becoming stern, Marissa frowned. "You're in no place to give me that tone. If I was a Shadow, why would I even think to call the ASH."

"I'm still trying to figure that out," Mark seethed under his breath.

"We'll deal with this as a family when your father gets back. You're just going to have to wait!" Returning to preparing dinner, she dismissed him. "You really should get back to school soon after missing a whole week..." she mumbled, rambling off as Mark left the room. He grumbled because he knew his dad would never confront an issue head on.

Marissa paused as soon as he was gone and frowned deeply to herself, maybe now that he was a Shadow, it wasn't right to keep it from him. She didn't know. That was the truth. She didn't know how to deal with this and she wanted to fall back on her husband before ever speaking to Mark about it. He didn't need something like *that* thrown on top of everything he had been through this week.

Supporting herself on the counter, she rubbed her face, stressing over it. Giving in, she clenched her fists and retrieved her cell phone from her pocket. It had been too long since she had spoken to her husband. Every day January was away made Marissa worry, but she would sacrifice for whatever paid the bills, and if work called January away for two weeks, she could accept that. But this was too much for her.

"Hello, this is January Halo," his voice came, filling Marissa with hope even though she still missed him dearly. He hadn't even checked the caller ID, answering his phone mindlessly as usual.

"Hey, Jan, it's Isa. How are things doing over there?" she asked trying to sound truly happy to hear his voice, because despite being heavy laden with the Shadows, she was happy.

"Fine," he muttered sounding like he was moving about wherever he was, in a hotel or eating somewhere by himself. *"How about you and the kids?"* he asked in a tone of mediocrity, unbeknownst to the wild troubles they had been through. Marissa didn't answer for some time, not sure how to tell him, but he broke into her thoughts. *"Is something wrong, Isa?"* His worry carried through the line.

Marissa bit her lip, ripping off some skin through her anxiety. "I don't know how to—" she stopped, her voice cracking and tears flowing against her will.

"Isa?" January's voice panicked. *"What happened?"* he asked with every vibe of his voice longing to hold her and comfort her.

Marissa supported herself on the counter trying to hold back the tears. "I don't know how to tell Mark the truth and not hurt him or if I even should."

It was likely that January sat down or acquired somewhere private to hold their conversation. *"You're not making any sense. What's going on with Mark?"*

Marissa tried to compose herself and sat at the island counter, resolving to just spit it out. "Mark is a Shadow. After all we feared, he's a Shadow!"

Silence rung on the other line for a long minute as January was left speechless. A long sigh of disappointed blew against the mouthpiece of January's phone. *"You need me to come home?"* he asked, offering. *"I can leave a few days early. You need me there..."*

Marissa didn't want to force him to come back early, but she needed him. "Mark's trying to find out what happened... why we always feared he was a Shadow... Should we tell him the truth? I don't even know..."

January sighed again, grunting as he was probably rubbing his temples as he often did. *"What nonsense are you going on about?"*

Marissa wavered a little. "We always knew Mark might be a Shadow, and we were right. He can turn invisible, make fire in his hands, and..."

"Marissa!" January's voice became firm. *"Don't take this out on yourself. There's no way you could have known this would happen. There were no signs when he was born... right?"* he stammered a bit, trying to force out the word.

Marissa pursed her lips. "Jan..." she whispered, growing more worried, "we've always known it was possible. There was a slight detection on Mark's test when he was born. You were the one who told me back then unless you—you didn't!" she realized. "Oh, please tell me you haven't forgotten all about it!"

January stammered. *"I uh... I don't know what you're talking about."*

Anger welled inside Marissa as January inadvertently confirmed it. "You did! You forgot all about it! Jan! How do you always forget about everything to do with Shadows?!"

"Calm down!" January urged, now sounding sorry. *"You know I forget things sometimes. You know I can't control that... just please, wait 'til I get home and we can deal with this then, okay?"* He tried to confirm, but only received a muffled response from his wife. *"Okay, I'm booking the flight for tomorrow. I should be back late tomorrow."*

Marissa dried her tears of grief and nodded even though her husband couldn't see it. "I miss you..." she whispered weakly.

She could tell January was forcing a smile on the other line. *"I miss you too, and I love you, Isa. Just hold on a day longer. It'll be all right, I promise!"* He tried to comfort her from afar.

It wasn't much help, and Marissa could not stop herself from fully letting loose her sorrow before she could continue cooking.

XXIV
INWARD MOTIVE, OUTWARD ACT, ONWARD FLIGHT

November 2, 2030

No part of the bed could have been comfortable from the way Sil tossed and turned through the night. Emilie hated seeing him like this, and after Mark and June went home, she stuck around quietly, hiding out in the Realm, and rarely making the family aware she was present. Sil was trapped in a nightmare, residual pain from his burns and a little subconscious homesickness.

All Emilie could guess by the way he shifted throughout the night was that it was going to take a while for him to adjust to life outside the ASH. In the quiet darkness, she drew near to him, resting her weight on the bed, and laying down behind him. He was cold, but he embraced her hand, and stopped fidgeting.

Emilie found herself able to sleep with him, closing her eyes against his cold back and slipping away until the faintest morning light touched her face. White light diffused through the window, and Emilie opened her eyes to the foggy silhouette of a bare November oak, and Sil sitting up.

Cross-legged on the mattress, Sil meditated, unmoving, training his breathing and opening his mind to the Realm. She could feel pulses in the Realm as he reached out, expanding his range gradually with each breath. He had been waiting a long time for this, and the freedom in the Realm was a welcome change. No part of her wanted to disturb his peaceful meditation, only taking note of his straight back and messy braid as she rose out of the bed vertically.

Without much in the way of keeping warm, she opened the window and slipped out into the cold air. Looking back only once, she watched Sil's eye peek open to see her go. As she exhaled, her breath came out in small clouds of fog, and she had never felt so happy and so free. However, as the cold pinched her cheeks, she started thinking about her mother.

As much as she wanted to put it off, she was going to meet her mother today. She didn't know a thing about the woman other than that she was Marissa's sister, and she was terrified to imagine what kind of person Hellen Meyvise would be.

It made her colder to fear that her mother had never forgotten her, and some form of love would flow from the grief. It froze her heart to acknowledge that possibility, because she had never loved her mother.

A sense of vertigo suddenly came over her and she felt something tugging her, wanting her to fly away from there. It might just have been her gut telling her to get out of there and fly to the farthest reaches of the world to never have to set eyes on her mother. But she felt drawn to the west after an urge she had never felt before. Curious of what the tug could be or if it was another Shadow, she flew after it as fast as she could.

At the speed of sound, she crossed over the Appalachians with incredible ease. The only thing that pained her was the cold. It stung her ears and shot at her face like a million needles. She didn't care, it was in her blood and she had never reached speeds like this before. She never wanted to stop, even if she died in midair.

A glint of light high above her tempted her to go faster, to climb higher, but even then, the air became thinner as she rose into the atmosphere. She was able to go fast enough to keep up with the distant airplane, but with how unbearably freezing the air was, she wasn't able to truly get nearer to it until it descended to land. Below her, she made out the airfield and a smile touched her lips as curiosity took hold of her reason.

Something occurred to her as she flew onward. Thousands of people, every day, were able to fly on their own, and within this airport, her power of flight seemed miniscule compared to the powerful jets that carried hundreds of people per trip. She ducked down behind the control tower, exploring as she always wished to, and watching from as close as she could get as a huge jet landed in the distance. In awe, Emilie identified the gangway that would be attached to the plane, allowing the passengers to enter the airport. A smirk touched her lips. It was too easy!

Entering the Realm, Emilie dashed down into the stairway and remained in the Realm until it was stretched out to attach onto the plane. Nothing excited her more, and no amount of waiting could dull the gleam in her eyes when passengers finally started appearing.

The sheer variety of passengers fascinated her, eyeing up men in suits glancing down at their phones for the time, small families fighting to hang onto their excited kids, and a young adult girl who appeared lost and confused as she toted a heavy backpack and dragged an oblong suitcase that was longer and thinner than a normal carryon and decorated with music notes.

Emilie wanted to help her, to try to look like one of the passengers, but she didn't even have a small bag with her to pretend was luggage. So, she stayed in the Realm. A man stepped out of the plane, catching Emilie's eye instantly. He was in casual clothes and pulled an obviously heavy suitcase.

He appeared rushed and had a distressed look in his eyes

as he paused and stared at the stairway for several seconds, almost directly at Emilie. He held up two people behind him, and he apologized half-heartedly before stepping off to the side and digging around his pockets for his phone.

Narrowing her eyes, Emilie gazed at him, intrigued, he looked to be in his late thirties with creamy-brown hair he kept pushed back, and dark brown eyes. The stewardess urged him onward and he walked haphazardly down the stairs, absorbing himself into his phone.

Seeing as there were no more passengers, Emilie followed him, floating behind him at a distance. Suddenly, the man stopped, appearing to be looking out the stairway's window for a few seconds before he looked back, feeling watched.

Nervously, he turned away and stepped down the stairs and into the hall which led into the airport. One step at a time, Emilie followed his movements, unsettling him, and she could tell he knew she was there. His footsteps were inconsistent, he kept glancing back until finally, he whirled around, and demanded to the air, "Who's following me?" His face was incredibly close to hers, and she held her breath, seeing instantly the humiliation in his eyes when he realized there was no one there. Sighing, the man relaxed a little, and turned about to continue on.

"Who are you?" Emilie asked, incredibly close to him on the opposite side, startling him a good deal.

He cursed quietly and jumped away. "You scared me..." he admitted before looking her over, growing confusion on his face.

Floating upward, which caused the man to pale considerably, she got even closer to his face. "You look familiar," she hummed, circling him and grinning as he stumbled to follow her. "Have you have been to the ASH? I could swear I've seen you before. Are you an ASO? Or were you one of the doctors Kimberly brought in for the Recluse?"

"Hold on, hold—" the man tripped over his suitcase and

stumbled. "You're a Shadow? How did you get here? The ASH is... miles away." He trailed off, confirming that he had a grasp on what the ASH was truly used for. "W-who are you?" he demanded in turn.

Gleefully, Emilie placed her feet on the floor and gave a wry bow. "Shadow Feather." She curtsied. "And your name?"

Skeptically, the man grasped at his cell phone in his pocket. "I need to get my luggage. Will you please excuse me?" He tried to be polite and pushed past, not anticipating how strong Emilie was when she held him back. "Excuse me!"

"I want to know your name," Emilie urged with benevolent eyes close to his face.

"You didn't give me yours!" the man insisted, pushing her shoulder so she drifted through the air. She followed him, of course, in awe by how unafraid he was of her powers. It was almost as if he had been around Shadows before, and not for a short period of time either.

He drew his hand out of his pocket, and protecting the phone from her view, he dialed a number and excused himself to a corner in the hall. "I just landed. Have you left yet?" he asked whoever was on the other line. "I know, but I don't want to get a taxi, and—" He stopped, glancing back at Emilie who was surely eavesdropping on him. "There's this girl following me. She said she's a Shadow."

Emilie could hear the caller on the other line. "*A Shadow? What does...*" it was muffled after that, but the man glanced over his shoulder and sighed.

"Crazy eyes, and she floats..." the man described her loosely. It did make Emilie a little nervous, but she didn't show it. The man started stammering uncontrollably, nervous or worse, as he listened to what seemed to be an interrupter speaking through the phone. "All right, all right... fine. Give the phone back to your mom." A hand drifted to his forehead and he massaged the bridge of his nose, exemplifying what seemed to be a nasty headache or migraine. "I'll see you soon?" he confirmed with his wife. "I love you…" his whisper was his only goodbye before the receiver hung up.

"You're January Halo, aren't you?" Emilie muttered happily.

He turned back to her, staring in shock that she knew his name. "How did you know?"

She crossed her arms and smirked. "I could hear Mark in the Realm through the phone."

Unconvinced, January turned away, nursing his headache as he walked. "And how do you know Mark? From the ASH, where you took him?" He trailed away, too bitter in his voice to require an answer. "I just found out he's a Shadow. I need to see my family. I need to see him for myself."

꙰

"Any luck?" Marissa said as Mark and Sil slammed the door shut behind them.

"Nothing. We can't find her anywhere, even through the Realm," Sil said, freezing both his hands in distress.

"I wonder if she went ahead to Aunt Hellen's without us," Mark said, flopping onto a stool at the kitchen island counter. He brushed the scarlet strike out of his face nervously. With no sign of Emilie all morning, and knowing her free spirit, they were starting to fear she had completely run away, never to be seen again.

"But Hellen lives an hour away and Emilie couldn't find her, by herself at least," Marissa said straightforwardly. Her phone rang but Marissa didn't care much and let it ring, her disheartened posture dominating both boys in their distress. It kept ringing, the song *Ode to Joy* played itself over and over. Marissa sighed. "All right, all right," she took the phone from her pocket and answered.

"Hello, this is Marissa," her voice changed completely when she answered the phone to seem friendly, bearing no baggage until she listened, not interrupting. "Oh you have, that was quick."

The two boys gaped, certain it could be Emilie on the other line. "Oh, it's just, we're a bit preoccupied here," Marissa grumbled in an already perplexed tone. "Should we come and pick you up?"

"Is it Emilie? Is she okay?" Mark interrupted. Marissa held up a finger signaling Mark to be quiet.

"A Shadow?" Marissa murmured with a still, somewhat concerned tone. "What does she look like?"

"Who is that?" Mark demanded, haphazardly grabbing the phone from his mother and holding it to his ear.

"Crazy eyes and she floats…"

"Dad? You're back already? Where are you? Is Emilie with you?" The words fell out of his mouth so fast, he could barely contain himself, but when he heard his father's voice, something changed in him.

Sil flustered when he heard it. Mark talked badly about his father with a scowl, but when Mark was truly with his father, in his heart, Sil could tell from a mile away that Mark still admired him.

Mark handed the phone back to his mother, a gleeful quiet look on his face as Sil broke into his thoughts. "Was Emilie there?" Sil asked unable to hold his breath any longer. "She isn't hurt, is she?"

"It wasn't Emilie. It was Mark's dad. He's at the airport. We have to pick him up," Marissa said, grabbing her keys off the peg on the wall near the door. "Mark, go get June. She's probably in her room playing video games."

Mark nodded and tread off down the hall. "Sil," Marissa continued, "you need to go ask the Addisons if you can come along." He nodded too and headed out the door hesitating to look back as Mark disappeared down the hall. Sil still struggled with the idea of having a family to answer to, and parents to love and respect, but even Mark had healing to be done in his own family, especially now that he knew he was a Shadow.

Mark's oblivious fascination with the Shadows had to end, and his disrespect for his father had to melt away, and even as he dashed down the street to the Addisons, Sil could feel Mark's heart, and how warm it was.

The Halos had a tiny car since they only had two children, and together with Sil, they filled the car, expecting Emilie would probably fly home without a care. The drive to JFK was long and sweet, but with how close they lived to Manhattan, the traffic usually prolonged the ride. It was even more over stimulating to Sil once they reached the airport, and to be surrounded by so many normal humans terrified Sil so completely, his entire focus became the Realm and finding Emilie.

January spotted them first and waved them over, prompting them to run as January gathered up his suitcases and let his family fall into his arms. He paid special attention to his daughter who innocently clung to his leg happily after practically licking her father's face with how many times she kissed him.

January hesitated, a wary look appearing in his eyes as he gazed closely at Mark. "Don't I get a hug from you anymore?" he asked with a smile. Mark stepped closer and hugged him tightly, squeezing him, as hard as he could. January did the same. He was sure to ruffle Mark's unruly black hair before releasing him and smiling into his face.

He looked directly to Sil, eyeing up his long white hair. "So, does somebody want to explain to me why she's following me around?" he asked, sounding quite annoyed as he rattled his suitcase forcing Emilie to exit the Realm.

She had been perching on the suitcase whilst hiding, so January probably only knew she was there because he had seen her vanish. However, it startled Sil a little to realize how good January was at recognizing Shadows in the Realm. Emilie beamed playfully, waving at Sil and causing fury to rise in his breath. "What are you doing here? We didn't have any idea where you went!"

January's eyes flashed as he stepped back, startled by the

power in Sil's voice as he displayed how infuriated he was by taking Emilie's arms and letting her float up to her feet. "You can't run off like that!" Sil's voice cracked, so terrified he shook her shoulders. "We don't know how people will react to us. Please be safe. I just don't want you to get hurt!"

Emilie didn't say anything, her wild unpredictable persona shattered. Her eyes fell, and she nodded.

He released her, and she wordlessly let Sil push her into the bustling crowd, vanishing into the Realm as they left. Mark couldn't fully understand their uneasiness about being around so many people, but he figured they were heading back to the car.

"Sorry, who was that? What's going on?" January let out his demands shakily.

Mark bent down to help his father with his bags and urged them in his movements to follow Sil and Emilie. "That was Sil. He's from the ASH too." With this short answer he stepped away from them, carrying the heaviest of January's bags.

"Mark," Marissa called hurriedly, scooping up June and urging along her family. "Sil's Arianne and André's son. And Emilie is Hellen's daughter, our niece," she explained, knowing Mark wasn't going to.

Tensing, January nearly stopped in his tracks. "That girl is related to us!" he gaped, completely at a loss. "Mark!" he called desperately, "slow down!" Hurrying his steps even though he was tired from the journey, January rushed to catch up with him. "We need to talk about this, to… try to understand what happened to you."

"Think we could talk in the car?" Mark glanced back as his only reply. He continued to the parking lot without looking back, trying to seem certain, like his old self to his father, but really, he was struggling to come up with an explanation for all this madness that made sense. He spotted Sil waiting at the car with Emilie sitting on the roof and being a nuisance.

You're nervous, Sil's voice in the Realm scared the wits

out of him.

Mark stopped in his tracks about six feet from the car and glared at the black pavement. *It's my dad. I don't know how to talk about Shadows around him.*

Sil didn't say anything aloud as Marissa unlocked the car from a distance and he opened the car door to sit inside. *Relax...* Sil breathed, letting a frigid cold come over Mark. *Let your father ask you questions. You don't have to explain everything in one go. You barely understand it yourself.*

Grumbling, Mark moved to the other side of the car and waited for his mother to hand his sister to him so he could buckle June into the middle of the backseat. Finally, he sat down inside and took a meditative pause to close his eyes and let his mind enter into the Realm.

It calmed his senses to do this, to feel the world within him and the hearts of the Shadows around him, and it distracted him long enough for them to get on the road.

"So, Emilie said she was Shadow Feather. What about you... Sil." The words came off January's tongue awkwardly, and he kept his eyes off the road to keep his headache at bay.

"Shadow Frost," Sil answered without any hesitation whatsoever. Uneasily, he twirled and unraveled his long braid, claustrophobic in the backseat.

"And... Mark?" January led into it, clearing his throat.

Mark felt his spine stiffen, every muscle in his body locked up and he was unable to speak to his father and unable to look away. January turned around in his seat to meet eyes with Mark and this unsettled him even more. Finally, he gazed anxiously at the floor of the car. "Fire. I'm pyrokinetic."

"Are you okay?" January's voice faded with every word.

Mark folded his hands in his lap, pinching his own fingers, and biting his lip, but swallowing his gut. He forced himself to blurt out what was on his mind as quickly as possible. "Are you a Shadow—"

"We talked about this!" Marissa cut him off.

"I want an answer from him! Because all I'm getting from you is lies!" The car fell silent. Mark's anger had finally shone through, and though his eyes stayed locked on his father's, the discomfort of snapping at his parents stung. January's gaze drifted out to the colored leaves which lined the street as they entered their neighborhood.

"I'm not a Shadow," January whispered.

Mark made out their house in the distance, his father breathed a sigh of relief when he was finally home. Being away strained January's nerves, stressed his psyche and made him shut down socially.

"If I was, I would have told you," January added in an even softer voice as the car came to a stop. "I'm sorry we sheltered you from the ASH, but Shadows who can't control their powers are dangerous."

Marissa turned off the car letting January fall silent, not exactly sure in his own voice. Mark eyed up his parents. She raised a brow and subtly gestured to their son with her neck. His father looked desperate, opening his mouth to protest, but his mother dismissed him wordlessly, fed up with his obsessive introversion.

"I'll leave you boys to talk." Mark's mother got out of the car and moved to let June out. June ran to the door happily unaware of her family's distress as she waited for her mother to unlock the house. "And don't worry about the luggage. I got it." This made January pale as he realized his wife had abandoned him to address their son alone.

Grumbling, January opened the door but remained in the car, just letting the cold air in to aid his headache. Each moment drew into a thousand before he finally spoke. "I admit, I can't totally remember everything about my past, but I'm still searching for the truth."

Skeptically, Sil leaned closer accidently causing the temperature in the car to drop further as his curiosity piqued. "How old were you when you lost your memory?"

January eyed Sil but gulped down his nervousness. "I was eighteen in my earliest memory." In his eyes, Mark could see his father searching his memory for more information but could barely summon anything. "I'm forty years old now."

Sil leaned back into the seat and drew his brows concerned. "Twenty-two years." He did the math, curling his finger under his chin. "And the ASH was built twenty years ago."

A growl emerged in the back of Mark's throat. "What does that have to do with anything?"

"I don't know," Sil admitted, finding January's nervous gaze and folding his hands in his lap. "It may be a coincidence, but it's an oddly close time frame."

"I assure you," January forced, "I've been tested for a Shadow at the height of the ASH, and it was negative."

"My test was negative," Mark seethed, pushing the car door open with his foot. "It doesn't prove anything."

Storming out, Mark stopped on the front lawn, anger boiling inside him with the reality that no one was being honest with him. Of course, the second he had a moment to forget about Sil and his father behind him, Emilie came into view, leaning against the garage doorway and grinning at him with her arms crossed. Somehow, she was ready.

XXV
TEARS OF THE YEARS

Smoothing her long brown hair over her shoulder, Emilie sat satiated upon the edge of the couch while Mark paced aimlessly. January had wandered into the back bedroom to sleep and deal with several hours of jet lag but this unresponsiveness killed Mark's psyche.

With a knowing smirk, Emilie wove her hair into a braid and chuckled to herself. "If you're this worked up about your father finding out you're a Shadow, then I have nothing to worry about."

Mark whirled at her, halfway between the television and the front door. "At least your dad won't be as evasive as mine. Aunt Hellen never got married, so you won't have to deal with that."

Startled, Emilie tossed the unfastened braid over her shoulder and leaned forward, floating slightly. "What do you mean? I don't have two parents?" She puzzled at a loss for the idea since it was very clear from the look in her eyes that she was fully aware how babies were made.

Preventing himself from finding humor in the thought, Mark plopped down on the floor in front of the television. Heaving a sigh, he forced himself to break out the gaming console he had been trying to avoid.

"I don't know the whole story. I was born the same day you were. She never liked to talk about it, but my mom told me as soon as I learned about Shadows." From the television cabinet, Mark removed and plugged in a seemingly high-tech console to a television hardly large enough to capture the whole screen. It looked a bit ridiculous since the console was only half the size of the screen.

"Ah..." Emilie hummed sarcastically and nodded, "because your mom has such a great record for telling you the whole story."

Mark pushed down his worry as he started up the dusty console. "It frustrates me so much..." he admitted, somehow trusting his wayward cousin with his feelings, "and the worst part... I feel like she takes advantage of my dad's amnesia, as an excuse to keep things hidden from me."

Clenching his fingers around the wireless controller, Mark gritted his teeth. "I know he knows more than he's saying." He felt his hands getting warmer, and hurriedly put down the controller on the carpet to stop himself from destroying it like his laptop. As far as he knew, his father didn't have a clue he had destroyed the expensive gaming computer. January didn't have a clue for much of anything.

Airlessly, Emilie floated up from the edge of the couch and knelt beside Mark, her knees barely touching the ground. "Sounds to me like you need to go talk to him, for your own good," she urged in a quiet voice.

Mark groaned, flinching when he felt Emilie's hand on his shoulder. Her fingers drifted up to brush his dark ebony hair behind his ear and she smirked with that same wry smile that irked him. "He won't tell me anything," Mark insisted, pushing her away and watching as she drifted without gravity.

In a retaliatory gesture, Emilie gripped both his shoulders and hoisted him up to his feet, forcing him to get away from the trap of video games that he used to distract himself. Once on his feet, Mark glared at her, unable to resist as she pushed him towards the hall. In another low disgruntled sigh, Mark gave in, first driving his heels in then murmuring, "Fine..."

Emilie beamed, more than pleased with herself as she watched his slow begrudging steps into the dark, unlit hallway. The whole house sank into silence while January slept, so Mark was particularly afraid that his mother would pounce on him from the kitchen when she spotted him going into her bedroom. Mark used the Realm, hiding himself in the sweet darkness to creep through the L-shaped hall and warily turn the creaky doorknob into his parents' bedroom.

Mark didn't bother knocking, doing everything within his power to keep his mother from finding out he intended to disturb his father's sleep. The bedroom was stuffy and almost pitch-black despite how the autumn sun peeked through the heavy curtain over the window on the far side of the room. January didn't stir when Mark closed the door behind him, not allowing it to click shut. "Dad..." Mark mustered to break the silence.

Buried under the covers, January jumped slightly and wearily he dug his face out from under the covers. His bleary eyes exemplified how irritated this made him. "What do you need?" he asked in a hoarse whisper.

Mark clenched his teeth for a second before he found his voice. "How did you lose your memories?" he asked quietly.

January groaned deeply and rubbed his face, attempting to bury himself a little longer. "Mark, can I please get a little rest before we leave to visit your aunt?"

"You're coming with us?" Mark burst, a little surprised since until this morning he didn't even know his father was coming home.

Sighing, January sat up and covered his eyes. From the looks of him, Mark could tell he had a headache, and jet lag had claimed his internal sense of time. "I was thinking about it. Do you need something? Why couldn't you just bug your mom?"

At this, Mark's nose wrinkled up in the darkness. "She won't tell me anything. I want answers!"

January tensed, and for that instant he seemed scared of the deep crimson glow in Mark's eyes but as he hesitated, Mark could see his mind jumping around. Grunting, January set his feet over the side of the bed. "The earliest memory I have was when I was eighteen. I had been living in a cheap apartment. I vaguely remember having a few friends, and other than that no clue. When your mother and I got married, we looked into my heritage because, you know, I've got a bit of an accent. As far as we can guess, I'm Scottish. I came over when I was young, and I have no known family except you, June, and your mom."

Rising to his feet, January placed one firm hand on Mark's shoulder, nearly pinching him. "Take it easy on us, Mark. We didn't spend a week with the Shadows, so we don't know what world you're coming from. Hang in there, it's just going to take some time for me to get used to this."

January's hand left his shoulder, and Mark's eyes fell despondently with a bitter nod. Mark pulled away to let his father sleep. January didn't sink back into the bed, watching Mark's back as he turned to leave, but a tenderness overcame January, when he acknowledged that their whole family was about to change.

Mark strapped his roller blades to his feet and tore out the front door to race down the sidewalk. The wheels under his feet felt great and getting his rage out like this was far more effective than video games. The cool wind nipped at his nose, but he ignored it even though he had dismissed his coat in the foyer.

He should have never given up skating. It cooled his head and got his heart pumping. Part of him felt withdrawal from his addiction to video games, but the other part missed being in the ASH and hanging out with Kip. He couldn't deny he felt miserable there, but Kip had been the purest form of a Shadow Mark encountered. He didn't want to fall back into video games or pick up where his life had been broken off. He wanted to be with Shadows, and to know more about them.

He felt graceful fingertips brushing against his shoulder and he looked up just long enough to see Emilie flying up beside him, following him with a queer grin. "Your mom wants to get ready to leave."

Mark scoffed and pushed himself harder. "I'm going to see Sil," he declared over the wind, rushing through the November fog. Emilie didn't slow in the air, and Mark could feel through the Realm, she felt the same, she longed to be with Sil. Maybe for romantic reasons, Mark didn't know for sure, but it was that same drive to be with Shadows.

She chuckled when they neared the gray-blue house. "And to think, you two didn't hit it off so well."

They didn't even have to step up onto the porch when the front door screeched open and Sil appeared, his cold golden eyes shimmering in the light of day. "I heard your tones in the Realm…" he murmured, a hint of worry in his voice as if he thought something was wrong. He poised a hand on his hip as his long hair fell in front of his chest like spider webs now that it was straight, and he smirked. "I can't seem to stay home for more than an hour with all the adventures you two are getting me into."

Sil had a strange aura about him for his choice of words, and Mark's heart softened at the warmth in Sil's eyes. "I think that's how this is meant to be. I feel like… I need to be with Shadows."

At this, Sil stepped down from the porch and onto the damp grass. "Haven't you figured it out yet?" he joked and strode over and leaned against Emilie's shoulder to annoy her. "'We are all Shadows.' Don't you know what that means? Ocie says it all the time." Mark shook his head, still oblivious and this made Sil laugh. It was a tad eerie to hear Sil laugh, but Mark enjoyed a little light in someone so dark. "It means we are strongest when we're together. That was Keller's plan when he made the ASH, to bring the Shadows together so they'd grow stronger."

Mark stared down at his hands a little nervously, recognizing there would be long-term consequences to destroying the ASH as he did. "Keller wasn't wrong to do what he did, but taking us away from our families, that was wrong. It makes me wonder what it would be like if you got to stay with your parents."

Sil shrugged, and finally tossed his arm over Emilie's shoulder, weighing her down. "Rita has some pretty wild stories from her home in Scotland. She said Shadows were abandoned after their powers surfaced, and they're picked up by a community of Shadows who live by themselves. Not too much difference from what the ASH was."

Mulling over these thoughts, Mark pressed his lips together. His dad was Scottish, could that give him any more excuse to start looking for a way to prove January had more to do with the Shadows than he could remember? Mark obsessed over these thoughts, not even noticing as a car pulled up behind them on the street and someone called out, "Come on, kids. I need to get to the store before we leave." Marissa was still rolling down the window when Mark turned to meet eyes with her.

Suddenly, Sil grabbed Emilie's arms and in one hurried motion, he hugged her tightly, despite how it pained his burns. "Good luck, Emilie."

She gasped, and Mark whirled about to see her aimlessly grasping at the air. Nothing startled her more than getting real affection from Sil, especially because she knew he meant it, and there was nothing coarse or cold about it.

He released her, and she stumbled back, half-heartedly letting gravity control her as she tried to pretend she could walk. "Th-thank you…" she gasped breathily.

Sil waved her off as she and Mark drifted to the car. "Best of luck with your mom. I hope she's as great as my parents." He waited on the lawn while the two of them got into the little car, crammed with June in the middle seat in the back. It wasn't until Mark had buckled his seat belt that he noticed his father wasn't in the front seat beside his mother. He had stayed behind. Mark fought to hide his disappointment and kept quiet as his mother drove them away from the Addisons.

"So, Emilie, it's your mother's birthday in a few days," Marissa spoke with her eyes squinting at the white sky while she drove. "I was planning to get her a gift before we drove out, can you think of anything you'd like to get her?" She opened a pocket on the ceiling of her car to release the pair of sunglasses hidden inside.

Emilie shuddered, drawing her brows together and gripping the seat belt's release button. "How can you talk while driving?" she wondered, terribly confused and nervous.

Marissa glanced back at her in her mirror and with a slight grin she chuckled. "I've been driving so long, it's easy to multitask. Why do you ask?"

By the way Emilie was quivering it was obvious that she didn't want to be in this car. It made her feel trapped. Forcing a chuckle, Mark nudged her shoulder over his little sister. "It's because she had to drive when we made our escape from the ASH."

Acknowledging Emilie's difficult position, Marissa's eyes grew tender as she denied herself a frown. "You'll be more relaxed when you learn to drive," she assured.

Scoffing, Emilie put one foot up on the back of the passenger seat and the other through the space between the seat and the door. "I'm never learning to drive. I'll just fly everywhere I go!" she insisted, crossing her arms over her chest stubbornly. However, a second later she reeled forward. "I got it!" She reached into her back pocket to retrieve the small piece of paper she had been keeping there. "Can we get zucchini?"

Drawing her brows together, Marissa laughed. "For your mom?"

Emilie nodded eagerly. "I have this recipe for zucchini chips that Kimberly gave me. I could make it for my mom."

"I think that's a great idea," Marissa declared as she turned in toward a shopping center. "What else do you need?"

Cradling the crumpled three-by-five card in her hands, Emilie blushed a little, pleased with herself. "Olive oil, bread crumbs, parmesan, and oregano. That's easy enough, right?" It wasn't a question. This was perfect, and Emilie burst out of the car as soon as they parked.

She zipped through the air despite how everyone urged her to walk like a normal person. Seeing Emilie with this pure happiness unmotivated by spite, only reinforced to Mark he wanted to stay with the Shadows forever, and he got the feeling, his family was going to seem very boring soon.

For an hour drive, Emilie remained chipper, and now that she had four small zucchinis in her lap, she seemed a little less as if she were about to jump from the car window and fly away. However, once they came to a stop, and Emilie saw the little house hidden among the overgrown garden, she stopped herself. Her expression fell blank, her face went pale, and her eyes grew dim. It wasn't so much that the house disappointed her, it was fine, and any four walls would make her feel cramped.

Mark noticed her demeanor, and somehow, he knew it had nothing to do with the sight of the house.

Emilie's feet planted on the ground, unwilling to take a step farther than the car door. "I can't do this," she whispered, her voice coarse and jumpy.

Mark came around the car to stand beside her. "Come on." He tugged her sleeve, meeting her gaze just long enough to see she was terrified. "Just see her," he beckoned, comforting her despite how afraid she was. "If you don't like it, we'll leave."

Clenching her fists, Emilie stared onward at the house making out through the outgrown garden that the door was painted forest green and it blended in like a hole in the forest canopy. "All right…" she breathed, "but you lead." Drawing up the zucchinis and other ingredients in a plastic bag, Emilie held them tightly and waited, proceeding after Mark took two steps ahead of her.

Emilie's elbows graced the scratchy thistles which made the walkway to the little house narrower. Though everything was overgrown, there was evidence of old flowers that would look magical in the summer. Now everything was brown and dying. Emilie sighed to herself, preparing her heart for the person she was about to meet. It caused her to panic, but she kept her feet firmly planted to the ground.

Marissa knocked on the door and the silence that followed made Emilie want to tear her eyes out. Each second the green door didn't move, made it seem more like a hole in the forest and it made Emilie want to scream, *"What is taking so long?"* Mark felt her distress in the Realm, as if she broadcasted her thoughts to him and he chuckled, taking her hand to give her something to keep her grounded.

The door creaked open, unoiled, and unused. The woman who lived here was a shut in, and the house they could see into was unnervingly dark. Marissa beamed when the door opened fully and declared endearingly, "Happy Birthday, Nini!"

The woman with light brown hair shuddered and her expression couldn't be further from happy. "It's not my birthday," were the first words Emilie heard from her, dark and depressed like the bags under the woman's eyes.

Marissa struggled to remain cheerful for her sister. "It's soon, and we brought you something." She moved aside from the door and gestured to her niece invitingly. "Emilie?"

Abruptly, Emilie found herself overcome by the first full sight of her mother's face. It only took one utterance of Emilie's name for the woman to look at her the same way.

Hellen tried to jump back but stumbled and clung to the door. This woman was broken and she had been lost for the last fifteen years, ever since she let go of her daughter. Emilie's arms sank around the four zucchinis she held, but she stopped herself from dropping them and inhaled sharply.

"I brought you these. I've got a good recipe I'd like to make for you."

The words were empty, and it became evident that Emilie was the exact opposite person her mother was. Hellen sputtered, her breaths shallow until she finally choked out the faintest, "Emilie?"

Her eyes grew sad, her lips taut with worry over this first impression. Emilie stroked her thumb along the smooth skin of a zucchini then she looked up, forcing herself to face her mother. Adopting a serious posture, because all other emotions felt weird, Emilie took a step forward, "Yes… I'm here."

Hellen's eyes widened, for it was all she needed. The klutzy woman, clattered past her older sister and before Emilie could rise from the ground, she threw her arms around her fourteen-year-old daughter. Holding her tightly, as if for the first time, Hellen sobbed uncontrollably, her tears dripping onto Emilie's clothes as the four zucchinis slipped to the ground, bruising their flesh as Emilie stood motionless and terrified.

"I thought you'd never find me!" Hellen said, muffled within Emilie's coat, and she could feel her mother's teeth as she wept.

Emilie sank, her feet lifting off the ground but her mother held her in place and with their weak legs the two of them drifted to the concrete walkway, and finally, Emilie gave in. Reluctantly, Emilie allowed herself to lower her guard just long enough to bring her arms around her mother's waist and in this fateful moment, she let her emotions flow. Tears welled in her eyes and she whimpered, stifling a cry as she pushed her mother away.

It was all to see her face, to look into her eyes, and to know this was her mother. Once she knew for sure, once the emotions rattled through her form, putting gravity over her body, Emilie gave up, tightening her grip around her mother's back as she wheezed gracelessly.

"I already have."

EPILOGUE

Ocie stepped into the dark room quietly, peering through the flickering lights and the smoke in the air. "Dad?"

Within a few seconds a soft cyan light illuminated through the soot sodden air and Keller appeared. "What?" he spat bitterly, broken.

Ocie gulped her fears and stepped through the doorway. "Someone is here to see you, someone... you know." Her nervousness shone through her hesitation.

Perking up a little, Keller looked past his daughter to see a man who was older than him, wearing a dark hood. Keller didn't move or say anything. All he did was send a tone through the Realm to beckon the man into the dim light to see who he was.

The man's emerald green eyes pierced the dark. "It's you!" Keller tensed and started to rise up, but then cowered. "I didn't think I'd ever see you again after... after..." he couldn't finish knowing his decision to make the ASH had blown back into his face as predicted.

Suddenly the man caught him off guard when he removed his hood and hurried to him. "You're hurt!" he pointed out seeing blood on Keller's forehead. A gentle green mist emanated from the man's hand over Keller's injury and in seconds it was healed. "You've aged, Ian. Has it really been twenty years?"

Tears welled in Keller's eyes. How could this man still show him kindness after all he had done? He bit his lip, dropping his gaze. "You haven't aged a day…" He never felt so ashamed, but somehow, he managed to be happy seeing his old friend.

The man grinned, the same dimpled smile. He never changed, always looking for ways to help. That was simply who he was. "I told you this would happen…" He smirked gently. "But I had to let you go through with it. That's how the Shadow works."

Keller felt where the cut had been on his forehead and was amazed as always to feel it was gone without any scarring. "What are you doing here?" he asked, trying not to sound skeptical.

The man gestured around, producing a light chuckle. "Look at this place. I'm here to help you pick up the pieces, and to help any Shadows who need a home," he offered.

Keller sighed, affording himself a smile. "Thank you…" He exhaled. "The Shadows wouldn't ever accept that help from me anymore."

The man gleamed brightly with a wrinkle in the corner of his eye. "All right, I can pay for any expenses you can't afford, and I'll be out of your hair before tomorrow!" he assured, stepping back gleefully and leaving the room.

Ocie stepped in after him, crossing her arms, a bit confused. "Who was that?" she wondered astonished that he would offer to contribute any sum of money to the ASH.

Keller picked himself up trying to do what his friend would do, put the pieces back together and let this place be a home for Shadows. "Not that it matters to you…" he whispered, stepping out of the room. "His name is William."

About E. Kathryn

Writer, Illustrator, musician, humanesque creature who doesn't get enough sunlight and lives solely on tea, E. Kathryn started writing The Shadows when she was thirteen years old. Brought up in northern Virginia with her six siblings and tons of animals, she was homeschooled and given the freedom to write to her heart's content. When she's not writing incessantly, E. Kathryn enjoys drawing, playing the violin, and collecting and consuming way more tea than she needs.

Stay Connected
EKATHRYNSSHADOWS.COM
TWITTER @EKsShadows
INSTAGRAM @e.kathryns_shadows

Book 2 of The Shadows:
Lævatein's Choice

www.ingramcontent.com/pod-product-compliance
Lightning Source LLC
Chambersburg PA
CBHW051957240626
47153CB00005B/1791